Blue Angel

· a novel ·

F r a n c i n e   P r o s e

a&b

First published in Great Britain in 2001 by
Allison & Busby Limited
Suite 111, Bon Marche Centre
241-251 Ferndale Road
London SW9 8BJ
http://www.allisonandbusby.ltd.uk

First published in the US by HarperCollins Publishers

A catalogue record for this book is available from
the British Library.

ISBN 0 7490 0580 7

Printed and bound in Spain by
Liberduplex, s.l. Barcelona.

Blue Angel

Also by Francine Prose

Guided Tours of Hell

Hunters and Gatherers

The Peaceable Kingdom

Primitive People

Women and Children First

Bigfoot Dreams

Hungry Hearts

Household Saints

Animal Magnetism

Marie Laveau

The Glorious Ones

Judah the Pious

To Howie

Swenson waits for his students to complete their private rituals, adjusting zippers and caps, arranging the pens and notebooks so painstakingly chosen to express their tender young selves, the fidgety ballets that signal their weekly submission and reaffirm the social compact to be stuck in this room for an hour without real food or TV. He glances around the seminar table, counts nine; good, everyone's here, then riffles through the manuscript they're scheduled to discuss, pauses, and says, "Is it my imagination, or have we been seeing an awful lot of stories about humans having sex with animals?"

The students stare at him, appalled. He can't believe he said that. His pathetic stab at humor sounded precisely like what it was: a question he'd dreamed up and rehearsed as he walked across North Quad, past the gothic graystone cloisters, the Founders Chapel, the lovely two-hundred-year-old maples just starting to drop the orange leaves that lie so thickly on the cover of the Euston College viewbook. He'd hardly noticed his surroundings, so blindly focused was he on the imminent challenge of leading a class discussion of a student story in which a teenager, drunk and frustrated after a bad date with his girlfriend, rapes an uncooked chicken by the light of the family fridge.

How is Swenson supposed to begin? What he really wants to ask is: Was this story written expressly to torment me? What little sadist thought it would be fun to watch me tackle the technical flaws of a story that spends two pages describing how the boy cracks the chicken's rib cage to better fit the slippery visceral cavity around his throbbing hard-on? But Danny Liebman, whose story it is, isn't out to torture Swenson. He'd just wanted something interesting for his hero to do.

Slouched over, or sliding under, the seminar table, the students gaze at Swenson, their eyes as opaque and lidded as the eyes of the chicken whose plucked head the hero turns to face him during their late-night kitchen romance. But chickens in suburban refrigerators are generally headless. Swenson makes a mental note to mention this detail later.

"I don't get it," says Carlos Ostapcek. "What other stories about animals?" Carlos always starts off. Ex-navy, ex-reform school, he's the alpha male, the only student who's ever been anywhere except inside a classroom. As it happens, he's the *only* male student, not counting Danny.

What stories *is* Swenson talking about? He suddenly can't recall. Maybe it was some other year, another class completely. He's been having too many moments like this: a door slams shut behind him and his mind disappears. Is this early Alzheimer's? He's only forty-seven. *Only* forty-seven? What happened in the heartbeat since he was his students' age?

Maybe his problem's the muggy heat, bizarre for late September, El Niño dumping a freak monsoon all over northern Vermont. His classroom—high in the college bell tower—is the hottest spot on campus. And this past summer, workmen painted the windows shut. Swenson has complained to Buildings and Grounds, but they're too busy fixing sidewalk holes that could result in lawsuits.

"Is something wrong, Professor Swenson?" Claris Williams inclines her handsome head, done this week in bright rows of coiled dyed-orange snails. Everyone, including Swenson, is a little in love with, and scared of, Claris, possibly because she combines such intelligent sweetness with the glacial beauty of an African princess turned supermodel.

"Why do you ask?" says Swenson.

"You groaned," Claris says. "Twice."

"Nothing's wrong." Swenson's groaning in front of his class. Doesn't that prove nothing's wrong? "And if you call me Professor again, I'll fail you for the semester."

Claris stiffens. Relax! It's only a joke! Euston students call teachers by their first names, that's what Euston parents pay twenty-eight thousand a year for. But some kids can't make themselves say *Ted,* the scholarship students like Carlos (who does an end run around it by calling him Coach), the Vermont farm kids like Jonelle, the black students like Claris and Makeesha, the ones least likely to be charmed by his jokey threats. Euston hardly *has* any students like that, but this fall, for some reason, they're all in Swenson's class.

Last week they discussed Claris's story about a girl who accompanies her mother on a job cleaning a rich woman's house, an eerily convincing piece that moved from hilarity to horror as it chronicled the havoc wreaked by the maid stumbling through the rooms, chugging Thunderbird wine, until the horrified child watches her tumble downstairs.

The students were speechless with embarrassment. They all assumed, as did Swenson, that Claris's story was maybe not literal truth, but painfully close to the facts. At last, Makeesha Davis, the only other black student, said she was sick of stories in which sisters were always messed up on dope or drunk or selling their booty or dead.

Swenson argued for Claris. He'd dragged in Chekhov to tell the class that the writer need not paint a picture of an ideal world, but only describe the actual world, without sermons, without judgment. As if his students give a shit about some dead Russian that Swenson ritually exhumes to support his loser opinions. And yet just mentioning Chekhov made Swenson feel less alone, as if he were being watched over by a saint who wouldn't judge him for the criminal fraud of pretending that these kids could be taught what Swenson's pretending to teach them. Chekhov would see into his heart and know that he sincerely wished he could give his students what they want: talent, fame, money, a job.

After the workshop on her story, Claris stayed to talk. Swenson had groped for some tactful way to tell her that he knew what it was like to write autobiographically and have people act as if it were fiction. After all, his own second novel . . . As hard as this is to believe, he hadn't realized how painful his childhood was until his novel about it was published, and he read about it in reviews.

But before he could enchant her with the story of his rotten childhood and his fabulous career, Claris let him know: Her mom is a high school principal. Not a drunken domestic. Well, she'd certainly fooled Swenson, and done a job on the class. Couldn't she have dropped a hint and relieved the tension so thick that it was a relief to move on to Carlos's story about a dreamy Bronx kid with a crush on his neighbor, a tender romance shattered when the hero's friend describes peeping through the neighbor's window and seeing her fellate a German shepherd?

That was the other story about animal sex. Swenson hasn't imagined it, and now he remembers the one before that: Jonelle Brevard's story about a Vermont farm wife whose husband keeps calling out his favorite cow's name in his sleep. . . . Three animal sex stories, and the term's just begun.

"Your story, for one, Carlos. Was I imagining the German shepherd?"

"Oof," says Carlos. "I guess I forgot." The class laughs—sly, indulgent. They know why Carlos repressed it. The discussion of his story had devolved into a shouting match about sicko male fantasies of female sexuality.

This class has only been meeting five weeks, and already they share private jokes and passionate debates. Really, it's a good class. They're inspiring each other. There's more energy in this bestiality thing than in years of tepid fiction about dating mishaps or kids with divorced dysfunctional parents drying out from eighties cocaine habits. Swenson should be grateful for student work with any vitality, any life. So why should he insist on seeing these innocent landscapes of their hearts and souls as minefields to pick his way through?

Why? Because they are minefields. Let his colleagues try this. The ones who think it's easy—no lengthy texts, no lectures, no exams to grade. The ones who envy him this classroom with its panoramic campus view—let them open those windows before some student faints. Let them spend class knowing their careers depend on finding a way to chat about bestiality so that no one's feelings get hurt. It's not as if someone couldn't write a brilliant story about a young man finding solace with a chicken. A genius—let's say, Chekhov—could produce a work of genius. But it's unlikely that Danny will. And for this class to pretend that Danny can turn his dead chicken into art should be an actionable offense.

The room has fallen silent. Has someone asked a question? It's come to seem possible that Swenson could just lose it and sit there, mute, while the class watches to see what happens next. When he first started teaching, he'd settled for nothing less than the whole class falling in love with him. Now he's content to get through the hour without major psychic damage.

"Uh." Swenson smiles. "Where were we? I must have blinked out." The students' laughs are forgiving. Swenson is one of them. Their chemistry teachers don't blink out, or don't admit it. Alcohol and drugs have taught the kids about consciousness lapses. Quick, inclusive half-smiles all around, then Danny says, "Do you think we . . . could we talk about my story?"

"Of course. Sorry," says Swenson. "What did the rest of you think? What did you like? What engaged you?" Long silence. "Who wants to begin?"

Begin? No one wants to be here. Swenson doesn't blame them. They look like cartoon characters hearing birdies tweet. Swenson was raised a Quaker. He can handle silence.

At last, Meg Ferguson says, "I liked how honest it was about how most guys can't tell the difference between making love to a woman and screwing a dead chicken."

"Well!" Swenson says. "Yes, sir. That's certainly a beginning. Thank you, Meg, for breaking the ice."

There's never any predicting. Swenson would have guessed that Meg would see the story as a hateful celebration of phallic dominance imposing itself on a defenseless bird.

5

The guys never answer Meg directly. They let a moderate woman start, then they jump in. Shy Nancy Patrikis, who has a crush on Danny Liebman, says, "That's not what the story's about. The boy cares about his girlfriend. And she really hurts him. So he's, like, taking it out on the chicken."

"Yo, Meg," says Carlos, "trust me. Guys can tell the difference between sex with a woman and sex with a chicken."

"You better hope so, girlfriend," says Makeesha. "Otherwise we all be in trouble."

"Excuse me," says Swenson. "Do you think we could find our way back from the male's lack of sexual discrimination to discussing Danny's story?"

"I thought it was disgusting." Courtney Alcott purses her lips, meticulously outlined with dark brown and filled in with pale pink. Courtney is Boston Brahmin. Back Bay Barbie, Swenson thinks. Her homegirl makeup and fashion statement, a misguided protest against the fresh-faced Euston tree-huggers, annoy Makeesha and Claris.

"Disgusting . . ." Swenson ruminates. "Could anyone be more . . . exact?"

Courtney says, "That part where Danny did it to the chicken."

It's not lost on anyone that Courtney said *Danny* instead of *Ryan*, the character's name.

"*Ryan*," says Swenson. "The character—"

"Whatever," Courtney says.

"Not whatever," says Swenson. "It matters. I don't think Danny wants us to think he did that to a chicken."

"Well, he thought about doing it to a chicken," says Meg. "Otherwise he wouldn't have put it in the story."

"Thinking isn't doing," Swenson hears himself starting to lecture. "Mystery writers aren't murderers. Necessarily. And we've gotten into trouble whenever we've assumed that the character is a stand-in for the writer."

When did they get into trouble like that? Then they remember: Claris. The little girl and the cleaning lady. Everyone looks at

Claris, a situation she defuses by hauling the conversation back to Danny's work.

"I . . . liked the story?" Claris says. "The last part just came as a shock? I mean, that scene in the kitchen kind of came out of nowhere."

There's an agreeing murmur, as always when Claris speaks. The students are swayed by her persuasive chemistry of intuition, authority, and common sense. Swenson should just go home and let her run the class.

"In that case," says Swenson, "what does one do to make the last scene seem less shocking? No matter what, it's going to be . . . a surprise. But it should be plausible and shouldn't, as Claris says"—he quotes the students whenever he can, it gives everyone a positive feeling of partnership in a group project—"appear to come out of nowhere. . . . If, in fact, you think that it does . . . come out of nowhere."

Swenson suddenly can't recall very much about the piece except for a few disgusting details. Occasionally he'll suggest another ending for a story, only to have the students look puzzled until someone gently informs him that the story already ends with the event he's suggested. Well, no wonder he thought of it. . . .

"I don't know exactly," says Nancy. "I'd maybe change the boy's character so we know he's the kind of person who could do something like that."

The class can get behind this. That's precisely what's needed. Connect the maverick chicken-rapist with the seemingly normal Long Island teen who, in the story, takes his girlfriend out for pizza. During the meal she tells him that she's met an older guy who works at a Northern Italian trattoria in Manhattan. She says that this new guy invited her to stop by his place, where he'll serve her their signature dish, polenta with mushrooms ("You hate mushrooms," the hero says, in the story's best line) and steak grilled over an open fire.

"Make the kid more . . . violent," suggests Meg. "Do we see the waitress in the pizza place? Make him be mean to the waitress. So then later when he goes home—"

Swenson glances at Danny, who has that stupefied look students get when their work is being discussed and, to compound the ritual sadism, they are not allowed to speak. Danny *is* the boy in his story. He would never mistreat a waitress.

"Is that our sense of the character?" Swenson throws a line out to the drowning Danny. "Someone with a mean streak? Or . . ."

"Listen!" says Nancy. "What if . . . what if his date orders *chicken* at the pizza place? Or better yet . . . what if the fancy dish the older guy promises her isn't steak but . . . chicken? So that when the kid comes home later and . . . does that to the chicken, he's really getting back at the girl and the older guy—"

"Yesss!" says Carlos Ostapcek.

"You go, girl!" cries Makeesha.

"Interesting," says Claris. The others are practically cheering. Danny grins, then beams at Nancy, who smiles back. Danny feels he's written a story that only needed this minor adjustment to reveal its secret identity as a work of genius. He can't wait to go back to his dorm and scroll it up on his computer.

Swenson thinks it's a lousy suggestion. Obvious, fake, schematic. O. Henry high school shit. You don't order chicken in a pizza joint, you don't molest poultry just because your rival's restaurant serves it. But it's always tricky when the entire class approves some damaging "improvement." Then Swenson can either keep silent or play the snobbish elitist spoiler. So what if he's the teacher? Why should his stupid opinion matter? "Do you all agree with that?" Please, won't somebody say no?

"I think it sucks," a high voice pipes up, and they all turn toward Angela Argo.

Angela Argo hasn't talked in class since the start of the semester when they went around the room awkwardly saying their names. A skinny, pale redhead with neon-orange and lime-green streaks in her hair and a delicate, sharp-featured face pierced in a half-dozen places, Angela (despite the heat) wears a black leather motorcycle jacket and an arsenal of chains, dog collars, and bracelets.

The quiet ones always spook Swenson. God knows what they're thinking. But the metallic Angela is a special pain in the ass.

Because she never speaks, and restricts her commentary to eloquent, disruptive squirming and sighing, her presence is a lit firecracker sparking in their midst. Swenson can hardly look at her because of the facial piercing. Now she rat-tats a spiked ring against the edge of the table.

"Angela, are you saying that to rewrite the story that way would . . . suck?" asks Swenson, reflexively ironic and reflexively sorry. What if Angela thinks he's mimicking her and retreats again into silence?

"It would suck big-time," Angela says.

Precisely at that moment, they feel the seismic tremor, the middle-ear pressure change that warns them, seconds in advance: the bells are going to ring. The Euston bells are in the cupola just above them. When they ring the hour, halfway through Swenson's class, the slow funereal chiming vibrates in the bones. Conversation stops. Let the professors who covet this classroom—who hear the bells ringing sweetly from across the campus—deal with this every week.

The students reflexively check their watches, then look sheepishly at Swenson for direction: their teacher whose puny power has been trumped by two hunks of swinging bronze. Sometimes Swenson smiles, or shrugs, or makes a gun with his fingers and shoots the tolling bells. Today he looks at Angela, as if to keep her there. As soon as it's quiet, he wants her to continue where she left off and rescue Danny—as Swenson cannot—from further ruining his story. But he can't predict what she'll say. He's never seen a line of her writing or heard her express an opinion. Maybe she'll tell Danny to rewrite the story from the chicken's point of view. But at least she's swimming against the tide and may create an eddy into which Swenson can jump and stem the flood rushing Danny to wreck what little he's got. As long as Swenson isn't the only one to ruin the collective good mood with his know-it-all pronouncements. . . . After all, what does *he* know? He's only published two novels, the second of which was so critically successful that even now, ten years later, he's still asked, though more rarely, to give readings and write reviews.

The bells strike twice for each hour. Each time, the students flinch.

Swenson stares at Angela, who stares back, neither curious nor challenging, combative nor seductive, which is partly why he can look at her with the whole class watching. Nor does he see her, exactly, but just allows his slightly out-of-focus gaze to linger on her until he senses restlessness in the room and notices that the bells have stopped.

"Angela? You were telling us . . . ?"

Angela stares at her hands, twisting a ring on one finger, then moves on to another ring, twists that one, five maddening fingers on one hand, five more on the other.

"I don't know," she says. "I guess I think the best thing—the one good thing—is that the end *is* so weird and unexpected. Isn't that the point? Anyone could do something like this. You don't have to be crazy, or have some babe ditch you for a waiter who serves Northern Italian chicken. Here's this loser on a date with a dorky girl, and he goes home miserable. And there's this chicken. And he just does it. Guys are always surprising themselves, doing crazy shit even though they don't think they're the kind of guys who would do crazy shit like that."

"Excuse me, Angela," says Carlos. "Most guys would *not* poke a chicken—"

"Carlos," says Angela, darkly, "trust me. I know what most guys would do."

From what authority does Angela speak? Is this some kind of sexual boasting? It's best that Swenson not even try to decipher the code in which his students are transmitting.

"Is something going on here? Something I'm not getting?" He feels them pulling together to screen their world from him. He's the teacher, they're the students: a distinction they like to blur, then make again, as needed.

"Moving right along," he says, "I think Angela's right. If Danny's story's not going to be just a . . . psychiatric case study of a guy who could go home and . . . well, we know what he does. The strongest story makes us see how we could *be* that kid, how the world looks through that kid's eyes. The reason he does it is not because his girl-friend has eaten chicken, or because her new boyfriend serves—as Angela says—Northern Italian chicken, but because he's there and the chicken's there. Circumstance, destiny, chance. We begin to see ourselves in him, the ways in which he's like us."

The students are awake now. He's pulled this class out of the fire, redeemed this shaky enterprise they're shoring up together. He's promised them improvement. He's shown them how to improve. The angriest, the most resistant think they've gotten their money's worth. And Swenson's given them something, a useful skill, a gift. Even if they don't become writers, it's a way of seeing the world— each fellow human a character to be entered and understood. All of us potential chicken-rapists. Dostoyevskian sinners.

"All right." Slowly Swenson comes to. For a second, the edges of things buckle and shimmer lightly. And there, among the fun-house curves, is Claris Williams, glaring.

What is Claris's problem? Did she miss the fact that Swenson's just kicked things up to a whole other level? Oh, right. It was Claris who suggested that the end of the story be tied down, like a rogue balloon, to the beginning. And now Swenson, with Angela's help, has not merely contradicted Claris but done so with a slashing inci-sion that's transcended the timid microsurgery of the workshop.

"Well," Swenson backtracks, "no one can tell the writer what to do. Danny will have to see for himself whatever works for him." He's so glad to have gotten through this that he can't bother much about their failure to agree on one thing that might help Danny's story. He starts to put his papers away. The students do the same. Above the squeaking of chairs Swenson shouts, "Hey, wait. What's the schedule? Whose story's up next week?"

Angela Argo raises her hand. He would never have guessed. Students tend to get very tactful—hesitant to make enemies—the week before their own work is to be discussed.

"Have you got it with you?" Swenson asks. "We need to copy and distribute—"

"No." Angela's almost whispering. "It's not exactly finished. Do you think I can come talk to you? During your office hours tomorrow?"

"Absolutely!" booms Swenson. *Office hours tomorrow?* He schedules two conferences with each student per semester, though actually, he'd rather not go into his office at all. He'd rather be home writing. Trying to write. If he has to be in his office, he likes to sit and think. Or jerk off, or make long distance calls on the college's nickel.

Of course, he can't tell the class that. He wants the students to see him as generous, giving—on their side. And he wants to be, he used to be, when he first started teaching. Well, anyway . . . he owes Angela for bailing him out, for helping him divert the class from the wipeout toward which it was heading.

Swenson says, "What time are my office hours? Someone remind me, please."

"Tomorrow morning," Nancy Patrikis says.

"*I* have morning office hours?" says Swenson. "Are we positive about that?"

"That's what it says on your office door." Danny's happy to play along, he's so thrilled that the class is over.

Clearly, there's no avoiding it. "All right, Angela. See you at nine."

"See you," Angela—half out the door—calls back over her shoulder.

On his way out, Carlos punches Swenson's upper arm and says, "Hey, Coach. Thanks. Good class." Nancy and Danny find each other—it's like Noah's Ark. Claris and Makeesha leave together, apparently reconciled since Makeesha criticized the politics of Claris's latest story. The disenfranchised Carlos with the feminist Meg, the furious first-family Courtney with the furious farm-girl Jonelle. Everyone's in a fabulous mood . . . .

A tide of satisfaction sweeps Swenson out the door and sends him, practically skipping, down the belltower's helical stairs. Not until he's halfway across the quad does he realize that he hadn't needed to mention the detail of the chicken's head, gazing back at its attacker.

As always, getting out of class, Swenson feels like an innocent man, sentenced to life, whose jail term has just been commuted. He's saved, alive, he's been reprieved . . . at least until next week. Hurrying across the quad, he nearly plows into a tour group inching across the campus. Rather than ruin his sneakers by cutting across the boggy lawn, he trails behind the high school students enduring the mortification of being here with their parents.

Deep in the Northeast Kingdom, an hour from Montpelier, sixty miles from Burlington, one hundred fifty from Montreal if you're desperate enough to wait at the border while the Mounties tweeze through each car to discourage Canadians from crossing to shop at the Wal-Mart, Euston's nobody's first choice. Students willing to travel this far to a college this cut off and inbred prefer Bates or Bowdoin, which have better reputations, the Maine coast, and the L. L. Bean outlet. Euston's conveniently located in the midst of the two-block town of Euston and the moose-ridden wilderness that its founder, Elijah Euston, so loved.

Recently, a public relations team advised Euston to *market* its isolation. And so the tour leader—Kelly Steinsalz, from last spring's Beginning Fiction—is explaining that the lack of distractions lets her concentrate on academics. The parents nod. The teenagers scowl. That's just what they want from college. Four years of concentration!

Swenson can't imagine how Euston looks to someone visiting for the first time. They couldn't have picked a better day. Warm vapors surround the handsome buildings, the gnarled maples and still-green lawns. What they cannot picture—and Swenson can, all too well—is how soon this soft green path will turn into a frozen white tunnel.

"Excuse me," says Swenson. No one budges. They're too busy miming presentability or disdain. Trapped, Swenson listens to Kelly Steinsalz describe Elijah Euston's vision: how a four-year liberal arts education far from the civilized world would nurture leaders who could go back into that world and change it. The parents are so deferential, so eager to make an impression, you'd think Kelly was director of admissions. Shyly, one mother asks, "Does it ever bother you that the school is so . . . small?"

"Not at all," says Kelly. "It means there's a community, everybody belongs. Anyway, it's not *small*. It's intimate. It's . . . close."

In Swenson's class, Kelly spent all semester writing a story about a cranky old woman named Mabel who thinks her ungrateful children have forgotten her eightieth birthday. At the end, Mabel's neighbor Agnes invites her to a melancholy dinner for two in the local diner—which turns out to be a surprise party attended by Mabel's whole clan.

Kelly redid the piece a dozen times. At every stage Swenson found "Mabel's Party" harder to deal with, he thinks now, than the most lurid account of sex with a dead chicken. Bring up sentimentality, they think you're saying they shouldn't have feelings. He couldn't make himself tell Kelly that revision wouldn't help. But she wasn't stupid. She got it, and at last demanded to know why she couldn't write a story with a happy ending instead of the stuff Swenson liked: boring, depressing Russian junk about suicidal losers.

Kelly explains how Elijah Euston founded Euston Academy to educate his six sons and seven daughters (one father whistles) but omits the sad story of Elijah's curse: three daughters died from diphtheria, two more committed suicide. Kelly describes the college traditions, but not the widespread belief that the campus is haunted by the ghosts of its founder's daughters, spirits with an appetite for the souls of undergraduate women.

Nor does Kelly mention the college's disturbingly high dropout rate among female students, the source of another quaint custom: every spring the senior girls ring the college bells to celebrate having made it. All this has become a rallying point for the Faculty-Student Women's Alliance, demanding to know why Euston is such an "unsafe" place for women that so many of them leave before graduation. Unsafe? It's not a safety issue. The women are just smarter, quicker to catch onto the fact that they're wasting their parents' money in this godforsaken backwater.

"Coming through! Coming through!" Swenson cries, and the group scatters.

"Oh, hi, Professor Swenson!" says Kelly. "That's Professor Swenson? Our writer in residence? Probably you've all read his book, it's called . . . ?"

Swenson nods politely but chooses not to wait and see if she remembers. He passes Mather Hall, the turreted Victorian firetrap in which he has his office, built on the site of the lake drained by Elijah Euston after one of his daughters drowned herself in its murky depths. He keeps going till he reaches the Health Services Clinic, a tiny prefab bungalow, neatly shingled and quarantined from the classrooms and dorms.

A bell announces Swenson to the empty waiting room. He sits in a plastic bucket chair under a poster of a perky blond cheerleader who never thought HIV could happen to her. No one's at the front desk. Is Sherrie back with a patient? Swenson should welcome the downtime. If he leafed through the women's magazines in the rack, he'd learn how important it is to have a quiet transitional moment. He clears his throat, scrapes the chair legs. . . . All right, let's try something faster-acting.

"Nurse!" he shouts. "Please! I need help!"

Sherrie rushes into the room, raking her tangle of dark curly hair. After all this time Swenson's still impressed by the stormy, rough-edged beauty his wife shares with those actresses spewing pure life force all over postwar Italian films. He loves the groove that time has dug between her eyebrows, the lively mobility of her

features, molting within seconds from alarm to confusion to indulgent, not-quite-genuine laughter.

"Jesus Christ, Ted," she says. "I heard some guy out here yelling
for help. It took me a couple of seconds to realize it was you."

"How'd you know I didn't need help?"

"Instinct," says Sherrie. "Twenty years of experience."

"Twenty-one," says Swenson.

"*I* need help," Sherrie says. "Is that how long I've been married
to some jerk who'd yell like that just to get attention? Jesus, Ted,
stop leering."

Such are the pleasures of intimacy: he can look as long as he wants.
Given the current political climate, you'd better be having consensual
matrimonial sex with a woman before you risk this stare. Sherrie's
outfit, a white lab coat over blue jeans and black T-shirt, might not
give every guy the first Pavlovian stirrings of a hard-on, but Swenson
seems to be having a definite response.

"Nurse, I think something's wrong," he says.

Those were the first words he ever said to her. The morning
they met—this was in New York—he'd gotten out of bed and
fallen, fell twice more getting dressed, went out for some coffee,
and the sidewalk came up to meet him. A brain tumor, obviously.
He waited till he fell again before he went to St. Vincent's.

The emergency room wasn't crowded. The nurse—that is,
Sherrie—walked him in to see the doctor, who was practically
delirious because the patient who'd just left was Sarah Vaughn.
The doctor wanted to talk about Sarah's strep throat and not about
what turned out to be Swenson's middle-ear infection. Swenson
thanked him, stood, and hit the floor. He'd woken with Sherrie's
hand on his pulse, where it's been ever since. That's what he used
to say when he told this story, which he hardly ever does anymore
since they no longer meet new people who haven't heard it. And
Sherrie used to say, "I should have known not to fall in love with a
guy who was already unconscious."

This always caused a complicated moment of silence at Euston
faculty dinner parties. Sherrie was kidding, obviously. The others

just didn't get it. Swenson cherished those moments for making him feel that he and Sherrie were still dangerous outsiders with no resemblance to these nerds and their servile wives dishing out the tabbouleh salad. Even after Ruby was born, he and Sherrie clung to that sense of being rebels, partners in crime passing for respectable citizens at nursery-school Halloween parties and parent-teacher conferences. But lately there's been some . . . slippage. He knows that Sherrie blames him for the fact that Ruby's barely spoken to them since she left for college a year ago this September.

Sherrie glances out the window to see if anyone's coming. Then she says, "Let's take a look. Why don't you come with me?"

Swenson follows her down a corridor into a treatment room. She closes the door behind them and sits on the edge of a gurney. Swenson stands between her legs and kisses her. She slides down so that she's standing. He moves his hips against hers, until Sherrie braces one hand against his shoulder and, toppling slightly, he steps backward.

Sherrie says, "What do you think it would do for our careers if we got caught having sex in the Health Services Clinic?"

But they aren't going to. This is just some primitive greeting, reestablishing their acquaintance, less real desire than the desire to raise their body temperatures after a long tepid day.

"We could claim it's therapeutic," Swenson says. "For medicinal purposes only. Anyway, we could fuck each other's brains out here and no one would ever hear us."

"Oh yeah?" says Sherrie. "Listen."

Someone's vomiting next door. Each volcanic eruption of retching trickles off into a moan. When the noise stops, Swenson hears liquid splashing, more retching, then more splashing. It's not the most aphrodisiac sound. He backs away from Sherrie.

"Great," says Swenson. "Thanks for bringing that to my attention."

"Stomach flu," says Sherrie. "Nasty. Not half so bad as it sounds. Ted, can you imagine? Kids come in here to puke. When we were their age, we knew enough to crawl off and dig ourselves a hole and throw up in private. No one went to student health unless we were overdosing on LSD and seeing green snakes crawl up our legs."

"Tough day?" says Swenson, warily. Something must have happened. Sherrie's never unsympathetic—anyway, not with the kids. He's driven her to the clinic at 4 A.M. for the cardiac emergencies that turn out to be freshman anxiety attacks. Or the truly scary but not yet fatal consequences of binge drinking. She's got patience for everyone but the morose faculty hypochondriacs who treat her like a servant and blame her for not being licensed to write prescriptions for antidepressants. Even so, she listens and never seems irritated. But since the start of this semester, Sherrie's been less tolerant of the lacrosse jocks weaseling out of exams, the wimp who jams his finger playing ball and demands a cast to his elbow. With those students she's all business, Nurse Ratchet instead of Mom.

"Let's blow this joint," says Swenson. "Let's go home and get under the covers."

"Jesus, Ted," says Sherrie. "We can't go home. We've got that meeting this afternoon. You know that."

He didn't know. Or maybe he did. Maybe he did and forgot. He wishes Sherrie wouldn't sound so annoyed, as if he were some helpless, irresponsible . . . child. He wishes she'd have more patience with his little memory lapses. Who could blame him for forgetting that the whole faculty and staff has been asked—is being forced—to attend a meeting to review Euston College's policy on sexual harassment?

All semester, Euston's been anxiously following a current case over at State, where Ruby goes, and where, last spring, a professor showed a slide in Art History 101: a classical Greek sculpture of a female nude. He'd said one monosyllable. *Yum*. That *Yum* blew up in his face. The students accused him of leering. He said he was expressing a gut response to art. *Yum*, he said, was about the aesthetic sense, not the genitalia. They argued that he'd made them uncomfortable. No one could argue with that. He shouldn't have used the word *genitalia*, certainly not in his own defense. The guy has been suspended without pay and is fighting his case in court.

There's a timid knock on the door. The vomiting kid, no doubt. Sherrie trills, "Come in," and they turn to see Arlene Shurley, suited up in her shiny white bush shirt and trousers. Arlene's a local Vermonter, a widowed grandmother whose lifelong uncertainty dribbles out in her shaky voice, constantly threatening tears. Sometimes, when she's on duty and phones Sherrie late at night, her tone makes their hearts skip. Someone must have died!

"Gosh, it's so pretty outside," Arlene says weepily. "And you can't help thinking how soon all the color's going to be gone and how long winter lasts. . . ."

Essentially, that's what Swenson thought as he trailed the tour group across campus, but it infuriates him to hear it from Arlene.

"In that case," he says, "you should be out partying, Arlene. Get it while you can."

Arlene smiles and mews, at once. Is Swenson flirting or mocking? He honestly doesn't know. Speech pops out of him, on its own. I need to see an exorcist, nurse.

Sherrie takes Arlene's arm and cradles the doughy knob of her elbow. She says, "We're late for the meeting. Call me if you need me, hon. Don't hesitate for a second."

Sherrie and Swenson cross the parking lot toward his five-year-old Accord. They know that it's an ecological crime to drive across campus, but they want to make a getaway the minute the meeting's over. Sherrie's Civic is languishing in the Euston garage, stricken with a computer chip ailment that causes the engine to die occasionally, though never in the mechanic's presence.

"What's with the car?" Swenson asks as he pulls out of the lot.

Sherrie says, "The garage guys say it's in denial. They can't help it heal until it admits it has a problem. Speaking of problems . . . what was that about? Picking on Arlene?"

"Sorry," says Swenson. "Nothing. Today I had the delightful task of teaching a student story that ends with a kid having sex with a chicken."

"Did the chicken have fun?"

"The chicken was dead," says Swenson.

"Too bad for the chicken," says Sherrie. "Or maybe it was better off. So how did the class go?"

"It went. We got through it without my saying anything that's going to have the Faculty-Student Women's Alliance camped out on my doorstep tonight. I still have a job. I think."

But now they're approaching the chapel, where, for all they know, Dean Francis Bentham is already informing the community that teaching a story about poultry sex is automatic grounds for dismissal.

Apparently, they've made it in time. A few die-hard smokers—tenured, of course—hover outside the door. Just as Swenson pulls up, they suck their cigarettes down to the filters and flick them, smoldering, onto the path. Holding hands, Swenson and Sherrie follow the smokers inside and find seats in the last row, creating a minor upset just as the room falls silent.

"Can I borrow your sunglasses?" Swenson whispers.

"Cool it," Sherrie says.

Slouching so low that his toes nearly touch the heels of the woman in front of him, Swenson can still see. The gang's all here: the tense, anemic junior lecturers, his own grizzled generation, even the retired emeriti. They've all crowded obediently into the austere chapel where, centuries before, the Reverend Jonathan Edwards, on the hell-fire circuit, the Sinners in the Hands of an Angry God Tour, terrified his listeners with descriptions of the damned cast into the flames and roasted, screaming, to ashes. In memory of that occasion, a burnished portrait of Edwards glowers from the chapel wall, peering over the shoulder of Dean Francis Bentham, who, when he rises to go to the lectern, glances back at the painting and fakes a tiny shudder as he tip-toes past. The faculty giggles, smarmily.

"Asshole," Swenson hisses.

The woman in front of them wheels around.

"Easy," Sherrie says.

Just as Swenson suspected from the inverted bowl of gray hair and the tense, aggrieved shoulders, it's Lauren Healy, the English Department's expert in the feminist misreading of literature and acting head of the Faculty-Student Women's Alliance. Swenson and Lauren always fake a chilly collegiality, but for reasons he can't fathom—a testosterone allergy, he guesses—Lauren wants him dead.

"Hi, Lauren!" Swenson says.

"Hello, Ted," Lauren mouths silently, redirecting them front and center.

In his natty blazer, crisp striped shirt, and perky burgundy bowtie, his china-blue eyes glittering in the gold-rimmed saucers of his glasses, Dean Bentham resembles a punitive pediatrician shipped over from England to cure the rude American children of their bad behavior. The dean was hired a half-dozen years ago in a fit of community self-hate; not even when he visited Euston as a candidate did he make a secret of his natural Oxbridge-assisted superiority to these touching but hopelessly naive colonial morons.

Bentham grabs the podium with both hands and leans down as if he means to kiss it, then straightens up, crackles a sheet of paper over his head, and says, "Dear friends and colleagues, I have here a copy of the Euston College policy on sexual harassment." He smiles at this terribly amusing symptom of their hangover from Puritan repression, at the same time suggesting the slightly perverted headmaster who would cane them in a minute for the mildest infraction. "One receives this paper in one's mailbox every September . . . along with updates on the health plan and cafeteria hours. All of which one tosses straightaway in the trash."

The faculty's chuckles are guilty and pleased. How well Daddy knows them.

"I know *I* throw it away, unread. Though it's my unpleasant duty to write it. But the current zeitgeist is such that—one knows about the grotesqueries at State, there's no need to add to the gossip—one has to understand that it's a whole new . . . cricket match out there. So I thought we might spend a moment or two going over it together."

A faint groan goes up from the room, the faculty's docile protest. Their dean lets them have their feelings, and then gets back to business.

Sherrie whispers in Swenson's ear, "This is so that if the college gets sued they can say they warned us."

Of course, it's just like Sherrie to get it right the first time, without the pointless ruminations on British cultural imperialism and Puritan moral baggage. Sherrie knows it's simpler, it's about indemnification. The college's fear of litigation is as intense as Jonathan Edwards's terror of hellfire. One expensive lawsuit could push Euston—with its alarmingly tiny endowment—over the edge.

"One," reads Francis Bentham in his ironic baritone. "No Euston College faculty member shall have sexual relations with a currently enrolled or former student, nor offer to trade sexual favors for academic advancement."

All right. They can agree to that, so long as it's not retroactive. In the old days, undergraduate paramours were a perk that went with the job. But already Bentham has moved from these clear prohibitions—as simple and as hard to obey as the Ten Commandments—into the fuzzy area of the hostile workplace, the atmosphere of intimidation. No matter. Like Jonathan Edwards's audience, Bentham's listeners drift from the subject of mass retribution to the juicier topic of each one's secret sin and its chance of being discovered.

Puritanism's alive and well. Thank God for repression. What if someone rose to say what so many of them are thinking, that there's something erotic about the *act* of teaching, all that information streaming back and forth like some . . . bodily fluid. Doesn't Genesis trace sex to that first bite of apple, not the fruit from just any tree, but the Tree of Knowledge?

Teacher-student attraction is an occupational hazard. Over the years, plenty of girls have had crushes on Swenson. He's not flattering himself about this. It's built into the system. Still, their interest is flattering, which in itself is attractive, and so their attention was sometimes returned in ways that couldn't have been more harmless. So what if he read Miss A.'s paper first, or looked to see if Miss B. got his joke? More often than not, those students worked harder and learned more. And those fleeting . . . attachments never led any further. Swenson should be canonized. He's the saint of Euston!

As hard as it might be for anyone, including himself, to believe, he's taught here for twenty years and never once slept with a student. He loves Sherrie. He wants his marriage to last. He's always felt . . . shy around women. Nor has he needed the dean to point out the moral implications of the power gap between teacher and student. So he'd managed to get past those . . . awkward spots with literary talk. Each friendly, formal professorial chat layered a barrier between him and the problematically attractive student until neither of them could have begun to dismantle that protective partition. By then it was way too late, too embarrassing and daunting, to face each other on any other terms—as male and female, for example.

How hard it is to remember their names, which proves that they meant nothing, nothing worth risking his job for, nothing that would have been worth his sitting here now, sweating lest some disgruntled loony rise out of his past to share her undying shame at having traded sex with him for an A in Beginning Fiction. But what Bentham's saying is that nothing *has* to happen. Any spark can set off the tinderbox of gender war. Best not to make eye contact or shake a student's hand. Every classroom's a lion's den, every teacher a Daniel. And every Tuesday afternoon, Swenson's job requires him to discuss someone's tale of familial incest, fumbling teenage sex, some girl's or boy's first blow job, with the college's most hypersensitive and unbalanced students, some of whom simply despise him for reasons he can only guess: he's the teacher, and they're not, or he looks like somebody's father.

Silence. Long silence. Dean Bentham glances coyly over at Jonathan Edwards's portrait, then flashes a grin at his audience and says, "Unlike your distinguished forefather, I don't mean to scare you. But one needs to know it's warfare, lest we poor settlers be . . . ambushed. Clearly there are still witch-hunters ready to burn one at the stake for the sin of smacking one's lips over the wrong Greek torso. Well, fine. Sermon ended. By the way, I have no fear that anything like this will happen here at Euston."

A pall creeps over the chapel, as if Bentham has been describing some fatal new epidemic that chooses its victims at random, as if he'd come here to preach the bad news of an angry God torching their miserable anthill. Then, inexplicably, everyone applauds.

Swenson and Sherrie duck out before they can be trapped in the quicksand of collegial conversation. But by the time they find their car, the mournful professors have clustered outside the chapel. The obvious thing to do right now is to peel out of the lot, spraying gravel like buckshot, scattering those gloomy groupings. But first Sherrie has to inspect her face in Swenson's rearview mirror.

"Christ," she says. "A giant pimple in the middle of my forehead. I could feel it growing every time Bentham opened his mouth. Look, Ted. Right here. See?"

"I don't see it," Swenson says.

"You're not looking," says Sherrie.

Exiting the parking lot, he threads his way through the campus, hopping over the speed bumps, crawling through the gates and the two blocks that comprise lovely downtown Euston. Then, only then, he hits the gas, and bingo, they're free—oh, the mystical ecstasy of taking off in the car!

How powerful, how safe he feels to have Sherrie sitting beside him, encapsulated, while the world slips by. Okay, a little piece of the world. Fine. All right. He'll take it. So what if it's one of those autumn evenings that drop so alarmingly fast, furry dark curtains behind which nature can work all night, freeze-drying the land-scape? So what if he knows the drive so well that the sights—how the sky expands as you round the second curve, stretching wide enough to display the blackened teeth of the mountains—the sights that used to thrill him have come to seem menacing and oppres-sive? He can't imagine how he could have been thrilled by the sight of mountains beneath which he will probably be buried.

A light fog rises off the ground, conveniently blurring the general store, the fly-specked mecca where he'd go for after-school ice cream with Ruby. He's thankful for the mist that softens the junkscape of the Turner farm, the rusted trucks, the busted fridges with illegally left-on doors beckoning neighbor kids to crawl inside and smother. He's glad even for the deepening blackness that separates him from Sherrie, walling him off in a lozenge of solitude in which he can face the fact that what truly depressed him about the meeting was neither Bentham nor his colleagues, neither the spartan Founders Chapel nor all that pilgrim self-regard, nor even the shock of finding himself, stranded all these long years, in the heart of the stony heart of Puritan New England.

No, what really bothers him—and he can hardly admit it to himself; if he weren't driving through the half-dark, he couldn't let himself think it—is that he was too stupid or timid or scared to sleep with those students. What exactly was he proving? Illustrating some principle, making some moral point? The point is: he adores Sherrie, he always has. He would never hurt her. And now, as a special reward for having been such a good husband, such an all-around good guy, he's got the chill satisfaction of having taken his high-minded self-denial almost all the way to the grave. Because now it's all over. He's too old. He's way beyond all that.

He was right to do what he did. Or not to do what he didn't do. He gropes in the dark for Sherrie's hand. Her fingers weave around his.

"What was that sigh for?" Sherrie says.

"Did I sigh?" says Swenson. "I was thinking I've got to do something about this molar." Turning toward her, he points to it with his tongue.

"Do you want me to call the dentist?" she says.

"No thanks," he says. "I will."

His marriage means everything to him. That's what he imagined telling the admiring students if it ever came to that—which it never did.

Sherrie says, "It'll sure make my life easier."

In a better mood, he'd enjoy the intimacy that lets his wife pick up an old conversation or start a new one without introduction, or explanation. Just now, it annoys him. Why can't Sherrie say what she means? Because he knows what she means. Crisis counseling is part of her job, and if the sexual harassment policy takes hold, she'll see fewer students destroyed by faculty Romeos. Sherrie has enough information to bust the entire school, but she's remarkably discreet and tolerant about what she sees in the clinic. She would not be discreet or tolerant if Swenson slept with a student. She used to boast about being Sicilian on both sides of the family, from villages where straying husbands were routinely thrown off mountaintops by the wronged wife's uncles and brothers. She used to say that if he cheated on her, she'd divorce him, and then hunt him down and kill him.. That she hasn't bothered to say that for years only depresses him more.

"Lucky you." He feels Sherrie flinch in the dark.

"Excuse *me*," she says. "What did I do?"

"My nerves are shot," Swenson mutters.

"Yeah, well, mine too," says Sherrie. "You would not believe the nightmares that came into the clinic today."

Swenson's supposed to ask, What nightmares? But he doesn't want to.

"You know," says Sherrie after a while, "you can relax. No one's going to fire you for teaching dirty student stories."

How dare she underestimate the horrors he faces each day! He'd like to see her go into the classroom and lie about what *she* loves most in the world, then crawl back into *her* hole and try to work on *her* novel. Just as he's deciding whether to say any of the hostile things that could start them squabbling for days, the mist thickens and forces him to pay attention to the road.

Sherrie fishes for a cassette and pops it into the tape deck. *Wake me, shake me, don't let me sleep too long.* The Dixie Hummingbirds. Terrific. So much for peaceful silence. Sherrie's been listening to gospel, which normally Swenson likes. This summer, driving the country roads, he'd turned up the sound and filled the car with glorious voices auditioning for the angel chorus.

Now he says, "I hate this song. It makes me want to pull off the road and kneel down in the drainage ditch and accept Jesus as my personal savior. Plus it makes me envy those lucky fuckers who believe it."

"Hey." Sherrie holds up her hand. "Don't blame me. All I did was put on some music."

Wake me? Shake me? Are the Dixie Hummingbirds really worried about sleeping through the Last Judgment? Here on earth, Swenson and Sherrie balance on the point between hellish recriminations and the purgatorial silence that passes for friendly camaraderie.

Sherrie switches off the tape.

"I'm sorry," Swenson says. "You can listen to it if you want."

"That's okay," says Sherrie. "You've been through enough for one day."

"I love you," says Swenson. "You know that?"

"Me you too," says Sherrie.

S wenson dreams that his daughter, Ruby, has called to say she's thinking of him and everything's forgiven. Struggling awake, he's snapped into the harsh bright morning, which greets him with three unpleasant facts, more or less at once.

One: the phone *is* ringing.

Two: it isn't Ruby, who hasn't called since she went away to college. She'll consent to talk to him if he phones her dorm at State, though talk is hardly the word for her murmurs and grunts, each one an eloquent expression of the rage that's been brewing since she was a high school senior and Swenson—stupidly—broke up her first real infatuation with arguably the sleaziest student in Euston College history.

Three: he seems to have spent the night on the living room couch.

Why doesn't someone answer the phone? Where the hell is Sherrie? It's probably Sherrie calling to explain why he's on the sofa. He'd know if they'd had an argument. Besides which, they never go to sleep without making up or at least pretending, though the embers may reignite first thing in the morning. Why didn't Sherrie wake him and make him come to bed? It's lucky the phone stops ringing before he's able to move. If it *is* Sherrie, he just might have to ask her why the hell she left him here. Once the phone stops insisting, he eases himself off the couch. He'll call Sherrie back when he gets a chance. But wait. She has to be in the house. He's got the only car.

"Sherrie?" he cries. Something's terribly wrong. Sudden death would certainly explain her leaving him on the couch. "Sherrie!" He can't live without her!

He rushes instinctively toward the sun streaming in from the kitchen. Glowing in the center of light is a sheet of white paper. A note from Sherrie, obviously, on the kitchen table.

"You looked tired. I let you sleep in. Arlene gave me a ride. Much love, S."

Poor Sherrie! Married to a lunatic convinced she'd abandoned him when she was only trying to let him get some shut-eye. Sherrie loves him. She signed her note: Much love.

Clutching the note, he drifts over to the window. Installing it was their second and final attempt to make the old Vermont farmhouse satisfy their needs or just acknowledge their existence. Mostly they've settled in and let the house do what it wants. Although (or perhaps because) they told the hippie carpenter not to make it look like a bay window in a tract home, it looks exactly like a bay window in a tract home. So what. The window does its job, lets them see Sherrie's garden from the table.

They'd inherited the garden from the old woman who sold them the house and who'd held out for a buyer who promised to maintain her flower and vegetable beds. Sherrie would have promised anything to escape the Euston residence hall where they were living as dorm parents, an existence so public that only thanks to desire's resourcefulness was Ruby ever conceived. But she'd kept her promise. Though almost nothing remains of Ethel Turner's flowers—perennial is a cruel jest here in northern Vermont—everything's been replaced with plants bought from the nursery or coaxed from seed. The garden's flourishing, thanks to an innate gift that must have come via DNA from Sherrie's grandparents. She'd spent her own formative years in city apartments and later, emergency rooms.

At this season, the garden looks like an archaeological tomb excavation in progress: tidy beds of clippings, thatches of straw, tender crowns tucked under layers of soggy leaves, evidence of rituals intended to ensure the dead's rebirth. And that, precisely, is the difference between Swenson and Sherrie. Sherrie believes that spring will come, whereas Swenson's always shocked when the snow melts and the first crocuses appear. He envies Sherrie's optimistic faith. Well, someone has to have it.

He peers into the refrigerator, less hungry than eager for clues about last night's dinner: leftover fettucine, sticky with butter and cheese. Sherrie tries to watch their diet but knows that there are times when nothing will do but big globs of cholesterol. They'd eaten on the living room couch, in front of the evening news, both of them so grateful for not having to talk that the low-level edginess of their car ride home from the meeting was smoothed out of existence, replaced by pure animal comfort.

As he reaches for the phone, he's thinking of how to tell Sherrie how much he loves her, treasures their life together. The phone rings, preemptively, startling him. His telepathic wife!

"Sweetheart!" he says.

"Er . . . um," says a female voice.

Oops. A student. Clearly. She doesn't know what to call him. Mr. Swenson. Professor. Ted. Definitely not *sweetheart*. Students never phone him at home, though he gives them his number at the start of each semester. He pretends he's joking when he tells them to feel free to call if their problem is life-threatening. A student with a life-threatening problem at . . . nine-twenty in the morning?

"It's Angela Argo?" the voice says. "We were supposed to have a conference at nine? I've been waiting outside your office? I thought I had the wrong day or . . . the wrong time? But we talked about it yesterday . . . ?"

Finally Swenson remembers. He was so grateful for getting through class, he would have promised anyone anything.

"You're right," says Swenson. "I'm sorry."

"No, *I'm* sorry," she says. "Did I wake you? I'm totally totally sorry."

"I was awake."

"Oh my God. Were you writing? Did I disturb you from writing?"

"I wasn't writing," Swenson says, more harshly than he intends.

"I'm really sorry," Angela says.

"Stop apologizing. Stay where you are. I'll be there in fifteen minutes."

"Okay," she says. "Are you sure?"

"Positive," he says.

For a moment he stalls by the phone. He should have taken early retirement. In one of the college's failed attempts to stave off financial ruin, the tenured faculty was offered a year's salary to get out. But like convicts who love their shackles, nearly all chose not to escape. He could be staying home, writing, reading, watching TV, instead of wasting yet another day of his one and only life.

Meanwhile he's got fifteen minutes to shower, shave, dress, drive to school, which itself takes fifteen minutes—an obvious impossibility. Forget the personal grooming. So this chick wants to write? Let her see how a writer *looks* at nine-thirty in the morning.

Swenson continues down the hall, slowing reflexively at the steps up and down between rooms. Each room was built as needed, in good harvest years. The earth settled before each addition as the segmented structure grew, perpendicular to the road. The front parlor faces on the nonexistent traffic, offering the world a buffer zone of the least inhabited room so as to protect the inner life of its bedrooms and kitchen. Farthest back is the attached dairy barn, reborn as Swenson's study.

Their other home improvement: Swenson's shrinelike office, skylit, soaring, unheatable, the sacrificial altar on which they pulped the whole advance for his unwritten novel. Half the time he worries that his publishers will ask for the money back. Half the time he worries because no one seems to have noticed. His working title is *The Black and the Black*, though he doubts he'll use it. His impulse—impossible to recall—was to recast Stendhal's Julien Sorel as a young sculptor, the son of a martyred Black Panther dad and a Social Register mom, a charming, amoral striver who uses everyone he meets in his ferocious scramble up the art world ladder. Race. Art. Ambition. Bullshit ideas. He doubts he'll ever finish. What a huge mistake to think he could write about single-minded ambition when all he can imagine, these days, is indolence and self-doubt.

He should be glad for his teaching job, not simply for providing income but for removing him from the dismal spectacle of the ministack of typescript dwarfed by his giant desk, an oak monstrosity he bought twenty years ago from a failing law firm. It cost Euston a fortune to ship it from New York, but they were happy to pay his moving costs and let Sherrie write her own ticket at the clinic. The desk is his sole reminder of how much he was wanted.

Where's his briefcase? He's always sure he's lost it, left it somewhere. There's never anything important in it, but usually several items, student manuscripts and so forth, that would be a time-consuming nightmare to replace. That's enough to make him panic, and he begins to shovel paper and books around, increasingly agitated until he finds the briefcase under a stack of yesterday's mail. A short stack: two magazine subscription offers, a begging letter from Greenpeace, an invitation to purchase travel insurance so like a real invitation he'd thought—before he opened it last night—that it might be to a party. He's still invited sometimes. He and Sherrie could go down to New York, stay with Sherrie's sister.... He throws the junk mail in the trash. Why would he need flight insurance? He never travels, never gets mail. He's dropped off the edge of the planet.

He'd just as soon not dwell on this as he runs off to meet some student. It's hard enough to leave the house, what with his obsessive-compulsive need to make sure all the lights are off, even in Ruby's room, which no one's used for ages. After her freshman year at State, Ruby got a summer job waitressing so she wouldn't have to come home.

He stands in Ruby's doorway and tries without success to remember its previous incarnations, how it changed from a nursery into a little girl's room and then froze forever, a teenage Miss Havisham's attic, plastered with the faces of actors, rock musicians, and athletes, whose stars have probably faded since Ruby put up their photos. The room had a living, evolving smell—first milk and talcum, then sneakers, nail polish, incense. But the dust and stale air have chased those poltergeist odors out.

Grabbing his corduroy jacket from a hook on the mudroom wall, he's snagged by the oversized mirror that decides at this most inopportune moment to show him his shocking face, the deep Buster Keaton furrows, the stubble, the messy graying hair, a guy who looks more like a divorced cop in a TV series than a well-respected middle-aged but still vital and attractive writer, teacher, husband, and father. Nasty white specks on his glasses, pouches under his eyes. Swenson scrapes something suspicious off his front tooth, then checks the troublesome molar.

Ugh. No time to think about that. It's off to work we go.

Running up the four flights to his office comprises Swenson's entire exercise program, but this morning the aerobic benefits are undermined by the stress of being late. By the third floor, he's panting. Chest pains? Possibly. Probably. Is this his fate—to collapse and die at the Doc Martened feet of this . . . leather-jacketed toothpick? Angela's sitting on the floor with her back against the wall, balancing an open book on the milky knobs peeking through the ripped knees of her jeans.

A few steps from the top, Swenson's able to read the title of her paperback, which is not, as he expected, the work of some trendy child author, but rather, *Jane Eyre*. She grasps the novel with talons lacquered eggplant purple, curling from fingerless black leather gloves studded with silver grommets. Her tiny hands—or perhaps their proximity to Charlotte Brontë's novel—give the gloves a prim Victorian decorousness. Otherwise her outfit is pure sci-fi unisex shitkicker. A streaked green and orange ponytail, spraying straight up from the top of her head, makes her look like a garish tasseled party favor.

"Good morning," calls Swenson, overheartily.

Glancing up from her book, Angela considers the bizarre coincidence that seems to have brought the two of them to this landing at the same moment.

"Oh, hi," she says, uncertainly.

"Sorry I'm late," Swenson says. "I lost track."

"That's okay. Don't worry about it."

Swenson grabs the banister, partly to steady his breathing and partly to keep from strangling this thankless brat who's dragged him out of bed—well, off the couch—practically at dawn and sent him racing here, risking his life.... That's okay. *Oh, is it?* His options are limited but clear. A stern, unpleasant lecture on manners and the value of *thank you*, or he can bite the bullet and get through fifteen minutes of her mumbling about her work or, more likely, about the reasons she hasn't done any work, and then he can mumble something back, and everyone will be happy.

He says, "Should we reschedule?"

"Oh, no no no. Please, no. I need to talk to you. Really. I was kind of liking it. Sitting here. Hiding out. It's like when I was a kid. I'd crawl under the porch and read when I was supposed to be at school."

"A reader," says Swenson. "Excellent."

"Yeah. I guess," she says. She leans on one arm to push off from the floor. Swenson reaches out to help her. She seems to think he's asking for her book, which she obediently hands over. While she stands, they negotiate the awkward exchange by pretending it was intended. As she gathers up her backpack, he leafs through the book, in which she's underlined passages. So. She's reading it for a course.

"How do you like *Jane Eyre*?"

"It's practically my favorite novel. I've read it seven times."

Swenson should have known. Under all that crusty leather beats the tender heart of a governess pining for Mr. Rochester.

"What I like," says Angela, "is how pissed off Jane Eyre is. She's in a rage for the whole novel, and the payoff is she gets to marry this blind guy who's toasted his wife in the attic."

"Come in," says Swenson. "Sit down."

As Swenson unlocks his office, Angela's still talking. "The trouble is, I'm reading it for Lauren Healy's class? Text Studies in

Gender Warfare? And everything we read turns out to be the same story, you know, the dominant male patriarchy sticking it to women. Which I guess is sort of true, I mean, I understand how you could say that, except that everything *isn't* the same."

Dealing with the lock and key spares him the always problematic dilemma of whether or not to agree when a student trashes one of his colleagues. Also, it's disconcerting that this sullen near-mute from class has turned into a chatterbox. He'd planned on one of those meetings in which the students chew their nails while he extracts ten minutes worth of conversation-like noise.

Swenson's study has the yeasty smell of sweaters left in a drawer. How long since he's been here? He honestly can't remember. He throws open a window. Air rushes in. He lowers the window.

"Is this too cold for you?" he says. "Yesterday was tropical. Today is freezing. The planet's out of control."

Angela doesn't answer. It's taking all her concentration to walk across the room. Even so, she trips on the rug and nearly falls as she bends to straighten the carpet. All of which moves Swenson to prayer. God, don't let her be on drugs.

"Oh, man," she says. "I'm always falling over shit."

"Try not to hurt yourself," advises kindly, paternal Swenson.

"I'll try not to. Thanks." Is Angela being sarcastic?

"Perhaps you'd be safer if you sat down," he says.

"Is it okay if I stand for a while?" She bounces from foot to foot.

"However you're comfortable," Swenson says.

"*Comfortable.* Ha. I wish," she says.

Oh, please, Swenson thinks.

Sliding into his desk chair, he plays with a stack of old mail, very official, tidying up. The doctor will see you now.

"So how's your semester going?" Swenson's on automatic.

"Mostly straight down the toilet." Angela gazes out the window.

"Sorry to hear that." Swenson's reply is more sincere than she knows. The answer to his question is supposed to be: fine. Students don't confide in him. He doesn't encourage them to. Their lives may be disintegrating, but they don't tell him. The poetry students confide in Magda Moynahan, who teaches the poetry workshop. But he never hears classroom gossip. Years after the fact, he's learned that a student was coming unglued and he never noticed. Well, he's got his own problems. He certainly doesn't need theirs, though from time to time he does feel a little . . . left out, worried by his obliviousness to the dramas around him. He lacks the most basic observational skills. No wonder he can't write.

Angela says, "I think I'll sit down now."

"Sure," says Swenson. "Go ahead."

Angela flops backward into the leather armchair across from his desk. First she crosses her legs on the seat in a failed attempt at a half lotus, then scoots down and pulls her knees up to her chest, then moves back and puts her feet on the ground and taps her ring on the chair arm. Swenson's never seen anyone have so much trouble sitting. What's she on? He doesn't think drugs. Protracted adolescence. Her leather jacket keeps making the sound of someone tearing off a Band-Aid.

She makes one last try at pretzeling her legs into some sort of yogic twist, then sits up straight and stares at him, a quivering punk Chihuahua. She's gone easy on the facial jewelry—only a silver coil snaking though the rim of one ear and a thin nose ring studded with a tiny green star that glitters under her nostril like a dab of emerald snot. She's left off the eyebrow ring and the upper-lip ring, so it's slightly less upsetting to look at her pale triangular face. Her eyes don't have a color, exactly: a newborn's gunmetal gray.

"So. What's the matter with school?" he says.

"My classes suck," she says.

"All of them?" he asks neutrally.

"Not yours!" Angela says. He didn't think she was including him, though now he wonders why he didn't. "Your class is the only one I go to. The only one I like."

Why me, Lord? thinks Swenson. How did *I* get lucky?

"What's funny?" Angela says.

"Nothing," says Swenson. "Why?"

"You smiled."

"I was flattered," he lies. "That you're enjoying my class."

She says, "Writing's the only thing I care about in the world."

"I'm delighted." Another lie. "We want our students to care. But you can't cut your other classes. If Tolstoy slept through his classes, they'd fail *his* ass out of Euston." Why the tough talk? Speaking her language? It's a reflex, sometimes, with students.

Angela flinches. A fragile flower under all that armor. Often they're the most delicate, the green-haired and the pierced. Most Euston students opt for the outdoorsy look of ecologically conscious future CEOs. Angela's fashion statement represents a decision to abandon all hope of ever fitting in.

"Can I smoke in here?" she asks.

"I'd rather you didn't," says Swenson. "You leave, I get to live with the smoke all day. Look, I used to smoke, so I know—"

"It doesn't matter! I don't actually smoke!" She throws her hands in the air. "Anyway, I'm not *sleeping* through my classes. I'm at my computer. Writing fiction."

"Well, good," says Swenson. "That's wonderful. Does that mean you'll have something for us to look at in workshop next week?"

"I'm writing a novel," Angela says.

"A novel," repeats Swenson despairingly.

He can imagine. Or maybe he can't. Often he's surprised when the captain of the men's lacrosse team hands in a Gothic bodice ripper. Last year a boy with blue hair and matching fingernails spent a whole semester on a novel entitled *King Crap*. The first ten pages were printouts of the words *King Crap* in different typefaces. One year two indistinguishable girls—not twins, as Swenson first assumed, but friends—worked collaboratively on science fiction stories about two androids named Zip and Zap. One girl wrote Zip's part, the other wrote Zap's. Years later, he saw a film about two best friends who conspired to kill one girl's mother, and the murderers' wacky intensity reminded him of those students.

"What's the novel called?" he asks.

Angela says, "Can I check out your bookcase? I think it might calm me down."

Swenson can tell her not to smoke. But he can't exactly forbid her to get up and look at his books. He wants to say, This is a conference. Let's keep it short and tidy.

"Go ahead," he says. "Feel free."

"We can keep on talking," she says. "It would just make me feel less weird."

Angela sidles along the walls, inspecting his vintage postcards and framed photos, pausing to stare at Chekhov, Tolstoy, Virginia Woolf.

"God, I can't believe this," she says. "I've got the same postcards on *my* wall."

It's been so long since anyone—including himself—has noticed what he's chosen to surround himself with. Years ago, the girls who came to his apartment would check out his books, his possessions. It used to be sexy, sitting there with nothing much to look at besides the girl's ass as she cruised his decor. But this isn't sexy at all, maybe because he can *see* Angela's ass, two white, symmetrical crescents exposed by her fraying jeans.

Angela prowls his bookcase, then pounces, sliding a book from the shelf. She shows it to Swenson. Naturally. It's Stendhal. *The Red and the Black*. He can't remember if he told the class, in an unguarded egotistical moment, that he was working on a novel loosely based on Stendhal's. Somehow he doesn't think he did. Is it coincidence or ESP that makes Angela say, "I love this book almost as much as I love *Jane Eyre*"?

"Why's that?" Swenson asks warily.

She says, "I love how Stendhal gets, you know, like, inside and outside Julien at the same time, so you can imagine doing what Julien's doing, and meanwhile you're thinking you would never do something like that."

That's the problem with Swenson's novel. He's never gotten inside his hero, Julius Sorley. Even the name has never fit. He's remained on the outside, watching.

Angela's returned to the chair. "Are you all right? You looked upset for a minute."

"I'm fine," he says.

"Me too," she says. "Sort of. I'm feeling better now. Okay." She takes a deep breath. "My novel is called *Eggs*."

"Nice title." Swenson shudders, imagining a three-hundred-page ovarian stream-of-consciousness homage to Anaïs Nin. "And what's it about?"

"I'd rather not say. I brought you the first chapter. We can talk about it after you've read it. Look. I might as well tell you before you figure it out for yourself. My writing's awful. It totally bites."

"I'm sure it doesn't," says Swenson. "Can we put the chapter up for next week's workshop?"

"Could you read it first? I could give it to you chapter by chapter? I've got half of it written. I started it last summer?"

Chapter by chapter. The three most frightening words in the English language.

"Let me read the first chapter," he says. "Then we'll see. Maybe it will be helpful to do it in class. Or we might decide not to."

"*You* decide." Angela wrestles with something stuck in her backpack and at last yanks out an envelope, crumpled in the struggle. Clearly, some thought has gone into selecting the tangerine-orange folder.

"Shit," says Angela. "Look at this thing." Vaulting out of her chair, she presents it, with an ironic flip, to Swenson.

"Well, thanks," she says. "Thanks for your time. And I'm totally totally sorry if I woke you up or stopped you from writing or anything."

"Not at all." Swenson's full of smiles. The conference is almost over.

Almost. Angela hesitates. "Could we talk about it next week? I don't want to be pushy. But if you finish before then, you can call me, or E-mail me. Or something. I know I'm being pushy. I need to know what you think. This makes me so nervous. No one else has seen it."

"I'll read it by next week." Hey, the conference is over. Can't this girl take a hint?

"See you," Angela says. "Thanks again." She turns to wave at Swenson as she opens the door and, turning back, plows into the doorframe. "Ouch. Listen, there's one other thing. There are like four or five typos in there. I meant to fix them—"

"Don't worry about typos," Swenson says.

"Okay, sorry," she says. "Sorry. See you soon."

"Later," Swenson says.

He waits until he can no longer hear her clomping down the stairs. Then he slides her envelope into his briefcase, behind his two-day-old *New York Times*. He'll get to it, eventually. For now . . . out of sight, out of mind. He should go home and look at *his* novel. But once more he's siphoned all his creative juices into a brain-numbing chat with a student. He's ruined the day for writing, and his punishment is to face yet another of the problems with *not* writing, which is: how to kill all that time.

Surely he has phone calls to make. Too bad it's only been two weeks since he called his editor, Len Currie. Len's publishing house has a contract for Swenson's next novel. No one bothers mentioning that the deadline's two years past. Every six months, he phones Len, who always seems pleased to hear from him and spends their brief conversation bitching about his workload.

On the other hand, it's been at least a week since he's driven to Montpelier and blown an hour at the bookstore, drinking espresso and skimming little magazines that he's too cheap to buy, though he knows he should support them for the sake of the literary community. The literary community. Isn't it enough that he's patronizing Bradstreet Books, when he could drive the same distance in the opposite direction and drink much better coffee at the Burlington Barnes & Noble?

Such trivial ideological quibbles are what nag at a writer's mind. Hence, to decide between bookstores is to be a writer.

Adam Bee's souped up the cappuccino machine so he can yank the lever to greet his customers and a few puffs of steam will sail out. Toot toot. Glad to see ya! Swenson does a mock salute to the little engine that could, wishing guiltily for the anonymity of the big chain bookstore. That can't be good for the cappuccino machine, about which Swenson feels protective. It's the one major upgrade since Adam Bee opened Bradstreet Books, in the early seventies, when he came to Montepelier—on the lam, it's rumored, from a Weatherman bombing indictment.

"*Ola!*" cries Adam, an aging gnome whose gray beard sprays halfway down his zeppelin-like belly.

"Hey, man," says Swenson. "How ya doin'?"

"I think I'll be okay," Adam says. "The usual?"

It's a bar conversation, transposed to a book store. Swenson wishes he *were* in a bar. "The usual," he says.

The machine makes what sounds like its last gasp as Adam pulls Swenson's double espresso. "How's the writing?" Adam asks.

Go to hell, thinks Swenson. But Adam's just making small talk. How's the farm? The wife? The kids? He's not tormenting Swenson, who believes that Adam has patronized him for years, ever since he witnessed one of Swenson's many character-building humiliations: a bookstore reading Swenson gave together with Magda Moynahan.

Adam had begged them to do it. They'd called it Writers of Euston. During a blizzard, naturally, and naturally, no one showed up. Rows of empty chairs. Wine and cheese cubes set out, and no one to consume them but Adam, Magda, Swenson, and a pair of those ghoulish androgynous slaves Adams hires out of Goddard.

There was one actual customer. An old woman in the back row. So they felt they had to go through with it. She'd come out in the storm. Swenson had begun to read the dramatic opening of *Phoenix Time*, the chapter that every critic cited for its unsentimental power, the section in which the teenage hero's father sets himself on fire as a protest against the Vietnam War. A few minutes into the reading the old woman raised her hand and asked him to read louder. When he gently suggested that she move up front, she'd told him she might need to leave in the middle.

Who knows if Adam even remembers? Probably only Swenson's condemned to relive it each time he comes to Bradstreet Books. He takes his coffee to the table farthest from Adam, making a wide circle around the territory that two young earth mothers have staked out with their baby strollers. He sips the bitter, watery brew. Yes, sir. This is the café life. Now what should he read?

If he braves the fiction section, he'll have to avoid the *S* shelf, where he'll notice—as if he didn't know—that his books are out of print. Of course, he has boxes of them at home, and could give them to Adam to sell on consignment. But that would be too humiliating. He'll just pretend not to care. So no Christina Stead for him. No Wallace Stegner. No Stendhal. Anyway, choosing a book would represent too great a commitment. His espresso would be cold long before he decided.

He grabs a copy of *Fiction Today*. Let's see who's doing what. The first story, by a writer whose name he faintly recognizes, describes a father cold-bloodedly executing the family poodle. He skims through it, then begins another story, by another vaguely familiar name, a woman's this time, and stops when the mother backs her car over the narrator's kitty. Is this some kind of theme issue? Or didn't the editors notice? Have his students been reading this? That could explain a lot. They're too young and sweet to kill off their pets, so they have sex with them instead. He *wishes* his students were reading this. He slides the magazine back on the shelf and picks up *Poets and Writers*, paging past the ads for summer conferences (to which he has not been invited) and anthologies (to which he has not been asked to submit), past the interview with the semifamous novelist discoursing on how she warns her students about the perils of putting descriptions of food in their stories.

He might as well read Angela's chapter. At least it's something he has to do. A false sense of accomplishment is better than none at all. He reaches for his briefcase. Now where did he leave it? He hopes not in his office. Did he stop between there and here—somewhere he'll never find it?

He runs out to check his car. The briefcase is on the front seat. Back at his table, he takes a fortifying gulp of espresso and finds the tangerine-colored envelope. "*Eggs*. A novel by Angela Argo." He steels himself, reads the first line, then reads on, without stopping.

Every night, after dinner, I went out and sat with the eggs.

This was after my mother and I washed the dishes and loaded the washer, after my father dozed off over his medical journals, it was then that I slipped out the kitchen door and crossed the chilly backyard, dark and loamy with the yeasty smell of leaves just beginning to change, noisy with the rustle of them turning colors in the dark. For a moment I looked back at the black frame of our house, the whole place jumping and vibrating with the dishwasher hum. Then I slipped into the toolshed, where it was always warm, lit only by the red light of the incubator bulbs, silent but for the whirring hearts inside the fertilized eggs.

The eggs took twenty-one days to hatch. I wasn't having much luck. I blamed myself completely. I believed I was being punished for thoughts I shouldn't have had, for wanting only to think of them in the warm dark shed, with my eyes shut and the unborn chicks floating in their shells.

I checked the thermometers on the incubators and put marks on my charts. I began to think I'd made mistakes, put X's in the wrong boxes. I went back and started again. If the heat varied, the chicks wouldn't hatch or would be born deformed.

43

The eggs were my eleventh-grade biology project. Officially, that is. Underneath those neat charts, those notebooks, the racks of fertilized eggs, my real project was black magic, casting spells for things I shouldn't have wanted, and longed for, and finally got.

My father's patient, Mrs. Davis, had a stroke in her henhouse and died and came back to life in a whirlwind of feathers. She decided she hated chickens and asked my father if he wanted the incubators instead of medical fees. Why would a doctor want incubators? Because I needed a science project.

From the hospital, Mrs. Davis told her son to kill the chickens. Her grandson—a kid I knew from school—brought us two dozen chickens, plucked, in plastic bags specked with blood. The grandson clutched three bags in each hand, four chickens in each bag.

My mother cooked chicken with spaghetti, chicken chunked with pineapple, chicken almondine, chicken curry. The chickens were always stringy, with a swampy edge. But my mother said we should eat every last goddamn chicken some poor old woman had slaughtered just to please my dad.

My father said, "They weren't killed for me. Damn it, you know that. They were killed for the sin of seeing poor Alice Davis almost drop dead."

My mother said, "Maybe they wanted her dead."

My father said, "The clot that lodged in the woman's arterial pathways didn't give a damn what some chicken wanted."

The plan was that in a few weeks, when Mrs. Davis felt better, my father and I would get the incubators, and Mrs. Davis would teach me how to hatch the eggs. Meanwhile I ordered pamphlets from the USDA because my father couldn't believe that anything could be learned from an old woman without front teeth. I couldn't understand the pamphlets, though I read them over and over. I was thinking, as always, about something else altogether.

Mrs. Davis walked with a cane, her right arm hooked to her belt. One eye didn't blink. Her mouth pulled down at one corner. On the fingers of her good hand she counted off the basics: constant temperature and humidity, turn the eggs several times daily.

The fixed eye and twisted lips flirted with my dad. "After a week you hold the eggs up to a light to see which have chickies, and you throw the empties away or they'll ruin the others."

My father shifted her crooked stare onto me.

"My daughter's in charge of this," he said. "This is her science project."

"Science project?" said Mrs. Davis. She turned to me, but her crazy eye stared at him. You could tell she thought I'd wreck the whole thing. She frothed at the mouth describing what would happen if I let the eggs get too hot or cold. Newborn chicks crumpling on matchstick legs, hatchlings tearing off flesh still stuck to the shell, chicks dying with their beaks sticking out of the eggs, one-eyed monsters gasping.

I was only half listening. The other half was wondering what Mr. Reynaud would say if I got to tell him about this tomorrow after orchestra practice. I had a gigantic crush on my high school music teacher, and I spent every minute, outside of his class, thinking about him.

Swenson puts down the manuscript. Is that the whir of the incubators? No, it's the cappuccino machine. He leafs through the pages, as if one more quick look will disclose the secret of how they could have been written by Angela Argo. Where did Angela learn a phrase like *arterial pathways*?

Once you've met enough writers—and in his former life, Swenson met plenty—you stop expecting the person to match the work. But this particular gap seems so wide that he has to . . . well, he has to at least consider the possibility of . . . plagiarism. A few years ago a student told Magda that a classmate's poem was stolen from Maya Angelou's Clinton inauguration ode. Hadn't Magda recognized it? To Magda's credit, she hadn't. Months of her time were eaten up by distasteful meetings with the plagiarist's parents, the dean, and the consulting shrink.

But what kind of psycho plagiarist begs you to read her work, comes to your office and tells you that writing is her whole life?

Plagiarists hand in their papers late. You have to remind them ten times. And then there was Angela's passion for *Jane Eyre*, for Stendhal. Maybe the girl's a writer. Stranger things have happened. Corrections dot the manuscript, neat deletions and additions, words crossed out and in every case replaced with better words.

Swenson jumps as Adam plunks a coffee cup down on the table.

"Easy," Adam says. "Relax. This one's on the house. You look stressed, big guy. Writer's block? Family shit? Anything I can do?"

"I'm fine, I'm fine," says Swenson. "Grading student papers." His eyes roll up in an arc of exasperation.

"I bet you'd rather be writing your own book," says Adam.

"You got it," Swenson says.

Adam scratches the back of his neck, pushing forward the long gray ponytail gathered in a black scrunchee. "Well, I guess The Man doesn't pay us for doing what we love. If you think *I'd* be pulling the crank on a cappuccino machine . . ."

"What would you be doing?" asks Swenson. Why would someone run a bookstore if he didn't love it? Though now he can't remember Adam ever mentioning a book.

"What would I be doing?" Adam repeats thoughtfully.

Wait. Swenson doesn't want to know. This is way more intimate than he needs to get with Adam Bee.

"Herb farming," Adam says.

"Go for it," Swenson says. "Guys are making fortunes. And if you get busted we'll just forget we ever had this conversation."

Adam says, "I don't mean weed. I'd only grow that for personal use. I can't even smoke anymore, some pre-emphysema thing. No, I mean medicinal. Gingko. Saint John's wort. Ginseng. The new frontier, man. Anti-AIDS. Anticancer. But my knees are going, I'm your basic old dog what can't learn new tricks. . . ."

As Adam hovers over Swenson, waiting for him to taste his coffee, his vulnerable belly grazes Swenson's ear. Their tableau—one standing, solicitous, the other seated and frostily grateful–makes Swenson feel like a melancholy provincial in Chekhov or Turgenev, attended by the family retainer, Old Gerasim or Mumbles with secret longings of his own, the tiny cottage, the white horse, hopeless and unobtainable. Swenson hates it that Adam can't grow his herbal hippie joy juice.

"Do it," Swenson says. "Hire some kids to do the grunt work." He could hardly sound more phony or feel more sincere. He stares up into Adam's rheumy eyes. Adam's younger than he is!

"Don't spill your coffee," says Adam. "You might have a hard time explaining it to the student who wrote that paper."

The student? Swenson stares at the manuscript as if for the first time. And then he has the strangest desire to tell Adam that he's just read the most interesting first chapter. Something actually good. It occurs to him that his new sympathy for Adam may have some connection to his having read Angela's work. Isn't that what he told the class yesterday, that good writing can make you *see* your fellow humans? It doesn't make you a better person. It just sort of . . . opens your pores.

"The students would understand," Swenson says. "They'd all be dead without coffee."

"Jeez," says Adam. "Dead? I hope not."

Adam stares at him quizzically. Swenson no longer cares. God bless Adam, God bless Bradstreet Books. Swenson's going home.

S wenson springs up the belltower stairs in an energized mood
quite unlike his normal resentment, ennui, and dread. Teaching
is a lot a more fun if he has even one student who might benefit
from, or understand, what he's saying.

Two nights after he read her manuscript, Swenson called Angela
Argo. He'd been wasting far too much time trying to decide when
to call, what to say, if he should phone at all. His impulse was the
correct one—generous, unselfish. He almost never gets to be sincerely enthusiastic. But the last thing he wanted was to make
Angela self-conscious with the sort of praise that might keep her
from experimenting and making the necessary mistakes.

Finally, one night, he'd called from home. He was surprised to
hear, on Angela's machine, Robert Johnson's honeyed crooning.
You better come on in my kitchen because it's going to be rainin' outside.
Then Angela's voice, "Leave me a message if you want. Okay. Wait
for the . . ." *Beep*. He'd forgotten what he planned to say and almost
hung up, then babbled semicoherently about how he'd really liked
her chapter but unless she desperately wanted to have her work discussed in class, she should just keep on with it, they could talk
about it in conference. *Beep beep*. No tape left to trick him into saying that it would be hellish to hear her classmates tell her how to
"improve" her work.

Only after he'd hung up had he realized what trouble he'd made
for himself. Now he'd have to call around to find a student story to
discuss, and get it photocopied and distributed. Saintly Ruth Merlo,

the department secretary, saw him moping around the office and volunteered, angelically, to take on the extra work.

So today—unless he's got it wrong—they're doing Back Bay Barbie's story. Oops. Courtney Alcott. When he'd asked Courtney if she was related to Louisa May, she didn't know whom he meant.

It's Courtney's week to be bound and gagged and forced to watch her darling dismembered before her eyes. As always, Swenson's overidentified with the student whose story they're doing. He always tries to give the condemned an encouraging nod or wink. Now, he seeks out Courtney, but before he can find her, his gaze snags on Angela Argo, rooting ferociously in her backpack. How could this twitchy ferret have produced the pages that Swenson has—he checks to make sure—in his briefcase? This girl just doesn't seem capable of having written those complex sentences, that disturbing scene in the henhouse.

When the class has settled down, Swenson says, "So I assume that everyone's had a chance to read Courtney's story?" For some reason, this is hilarious.

"Enlighten me," Swenson says.

"We never got it," says Carlos. "Courtney screwed up, man."

Courtney covers her face with one hand and with the other plays with her medallion: a silver bulldog snarling at the end of a thick silver chain. "I got the copies." Her cartoon-mouse voice squeezes out through the lattice of her pearly inch-long nails. "But I put them in my bag and I, like, forgot to hand them out."

"I guess Courtney really didn't want us to do her story," says the forgiving Nancy.

"Somebody should've given the copies to Claris," says Makeesha, with inarguable logic. "Those stories be handed out by now."

Courtney says, "I've got the copies with me. We could read it now. It's short."

"Courtney could read it to us," suggests Meg. "We could read along with her."

What is Swenson supposed to say? Courtney's *not* going to read her goddamn story out loud while we sit here and suffer!

"Courtney?"

"I could do that." Courtney always seems to be chewing gum, even when she isn't.

So be it. Swenson takes a copy—short, it's true—and passes along the stack. "Well, thank you, Courtney. For coming to our aid and bringing us something to talk about."

Courtney takes a deep breath. "I really like this story. It's the first thing I ever wrote that I thought was, like, totally good."

"I'm sure the rest of us will, too." Oh, dear Lord, Swenson prays silently. This could really get ugly.

"It's called 'First Kiss—Inner City Blues,'" says Courtney.

"That's two titles right there," says Makeesha.

Courtney ignores her, and begins:

"'The summer heat sat on the hot city street, making it hard for it to breathe, especially Lydia Sanchez. Lydia sat on the filthy, garbage-laden front steps of her brownstone tenement home, watching kids play in the gutter in the water rushing out of a broken fire hydrant. Just yesterday she used to be one of those kids. But she wasn't now.

'Lydia was miserable. That morning she'd yelled at her mother and hit her baby brother, then she felt even worse. She was used to the crime-ridden, drug-infested city streets of her neighborhood. She didn't let any of that get to her anymore. But this time was different.'"

Courtney must have worked hard on the opening section. From there on, the grammar and syntax deteriorate, making it hard to follow, on the simplest plot level, the story of Lydia, who has a "huge thing" for "this good-looking guy" named Juan, who belongs to a "vicious tough inner-city gang" known as the Latin Diablos. Juan wants Lydia to join the "girl-part" of the gang. He comes along and kisses her while she's sitting and brooding among the "crackheads and junkies like human garbage on her front steps. After all, it was Lydia's first kiss. So it really meant a lot."

Lydia's almost persuaded to go through the "terrifying gang initiation" to become a Latina Diabla. But then her mother tells her that a baby down the block—a "cute precious girl" Lydia used to babysit for—was accidentally killed in a drive-by shooting. Who did it? Guess. The Diablos.

Relieved to be almost finished, Courtney sails into the grand finale. "'Right at that moment Lydia knew she could never be part of Juan's world. She could never love a man who could be part of something like that. She needed the strength to tell Juan she didn't want to. But would she be able to? Could she? Lydia honestly couldn't say for sure. At least not for the moment.'"

That's it. The end. That's all she wrote. Most of the students are still reading, giving Swenson a moment to think of something to say, some way to improve this heartbreaking, subliterate piece of shit, heartbreaking because, for all he knows, it represents Courtney's personal best.

He refuses to accept that. It's his job to refuse to accept that. Courtney can do better. Too bad that classroom etiquette prevents him from saying so. God forbid he tell Courtney—or anyone—to bag it and start over, as if no real writer would do that, as if he himself hadn't pulled the plug on dozens of stories and novels.

And now they're all looking at him with the same panic he fears they see on his face. Or maybe they loved the story and are moved too deeply for words. Certainly, he's been wrong before. . . . He waits a beat, then says, "At least it isn't about someone having sex with an animal."

"Compared to this," Makeesha says, "that chicken thing was genius. This is just more of that totally racist shit white folks are always laying down. Like every sister and brother on the street is a gang member killing babies and doing dope. What's that shit she calls the brothers? Human garbage?"

"Hang on, Makeesha," Swenson says. "Let's get back to that in a minute. We usually start off saying what we *liked* about the story."

He's asking the impossible, but Angela's hand shoots up. "I like the name, the Latin Diablos. And then the Latina Diablas, it's like the Ladies Auxiliary or something. They're pretty good gang names."

Some new confidence or authority shines in Angela's face. Her entire metabolism seems less speedy and frenetic, as if some hand has steadied her and made her stop tapping and squirming. Could she have been so changed by Swenson's message on her machine?

Claris says, "Is *Diabla* a Spanish word? Is the devil ever female?" Swenson often wonders what Claris is doing at Euston.

"I'll bet not," says Meg. "They'd never let us have that much power. Even the devil has got to have a dick."

Swenson shakes his head. The students chuckle, sympathetically.

"Let's see," says Carlos. "As you know, guys, I'm half Dominican. And I don't know about *Diabla*. *Bruja*, maybe. That means 'sorceress.' I guess that's a little different."

"You could change it to the Latino Brujos," Angela says, excitedly. "And the Latina Brujas. That would be good, too."

Makeesha says, "Have we finished the part about the stuff we like? Because I got some other shit to say."

"Have we?" says Swenson. "People? Anyone want to mention something they admired about Courtney's story?" Courtney's staring at the wall. "I thought it represented an attempt to deal with some larger social problems. Did anyone pick up on that?"

No one speaks. No one's going to speak. His students aren't idiots. Swenson sighs. "All right, Makeesha."

Makeesha says, "I think it's, like asking for it, to pretend you know shit about shit you don't know about. Yo, like where did *you* grow up, Courtney? In some mansion in Boston? And you be acting like you know what's going on inside this sister's head when she be chilling on the street."

And where did Makeesha grow up? Dartmouth, Swenson seems to remember. She slips in and out of homegirl talk for the authority it gives her.

"Makeesha," Swenson says, "are you saying you don't think it's possible to imagine something unless it's happened to you?"

"I'm not saying that," she answers. "I'm just saying there's some things you can't imagine, some stuff you ain't got no business trying to imagine if you—"

Angela interrupts her. "That's not true, Makeesha. You can imagine anything if you do it well enough. I mean, like, Flaubert wasn't a woman, and you can read *Madame Bovary*, and it's amazing how much he knew about women. Kafka wasn't a cockroach. People write historical novels about the times before they were born—"

Carlos catches the pass and runs with it. "You don't have to be a space alien to write science fiction, man."

"Angela and Carlos are right," Swenson says. "If you really work at it, you can get under anyone's skin. Regardless of its color." Does he really believe that? He chooses to, for the moment.

"Yeah," says Courtney. "That's what I think, too. Why shouldn't I be able to write about some homegirl if I want?"

Hold it, let's back up a step. Something's gone terribly wrong if Courtney has mistaken his defense of the imagination for an endorsement of her story. To say nothing of the fact that Courtney has, by speaking, shattered the most sacred covenant of the workshop.

"All right-eeee. . . ." Swenson draws out the word, pneumatically, letting Courtney down easy. "The question is whether Courtney's done it. What do the rest of you think?"

Claris says, "I didn't believe it. Lydia and her boyfriend seemed a little . . . generic. They could have been *any* girl and boy, *any* city street."

Swenson says, "Bravo, Claris. Once more, you've nailed the problem. So how can Courtney fix it? How can she make us believe that Lydia and Juan are a *particular* couple on a *specific* street, not some abstract composite? Anyhomey."

"Anyhomey," says Makeesha. "That's the problem right there. These dudes don't have faces."

"So what do we do?" says Swenson.

"Describe what they look like?" Danny says.

"Tell us what city it is?" ventures Nancy.

"That might help," Swenson agrees.

"Maybe we should know where they're coming from," says Carlos. "Are they Mexican? Puerto Rican? Half Polish and half Dominican? Let me tell you, man, it makes a difference."

"Sure," says Swenson. "Why not? What else?"

"Give the sister and brother somethin' to *say*," suggests Makeesha. "Give 'em some brains. Some personality."

"Now we're getting there," says Swenson. "How would you do that, Makeesha?"

But before Makeesha can answer, Meg suggests, "Maybe by the end of the story she should be a little more . . . conscious. I mean, of her oppression . . . as a woman of color?"

There's a silence after this. No one wants to touch it.

"Details," Angela says at last.

Bless her, Swenson thinks.

"Okay? Like what?" says Courtney, with an edge in her voice honed by generations of Alcotts not bred to take instruction from punks like Angela Argo.

"*Garbage-ridden* and *filthy* don't exactly *do* that street." Angela's rolled up Courtney's manuscript and is waving it like a brush with which to paint a streetscape of Lydia Sanchez's block. "What makes it *her* house, *her* front steps? Put in . . . a laundromat. A bodega."

"Plantains," Claris suggests.

"Plantains nothing," says Carlos. "A *cuchifrito* stand. Let's see some greasy fried pig ears steaming up the window."

"Give the gang dude some tattoos," Danny says.

"Born to Lose," Jonelle says sourly.

"Latins don't do Born to Lose," says Carlos. "They do *Mama. Mi Vida Loca. Mi Amor.* Stuff like that."

"So what are you saying?" asks Courtney. "That I'm supposed to do . . . research?"

"No," says Angela. "Close your eyes. Concentrate till you see the street and the girl and her boyfriend. Till you're sort of . . . dreaming them. Then write down what you see."

Okay. Angela wrote that chapter. Why did Swenson doubt it?

"All right," Courtney says. "I can do that."

No, you can't, thinks Swenson. Courtney's heroine will be Natalie Wood in *West Side Story*. But so what? Courtney's charged with faith in the power of observation to make something come to life on the page, in the power of language to make something walk and talk. That's all Swenson can hope to give them, and together they've bled it out of Courtney's turnip of a story. Meanwhile they've avoided the dangerous question of whether the sharpest details, the most gorgeous embroidery can cloak the clumsy contrivances of a plot about a girl who decides not to join a gang responsible for the death of a child. They don't have to mention that. They've performed the weekly miracle of healing the terminally ill with minor cosmetic surgery.

"Wait a minute," says Jonelle. Swenson waits for Jonelle to say— as she often does—that the story was perfect just the way it was, and they should have left it alone. Nearly every class has a self-appointed guardian of the writer's tender feelings, an aggressive protector less inspired by kindness than by the need to negate the time and effort they've expended.

Jonelle says, "You didn't give Courtney a chance to say something at the end. Like if there's anything else she wants to ask us, or what."

Usually, the writer just thanks the class. Still, they need it for closure. "Sorry, Courtney," says Swenson. "Last words? Last thoughts?"

"Thanks, guys," says Courtney. "I think I know where to go from here."

It's like a benediction. Or like the end of Quaker Meeting, the rising and shaking hands, faces warmed by the hour spent by the fire of the Inner Light. Before Swenson knows what he's doing, he glances at Angela Argo. Messages crackle back and forth, and it's understood that Angela will stay after so they can discuss her chapter.

"Wait!" he says. "Before everyone leaves. Whose story are we doing next week?"

Carlos hands over a manuscript. "One for the crapper," he says.

"Oh, I doubt it," Swenson says. "Thank you, my man!"

From the corner of his eye, Swenson sees Angela stand up. Is she getting ready to leave? Was he wrong about their wordless agreement? "Angela?" His voice cracks. Carlos gives him a funny look.

"Since we're ending early, if you want to stay, we can talk about your manuscript. . . ."

Angela says, "I was counting on it. If it's all right with you. I was just standing up to stretch. I mean, if you want to, if you have the time. I'd hate to bother you. . . ."

"Of course I do," says Swenson. "That's why I suggested it. Should we stay here and talk, or should we go to my office?" Who's in charge here? Why is he asking *her*?

"Your office. I mean, it's more comfortable there. It's not, like, you know, a classroom. I mean, if that's all right with you." Angela can hardly speak.

"We're on our way," Swenson says. "See the rest of you guys next week."

Swenson finds it trying to walk anywhere with a student. Conversation's tough enough when everyone stands in one place. Forward movement creates so many chances for awkward stalls and collisions, decisions about who goes first, right or left, mini-crises that make one conscious of authority and position. Does the student respectfully stand aside and usher Swenson through the doorway, or does Swenson, in loco parentis, hold the door for the kid? And is everything different depending on whether the student is male or female?

You bet it's different if the student is female. Crossing the quad with Angela, Swenson's acutely aware that he might walk one inch too close and someone will report them for holding hands. At least the quad's nearly empty. Another advantage of ending class early is that they're spared the traffic jam between classes, the saying hello to everyone just in case you happen to know them. Looking up at the high windows of granite Claymore, Thackeray, Comstock Hall, he wonders who's looking down.

Angela says, "Doesn't it creep you out to think about everyone watching? You could be, you know, just like *walking,* and, like, Lee Harvey Oswald could be drawing a bead on you. Probably some psycho you gave a crummy grade to—"

"Relax," Swenson says. "My courses are pass-fail. Everyone passes."

"That's good." Angela smiles. They're moving much too slowly. It's his job to set the pace. But his legs feel bizarrely wooden. Last week, waiting for Sherrie to finish at the clinic, he read an article about a woman who had a stroke preceded by this same trudging-through-water sensation. The woman was younger than Swenson.

Angela says, "That was a pretty good class."

"Thank you," Swenson says.

She says, "Actually, it was a miracle. Considering how Courtney's story sucked."

Students don't tell teachers that another student's story sucked. They're supposed to show solidarity; the teacher is management, they're labor. And the teacher has a professional (a parental) responsibility not to let students (the siblings) be nasty about each other.

"Ouch," says Swenson.

"You know it did," Angela says.

"Courtney will get better." Is Angela a colleague with whom he's discussing a student's potential? Shouldn't Swenson remind her what the protocol is?

He doesn't. And now his punishment comes barreling toward them down the path. He feels like a bowling pin watching a strike roll in. But how can he call it a punishment to run into the only colleague he actually likes? Because for some reason he just doesn't feel like seeing Magda right now.

Swenson and Magda Moynahan kiss on the cheek, warmly, decorously, as they do when they meet for lunch, though it's not exactly natural with Angela Argo watching, but more of a performance. They may *look* like teachers, but they're humans, they have friends. A swatch of Magda's wavy black hair sticks between Swenson's lips. Getting it loose takes some doing with both women watching.

"We're on break," says Magda. "I forgot some poems in my office." Magda's always breathless, always forgetting something, her flyaway beauty torqued by panic and distraction. The author of two well-received books of poems, she's divorced from a more famous poet, Sean Moynahan, who has recently remarried a young female poet with a growing reputation, a pretty girl who could be Magda's twin, minus twenty years. Swenson and Magda have lunch every few weeks and exchange Euston gossip.

"We got out early," Swenson explains. "Angela and I are going off to have a conference about her novel."

"Angela," says Magda. "How are you?"

"Oh, hi! I'm fine!" says Angela, sweetly.

"Let's have lunch, Ted," says Magda.

"Next week?" Swenson says.

"Call me," says Magda.

"Beautiful," says Swenson. Everyone smiles and walks on.

"Did you take . . ." Swenson's unsure how to go on. What do Magda's students call her? "The Beginning Poetry Workshop?"

"Freshman seminar," Angela says. "My poetry ate it."

"I doubt it."

"Trust me. It did. I was writing all this weird sexual stuff."

Swenson makes a mental note to ask Magda about Angela's poems.

"The class wasn't so great," says Angela. "Magda was sort of . . . stiff. I felt like my work made her nervous. Like on a . . . personal level."

It's one thing for Angela to trash a classmate's story, or to be snide about Lauren Healy's class, but it's quite another for this twit to criticize his best—his only—friend at Euston. Swenson isn't going to touch the question of what sexual stuff Angela wrote that made Magda nervous on a "personal level." Besides, he has to admit that some infantile part of his pyche is pleased. You *want* your students to love you best. . . .

At the entrance to Mather Hall, Swenson says, "Go on up. I'll get my mail and be there in a minute." He'd rather not follow her up four flights in that face-to-ass configuration. Obligingly, his mail box produces a few party-colored flyers for him to wave at Angela, who is watching from the top of the stairs. Stepping aside as he unlocks the door, she stumbles only slightly. This time, at least, she finds the chair and manages to twist her legs into the yogic contortion she seems to require for comfort. Swenson paws through his briefcase, and after a scary moment finds the orange envelope and hands it across the desk.

"I assume you got my phone message," he says.

"I saved the message tape," says Angela. "I played it a million times. Gosh. I can't believe I just told you that? Can we forget I said that about replaying your message? Was I supposed to call you back? I was too embarrassed. I thought you'd think I was trying to make you say even more nice stuff about my work."

"I didn't expect you to call," says Swenson. "Wasn't that Robert Johnson on your answering machine?"

"I can't believe you recognized him. Wasn't he the best? Did you know he died when he was, like, sixteen? His girlfriend got jealous and poisoned him with a glass of wine?"

"I do know," Swenson says. "Well . . . I don't have much more to say beyond what I told your machine."

"Did you find the typos?" she asks.

"Most, I guess. I marked them. I made a few marks on the page. Otherwise . . . just keep writing. Be careful whom you show it to. For God's sake, don't bring it to workshop. Don't let anybody tell you anything. I mean no one. Not even me."

"Oh my God," says Angela thickly. Swenson watches, mildly horrified, as her eyes film with tears. "This makes me so happy." She swipes at her eyes with the back of her hand. "It's not just because you're the teacher. It's 'cause I really admire your work. *Phoenix Time* is like my favorite book in the universe."

"I thought *Jane Eyre* was," says Swenson.

"This is different," Angela says. "Your book saved my life."

"Thank you." Swenson doesn't want to know why. He's afraid he already does. When he used to give readings from *Phoenix Time*, listeners would come up afterward to say that his book was exactly like their lives. Their dads were crazy, too. At first he'd encouraged them to tell him their stories, he'd felt it was his duty to listen to the grisly tales of alcoholics, alimony deadbeats, emotionally distant workaholics. As if that were what he'd written. Hadn't they read the chapter in which the boy sees his father incinerate himself on the TV evening news? Were they saying that happened to *them*? He learned to say, solemnly, "Thank you." A simple thank you was enough.

But not, it seems, for Angela. "All the time I was in high school, my dad was determined to kill himself. And I didn't know anyone else—not in my school, that's for sure, not in middle-class nowhere New Jersey—I'd never heard of anyone who went through anything like it. After my dad finally did it, I got kind of . . . weird. That's when my therapist gave me your book. I read it a million times. It made me realize that people survive stuff like that. It really helped me. It saved me. Plus it's a great book. I mean, it's right up there with Charlotte Brontë and Stendhal."

"Thank you," says Swenson. "I'm flattered."

It's true. Swenson feels terrific. It's gratifying to think that his novel helped this girl. When interviewers used to ask him how he pictured his ideal reader, he said he wrote books for nervous people to take with them on airplanes. Now he thinks his answer should have been: schoolchildren in middle-class nowhere New Jersey, girls who think that theirs is the only life scarred by grief.

Angela says, "Can I ask you something?"

"Ask away," says Swenson.

"Did that stuff in your novel, like, really happen?"

"I thought we talked about that in class. About not asking that question—"

"This isn't class," says Angela.

"It isn't," Swenson agrees. "That's really how my father died . . . . My mother and I really did see it on TV. It was sort of a celebrity death. For about fifteen minutes. And that scene in the Quaker Meeting House, when the old man comes up to the kid and says his life is going to rise from the ashes of his father's. That really happened, too." Swenson's said this too many times for it to qualify as a confession. In fact, it's the prepackaged betrayal of his own painful past—lines he'd robotically delivered to interviewers when *Phoenix Time* came out. "You do know about Vietnam, right? And the antiwar movement?"

Angela flinches, then rolls her eyes. "Please," she says. "I'm not retarded."

Regretting his condescension, Swenson searches for some fresh detail that he hasn't recycled again and again. "I'll tell you a funny thing. It's gotten to where I sometimes can't remember what happened and what I made up for the novel."

"*I'd* remember," Angela says.

"You're still young. What about the stuff in your novel? How much of *that* is true?"

Angela recoils. "Oh, man."

Her discomfort is contagious. But would someone tell him why that question was perfectly fine for her to ask him, but a violation—prying—when he turned it around?

"Of course not," Angela says. "I just made it up. I mean . . . well, I did have this friend who hatched eggs for her science project. But I invented the rest."

"Well, that's good," says Swenson.

"So, fine . . . I was just wondering if there was anything you think I should do to fix those pages I gave you."

Hasn't he just told her not to ask for advice? "Let's see it again." Angela hands back the manuscript, and he skims through it. It really *is* good. He was right about that. If only its author weren't quite so draining.

"This last sentence," he says. "You could lose it, and the piece would be stronger. You've made all that clear already."

"Which sentence?" Angela scoots her chair forward so their foreheads are practically touching over the desk.

"This one." Swenson reads: "'I had a gigantic crush on my high school music teacher, and I spent every minute, outside of his class, thinking about him.' We know that from the previous sentence. You could end the chapter with: 'The other half was wondering what Mr. Reynaud would say if I got to tell him about this tomorrow after orchestra practice.'"

Swenson finally gets it. How could he have read the manuscript—twice—and somehow never noticed that it's about a student with a crush on her teacher? Why? Because he didn't want to know. This conference has been exhausting enough without his having to deal with that.

"When did you start writing this . . . novel?"

"Early last summer. I was staying with my mom again and having a nervous breakdown." Angela takes a pen out of her backpack and draws a line through the final sentence, looping jauntily at the end, with a pig's-tail curl. "Anything else?"

"No," says Swenson. "That'll do it."

"Can I give you another few pages?" She's already got out a fresh orange envelope and is handing it to Swenson.

"Thanks," he says. "We'll talk about it next week after class? Like this . . . again?"

"Cool," says Angela. "See you then. Have fun!"

Leaving, she slams the door by accident and calls from the other side, "Oh, man, sorry! Thanks. See you!" Swenson listens to her footsteps running down the stairs. Then he takes out her manuscript and reads the opening paragraph.

> Mr. Reynaud said, "A little-known fact about eggs. During the equinox and solstice you can balance an egg on its end." This information struck me as more meaningful than anything I was learning about incubation and hatching. Everything Mr. Reynaud said soared above our high school class to something as large as the universe, the equinox and the solstice.

Swenson counts four pages—all he'll see this week. He reads slower, as he does when he's getting near the end of a book he likes. What the hell's going on here? This is a student novel. He reaches for the phone and dials.

A young man with a clipped British accent says, "Len Currie's line. May I help you?"

"Is Len there?"

"He's in a meeting," says the young Brit. "May I take a message?"

"I'll try later." Swenson hangs up. What exactly was he planning to say to Len? He can thank his lucky stars that the assistant blew him off.

Well, that's enough for one day. Swenson's earned a rest. Sherrie's waiting at the clinic. It's time to pick up his wife.

Dinner's a celebration. Of sorts. Sherrie's car's been fixed. Swenson's attention drifts while she explains what the problem was. The garage only charged them—he can focus on that—half as much as they'd feared. So that's what they're celebrating: painless car repair. Tonight, all over America, writers are toasting works of genius, six-figure advances, successes and romances, new friendships and BMWs. While Swenson, on his desert island, clinks glasses with his wife because the Civic only needed a two-hundred-dollar alternator.

What's so bad about that? They're drinking a nice Montepulciano, tied with a grapevine twig that's traveled all the way from Abruzzo to amuse them in Vermont. They're eating chicken with garlic, white wine, and fennel fresh from Sherrie's garden. In the salad are the last tomatoes, ripened on the windowsill, because Swenson has the good luck to be married to a woman who can work all day at a clinic and still have enough consciousness about the small pleasures of daily life to leave the tomatoes on the sill—just to make his salad. Earlier, when Sherrie was cooking, Swenson came up behind her, pressed his hips against hers, and she'd arched her back against him. . . . Not bad for forty-seven years old, twenty-one years of marriage. Good wine, good food, dinner in a state of mild arousal. Swenson's not a lunatic. The world is a vale of tears. He's got nothing to complain about. Nor is he complaining. Exactly.

Sherrie gazes out toward her garden, though it's already too dark to see. No doubt she's thinking of all the things that need to be done before winter. But what about Swenson? Hello, I'm over here, a few steps higher up the food chain than some plants that will survive or not, regardless of what Sherrie does.

After a while she says, "You know what, Ted? I feel weird sitting here eating fennel when the rest of the fennel patch can watch us through the window."

For a few seconds Swenson's charmed. Then he thinks, She's making sure I remember she grew the goddamn fennel.

He says, "Relax. Nothing can see in. *If* the vegetables were watching."

"Jo-oke," trills Sherrie. "Sorry."

"The fennel's great," says Swenson.

Sherrie throws her whole self into mopping up sauce with bread. Swenson loves to watch her eat. But tonight he makes the mistake of glancing past her, at the wall. On top of the flowered wallpaper that was here when they moved in, with its spreading fissures and sugary brown blotches, Sherrie's hung a row of holy pictures that she inherited from a great aunt. She'd put them up ironically, but they've stayed up in earnest, clasping their hands, some in ecstasy, some in torment, one crucified upside down.

Swenson thinks of Jonathan Edwards looming over the dean's head. Why does religion make people want to put scary images on the walls? So they'll know what they're doing in church, what they're putting in time to avoid. Give him the old Quaker Meeting House, nothing on the walls, nothing terribly frightening unless you were Swenson's father, who had the scary pictures inside of him, and was encouraged by his religion to spend an hour every Sunday touring his inner chamber of horrors. One morning after Meeting, when Swenson was twelve, his father took him out for breakfast at the Malden Diner and calmly explained that he'd come to believe that everything wrong with the world was his personal fault. As he said this, Swenson's skinny father ate three consecutive full breakfasts. It wasn't very long after that he set himself on fire on the State House steps.

Sherrie wheels around, then turns back. "Christ, Ted, the way you were looking at that wall, I thought one of those saints had started weeping."

"I wasn't looking at the wall."

"I thought you were," says Sherrie.

"I wasn't looking at anything."

Sherrie helps herself to more salad. She's not going to miss the last tomatoes just because Swenson's cranky. "Another crazy day at work. Mercury must be in retrograde, or something. This girl came in and said she was getting bad vibes from the ghosts of Elijah Euston's dead daughters."

"What were *you* supposed to do about that?"

"Valium," Sherrie says.

It actually cheers Swenson up to hear that clean-cut Euston kids are scamming to get drugs. "Probably one of my students."

"Freshman. Theater major," says Sherrie. "And then this disgusting thing happened. Some creep, this new guy in admissions, comes over with an application from some high school kid. The good news is the kid's got astronomical SAT scores. The bad news is he's got testicular cancer. They want me to call Burlington and ask about his chances. They don't want to waste a place in next year's class if the kid's not going to make it."

"Is that how he put it?" Swenson asks.

"No," Sherrie says. "That would have been illegal. But that's what he meant. I wasn't going to call Burlington. Or let them turn the poor kid down. So an hour later I call admissions and tell them that the guys at the medical school promised the kid would be fine. I'm feeling like a hero. And then it hits me that they could admit the guy and I could spend the next four years with a very sick kid on my hands."

Swenson certainly hopes not. He doesn't want to spend the next four years discussing testicular cancer. Listening to Sherrie's stories about the clinic has begun to feel like hearing someone's hypochondriacal symptoms. It's not Sherrie's fault that whatever she sees in her office has started sounding like something Swenson's fated to get.

The fact (which he would never say, and rarely admits to himself) is that he's not very interested in what happens at the clinic.

He married Sherrie under false pretenses—pretending to be enthralled by what she'd chosen to do with her life. But he *had* been fascinated, and not just for romantic reasons. A few days after he woke up on the emergency room floor with Sherrie's cool hand encircling his wrist, he'd started writing a story about a doctor so infatuated with a jazz singer that he ruins his career to satisfy her unquenchable thirst for love disguised as a ravening hunger for morphine and diet pills. As the story grew into his first novel, *Blue Angel*, it developed its own needs—a craving for medical information. So he went back to St. Vincent's and found Sherrie waiting for him. They fell in love so quickly, it seemed like research for the story of a man whose passion for a woman leaves him no viable option but to wreck his life. Except that Sherrie saved his. Everything changed when he met her.

That summer, they saw *The Blue Angel* at the Bleecker, and as Swenson watched the professor degraded into a slobbering clown for the amusement of the nightclub singer, Lola Lola, played by Marlene Dietrich with her smoky voice and the thighs that grabbed and held your attention, he knew where his book was going. The film gave him the name of the nightclub where his singer worked— and the title for his novel. For the first time, he felt that he was onto something larger than revenge on a doctor so starstruck by Sarah Vaughn that he'd ignored Swenson's ear infection. He understood that this period in his life—being in love instead of *wanting* to be in love, writing instead of *wanting* to write—had been arranged by magic, that a mantle of grace had settled on him and could as suddenly be whisked away. But not suddenly, as it turned out. Slowly. Thread by thread.

Sherrie says, "Arlene told me the most insane story at work today. These cousins of hers took their daughter to some amusement park near Lake George. They went to buy cotton candy and let go of the kid's hand and looked down . . . the kid disappeared. So they ran to park security, and the guards said, 'This happens all the time.' They closed off all the exits but one. The guards said, 'Stand there and look for your child. Look at the shoes, concentrate on the shoes. Everything else will be different.' So they stand at the exit, and they see the shoes and go, 'That's her! That's my child.' The kidnappers had dyed the kid's hair and changed her clothes, but they couldn't do anything about the shoes. Kids have such different sizes."

"That's ridiculous," Swenson says. "What do you mean, this happens all the time? Didn't they catch the kidnappers? Do lots of kidnappers do this? Why bother changing the kid's clothes and dying her hair—where? in the public bathroom?—when they can just hustle the kid out of the park and split before anyone notices?"

"Why are you shouting at *me*?" Sherrie says. "I told you it was insane. That's why I brought it up. Forget it, Ted, okay?"

"Sorry. It's just that typical tabloid country bullshit Arlene always talks."

Sherrie laughs. "Poor Arlene. She was hyperventilating, the story turned her on so much."

"Her cousins told her this? They said it happened to *them*? Are they pathological liars?"

"God knows," says Sherrie. "God knows at what point the fantasy takes over."

"Or maybe the wishful thinking," says Swenson.

"Don't say that." In the silence that follows, Sherrie plays with a piece of fennel, sawing along one bumpy ridge with surgical precision.

Finally Swenson says, "Speaking of missing children . . . this morning I thought about leaving early for class and driving over to Burlington and going by Ruby's dorm and ringing her buzzer, finding her somewhere, somehow, taking her out for coffee. . . ."

"And?"

"I didn't."

"Maybe you should have," says Sherrie. "Maybe it would've helped."

"Time's what's going to help," Swenson says.

They know that, and neither believes it. Ruby doesn't forget. Since she was a baby, she's always been the most stubborn person

alive. A passing fright, some toy she had to have, she could keep it
going forever. Why did they imagine that would have changed?
Because everything else has. Their funny, gangly little girl turned
into a chunky teen with dirty hair and the sullen blankness you see
on vintage farm-family photos. Ruby retreated further and further.
Sherrie said it would pass; girls get lost at a certain age. Sherrie
brought him a book about this, which he refused to read. It
depressed him that he was married to a person who would think
that some self-help piece-of-shit bestseller had something to do
with their daughter.

Eventually, they convinced themselves that really they were
lucky. Ruby was fine. She got Bs in school. Half her classmates
were pregnant or on drugs, even (or especially) up here in idyllic
Euston. And then, at the start of Ruby's senior year, Arlene Shurley
came into the clinic and told Sherrie she'd seen Ruby with a guy
driving a red Miata.

There was only one Miata on campus, a sleek red rose of a car
tucked neatly into the buttonhole of Euston's most troubled student. A southern senator's youngest son, entitled and alcoholic,
Matthew McIlwaine had transferred in as a sophomore after being
thrown out of two colleges, in the first case for passing bad checks,
in the second for date rape. His presence at Euston was a scandal
that died out within weeks, after the announcement of the library's
new McIlwaine wing. The kid looked like a male model: that narcissistic, that pretty. What was he doing with Ruby? Swenson didn't
want to imagine. Sherrie said that transfer students were often very
lonely.

They should have been glad that Ruby *had* a secret, glad that she
had a boyfriend. It used to bother Swenson that her friends at
Central High were the homely-girl clique. Any boyfriend, any girlfriend would have been fine—anyone but Matt. Who could blame
Swenson for wanting to save his child from a felon and a date
rapist?

Swenson talked to Matt's advisor, then to Matt, who promptly
cut Ruby loose. That's how Swenson saw it: a cat played with a

mouse, something distracted the cat, and the mouse ran free. He'd thought the mouse would thank him.

Swenson and Sherrie know it's important not to blame each other. Sometimes it's weirdly sexy, this sharing of their grief, the two of them, connected this way that no one else can feel. But the wedge of all they can't say is busily doing its damage. Sherrie's totally innocent. She'd warned him that it wouldn't work, that Ruby wouldn't forget. And though Sherrie would never accuse him of having done everything wrong, he knows that she must think so. So he can blame her for blaming him, and because he's the one to blame.

Sherrie drains the last of her wine. "Ruby will get over it. Basically, she loves us."

"Why would she?" says Swenson. "I mean, why would she love *me*?"

Sherrie sighs and shakes her head. "Give me a break," she says.

After dinner, Swenson goes to his study. He picks up his novel, with a queasy lurch of misgiving. Holding the pages at arm's length—admit it, he's getting farsighted—he reads a sentence, then another.

> *Julius walked into the gallery. He knew everyone there, and knew precisely how many of them wanted to see him fall flat on his face. Over the head of a woman air-kissing him on both cheeks he saw his work—the same lines that had writhed on the subway tiles—dying all around them on the gallery walls.*

Who wrote this hopeless moribund crap? Certainly not Swenson. Dead on the walls, dead on the page—a coded warning to himself. He dimly remembers how it felt when his work was going well, how sitting down to his desk each day was like slipping into a warm bath, or a warm silky river, a tide of words and sentences floating him away. . . . He opens his briefcase and takes out Angela Argo's manuscript. He's not going to read it. He'll just take a peek. Then he starts to read and forgets whatever he was thinking, and then, little by little, forgets about his novel, Angela's novel, his age, her age, his talent, her talent.

Mr. Reynaud said, "A little-known fact about eggs. During the equinox and solstice you can balance an egg on its end." This information struck me as more meaningful than anything I was learning about incubation and hatching. Everything Mr. Reynaud said soared above our high school class to something as large as the universe, the equinox and the solstice.

I never tried to balance an egg during the equinox or the solstice. I don't believe in astrology. But I knew that my life was like that egg, and the point it balanced on were the few minutes I got to stay after class and talk to Mr. Reynaud.

The last ten minutes of practice were hell: how much time was left, how long the piece might take if Mr. Reynaud stopped to yell at the snare drum for missing his cue and we had to start over and finish just as the bell rang. That was how I finally learned math, figuring it all out. If the music ended early—the remainder was what I got. If not, I had a desert to cross—a night or a day or a weekend.

I was first clarinet. I made sure the others came in on time. I tapped the beat with my foot. Did Mr. Reynaud think that tapping the beat was babyish and stupid? I imagined him watching my foot. I concentrated on the measures, holding the clarinet in my lap. Mr. Reynaud glanced at my clarinet as his eyes skimmed over the band.

He'd taught us to pick up our instruments three measures ahead of our cue. We knew to put them in our mouths and come in on the downbeat. We did, more or less together, the others maybe a second behind, and then the piping of the woodwinds drove all that out of my head, the crispy bubbling precision of those perfect notes of Bach's Fifth Brandenburg Concerto, simplified for high school kids, but still miles beyond us.

Three measures from the end, the world came back. Was Mr. Reynaud watching my foot? As if my stupid ankle was all he had to worry about as he swooped his arms above us.

It had begun one afternoon the previous spring, on the way home from the All-County tryouts. The Cooperstown High School Orchestra had won the competition with a piece called "The Last Pow-Wow," corny disgusting tom-toms, moaning cellos supposed to be warriors chanting in the longhouse, then a scream of piccolos, someone scalping somebody. The crowd in the high school gym went wild. The judges were nodding their heads. Our tinkly pitiful Mozart sounded totally pathetic.

Mr. Reynaud drove the van with the instruments and the section leaders, his elite squad. Normally we talked nonstop. Who liked this one, who liked that one, as if Mr. Reynaud wasn't there. Actually, it was all for him: a display of our cool teenage lives. But after the tryouts we were too disappointed to talk. We'd lost, and it was our fault.

Mr. Reynaud hit the brakes. The van changed lanes. The band instruments shifted, the high hat clanged. A car horn blared and faded. From over Mr. Reynaud's shoulder, I watched the speedometer climb. He'd always driven like my parents: a few miles under the limit. Now he was all over the road, cutting off other cars. I thought we were going to die.

He cut across three lanes of traffic, pulled into a rest stop, and said, "Okay, everyone out. Forward march."

We looked at him. He meant it. We knew he'd been a Marine.

He'd nearly killed us in the van, but we were fine with him marching us way out into the woods beyond the deserted rest stop. This was one of those crazy stunts that made him a popular teacher. Once at rehearsal he made us switch instruments with someone in another section and rehearse the hardest piece on instruments we couldn't play.

We followed him along the path past the map under its grimy glass, past the heavy trash cans. We entered the spongy forest. We kept losing sight of Mr. Reynaud as we trailed him into the woods. He held his shoulders very straight. We followed his dark angry head.

"All right, stop," he said. "Look around you. This is where the Indians lived. Do you think for one second they played that corny Hollywood shit? Real Indian music was nothing like that!"

He didn't blame us for losing. The proof was that he'd said "shit." He only cursed around the section leaders, so we knew he still liked us.

"All right," Mr. Reynaud said. "Everyone back in the van."

The others started back to the van, but I couldn't move. Suddenly I felt sleepy.

Mr. Reynaud grabbed my arm.

I was so scared I smiled. Mr. Reynaud's face was close to mine. I stared into his eyes. I could hardly focus. I saw my own contorted face in Mr. Reynaud's glasses. He opened his mouth. Then he shut it again.

"Go ahead," he told me. But he was still holding my arm. "Sorry," he mumbled. "I didn't . . ." And then he let me go.

It's only their third conference, but Angela's so much calmer that she only writhes a little as she falls into the cracked leather chair. Well, she's got a right to be calm. Swenson called *her* and arranged this meeting. Probably she assumes that he does this with all his students. She crosses her legs beneath her. "Well? What did you think?"

Swenson says, "What are those words on your hand?"

Angela scowls at the smeary ballpoint. "Oh. There's a lunar eclipse this weekend. I didn't want to forget. Come on. What did you think of my novel?"

"Do you play an instrument?"

"Actually, no. I failed second grade music. Flunked soprano recorder."

"Then how do you know so much about music?"

"I have friends. I asked. I made it up. You hated it. That's what you're saying, right?"

"Not at all. I thought it was terrific. I've marked a couple of places you might want to look at and change."

"Shoot." Angela takes out her pen.

"They're nothing. Like here. A grammatical thing. You say, 'As if Mr. Reynaud wasn't there.' Technically, it's *weren't*. *Weren't* there. But you can do it either way."

"Did you mark that?"

"I did. And over here . . . this is about . . . plausibility. Would she really be able to see her face in his glasses? Or did you just want it there, so you decided to finesse it?"

Angela drops back in her chair. "Whoa," she says. "That hurts. Let's look in *your* glasses. Okay. Forget it. Sorry. Isn't it enough that she thinks she can see her reflection? I mean, she's pretty stressed out at that point in the story."

"Leave it in." Swenson's not going to argue. "Maybe you'll look at it later. . . ."

"What else?" Angela says.

"Well . . . here. This same sentence. If you do decide to keep it. 'She sees her own contorted face.' *Contorted* tells us nothing."

"It could mean anything," Angela says.

"Exactly," Swenson says.

"Make sure you mark that," Angela says.

"I already did," says Swenson.

"I can't believe I did that," Angela says. "Thank you, thank you so much!"

Encouraged, Swenson checks the manuscript one more time. "Okay, look. This scene in the van. It goes by a little fast. Does she really think they're going to get hurt, that they're going to get in a wreck? So when he pulls over there's real relief mixed in with this new terror . . . ?"

Angela nods, then quits nodding. Swenson watches her think.

"You're right," she says. "I knew that. I was just kind of rushing ahead so I could write the part when they're in the forest. That little moment she spends alone with him is so important to her, everything changes after that. . . ."

After a silence, Swenson says, "Do you have other readers for this? I mean, are you showing it to anyone else?" He vaguely recalls her saying no one else has seen it. But for some reason he wants to be sure. . . .

"No one," says Angela. "I mean, no one except my boyfriend. Oh, my God, what do you think it means that I just called my boyfriend *no one*?"

"I'd hate to speculate," says Swenson. "And what does your boyfriend think?"

"He thinks it's great." Angela shrugs and turns up her palms.

"Look. I brought you more pages." Angela pulls a new orange envelope from her bag, and they exchange orange envelopes. Angela almost drops hers, and giggles.

Looking at the floor, she says, "Actually, it's just a paragraph that I wanted to add onto the end of what I already gave you. I've got more, whole chapters, but I thought I'd take it slow. I don't want to scare you. Working with you is amazing. It's making me want to write. I can't get it down fast enough. I have to make myself rewrite it until I'm not embarrassed to show it to you, which is usually after about a zillion revisions. Will you write a note for me when someone catches on that I'm not going to any of my other classes and the dean gets on my case?"

"I can't do that," Swenson says. "But I'll be glad to read what you've written."

"See you Tuesday," Angela says.

"Tuesday," Swenson says. He listens to her footsteps running down the steps and then opens the envelope.

> *The next day, I could hardly play. I'd forgotten how to lose myself in the music. I wondered why had Mr. Reynaud grabbed my arms in the woods? And that became my real science experiment: analyzing the data with more attention than I ever gave to those poor hopeless eggs I tried to hatch in our backyard toolshed.*

Swenson puts down the page and picks up the phone. But whom is he going to call? He phoned Len Currie last week. He doesn't feel like talking to Sherrie. He dials Magda Moynahan's extension.

"Ted!" says Magda. "How are you?"

Among the things he likes about Magda is how happy she sounds to hear him, as opposed to all the unwelcome calls she seems to have been expecting.

"I've got a student here," she says. "Can I call you back?"

"Don't," says Swenson. "Let's have lunch and talk then. How about tomorrow?"

"Fine," says Magda. "The usual place, I assume."

"Right," says Swenson. "Should we drive out together?"

"I'll be coming from Montpelier. I'll meet you there at twelve-thirty."

Expecting Magda to be a few minutes late, Swenson arrives a few minutes later and is irritated when Magda's later still. Without a newspaper or a book, he has only his glass of headache Chardonnay to mediate between him and the Maid of Orleans's grim ambience. The windowless, dark-paneled steakhouse was built in the late fifties by a family from Quebec. In honor of their patron saint, Joan of Arc, they decorated the place like an S&M club: armor, crossed axes, spiked maces dangling from the rafters, loops of the bicycle chain no doubt used to "distress" the woodwork. Where do you shop for *objets* like that? Nowhere, not anymore.

Three generations of owners have polished the suits of armor, preserving the decor of this place where Euston faculty meet for friendly collegial lunch. Students never come here, so you can complain about them without the fear that they'll be at the next table. On rare occasions, when a department is recruiting, they take prospective faculty members here, calculating that if they go all the way to Montpelier, where the food is better, the candidates will figure out that you have to go all the way to Montpelier. And they charm the interviewee with a Euston faculty joke: The cuisine at the Maid of Orleans has been tied up and burned at the stake.

Today, two-thirds of the tables are filled with predictable combinations of administrators and professors. Swenson's greeted everyone on the way to his seat. He never comes to this place except with Magda. You can have lunch here with a female colleague without exciting gossip or speculation. Lovers wouldn't go near it unless they wanted the world to know. You might as well embrace in the middle of Euston Quad.

Still, Swenson and Magda do have one of those friendships that can, for no clear reason, jitter for a few weeks or months on the edge of flirtation, a giddy brink from which they're pulled back by the gravity of their working together, Swenson's marriage, Magda's ex-marriage, their knowing each other too well. A tinge of romance lingers, as evidenced by the fact that now, as Magda rushes in, Swenson's surprised, as always, by how pretty she is.

Swenson half-rises. Magda kisses his cheek. He hugs her, clumsily patting her back. She shrugs off her coat and leans forward, elbows on the table, her eyes so focused on his that, if this weren't the Maid of Orleans, a stranger might think they *were* lovers.

Women tend to like Swenson, mostly because he likes women. He's interested in what they have to say, doesn't think they're plotting to kill him. That's why he's got a good marriage, why librarians and department secretaries will do anything for him, why he's the only sucker at Euston who never slept with his students. Women have told him that his lack of obvious hostility sets him apart from most men. Maybe what they mean is: they don't want to sleep with *him*.

Magda might have—she almost did—one night at her apartment. This was during one of their more intense spells of attraction, so Swenson had looked forward all day to dropping off some papers at Magda's, where he responded to the complex nuances of the situation by drinking a bottle of wine within the first twenty minutes. He slid deeper into Magda's couch, closer and closer to Madga, and—at the very moment when they might have, should have, kissed—he'd realized he was way too drunk. He'd rocketed up off the couch and run out the door. A lot depends on their never—never once—mentioning that evening.

"What were you doing in Montpelier?" he says.

"The bookstore," Magda says. "Look."

He squints at the title. *"Great Dog Poems?"*

"There are some terrific poets in this," she says. "Real writers, I'm not kidding."

"Don't tell me," Swenson says. "First you're going to get a dog. And then you're going to write a poem about it."

"Ted," she says, "I *have* a dog."

"Check," he says unsurely. What kind of dog does Magda have? An Irish setter? Or is he imagining this because Magda has the coloring and the temperament of a setter? He thinks perhaps he met the dog, that night at her house. Mostly he remembers seeing her wall of books lurch and start to rotate, gradually picking up speed.

Swenson says, "Didn't I meet your dog?"

Magda sighs. "This is not about my dog. This is about one of my freshmen having written the world's worst greeting-card poem about the death of a dog. I know for a fact it's *his* dog, so what am I going to say? I'm sorry about your puppy. And by the way, your poem stinks. So I thought if I could show the kid some good poems about dogs or the deaths of dogs, at least we'd have someplace to start."

"You're a great teacher. You know that?"

"Thanks a lot," Magda says.

"It's true. You take it seriously. Plus, your students love you." Swenson remembers Angela saying she disliked Magda's class.

"Ted? Is something wrong?"

"Sorry. I was just thinking: In my class they'd be writing stories about having sex with the dead dog."

"Huh?" says Magda. "Excuse me?"

"I mean a dead chicken. Listen, is your class weird this semester? What's with these kids, huh? Everyone's writing stories about having sex with animals."

"Safe sex?" Magda says dubiously.

"Danny Liebman handed in a masterpiece about some kid coming home from a date and sodomizing a raw chicken he finds in the refrigerator."

"Disgusting," Magda says.

"I wish you'd said that in my class."

"What *did* you say?"

"I took the technical route. Accuracy of detail. I said chickens in suburban refrigerators usually don't have their heads on." Swenson knows he's lying to make a better story for Magda.

"Chickens. That's a big sexual harassment suit just waiting to be filed."

"Tell me about it," says Swenson. And they both fall silent.

Then Magda says, "How's Angela Argo doing?"

Swenson's glad she asked. He was going to bring up the subject. But just at that moment, the waitress arrives. Gruff, good-natured Janet.

"How we doin'?" Janet says.

"Excellent," says Swenson.

"Ditto," says Magda.

"Sure. Right," says Janet. "A-plus."

Swenson orders what he always orders, the choice every insider—and who else comes here?—makes without deliberation: the grilled steak sandwich, charred (as the menu says) to perfection, layered lovingly on a buttered hard roll and served with mashed potatoes and gravy.

"I'll have the same," says Magda.

"Why did I bother asking?" Janet turns and leaves, pleased and disappointed with them for not surprising her more.

Praise Janet, and the Maid of Orleans, and the fact that the ordering has gone quickly enough for them to get back to what they were saying.

"Why do you ask?" says Swenson.

"Ask what?" says Magda.

"About Angela Argo." Swenson sounds like Angela on the first day of class when *she* had to say her name and rolled her eyes so far back in her head he'd thought she was having a seizure.

Magda gives him a searching look. Information zaps back and forth, complex but unclear. Well, if Magda knows so much, she can explain it to Swenson. Anyway, she's got it all wrong, because what she says next is, "Ted, if you sleep with Angela Argo, I'll never talk to you again."

What a weird thing for Magda to say! And how, precisely, did they get from Danny's story to the possibility of Swenson's sleeping with Angela Argo? She saw them together yesterday. Could Magda possibly think . . . ? Did she pick up some signal as yet invisible on Swenson's male radar screen? Even Swenson, so warm toward women, feels an edge of chill. They *are* another species. You really have to watch it.

"God, Magda, where is this coming from? Are you nuts? You were at that meeting. If I were going to risk my job, it wouldn't be for Angela. Anyway, you know I don't do that kind of thing."

Magda certainly does know that. The tension leaves her face. "So? What's Angela up to now?"

"Writing a novel," Swenson says. "It's good. I mean really good."

"I'm not surprised," says Magda. "Though the stuff she wrote for me was awful. But I could tell she was gifted. She's also major trouble."

"Trouble how?"

"Well," says Magda, after a beat, "it's as if she has . . . no center."

"Meaning what?"

"She lies."

"Lies about what?" Swenson's holding his breath.

"Little things. For example, she borrowed some books—Rilke, Neruda, Stevens—from another student, and when he asked for them back, she said she never took them. He sneaked into her room and found them on her desk. It was complicated, because I think the kid had a crush on her. But the fact was, she *had* the books."

"Stealing books? Not the world's worst crime. I wish more kids wanted books enough to steal them. And how does that stack up against the guy sneaking into her dorm room? So . . . was this the kid who's her boyfriend now?"

"I didn't know she had a boyfriend. I'm pretty sure she didn't then . . . . Anyhow, it was a mess. But eventually it turned out to be a sort of bonding thing for the class. I don't think anyone told."

Such things never happen in Swenson's class. No one *bonds*, as Magda puts it.

"I don't know," says Magda. "Maybe it was just me. Angela was one of those students I always think I'm failing. I know I just told you her poems were bad . . . but in fact they were sort of strong. Maybe I just couldn't deal with them. They were so . . . furious and dirty."

"Furious and dirty? Yikes. What were they about?"

"Dramatic monologues, I'd guess you'd call them. Or dialogues, maybe. All supposedly transcriptions of phone-sex workers on the job."

Why did Magda never include *this* among the horror stories she'd told him last spring over lunch?

"I told you about it," Magda says.

"You didn't."

"You just don't remember. You weren't paying attention. The point is, they were freshmen, Ted. I felt I had to be careful. I felt I had to vet which ones we discussed in workshop."

What a time for their food to arrive! But by now their conversation has enough tensile strength to hang in there for a few bites.

Magda swallows first. "Also . . . there was something else. The phone-sex worker in the poems calls herself Angela 911."

"Jesus H. Christ," says Swenson. "So now Euston's admitting former phone-sex workers?"

"Former or current. Hard to tell. I had a feeling it might be true. Also there was something about the way the other kids treated her. Fear. Respect. I don't know. My rule is: Don't ask, don't tell. You know when a kid is writing about his dead dog. But unless they volunteer—"

"Me, too," interrupts Swenson. It's a relief to switch from the subject of Angela's steamy poems to the subject of workshop procedure. It reminds them of their mission here. Colleagues, talking shop. "Don't ask. Don't tell. Don't want to know."

"Certainly not about this. But again, she was a freshman. I wondered if I should alert someone. I thought about telling Sherrie."

"Sherrie? Did you?"

"No. I didn't want any mental health stuff on Angela's record. And . . . I'm not proud of this, but I didn't want to get involved. You know how it is. Just hang on, the semester will be over. In any case, I didn't have to ask. Angela made sure I knew. There was a lot in the poems about the phone-sex worker's sexually abusive father. And one afternoon, in conference, Angela hinted that it might be true."

"What did she say?"

"I can't remember. I went into panic mode. Of course, half the student population claims to be incest survivors."

"Not to me they don't," says Swenson.

"Lucky you," says Magda. "But there were things about Angela . . . well, I could believe it."

"Meaning what?" Swenson says carefully.

"I don't know. It's not just Angela. It's her whole generation. Sometimes I worry that they think there's something wrong with sex altogether. It's as if they secretly believe that having a sexual thought or desire means you're a terrible person."

"Unless it's for an animal," Swenson says. Then he says, "Jesus. Poor kids." He stops, struck by the oddness of his having this conversation with Magda. Both of them have worked fairly hard to thwart the wayward sexual impulse. Maybe Angela was right about Magda having some kind of . . . problem. One thing that's for certain is that Magda hasn't read Angela's novel. Yet the chance that Magda's right about Angela and her generation makes Swenson feel somehow relieved.

"The father in her poems . . . was that the father who killed himself?"

"Killed himself? She never mentioned a suicide. You know, Ted, I had the funniest feeling about her. That all of it could be invented, and *she* might not know the difference."

"The novel's for real," says Swenson.

"I'm glad to hear that," says Magda.

"You don't still happen to have any of those poems, do you?" Swenson stares down at his plate. He knows he must sound insane. How many examples of student work has *he* saved in his files?

But Magda doesn't seem surprised. "Well, this is very strange, too." She takes a small bite of her sandwich and wipes her mouth with the back of her hand. Swenson gazes at the back of her hand. He wants to reach over and stroke it. "This will show you how driven Angela is. End of spring semester, I get a phone call from Betty Hester. At the library."

"I know Betty," says Swenson. "Mother Hubbard."

"Oh, Ted, no. That's mean. Anyhow, Betty tells me that one of my students—Angela, obviously—has printed out a volume of her poetry, nicely designed, typeset on the computer. She's stitched it together, a real book, and presented it to the Euston library as a souvenir of her freshman year. She thought Betty should shelve it in the modern American poetry section.

"Betty thanked her. She thought it was sweet. But then she actually *read* a few lines and figured out what was what. That's when she called to ask me: Should she turn down Angela's gift? I asked if the college had a rule against shelving books by students. Betty said they didn't. The situation had never come up. I told Betty what I thought: that Angela could come looking for her book and was quite capable of making a fuss with the administration if it wasn't shelved or checked out."

"Angela?" Swenson's trying to square the litigious harpy Magda seems to have in mind with the awkward sparrow he knows, begging for crumbs of praise.

"Angela," says Magda. "Finally I told Betty that if she catalogued and shelved the goddamn thing, no one but Angela would ever check it out. No one would ever see it. She could ditch the book as soon as Angela graduated. Of course, the truth was . . . I was the one who didn't need trouble with the administration. The poems were written in my class. I don't have tenure, remember?"

"So the book's in the library?" Swenson says.

"As far as I know."

"I might take a look at it."

"Be my guest," says Magda. Suddenly they're both aware of their half-eaten sandwiches and guiltily apply themselves to finishing their food.

"I was hungry," Swenson lies.

"Me, too. I guess," says Magda.

"By the way, Ted." Magda pushes away her plate. "While you're at the library, check out Ackerley's *My Dog Tulip*. Pass it on to your students. It's the best thing ever written about having sex with a pet."

"Thanks," says Swenson. "I knew I could count on you."

"We're friends," says Magda. "Right?"

The last sighting of Elijah Euston's ghost took place in the library several years ago. A freshman working late in the American history stacks saw an old man in a black frock coat, sobbing, his face buried in his hands, with only his powdered wig showing. Why was Elijah crying? Because of the tragic fates of his daughters or the decline of the college he founded with such high hopes?

Swenson jogs up the library steps, steps intended to make you feel you should be climbing them on your knees. Whether or not the library's haunted, Swenson never feels closer to Elijah Euston than he does in this British cathedral transplanted to northern Vermont. Euston didn't live to see it finished but left elaborate instructions for the stonemasons, stained glass makers and wood-carvers on how to build his temple to higher education.

Swenson's spirit used to soar on the updraft of transcendence that the library's vaulted arches were designed to produce. Every so often he still gets a buzz in the presence of two thousand years of poetry, art, history, science—the whispery proximity of all those dear dead voices. But lately, he's more likely to feel the dizzying chasm between what Elijah Euston dreamed and what his dream has become, between the lofty heights of Western culture and the everyday grubbiness of education at Euston.

It's the same mild vertigo Swenson suffers whenever he passes portraits of Euston's past presidents, or Jonathan Edwards scowling from the Founders Chapel wall. That's what tradition means these days: those stirrings of inadequacy in the face of our ancestors' hopes. Or maybe Swenson's just edgy as he enters these hallowed halls to find a student's dirty poems.

As always, the library's empty. Where do the students work? Swenson's footsteps ring against the stone floor of the entrance hall. He feels at once tiny, overwhelmed, and disruptively huge and noisy. At least no one's around to ambush him with maddening conversation.

Then he sees Betty Hester at the checkout desk. A tall upright tea cosy of a woman, Betty wears a homespun eggplant-colored dress with a skirt roomy enough for her whole clan—the six children she's raised while working at Euston and obtaining the requisite Library Science degrees—to live comfortably underneath it.

"Ted!" hisses Betty. "We haven't seen you in decades. Too busy writing to read?"

"If only!" Swenson shrugs modestly to deflect Betty's assumption, meanwhile leaving open the chance that she might be right.

"Oh, you artists. How's Sherrie?"

"Fine," says Swenson. "The kids?"

"Just dandy. Well! Is there something I can help you with today?"

"Thanks, no. I'm at one of those slow points. . . . I thought I'd just drop in and browse, see if inspiration strikes."

"Oh, a real reader!" Betty says. "People like you are the reason this place still exists."

With newly wary eyes, the paranoia of a pervert, Swenson observes that from the checkout desk Betty can see the card catalog, which he still prefers over the frustrating computer. Does he imagine that if Betty sees him head for the As, she'll guess he's here to find *The Complete Dirty Poems of Angela Argo*? And now inspiration *does* strike. He can go to the As, look up Magda's suggestion—Ackerley's *My Dog Tulip*—and while he's in the neighborhood . . .

He scribbles the Ackerley call number on a slip of paper and then, with studied casualness, finds "Argo, Angela. *Angela 911*. Privately printed."

No need for Betty to notice that Swenson's breathing quickens. And now he can only hope that Elijah Euston's ghost has gone back to wherever it normally lurks as he takes the stone stairs that corskcrew up to the literature section.

Not an extra molecule of oygen up here in this smog of mildew. He traces his index finger along the rows of books and stops at a volume sewn with shiny red thread, shelved next to A. R. Ammons. His fingers fly away from it as if from a hot iron. His lungs seem to be shrinking in response to the lack of air.

He steadies himself, then slides the book—the booklet—from the shelf. No wonder Betty was freaked. On the cover is the title, *Angela 911*, in bold red letters. And below that is a photo, downloaded from a computer, of the Venus de Milo, with a pair of arms crudely drawn in. One hand covers the statue's crotch. The other holds a phone receiver.

Hearing—imagining?—footsteps, Swenson stops and listens. He peers down the row of bookshelves. The manuscript shakes in his hands. He finds the dedication page: "To my Mother and Father." How thoughtful—dedicating dirty poems about incest and phone sex to your parents. He shuts the book. Is someone coming? Perhaps the bookshelves are groaning with age, the floors shifting under their weight.

The light is too dim to read by, but he hesitates to go to a carrel, where someone might catch him with the book, too far from the shelves to slip it back. He restores it to its proper place, leaves, finds the Ackerley book, returns and gets Angela's manuscript, which he slips under the Ackerley. Then he walks to the farthest desk, a cubbyhole wedged in a corner—a carrel no one would ever pass on the way to anywhere else.

He pages to the first poem and reads:

> I'm the father of four daughters.
> Three of them are sleeping.
> One is awake and waiting for me.
> That's why I called you tonight.

Are you sleeping? Don't sleep. Listen.
I keep thinking of her hard tiny breasts.
My fingers between her legs.
Her hips pushing up against my hand.
Are you sleeping? Listen.
I hear her cry
The pigeon coo she made as a baby
But now the cry is for me, it's mine.
Her bones are a pigeon's bones.
I lie on them gently, gently,
My penis against her smooth thigh.
That's why I called you.
Listen. Don't sleep. Listen.
I said, I'm not sleeping.
I'm waiting for you.
Oh, you make me so hot.
Pretend that you're lying on top of me.
Pretend that I'm your daughter.

Okay. She's no Sylvia Plath. It's a good thing her fiction is better than her poems. Meanwhile he's aware that these uncharitable thoughts are merely attempts to distract himself from the fact that he has an erection. What kind of monster is he? Aroused by a poem about incest, the abuse of an innocent girl! All these years he's been fooling himself about his so-called moral principles, his inner life, his duties as teacher and husband and father—the father of a daughter. Suppose someone did this to Ruby? Suppose someone did this to Angela?

Swenson's hardly human. He's an animal. A beast. He crosses and uncrosses his legs, closes his eyes and inhales. The dust makes him cough. Think of lung cancer. All those years he smoked. There now. His hard-on's subsiding. Really, he's got to calm down. Stop being so tough on himself. An erection isn't a capital crime, it's neither rape nor molestation. Not even Catholics believe that bad thoughts are as bad as bad deeds. In high school, when he got erections during boring math class, he'd imagine his parents were dead. And now they *are* dead, and he himself will be dead, as will Sherrie and Ruby. Well, that takes care of it nicely. The industrial-strength antiaphrodisiac.

Anyway, Angela's poems—their trite erotic content—weren't what got him hard. Nor the fact that they were written by a student he can picture in his mind, a girl with a side he wouldn't have guessed, or maybe he could have guessed, and wisely chose not to. He's forty-seven, nearly done with the necessity of evading erotic sabotage. Having chattered his way through flirtations with so many *pretty* students, he'd have to be mad to lose it, so near the finish line, for scrawny Angela Argo. His hard-on wasn't about the poem. Or Angela. Certainly not. It's the whole situation: the airless library, the aura of taboo, reading any reference to sex, no matter how banal, in this . . . hushed, ascetic, hallowed temple to scholarship and study.

He wants to read the rest of the poems. But not here in the stacks. It would be different at home. Cleaner. Less furtive and weird. But first there's the little problem of getting it past Betty Hester.

Probably he should just steal it. He'd be doing Betty—and Magda—a favor. Why didn't he bring his briefcase? He could tuck the book under his arm and walk it through the front door. With his luck, it's been magnetized and will set off the alarm they installed a few years back on the foolishly hopeful premise that students want to steal books. Angela steals books, Magda said. And now, it seems, so does Swenson.

He wants the book. He should have it. But he can't risk checking it out, generating a permanent record stored in the computer. Why doesn't he just photocopy? It's only fifteen or twenty pages. He's so pleased by this easy solution that he hurries downstairs, then stops when he remembers that the library copy machine is near the card catalog—plainly visible from Betty's desk. Copying will never work. He's got to keep a cool head. Avoid all eye contact with Betty and make it clear through gesture, or lack of gesture, that he brought the bound manuscript into the library and can simply take it back home.

From the corner of his eye he sees that Betty's not at her desk. Then, from the reference stacks behind the desk, Betty shouts, "Oh, hi, Ted! Be with you in a sec!" Where's her professional duty to maintain the tomblike silence?

Swenson forces a smile. It's vital not to panic. For him to go to the trouble of checking out a student's work for a previous class is not only well within his rights but a sign of superhuman dedication. What has gotten into him, a respected novelist and professor, terrified he'll get busted for borrowing some amateurish, slightly titillating poems? You'd think he was a kid getting caught with his first dirty magazine.

As Betty takes the Ackerley, Swenson surreptitiously transfers Anegla's book to his other hand. That's his. He's not surrendering it. It's none of Betty's business.

"Ted?"

"What?" he temporizes. Busted for possession.

"Your card?" says Betty, sweetly.

"Oh!" Twisting sideways to keep *Angela 911* out of Betty's view, Swenson gropes with his free hand until he finds his wallet.

Betty says, "Hmm. *My Dog Tulip*. I don't believe I know this."

"Professor Moynahan recommended it," he says. And then unnecessarily, "My students seem to be writing stories about people who fall inappropriately in love with their pets." Why did he say *that*?

"Well, I suppose that happens." Zapping the book with the quivering beam of red light, Betty seems reassured by whatever message comes up on the computer screen and surrenders the Ackerley, all checked out and ready to go.

"Thanks," booms Swenson in an effort at hearty closure.

Then Betty points and, in the unmistakable tones of a grade school teacher ordering a child to bring up the passed note or spit out the contraband gum, says, "And that one, Ted?"

Oh, that one's mine, Swenson should say. He doesn't have to show her. But he hands it over, a transaction in which far more is

exchanged than Angela Argo's manuscript. A silent interrogation—
all body language and facial expression—ensues over the question
of whether he'd merely forgotten or intended not to declare it. The
faintest tremor of suspicion . . . then the moment passes. Betty
rotates the manuscript and together they study the Venus de Milo,
the naked torso talking on the phone and grabbing her crotch.

"Oh, dear," Betty says. "I believe I know the author. Is she one of
your students?"

"You got it," Swenson says gratefully.

"How fortunate for her."

Swenson's eyes film with tears of relief. It's been an emotional
day—lunch with Magda, then that little incident with himself, up in
the stacks. Bless dear Betty for making it clear that borrowing a student's poems is neither a perversion nor a punishable offense.

Betty checks out the book and gives it to him. It's all he can do
not to grab it before she changes her mind.

"How's Sherrie?" says Betty. Didn't she already ask?

"Fine," Swenson says. Again.

"And Ruby?"

"Fine."

"Give them my love," says Betty.

"And mine to yours," says Swenson.

As Dean Francis Bentham opens the door of his Main Street Victorian, a cloud of acrid smoke billows out at Swenson and Sherrie.

"Welcome to the crematorium, chums!" Francis waves them inside. "Enter at your own risk. We're in the midst of a crisis. Let's just say a head-on crash between high tech and haute cuisine."

"Is something burning?" asks Sherrie.

"Dinner," Francis says. "I suppose I should have taken the new Jenn-Aire for a test run. A maiden voyage, what? The range-top grill is the problem. Not vented properly, I guess. The minute I put on the sausages, they erupted like volcanoes."

Swenson and Sherrie exchange quick looks. Both think, Serves him right.

Francis makes a major production of serving roast hunks of meat. It's partly the British tradition he's hanging onto so tenaciously in the savage vegetarian colonies, and partly his private dig at the health-conscious squeamishness of Americans in general and of academics in particular.

Swenson likes red meat. He's glad to get it. They rarely eat it at home. He certainly prefers it to the ectoplasmic zucchini casseroles so popular at faculty dinners. But he doesn't think food should be used to make a point about status and power. Who cares if you've got tenure? The dean can serve you what he wants. And you can either eat it or shut up and go hungry. Also, it occurs to Swenson that he'd better get his tooth fixed before he attends too many more of these flesh fests. He probes his molar with his tongue. He'll chew on the other side.

He and Sherrie used to go to faculty dinner parties, but when Ruby was born they got out of the habit, and by now they've lost the impulse—besides which, they're rarely invited. In a community like Euston, turning down invitations makes you seem briefly more desirable. But fairly soon the magic wears off, and you stop being asked.

It's been a while since they've participated in one of these protracted peeps into the abyss. Deadly conversations, banal beyond belief. Did Mrs. Professor X really and truly see a red-crested titmouse at her bird feeder this morning? Could Professor and Mrs. Z possibly have ordered a double sleeping bag and been obliged to send back the single they received by mistake? The gossip, from the tepidly mean to the libelous and cruel. And the vile food, memorable only by decade, as generations of wives discovered the joys of olive oil, garlic, paella, sun-dried tomatoes, crudités with yogurt dip, parched chicken breasts, falafel—and now the ascetic vegans with their soy cheese and faux sausage.

Swenson wouldn't be here if Sherrie hadn't answered when the dean's secretary phoned. Sherrie thinks it's suicidal to keep insulting his colleagues. He might need to ask for a favor someday, for a string to be pulled—or just tweaked. And Bentham will think of him as the man who wouldn't come to dinner.

Having forgotten that the party was tonight, Swenson's spared himself the anticipatory dread, so that now the full horror assaults him. Their host ushers Swenson and Sherrie past the massive Victorian pieces that Marjorie Bentham has draped with folksy weavings from their junkets to third-world conferences. The house suggests an English country manor with the obligatory scuffings inflicted by the Benthams' three outdoorsy, oversize, puppylike children: one now at Princeton, one at Yale, one in boarding school. Tonight, the details of that scruffy aristocracy are obscured by smoke. Bentham coughs, allowing—almost requiring— Swenson and Sherrie to hack politely after filling their lungs with particulate flakes of charred protein.

"Be good chaps," says Bentham, "and toss your coats over there. I'd take them, but—" He models two transparent speckled gloves of grease. It used to be the wives who were responsible for the dinners, but now often the cooks are men, who preempt any suspicion of feminization with fierce territorial possessiveness about what goes on in their kitchens. Men who, like Francis Bentham, use the ladle to remind their guests of the manly pleasures of animal muscle.

Why is Swenson being so harsh? Of what are these people guilty? Dull dinner parties aren't crimes. They're not making child snuff films. Why not see this scene as Chekhov might: a gathering of lost souls pretending they're not expiring from boredom and angst in some provincial outpost? Chekhov would feel compassion for them and not judge them, as Swenson does. And who is he to judge? A guy who gets a hard-on over girl-student erotica.

The memory of his afternoon—the incident in the library—makes him feel as if his skin is coated with a thin film of sticky lotion. What if the soot from Bentham's kitchen adheres and coats him with black? So now he's imagining himself as a Hawthorne character whose sin manifests itself at a faculty dinner party. What is his crime, exactly? Borrowing some poems? It's not as if he hurried home and rushed off to his study to read them. They're where he left them, on his desk.

Speaking of Hawthorne . . . here's Gerry Sloper, Mr. American Lit, his florid face dimly visible through the miasma of sausage fumes. Whom else has Bentham invited? Swenson prays that the guest list will venture beyond the English Department. Sometimes the dean makes an effort to include new faces, insofar as there *are* any at Euston. On the way over, Swenson let himself hope that Bentham might have asked Amelia Rodriguez, the sexy, unsmiling Puerto Rican martinet recently brought in to head—to *be*—the new Hispanic Studies Department. The disapproving Amelia might at least generate a faint hum of the exotic, a promise of masochistic excitement as the guests took turns failing to amuse her.

But Amelia's isn't among the group in the living room, the all-too-familiar bodies perched on the edges of sofas and chairs, balancing drinks and nibbling Triscuits smeared with some sort of fecal material. Who knows how long they've been knocking back those vodkas and double scotches. They may have given up red meat, but some things are still sacred.

"Marmite!" cries elderly Bernard Levy, their eighteenth-century man. "Why, I haven't had Marmite since my *wunderjahr* at Oxford!"

"Oh, do you like it?" says Marge Bentham. "Most Americans don't." Encouraged, she picks up two more crackers and waves them at Swenson and Sherrie, biscuit treats offered witholdingly so they have to trot over to get them.

Marmite! Is there no end to the Benthams' sadism? What will they be serving next—wobbly slabs of jellied calves feet? Steak and kidney pie? If Marjorie knows that most Americans—most humans—don't like Marmite, why is it the only hors d'ouevre? Swenson gobbles his Triscuit in one brave bite and tries not to make a face at the sharp wheaty splinters glued together with vile salty paste. Attentive as baby birds, the other guests wait for him to gulp it down.

Who's the audience for Swenson's magic trick? The Benthams. Gerry Sloper. Bernard Levy, the elderly Angophile, and his wife, the long-suffering Ruth. Dave Sterret, their Victorian man, and his boyfriend, Deconstructionist Jamie. The frosting, so to speak, on the cake is Swenson's number one fan, Lauren Healy, the feminist critic and head of the Faculty-Student Women's Alliance. He's thrilled to see Magda—a friendly face for his gaze to alight on in its frantic swoop around the room. But his pleasure turns into a low-grade unease that takes a while to diagnose: lunch today. Angela's poems.

"You need to wash that down with something, old man," Bentham says.

"Vodka. Straight up. A double. Please." Swenson feels Sherrie's eyes drilling him. Let *her* drink the white wine.

It's a purebred English Department crowd, just as Swenson feared. The tepid predictablity, the lack of interest or buzz. Easy, it's only dinner, not death and eternal hell. The guest list suggests that this isn't "pleasure" but business: one of the dean's periodic checkups on his various departments. Bentham will ask thoughtful questions and murmur soft grunts of comprehension as they cut their own throats, one by one, each sounding too jaded, too naive, too earnest, too complaining, until even the tenured will feel anxious about their jobs as Bentham sits back and watches how badly they're behaving.

The smoke has begun to dissipate, and their convivial moment of alliance against the elements ends. They regard each other in the unflattering light of their most cherished resentments.

"Please, sit down," says Bentham.

Two seats are vacant, a Queen Anne chair and a large hassock. Swenson and Sherrie dive for the hassock.

"Hello, Ted," Bernie Levy says in his cultivated accent.

Swenson is supposed to have forgotten how, twenty years ago, Bernie, who still had some fight in him then, battled Swenson's appointment, campaigned against hiring a novelist and starting a writing department. Some department: Swenson and Magda. Bernie needn't have worried. Oh, if only Bernie had won! Swenson might have stayed in New York.

"Our author in residence," Bernie says. "How's the writer's life, old boy?"

"Hello, Sherrie," Ruth Levy says grimly.

"Hiya, Ruth," says Sherrie.

"Fine," says Swenson. "Thanks."

"How *is* your work going?" asks Dave Sterret, the nicest guy in the room, battered daily into mellowness by his sadistic boyfriend, Deconstructionist Jamie.

"Some days fast, some days slow." Is that really Swenson talking? All you have to do is walk in here to catch a case of terminal banality.

"The creative life is such a challenge," says Ruth Levy. "So difficult—and so rewarding."

Deconstructionist Jamie shoots daggers at harmless, ga-ga Ruth, while Lauren Healy glares at Jamie, protecting the older woman from his patronizing, oppressive maleness.

"Can you talk about what you're working on?" Could Jamie somehow have intuited that Swenson's not working? And why should Jamie care? He hates books, or as he calls them: *texts*. And he especially hates the writers who deposit these annoying book-length paper turds that Jamie must dispose of.

Ever since he got tenure, Jamie has made no secret of his contempt for the rest of the department—everyone but Dave, with whom Jamie fell in love his first year at Euston. How strange that Bernie Levy fought Swenson's hiring and eagerly welcomed Jamie, the viper in their midst. Jamie has managed to communicate that he's never read Swenson's books, nor does he intend to, though sometimes he does inquire about Swenson's more famous and successful contemporaries. He likes to ask why such-and-such is so terribly overpraised.

Jamie says, "Is talking about one's writing strictly against the rules?"

"I'm going to help Marge," Lauren announces. "The poor woman's all alone in there." And indeed, Bentham's left Marge to clean up the wreckage. He leans dapperly against the mantel, twirling a drink in his hand.

"Excuse me, Jamie. What did you say?" says Swenson. It's one thing to skip a beat in front of your class, another at the dean's dinner.

"Are you working on a novel?"

"No wonder I didn't hear," Swenson says. "Yes, in fact. I am." Sherrie and Magda are watching, wishing they'd all drop the subject.

"What's your new novel about?" asks Bentham. "Have you told us? Sorry if I've forgotten."

What if Swenson had told them? How would he feel to learn that his wisp of an idea had already floated out of the dean's famously retentive mind.

"That's all right," says Swenson. "I don't think I *did* tell you. Or anyone. Not even my nearest and dearest." He nods at Sherrie.

"Don't look at me," says Sherrie. Chuckles, all around.

"I hear that's quite common among writers," ventures Ruth Levy. "Secretive. You know."

"As if we're all just dying to steal their ideas," says Jamie.

"Not even the title?" prods Francis coyly. "You won't even tell us that?"

"Well," says Swenson. "All right. It's *Eggs*."

He feels like that girl in *The Exorcist*. What demon made him say that? He wishes his head could swivel around to see where his voice just came from.

"What an interesting title," says Dave.

"Ted?" Sherrie murmurs worriedly. "I thought your title was *The Black and the Black*."

Dave says, "I suppose the wife's always the last to know."

"*The Black and the Black*," says Ruth. "Another interesting title."

"We get it," Jamie says.

"They're both good titles," says Magda.

Swenson wonders if Magda knows what Angela's novel is called. Did he tell her over lunch?

"Titles are tricky," says Swenson.

He can't bear this another minute. He gets up and starts to leave the room with the vague purposefulness of some nonemergency bathroom errand. And why not? A leisurely piss would provide a nice mini-vacation from the party.

"Here's another double for the road," Bentham says. More vodka glugs into Swenson's glass. He downs half in one gulp, so that his throat is still burning when, en route to the bathroom, he meets Lauren Healy, emerging from the kitchen with a rattan tray on which are neat rows of yet more Marmite crackers. Normally Lauren wears dark suits, but tonight she's put on a dress, dark cotton, gathered high over the waist, puffing discreetly over the breasts, at once matronly and girlish. Swenson checks Lauren out. Lauren watches him check her out. Now he's done it. Lauren draws nearer. Half his size, she peers up at him with a bleary pugnacious tilt.

"Ted, what are you doing here?" Lauren's whisper is oddly conspiratorial.

"What do you mean?" asked Swenson.

"You're not up for tenure. You don't want anything from Bentham. You're not lobbying for a sabbatical? Or a new faculty line? Are you?"

Is Lauren saying he's a cowardly suck-up for accepting the dean's invitation? Or a guy with such a nowhere social life he's glad to be asked, even here?

"Sherrie answered the phone. Otherwise I wouldn't be here, believe me."

Lauren cringes. Too late, it crosses Swenson's mind that she might have been flirting with him instead of trying to make him feel small. Well, he put a quick end to *that* with the mention of Sherrie. And the simple, chilly statement of fact: I wouldn't be here—where you are, with you—if my wife hadn't tricked me into it.

Lauren shakes herself like a small drenched pet, straightens her tray of Marmite, and leaves. Swenson treks off to the bathroom where he lingers, as planned, though it's hardly the leisurely piss of his dreams but rather a long, nervous prelude during which he stands there, embarrassed to be holding his dick, paralyzed by Marge's pristine, accusatory collection of fluffed-up dainty terrycloth towels and edible-looking soaps. He's so grateful for the few dribbles that finally oblige—his prostate must be shot—that he forgives himself the stain on his pants, though he knows Lauren will see it as yet another aggressive declaration of maleness.

He returns to the living room, which has emptied in his absence. After an instant of irrational panic, he hears voices from the dining room, where everyone's seated except for the rude, uncivilized, drunken novelist.

"Sorry." Swenson slides into the remaining chair, which with his luck, or perhaps Marge's thoughtful *placement*, is next to Francis Bentham and across from Lauren. If he had any balls he'd make them all move so he could sit next to Sherrie, who's eyeing him a little wildly from the far end of the table. But if he had any balls, he wouldn't be here in the first place. Years ago, at dinners like this, he and Sherrie would catch each other's eye and keep looking: Brief

out-of-body moments from which they'd return refreshed, as if
after a nap. Who knows if that would work now? Still, it would be
helpful to grab Sherrie's hand under the table.

The dean sends plates of food around. Somehow Marge has flayed
the sausages, peeled away the blackened skins, and pulverized the rest
into a species of pork gravy to pour—an impromptu shepherd's pie—
over mashed potatoes. Though it's hardly the blood feast from *Beowulf*
that the Benthams specialize in, the meal's been saved. The guests are
relieved. They lean over their plates of steaming hash, periodically
bobbing up to compliment Marge on her cooking and her improvisa-
tional skills, pretending the gravy doesn't taste smoky and charred.
Meanwhile, they wash the whole mess down with streams of the vine-
gary red wine that the dean pours from a sweating glass carafe.

"Comfort food!" says Lauren, bullyingly.

"Mmm," agree the others.

"Very good, Marjorie. Well, friends," says Francis, "what's new
out there in the trenches?"

Everyone keeps eating. Let someone else begin.

"How do Euston's best and brightest seem to you? As opposed to
last year's? As compared with any year's . . . ?"

"Well," begins Bernie Levy, "I don't suppose it'll come as a
shock if I say that each year's entering class seems to have read less
than last year's worst students."

"Right," Deconstructionist Jamie sneers. "I guess those high
schools are really slacking off on their Dryden and Pope."

"What about you, Jamie?" says Francis. "Are your students cut
from brighter cloth?"

Does Jamie intend to tell the dean that the five or six misfit
seniors who elect to take his Literary Theory seminar are brighter
than Bernie's? Even Swenson, who has no great love for Bernie,
tenses with anticipation.

"I have mostly upperclassmen," says Jamie. "So by the time they
get to me, I can't blame their high school teachers. It's these
guys"—he gestures at his colleagues—"who have messed up their
minds." Jamie laughs. Alone.

Gerry Sloper says, "I had a sort of interesting thing happen in class the other day. It made me realize where the students are at— how different from myself at their age."

"I was never their age," Bernie says.

"We believe it," Dave says affectionately, mopping up after the ravages of Jamie's casual meanness.

"*Sort of* interesting," says Jamie. "God help us."

"Gerry," says Bentham. "Please. Proceed."

"Well," says Gerry, "this was in my Intro to American Lit. We were doing Poe. I thought I'd give them a little bio . . . a little . . . gossip, really, to make it more immediate, give it a personal touch—"

"Personal!" says Bernie. "That's what we've been reduced to! Fodder for the talk show."

"Wouldn't it be great?" Jamie says. "Poe and the thirteen-year-old child-bride cousin discussing their marital arrangements with Sally Jessie Raphael?"

"Interesting," says Ruth.

"Jesus Christ, no," says Swenson.

"Oh, Ted," says Lauren, "you're so predictable. Always taking the male writer's side."

"Anyway," says Gerry, "I told them about Poe's problems with alcohol and opium. Winding up in the gutter, details like that. Any reference to substance abuse always gets their attention. But when I got to Poe's marriage, the class got very quiet. I kept asking what the matter was, none of them would answer. Until finally one young woman said, 'Are you telling us that we've been studying the work of a child molester? I think we should have been told that before we read the assignment.'"

"No way," says Dave.

"Way," Gerry says.

"A child molester?" says Magda. "Oh, poor Edgar Allan!"

"Edgar Allan, is it? Listen to Magda!" Dave says. "Oh, you poets! On a first-name basis with the dead."

Magda likes being called a poet and turns to smile at Dave.

"Fascinating!" Coquettishly, the dean cups his chin in one hand and tilts his head in measured increments toward each guest at the table. "Are the rest of you finding a heightened consciousness about those . . . issues . . . ?"

Another mystery solved! All this is just a follow-up, one in a series of dinner-hour departmental reviews of the basic points covered by the recent faculty meeting. Is sexual harassment Bentham's private obsession? Or his professional duty? Ceaseless vigilance on behalf of the college's legal status, its budget, its reputation?

"We all have to watch our backs," says Bernie. "I never talk to a female student in my office alone without the door wide open. And I keep a tape recorder in my desk that I can activate if things get dicey."

Everyone stares at Bernie, straining to imagine the scenario in which a student fantasizes that Bernie's about to grope her with those mottled spidery fingers.

"What about the rest of you?" says Francis. "Does the problem seem dangerous here at Euston? Or is it just our . . . sensitivity to the current academic climate?"

"It's very dangerous," says Dave Sterret. "Sensitive as in . . . top secret. Sensitive as in . . . explosive."

The guests deepen their involvement with their charred shepherd's pie.

For years before Jamie came to Euston, Dave, as faculty adviser to the Gay Students Alliance, dated its best-looking guys. The department heaved a collective sigh of relief when Jamie and Dave fell in love, though by then, knowing Jamie, they worried about poor Dave. Swenson used to wonder how Dave—a tall, thin, painfully awkward guy with a face badly scarred by acne—got so much action. Apparently, Dave Sterret has hidden depths, some well of integrity or bravado that's led him to take on the dean's question, despite a past that might keep a lesser man focused on his mashed potatoes.

Dave says, "We were doing *Great Expectations* last week. And one of my students—a big beery jock—asked if Dickens meant there to be a homosexual thing between Pip and Magwich. Was this kid trying to bait me? They all know I'm gay. I said I thought there might be critical writing on the subject, which the kid could look up for extra credit. But I didn't think that Dickens meant us to read a gay subtext into the book. And finally we had to consider what the writer intended."

"What the *writer* intended?" cries Jamie. "I can't believe I just heard you say that, Dave. Have I taught you *nothing*?"

Dave's used to this. He hardy misses a beat. "I thought that was the end of it. But the next day, a young woman—stuff she's said in class makes me think she might be some sort of born-again evangelical—came to my office and told me that the discussion had made her feel very unsafe. The way she said that word . . . *unsafe* . . . I'll tell you, it gave me the chills."

"Why?" demands Lauren. "It's an ordinary English word with a perfectly valid meaning."

"Oh, dear," says Jamie. "*Semantics*, now!"

"What did you do, Dave?" asks Magda.

Dave says, "I reminded her that *I* didn't start the discussion. I said I wanted students to feel free to bring up any questions they had. I gave her a two-minute sermon about academic freedom. And then I went home and took to my bed with a major case of the vapors!"

"Oh, my," says the dean. He looks from Dave to Gerry and back again. "And both of these incidents—the Poe and the Dickens— you say happened *last week*?"

"Well," says Gerry, "within the last few weeks."

Bentham shakes his head. "Statistically speaking, I'd say this indicates that things are heating up. What about you, Lauren? Has this come up in your classes? I'd imagine it might be a flash point in the field of gender studies."

Swenson tries to recall the title of Lauren's senior seminar. *Huck as Hermaphrodite: Masks of Gender and Identity in Twain—or Was It Samuel Clemens?* It was the department joke when the course list first circulated. But by now everyone knows that Lauren's classes fill up fast. The memory of Angela's contempt for Lauren's reading of *Jane Eyre* glows in the center of Swenson's chest, a bright star of protection.

"Of course, it comes up," says Lauren. "I *bring* it up. I want to make sure they know that I'm on their side. I want them to feel that the classroom is safe—that word Dave finds so 'chilling.' I want them to be aware that they can talk to me, that if they're having a problem with these issues, harassment or whatever, the kids can confide in me, and I'll take them seriously. I feel it's my duty, as one of the few women. . . ."

Lauren never lets them forget that she was the first woman given full tenure in the English Department and is still the only tenured woman. "We all know Euston's history, beginning with Elijah's poor martyred daughters. In any case, I find that the whole mood in the classroom changes after we work our way through this. Clear the air. After that, we can pretty much talk about any-thing—*safely*—without any threat or discomfort. . . ."

So that's what Swenson's doing wrong. If he had any brains—or the vestiges of a survival instinct—he'd urge his students to confide in him, say he wants them to feel safe. After that they can have the world's most relaxed discussions about teenagers having sex with whole flocks of chickens.

"Magda?" the dean asks. "What about your class?" Speaking of untenured women, let's hear from our little poet.

At the faculty meeting, Bentham told a story about a hiring com-mittee that called up a male candidate's former student to ask how the candidate had interacted with the women in his class. When the student said that one of those women—a friend—was visiting him and would be happy to answer his question, the interviewer said that female students would be contacted later by a female member of the hiring committee. This cautionary tale had gotten a laugh, or at least a horrified chuckle. A tornado was brewing out there. Head for the basement, Dorothy.

Magda says, "I don't know. It's tough. I keep making these awful mistakes."

A tremor shakes Magda's throaty voice. Swenson wants to help her up and lead her away from the table. Magda shouldn't be telling them this. These people are not to be trusted. They will do her more damage than the most neurotic student.

"What sorts of mistakes?" asks the dean.

Marjorie asks, "Does anyone want another dab of shepherd's pie?"

"What mistakes, Magda?" the dean repeats.

"Lord." Magda sighs. "Miscalculations. Okay, here's an example. I noticed that my students seemed a little narrow in their ideas about what you could say in a poem. So I read them that Larkin poem that begins, 'They fuck you up, your mum and dad.'"

"Oh, I adore Larkin!" Saintly Dave rushes headlong into the hideous silence. Everyone else has gone rigid. Does Magda not *want* tenure?

"I realized it was . . . dangerous." Magda turns up the charm, determined to present herself as a teacher who stays up nights wondering how to help her students. "I thought about it a long time. I knew I was taking a risk. But their response was way worse than I'd thought. They all turned white as sheets."

Swenson refills his wineglass. How much has Magda been drinking? Is she on a suicide mission? Everyone's heart is breaking for her, even heartless Jamie.

"Maybe the problem wasn't the language," Jamie says. "Maybe it's Philip Larkin. Talk about *overrated*. All that bitter, self-pitying, narcissistic whining from that squalling infant posing as a middle-aged librarian!"

"His misogyny!" Lauren says. "And the total absence of one positive, life-affirming line in the man's entire oeuvre!"

Swenson can hardly stand it. He loves those beautiful poems that tell more of the truth than anyone wants to hear. Nor does it help to think that this is one of the few, the very few dinner tables in the world at which most, or any, of the guests have heard of Philip Larkin.

"Magda, my dear," says Bernie, "if your point is that you wanted your students to 'loosen up,' there *are* other models. Swift, for example. Swift, as you no doubt know, could get very . . . loose. Frightfully scatological."

Swenson drains his wineglass. He has the strangest sensation. His desire, his need to speak is burning a hole in his head. Is that the stench of his own charred gray matter, or the Benthams' sausages? The pressure is explosive, but he can't afford to blow. The group's coming down on poor Magda for saying *fuck* when he spends hours of classroom time on graphic descriptions of bestiality. A man with Angela's dirty poems on his desk shouldn't go anywhere near this.

The thought of Angela cheers him. It calms him, in a way, to let his churned-up feelings settle on the fact of her existence. It's almost as if she's become a place to which he can retreat. She reminds him that there is a world beyond this soul-eroding dinner, a world of kids with a passion to write, some of whom actually can.

Of course, it's at this most inappropriate moment, in this most inconvenient setting that Swenson finds himself starting to wonder if he might not be developing the teensiest bit of a crush on Angela Argo. He's certainly been thinking about her, looking forward to seeing her. No. What he's looking forward to is reading more of her novel.

He looks down the table at Sherrie. Sherrie sees him, stares back at him. Sherrie loves him. She knows him. They have a child, they've shared twenty-one years, a sizable chunk of their lives. But Sherrie's putting up with this dinner, which he doesn't think Angela would. Sherrie's compromised, as he has, while Angela probably still believes she'll never have to. Sherrie just wants to get through this. Angela would be taking a stand against all this drippy self-satisfaction. She'd be spinning her eyes and gouging holes in the Bentham's glossy table.

Swenson owes it to Angela to say what he's been thinking. He feels as if he's growing nose rings, green hair's springing out of his head. His forehead heats up, his cheeks warm, his skin seems to tighten and shrink.

"I've got an idea," he hears himself say. "A new approach, so to speak." The other guests turn to watch his face turn pink, like a stir-fried shrimp.

"What's that, Ted?" says Bentham.

"I think we've been giving in without a fight," says Swenson. Sherrie and Magda exchange anxious looks. He winks at them and keeps going. "We've been knuckling under to the most neurotic forces of censorship and repression. In fact we should be helping them get beyond their problems. We should try desensitizing them, the way the Scientologists do. . . ."

"Oh, Ted," says Lauren, "are you a Scientologist? I had no idea. How amazing!"

"Ted's a Quaker," says Dave Sterret, the only one who's read—who makes a point of having read—Swenson's work. In fact he often refers to details, as if he's being tested.

"Not anymore," says Sherrie. "Ted's not a Quaker anymore." Sherrie, the expert on his spiritual life.

"Of course I'm not a Scientologist. What do you think I am, Lauren? An idiot? I've just read about their process. And it's got its points. They hook you up to a lie detector and read you a list of words guaranteed to pack an emotional punch. Mother. Father. Child. Sex. Death. And then they say them over and over, until the graph stops spiking.

"So why don't we do something like that for these wimps, these . . . whiners bitching about sexual harassment. Lock them in a room and shout dirty words at them until they grow up. Shit shit shit. Fuck fuck fuck. Like that. You get the idea."

Well, he's got their attention now. The guests all listen politely as he goes on braying obscenities like some sidewalk psycho. "Motherfucker. Penis. Words like that. Nothing fancy or kinky. Ordinary, honorable, time-tested Anglo-Saxonisms. We'd be doing them a big favor, educationally, morally, spiritually, helping them mature faster than if we coddle them, indulge every whim and neurosis."

"Ted . . . ," says Sherrie. "Ted's got Tourette's. Late-onset adult Tourette's. A very rare condition."

No one laughs.

Swenson says, "That's a great idea. Hire the handicapped. Find people with Tourette's to say the dirty words."

His colleagues gaze woozily down at their food or into some middle distance.

"Well!" says Marjorie Bentham at last. "Freeze! No one move! Everyone stay exactly where you are while I clear the table."

"That was wonderful, Marjorie," Magda says.

"Are you sure we can't give you a hand?" says Lauren.

More compliments, more offers of help. None of them—not even Sherrie—is up to eye contact with Swenson. From down the table Magda sends him a smile so supportive and stricken that it dawns on him, at last, just how badly he's blown it.

"Marjorie's spent all day making the sweet," announces the dean with pride. And Marjorie appears in the doorway with her twenty-four-hour production: a giant free-standing pudding, its outer layer—strawberry jello?—trembling under the load of tiny silver candy ball bearings and multicolored sprinkles. A blazing toxic rainbow.

"Jam trifle!" Marge solves the mystery for them.

The guests say, "Oh!" and smile in unison as if she's taking their picture, a formal group portrait of adult men and women simultaneously rescued and menaced by dessert.

A bad sign: leaving the Benthams', Sherrie hurries ahead and gets in the driver's seat. Another bad sign: silence, and the fact that they're both holding their breath as they pull out of the driveway and cruise past the grand houses on Main Street, whose lights appear to be blinking out, house by house, as they pass.

"Jesus, Ted," says Sherrie. "What the hell got into you? I kept expecting your head to swivel around and for you to projectile vomit."

"You want to hear something weird? I was thinking about *The Exorcist* too, just recently. I was feeling like that kid. . . ." Swenson laughs with wild relief. How lucky he feels not to be enacting the more standard scenario: the sourpuss wife scolding the errant husband for transgressing against the standards of social decency and offending the powers that will decide on his next minuscule salary raise. Sherrie hasn't turned into his mother, reproving her naughty child-husband. They're both still unruly children, still the rebel kids, preserving some vestige of big-city badness here among these bloodless New England wusses.

"Glad you enjoyed yourself," Swenson said. "Jesus, why *did* I do that? It was Jamie trashing Philip Larkin that sent me over the edge."

Sherrie's silent till after she's made the turn by the Euston dairy co-op. "Magda's got a huge crush on you. You know that, don't you, Ted?" Is Sherrie curious? Jealous? Proud? Or just making conversation?

"Magda's not my type," he says. "All that wired Irish Catholic hysteria. If I'd wanted that, I would have married Mom." He feels disloyal to Magda and also guilty for lying, since the qualities he's just dismissed are what he finds appealing. But it's a quick way of changing a subject that he's not quite ready to change.

"What makes you say that?" he asks.

"The way she looks at you," says Sherrie. "Total adoration. Poor thing. I wanted to kill her."

"You were projecting," Swenson says. "The total adoration."

"Right," says Sherrie, and laughs.

"I'm flattered. But I don't think Magda's attracted to me. It's too late. I'm too old. I've lost it. *No one* gets a crush on me. Not even students. Do you think *anyone* would find me attractive anymore?"

"I do." Sherrie puts her hand on his thigh. Swenson puts his hand over hers and slides it closer to his crotch. Oh, he's a very lucky guy, to have a beautiful wife who's turned on by his bad behavior at a faculty dinner party.

Their hands stay locked until Sherrie retrieves hers to turn into the driveway. She reaches the house before him—getting out of the car, Swenson realizes he's drunker than he'd thought—and is waiting for him in the hallway when he finally gets through the door. They embrace. Swenson runs his hand down her back and pulls her against him.

He says, "Wait up for me a minute. I'll meet you in the bedroom. I had this idea for something I'm working on. I need to jot down a few notes before I lose it."

"Okay," says Sherrie. "Don't be long. I'm about to pass out."

And now Swenson knows he is sinking, has already sunk beneath the level of decency, honesty, and self-preservation. His attractive, grown-up wife is waiting for him in bed, and the rat he's turned into is streaking through the dark, scurrying off to his rathole because he can't wait till morning to read a filthy poem by a child.

Swenson finds *Angela 911* hidden under some unpaid bills. He opens the book at random and concentrates to keep the words from sliding all over the page.

He says: Is this 859–6732? Is this Angela 911?
Angela, is that you?
I say: What would you like to do tonight?
He says: Hush. Don't talk. Listen to what I'm doing.
I'm coming up to you from behind.
My hand is over your mouth.
I say: Honey, how can I talk on the phone
With your hand over my mouth?
He says: Don't call me honey.
My hand is over your mouth.
I'm bending you over a trash can.
I'm pulling up your skirt.
I'm slapping your thighs, just lightly.
Making you open your legs. You push your ass against me,
Helping me find your cunt.
I say: Honey, you know I can't talk.
Bye now. I'm hanging up.

Swenson puts down the manuscript, switches off the light. He doesn't want to think about the poem, doesn't want to think at all.

Navigating by faint moonlight, he gropes and stumbles to his dark bedroom. Is Sherrie sleeping? He undresses and gets in next to her. He runs his hand down her thigh.

"Ted," she says sleepily, "listen."

He puts his hand over Sherrie's mouth. She pries his hand away and gently licks his palm with one swift silky stroke that transmits a shower of sparks directly to his groin.

"Don't talk," says Swenson.

"Okay," Sherrie says. "Not a word. I promise."

Sometimes, when Swenson can't remember what happened in class last week, he looks to see which student seems most wounded or aggrieved and tracks that information back to whose story they demolished. Today, it's a real contest. Everybody's scowling, though Courtney's special ferociousness as she sits, shoulders high and rigid, hands knotted over her books, offers a helpful memory jog. "First Kiss—Inner City Blues."

But the rest are also projecting massive discontent. Did the college announce a new policy banning keg parties or binge drinking? Maybe it's just that low point that comes at midsemester, though it's early for that. Or could they all somehow suspect that their teacher spent the week rereading Angela's poems? Isn't this what one hears about bullfighters and lion tamers? On the day of the accident, they could *taste* the animal's ugly mood.

In this cage of snarling beasts, Carlos looks the most frightened.

"Carlos," says Swenson. "My man!"

"Yo," says Carlos, gloomily.

The only seat left at the table is between Angela and Claris. Swenson inserts himself exactly halfway between them, where he sits, unable to breathe, hoping only that if he passes out, he'll fall into Claris's lap and not in the more incriminating direction of Angela Argo. Is anyone alarmed by the icy droplets beading up on his forehead? Does anyone notice? Apparently not. Well, that's fine. Just asking. An ominous interior voice pretends to offer him comfort, droning its three-word mantra: No one knows. No one knows. No one knows that Angela's poems are in his office at home, locked in his filing cabinet. Or that her filthy free verse has traveled here in his head, like some malarial mosquito sneaking across the ocean in an airplane's passenger cabin. The poems about the incest, the ones about the rapes . . .

But Carlos's work is what's happening here. Swenson needs to stay focused on the story, which he skimmed way too fast this morning. It's not bad, but it's disturbing, and the students don't like to be disturbed, so by the time they've finished working over the unfortunately titled "Toilet Bowl," they will have defused its power to unnerve them.

"Toilet Bowl" opens with its sorry, "fat white fish" of a hero having his face dunked in the eponymous commode by other inmates at a state reformatory for boys. As the story progresses, the hero is pushed toward the suicide that the reader can see coming from the second paragraph. And in the harrowing and surprisingly successful penultimate scene, the boy is talked into killing himself by a bunkmate who tells him a rambling, sadistically detailed story about the mercy killing of a dog, and why it was such a mercy.

Swenson says, "Carlos, read us something."

Carlos takes a deep breath. "Man. This is tough."

Jonelle says, "Everyone's got to do it, Carlos. Come on. You're the ex-Marine."

"Navy," says Carlos. "If you don't mind."

"Come on, people," Swenson says. "It *is* hard. Give Carlos a break."

Angela says, "Yeah, man, it's torture. I mean, I'm so terrified of you guys talking about my work that I'm just not bringing it in this semester."

Like every class, this one is attentive to infinitesimal shifts of status and position. Everyone knows that Swenson has been reading Angela's manuscript. Now she's signaling them that her seemingly special treatment is not a sign of superior talent but actually a concession to her childish fears. She's like some furry animal, rolling over and playing dead in their furious Darwinian struggle.

"Right!" says Nancy. "Angela got trashed so bad in Magda's poetry seminar last spring that she doesn't want to risk it again."

So that's how they see Angela: a writer of mediocre pornographic poems. In any case, they've read her poems, discussed the least dicey ones in class, the very same poems that Swenson is so ashamed of reading in secret. But they were assigned to read Angela's poems— and Swenson's volunteering. Oh, why can't he just lighten up and be proud of himself for taking a genuine interest in a gifted student?

"That's right," Swenson says. "We all know that having our work talked about in class isn't exactly fun. So let's all shut up and give Carlos our most generous attention."

"Okay, Coach. Here we go. Let's do it." Carlos clears his throat:

"'Eddie was glad there were no mirrors on the bottom of toilet bowls. He would have had to see his fat pale jellyfish sea-monster face, bobbing around like some sort of undersea creature, the terror in his filmy blue eyes and his neck twisting back to choke down disgusting shit water and beg his torturers for mercy. . . .'"

Swenson lets Carlos go on for awhile. "Thank you," he says at last. "It's a brave story. Really. Let's hear what the rest of you think. Remember, let's start off with what we like. . . ."

"Well," says Makeesha, "that first paragraph is typical of the whole problem. What dude with his head being dunked in a toilet would be thinking about why they don't have mirrors in the bottom of the bowl?"

Danny says, "Makeesha's right. That stuff about the mirror in the toilet bowl felt more like Carlos wanting to describe the kid than like anything the kid himself would be actually thinking—"

"Actually thinking?" says Angela. "How do you know what you'd be actually thinking if someone was stuffing your head down a toilet bowl?"

Go, Angela, thinks Swenson. It irritates him that Carlos shoots Angela a grateful glance. He's never noticed her before. Just for that, Swenson won't remind the class that they're still supposed to be discussing what they liked about the story.

"Frankly. . . ." Whenever Meg says *frankly*, or *personally*, they'd all better run for cover. "The whole subject bored me. Personally, I'm sick of this shit about guys nearly killing each other so they won't have to admit that what they really want to do is suck each other off."

"Meg," says Swenson, "please. We're supposed to start out with what we *liked* about the story."

Carlos says, "And I'm sick of your shit, Meg. If you think the only thing guys want is to suck each other's dicks, no wonder you're such a dyke!"

And now Swenson has an almost cinematic image of himself in Francis Bentham's office, answering Meg's charges that she was called a dyke in his class. But not by Swenson. It's not his fault. He's innocent. Innocent!

"People," he says, "surely it's possible to do this with civility and intelligence. I want to remind all of you that we're talking about language in this class, and some kinds of language will not be permitted."

"What do you mean?" says Makeesha. "Brothers and sisters be talkin' this way—"

Swenson ignores her. "Carlos, aren't you supposed to shut up until the others are finished?"

"Sorry, Coach!" Carlos makes a zipping motion across his lips.

"Claris," says Swenson, desperately, "What did *you* like about Carlos's story."

"It's got some . . . good moments," Claris concedes. "I liked the last scene. The part where that other kid, what's his name, tells the story about the dog—"

"Doofy," Nancy says.

"I liked the guy's name," says Danny. "Doofy. That's pretty good. Especially considering that he wasn't doofy at all. He was, like, kind of—"

"A snake," says Meg.

"Doofy," says Claris. "That's right. Anyway, I liked his crazy speech about shooting the dog that's been run over by the truck. I liked how over the top it was even when he's trying to make Eddie feel like he's the dog."

"That part about the dog blood and guts and brains, it was sort of like Quentin Tarantino." Jonelle doesn't mean this as a compliment.

"It was too obvious," says Courtney. "Connecting the kid with the dog."

"It was *supposed* to be obvious," Claris says. "But I still didn't believe that Doofy's story would actually push Eddie into killing himself."

Once more, Claris is right on the money. The ending's completely implausible. Eddie dives out the dorm window and breaks his neck on the pavement.

Jonelle says, "It was too predictable. It was a total setup. From the first line we knew that Eddie was going to do it."

"Where?" bursts out Carlos. "You show me, Jonelle. You show me where the story says that in the first sentence."

"Carlos," says Swenson, "please. Stay calm."

"You know what I thought?" says Courtney. "I kept trying to fig-ure out where I'd read it before. And then I realized I saw it in a movie, some movie just like Carlos's story, except they were sol-diers, Marines or something, some fat stupid soldier in a barracks and everybody's being mean to him and he blows his head off in the bathroom and they go to Vietnam. Or something."

"*Full Metal Jacket!*" says Danny. "Kubrick! One of the all-time great films!"

"I thought it was boring," says Courtney. "But still better than Carlos's story."

Just then the bells start ringing. Courtney's statement hangs in the air. And now—without the distractions of protecting Carlos from the class's blood lust—Swenson feels the floor shake as Angela's legs bounce under the table. For as long as the bells ring he thinks about reaching over and sliding his hand between Angela's legs. He imagines this so vividly, he can feel her against his hand. It takes a few scary seconds to realize he hasn't done it.

The bells stop. "Okay," he says. "Where were we?"

Angela says, "You guys are all being way hard on Carlos. There's good stuff in his story, and it's *nothing* like a movie. The scene where Doofy goes on about the dog is pretty amazing."

Swenson thinks, She did it for me. I needed her to say that. Carlos gazes at Angela with naked adoration.

"Well," says Swenson, "it looks as if opinion is divided. I don't know how helpful this was for you, Carlos. Is there anything you want to say?"

"Thanks, Angela," Carlos says. "At least somebody understands me."

As the class breaks up, Carlos waits at the door for Angela. But Angela hangs back, waiting for Swenson. What's being communi-cated here could hardly be more obvious if the most desirable doe were sidling up to the buck who'd just won the antler-bashing contest. Carlos may be younger and stronger, but Swenson is the teacher.

From the doorway, Carlos sees all, comprehends all, and leaves, but not before giving Swenson a knowing—a monitory—look.

Swenson says, "Angela, I guess you saved another class from the dumpster. I thought they'd tear poor Carlos limb from limb and feast on his bleeding carcass."

"I just told the truth," says Angela. "His story wasn't so bad."

"Well, thanks again," says Swenson.

"Don't thank me too fast," says Angela. "Nothing's for free, you know." She fixes him with a cool stare, and suddenly all Swenson can think of is the clinical, practiced, zombified voice of her poems. He feels as if he's calling Angela 911 and requesting some repugnant sexual service. But nothing like that's happening here, it's entirely his own projection. . . .

"What's it going to cost me?" This comes out more flirtatiously than he would have liked.

"Time," says Angela. "Hard time. Was that paragraph I gave you okay?"

"Oh, fine. A good addition. But I *will* read more than a paragraph—"

"Great. I was hoping you'd say that. I've got another chapter for you. I'm a little worried about this one. In fact . . . I think it sucks. I'm trying to write this part from the mother's point of view. Look, I'm only joking about this being payback. I know I've been loading you down with stuff, so if you don't have time, I can wait till next week, whenever you feel ready."

"Don't be silly," Swenson says. "I'd be delighted. Just promise not to be upset if it takes a few days."

"I won't," says Angela, handing over another orange envelope. "I'll be waiting by the phone. . . . Oh, listen, could I ask you *another* favor?"

Swenson tenses, reflexively.

"My mom and stepdad are coming for parents' weekend? They'll probably stop in and see you? So could you do me a favor and tell them I'm not just blowing their money? My grades suck so bad my stepdad keeps threatening to take me out of here and make me go to some, like, community college—"

"Would they *do* that?" How anxious Swenson sounds!

"Probably not. At this point I probably couldn't get *into* community college."

"I'll do what I can," says Swenson. "I'm looking forward to meeting them."

Out of breath from the hike across campus and the healthful cardiovascular trot up four flights of stairs, Swenson locks his office door, sits at his desk, and starts to read.

> *All that summer, Mr. Reynaud was away with his family at a summer program for music teachers. That was where I imagined him as I lay in a deck chair in my backyard, working on my tan. I pictured him in an auditorium paneled with gleaming wood and acoustic carpet. I saw him press his hips into the back of his bass as the harmonies of a Bach chorale floated up the steps of the theater.*
>
> *At the start of junior year, when I saw him in the band room, I was confused for a second. What was he doing there in real life, outside my imagination?*
>
> *"How was your summer?" I managed to say.*
>
> *He rested his hand on my upper arm, where he'd grabbed me the previous spring. I felt as if he'd let me go for the summer and with one touch reeled me back in. I held my arm as I sat down. I watched him greet each student, hugging the section leaders, so I knew his touch meant nothing. I wasn't the only one.*
>
> *The girls were still in sleeveless T-shirts. The violinists' arms looked like pale sausages trembling in their casings as they sawed away at their bows. The windows were open. The air smelled of burning leaves. Shouts from football practice rolled in on the spongy heat. I was sweating, my hair stuck in points like dirty paintbrush tips.*
>
> *For once, I hoped class ended late. The last thing I wanted was to stay after and attract Mr. Reynaud's attention. Also I hadn't slept well. I'd woken up feeling sick. I wondered if I'd caught something in Mrs. Davis's henhouse.*

I packed up my clarinet and was leaving when Mr. Reynaud called me back.

He said, "Where was everyone's head today?"

I said, "I don't know. It's hot."

"Are you all right?" said Mr. Reynaud.

"I'm fine," I said. "Really, I'm fine. I went to this weird farm last night for my science project. . . ."

"What science project?" said Mr. Reynaud.

"I'm hatching chicken eggs."

"Sitting on them?"

"In incubators," I said.

That was when he told me that during the equinox and the solstice you can balance an egg on its end.

"Wow," was all I could say.

"I grew up on an egg farm," he went on. "So if there's any help you need, anything you don't know, don't hesitate to ask. I'd be glad to pass along the wisdom gleaned from all those years of reaching up under hens."

At that moment the bell rang and saved me.

He'd forgotten to give me a late pass. I had to run to my next class, so it wasn't until after school that I had time to wonder. Had he really offered to help me with the eggs? Also it was a little strange, the part about the egg farm. I remembered him telling the band he'd grown up in the slums of Chicago.

The final sentence is meant to cause a shiver of unease, but Swenson finds it, finds the whole chapter, wonderfully reassuring. Now he remembers what drew him to Angela Argo—not those awful dirty poems. The girl has demonstrable talent that he's being paid to encourage.

He's glad he's got a few pages left. He puts off reading them for a moment. They're all he'll get this week. Obviously, he could ask to see as much of the book as she has. She'd be only too happy to oblige. But then he'd have to wait for her to write more chapters. Anyway, that would threaten the fragile pretense that she is presuming on his good graces, asking favors above and beyond his pedagogical obligations.

Stuck to the next page is a yellow Post-it on which Angela has scrawled, "This is the section that's really messing me up. The mother's POV."

Only after what happened later did I begin to understand what was really going on during those autumn evenings when she told her father she didn't want him to come to the shed and help her do whatever she was doing to those eggs.

As always, he pretended that what hurt him was a joke. Ha ha, his teenage daughter said she had to do her science project herself. I watched him watch her go.

"She's quite a kid," he said. "The clarinet, the perfect grades, and now this thing with the eggs."

Then he went off to his medical journals, his giant tumbler of Scotch, his nap in front of the evening news. Sometimes I watched him sleeping with his mouth open, his glasses slipped to one side, and I wondered what had happened to the handsome young doctor who had reached out and saved me years ago as I fell over and slumped toward the emergency room floor.

And now Swenson *does* have the shivers, a tightening over his scalp. The doctor breaking the patient's steady slide toward the emergency room floor—could that be just concidence? Possibly, but not likely. More probably, it's been stolen straight, perhaps unconsciously, from his novel, *Blue Angel.* Which, in turn, was borrowed from his life. He reads on.

That was in Boston, in the fifties. I was living in Copley Square. I wanted to be a jazz singer. My boyfriend played the guitar. He said he was a gypsy. He said his name was Django. But once an old woman— his grandmother—called. She sounded Italian. She asked for Tony.

Nothing led to his hitting me, not one word or a gesture. It had never happened before. He had gone to play at a club and came home

and pulled me off our mattress and punched me in the face. I remem-
ber his anger having a smell, the smell of burning truck tires, a diesel
laying tread on the road as it crashed into my face.

Swenson looks up from the manuscript. All right, she's read *Blue*
Angel. His heroine was a jazz singer, recovering from a violent affair
with a musician. So how is he going to handle this? Does he let Angela
know he's noticed the striking correspondences between her novel
and his? Such things happen—quite innocently. A phrase, a fragment
of description, even a minor plot point lodges in one's mind and
emerges in one's work without one's knowing where it came from.
That's what he could tell her: make it very abstract, theoretical. Take
a leaf from Francis Bentham's book—keep the pronouns third-person
impersonal. Sometimes the work of others lodges in *one's* mind. . . .
But even that could ruin everything, destroy the trust between them.
Angela's so skittish, she might think he was accusing her of plagiarism—of plagiarizing *him*. Better not to mention it, just say that the
part about the mother's past seems extraneous, distracting. Angela
said *she* had her doubts. He'll suggest she cut the whole section.
   Something else is bothering him. . . . All right. He's got it now.
The part in *Blue Angel* about the singer's boyfriend was loosely
based on life. When he first met Sherrie, she'd just gotten rid of this
guy. . . . Now wait a minute. This is strange. Sherrie's real
boyfriend played guitar. The guy in the novel—the character—was
supposed to be a drummer. And now Angela's restored him to
what he really was. It's not so odd, especially if Angela was con-
sciously or unconsciously echoing his novel. She'd naturally pick
another instrument for the guy to play. How many jazz instruments are there?
   He finds his place and resumes reading.

   I was young. I healed quickly. The bruises disappeared. But one
   morning I woke up, got out of bed, and fell on the way to the bath-
   room. When I tried to stand the room spun until it threw me onto the
   floor. This time, I was really scared. I thought the beating had dam-

aged my brain. I called a cab. I went to the hospital. The doctor was
young and handsome. I didn't want to tell him that my boyfriend
had almost killed me. I said I didn't know what was wrong. I let him
look in my throat. He said I had an ear infection. I was so grateful I
jumped up to thank him. . . .

I woke up on the floor. Nurses came running in. The handsome
doctor was taking my pulse. Reader, I married him.

And that's it. The manuscript breaks off there, which is just as
well because Swenson's concentration is shot. This time he doesn't
have to stop and figure out the problem. The jazz singer in his
novel—like the real one who preceded him to the emergency
room—had strep throat. It was *Swenson* who had the middle ear
infection, a detail not in his book.

There's no way Angela could know that. It just doesn't seem
possible—logical—that she could be so tuned into him that she
picks up details from his past on some sort of writerly radar. But
weirder things happen all the time. He remembers writer friends—
years ago, when he still had writer friends—talking about the
uncanny coincidences that so often seemed to occur. You invented
a character, imagined an event, and within days you met that person or experienced what you'd imagined.

There's got to be some explanation here, less arcane than clair-
voyance. Could he have told the class—during one of those out-of-
body journeys from the here and now—how he and Sherrie met?
Did he use it as an example of how a real incident gets altered on its
way into a novel? Swenson doesn't think so. He's learned to be
wary about bringing personal history into the classroom ever since
he read, on a student evaluation, that he was always wasting class
time with pointless personal anecdotes.

Or has he told the story to someone Angela might know? It's
been years since they told it at a faculty dinner. Perhaps he told
Magda, but try as he might, he can't picture the scene in which
Magda girl-talks with Angela about how Professor Swenson met his
wife.

Grabbing for the phone has become a kind of a reflex. Reading Angela's work seems to generate an instant need for telecommunication. But whom does he want to call? It doesn't seem quite the perfect moment to hear Len Currie complain about being a successful, well-paid, highly sought-after Manhattan editor. He doesn't want to call Sherrie, nor can he call Magda for another disguised interrogation on the subject of Angela Argo. Nor is he ready to call Angela and discuss this new chapter while trying to figure out how she tapped into the intimate facts of his past.

Fine, then. If the phone call's a reflex, let the reflex dial. Swenson's only dimly aware of his fingers pushing buttons. Hmm ... whose number is this? Well, he's just kidding around, but, hey, he seems to be dialing the phone-sex number from Angela's poems.

The question is how he remembers it. He forgets nearly everything else. The answer is: He's known for days that he was going to call.

He feels a flutter of light anxiety, like the turning of a page, specifically a page from the English Department phone bill. What will a call to a sex line at the college's expense do for his professional reputation? And why should it matter, really? Phone sex is hardly criminal. The idea that he might not be allowed to call a phone-sex line makes him want to call and stay on the line until they come and drag him away.

More likely, he'll have to give his credit card number. It'll never show up on the college bill. Anyway, he's not going to talk. He'll just see who answers. In fact he's pretty certain that the number was invented. He'll get some old geezer in Middlebury, some garage in Plainfield. He'll just see who answers, apologize, and hang up.

"Good evening," says a woman in the businesslike tones of an airline ticket clerk. "Intimate Phone Friends. Whom would you like to speak to tonight?"

Swenson can't answer for quite a while. No doubt she's used to that. Then, holding his hand over the receiver—no doubt she's used to that, too—he says, experimentally, "Angela 911?"

The woman says, "I'm sorry, hon. She doesn't work here anymore. Would you like to talk to one of our other beautiful ladies?"

"No thanks." Swenson hangs up. Adrenaline's pumping through him. He's practically sick with relief. But where did he think this was leading? What had he imagined? What would he have done if Angela 911 had answered?

Swenson leaves the office and drives home with a dangerously small portion of his psyche. The rest has better things to do, such as twisting itself around the question of how Angela knows so much about his past. More than likely it's coincidence. That's the answer he can live with. And though it gives him the willies, it's a lot less troubling to think about than the fact that he just called a phone-sex line from the college phone.

Since the Benthams' party he's been unpleasantly aware that Angela is occupying more than her share of territory in his mind. Nor has he forgotten that less than an hour ago, he was mentally groping between her legs while, on the surface, teaching a class. Fantasies aren't actions. Let's hear it for repression, and for his pretty white farmhouse appearing around the bend.

Sherrie isn't home yet. Being alone—briefly—in the house always makes Swenson feel calmer, more capable and grown-up. Though being alone for too long makes him feel like a panicky child. He goes to his study, looks up a number, and calls Angela in her dorm room.

Angela sounds sleepy.

"I read your chapter," Swenson says.

"Already? Wow. I'm flattered."

"Don't be," says Swenson, lamely. How pathetic is *this*? Admitting to reading a student's work the minute class was over. "The novel must be good. The plot's got me hooked."

"Did you totally hate the new chapter? Is that why you're calling so soon?"

"Not at all. I thought the first part was wonderful."

"Which part was that?" Is it possible she doesn't know? That first time she gave him a chapter, she knew about every typo. Her voice sounds hoarse. Was she sleeping? Or could he have interrupted her in the midst of fooling around with the boyfriend she mentioned so dismissively in his office? Don't these kids have voice mail? Why did she pick up?

"You said the first part was wonderful. So does that mean the second part sucked? The part about the mother? That's the part I'm worried about." Swenson hears the familiar Angela taking over from the impostor who answered.

"Well, I don't know," says Swenson. What if it's published some-day, and Sherrie or someone reads it? "I wasn't sure. I found myself skimming to get back to the story of the girl and her . . . music teacher. That part where the mother meets the father . . . in the hospital. I wasn't sure you needed it. It seemed a little extraneous. . . ."

His voice trails off. It *is* a good idea. Lose the mother's history. The girl's story doesn't need it.

Angela's sigh is impatient. "I could maybe cut the stupid Jane Eyre joke at the end. But I need the mother's point of view. For stuff that happens later. Stuff the reader will need to hear that can't come from the girl's point of view. It's technical, you'll see. . . ."

Technical! They're talking technique here, one writer to another. Swenson presses on his molar till a stab of pain calls him back to his real life. A life with a dentist. Sherrie. A home.

He says, "Where did you get that part about the ear infection and falling down in the hospital?"

"Huh?" says Angela. "Oh, that. Okay. This friend of mine in high school. She keeled over in the emergency room, and the doctor tried to ask her out. Until the nurse showed him her chart. Showed him how young she was."

"I see." Swenson's not going near *that* story.

A lull in the conversation. Time to say good-bye.

"So . . . how are things going? School? Work? Life in general?"

Just then he looks up and sees Sherrie in the doorway of his office. She's wearing her coat. Rain shines in her hair.

"Excuse me. I've got to go," he says, and hangs up.

"Who was that?" asks Sherrie.

"Oh, that? That was . . . Magda."

Sherrie says, "That's what I thought. You're leading her on, you know? Unless that's what you want to do."

"It's not," says Swenson. "Believe me. Anyway, you're imagining all that. I couldn't lead *anyone* on. I mean, no one would want to *be* led on by me—"

"Are you all right?" says Sherrie.

"You tell *me*," he says.

"I think you're going to make it," Sherrie says.

"I'm not so sure," says Swenson, then stands and kisses the top of her head.

On Saturday morning of parents' weekend, Swenson passes Kelly Steinsalz sauntering across the quad with her mother and father. Unlike the other students, power-walking ahead of their parents, Kelly, perhaps because she's had so much practice giving campus tours, walks slowly enough for her mother and father to keep up, which is not to say that they don't appear to be barely staving off panic.

"Kelly," says Swenson. "These must be your parents!"

"Professor Swenson!" Kelly says. "This is my mom and dad." Kelly's parents grin at him, and Kelly seems to glow, thankful for this proof that she exists here: a teacher knows her name. Instantly she forgives him for disliking her story, "Mabel's Party." What's a story, really, compared to this validation? Swenson accepts her gratitude, nods, and moves on, feeling he's finally taught her something—something about power, obligation, and kindness.

Smiling beatifically at the students and their visitors, Swenson could be an actor sent from central casting to play a beneficent college professor. At the same time, he feels as if he's transcended his ego and become pure soul, expanding outward to experience the pain of the parents, the middle-aged women so touching in their Birkenstocks and gunny sacks, their husbands, overgrown boys shocked to discover that *they're* not the students; the scholarship parents, the dads in baseball caps and feed hats, the minorities and country folk eyeing the pretty campus as if it were Jurassic Park.

How uncomfortable they are in the presence of their children! Who would believe that these intimidating strangers were attached to bottoms they diapered, mouths they pried open with spoons? These hulking boys and gum-chewing girls could be visiting dignitaries or important business contacts, that's how obsequiously the grown-ups trot behind them, keeping up their interrogations— how's the food? your roommate? your math professor?—questions their children ignore, walking farther ahead, so that the parents must speed up, intent, but possessing just enough peripheral awareness to compare themselves with the others: whose children are more sullen—or phony enough to pretend to enjoy this?

When he and Sherrie took Ruby to college, a year ago this August, they were near the low end on the spectrum of parent-child relations. No one's daughter was more withdrawn, pulling harder away, more mortified by their existence or encumbered by her own. Ruby's fury at them smoldered so intensely that Swenson could see other parents turning to look, distracted from their own dramas by whatever signals his family must have been putting out. By then Ruby hadn't spoken to them for weeks, and didn't speak all that day. When Sherrie went to kiss Ruby good-bye, she lowered her face like a toddler submitting to having her winter hat pulled on.

And what had Swenson and Sherrie done to deserve such rage? Broken up a romance with a liar, a fraud, an alleged rapist. Was the problem really the busted love affair, or their making Ruby see herself as a person so weak that her parents could make her go in the opposite direction from the way her heart led?

Every so often, Swenson sees Matt McIlwaine with another victim, always a freshman girl. Sometimes, when they pass close enough, Matt winks at him. Eventually, Ruby would have learned the truth, would have run to Swenson, her dad, her champion, her protector, which is how she used to see him when she was a little girl.

Swenson's dressed with care in a T-shirt and sports jacket. Joe Professor on Saturday, professional but not off-putting. He changed shirts twice, jackets once, adjusting his appearance for the imaginary range of parents who might walk into his office. It's understood that he'll be there from nine-thirty till twelve so visitors can drop by, no appointment necessary. He's implying that this open-door policy applies year-round for their children, which is only fair, considering what their families are shelling out.

Swenson arranges his books and papers to convey the impression of a desk he's worked at, a work in progress, so to speak, though not the work of a slob. He scoots a second chair over from the window, a chair sufficiently similar to the one in front of his desk to spare the mothers and fathers the revealing negotiations about who gets the more comfortable seat. He often sees too deeply into the parents' marriages.

He gazes out his window down at the groups sleepwalking across the quad. He needs to appear to be doing something when the parents walk in. Scanning the stack of books on his desk, he pulls out *My Dog Tulip*, which he hasn't looked at since he used it for cover to borrow Angela's poems. The poems are in his desk at home. He should get them out of his house. He doesn't need to think about them with the parents about to walk in. Hi, I'm Ted Swenson. I'm a big fan of your daughter's dirty poetry. He opens *My Dog Tulip*.

> As soon as he made his wishes clear she allowed him to mount her and stood quietly with her legs apart and her tail coiled away when he clasped her around the waist. But for some reason, he failed to achieve his purpose. His stabs, it looked to me standing beside them, did not quite reach her. . . . They tried again and again, the same thing always happened, whenever he seemed about to enter her she protested, as though she were still a virgin, and pulled herself free. And now it was quite upsetting to watch, his continual failure to consummate his desire and the consequent frustration of these two beautiful animals who wished to copulate and could not manage to do so. Nor could I see any way to help them, except to lubricate Tulip, which I did, for they seemed to be doing themselves all that could be done, except unite.

Just then, someone knocks on the door. Oh, hello. Do come in, let me read you this brilliant depiction of canine sexual frustration. He props the book open, face down. The professor's reading! But suppose they recognize the book—not at all the heartwarming pet story one might expect from the title. How many parents have read Ackerley? Swenson can't take the chance. He hides it under some other books and calls out weakly, "Ye-es?"

The door opens, and a man—wispy beard, silver-rimmed glasses, *he* looks like the professor—sticks his head in, grinning shyly. The door opens wider to admit his wife, tall and also gray-haired, with a taut, eager-to-please smile.

"I'm Doctor Liebman? And this is my wife Merle?"

The woman says, "We're Danny's parents?"

"Oh, yes," says Swenson. "Please, come on in." Oh, yes, your son just wrote the most amusing story about a chicken.

"We just came to say hi!" says Danny's mom.

"To see how he's doing," the father says. "Just in a general way."

"He loves your class," says the mother. "It's the only one he talks about. Last week, on the phone, he was raving about a story by one of the other students, a story about a boy who commits suicide."

"Oh, Carlos's story." Swenson's proud of himself for remembering.

"Of course, as a mother, you worry when your son admires a story about a suicide."

"Mothers!" says the father. "What *don't* they worry about? If the kid likes *Crime and Punishment* they worry that means he's going out to bludgeon some old lady."

Bludgeon *two* old ladies, thinks Swenson. "I wouldn't worry. Danny's very together. He works hard. He wants to improve. There was a very interesting classroom discussion the other day about one of Danny's stories."

"*Danny's* stories?" says the mother. "He never mentions *his* stories."

"Interesting," says the father. "What was the story about?"

"Surburban life," says Swenson.

"Not about *us*, I hope." Mrs. Liebman giggles.

"I wouldn't worry," says Swenson.

Danny's parents thank him profusely and leave. Is someone waiting out there? Apparently, no, there isn't. Swenson finds *My Dog Tulip* and begins with Ackerley's description of meeting an old woman wheeling her ailing, bandaged dog through Fulham Palace Gardens in a baby carriage, a scene that segues into the writer's account of his affair with his Alsatian, a relationship as tender as any romance with a human. Swenson gladly exchanges his office for London in the late fifties, a world seen through the brilliant lens of Tulip and Ackerley's love. He loses himself, loses all sense of time, and is shocked by the sound of someone knocking on the door.

A woman walks in and says, "I'm Claris's mother."

Fiftyish, unsmiling Mrs. Williams has no interest in deploying what's left of her daughter's beauty. Life as a high school principal has given her the authority to turn Swenson into a meek kid to whom she can lay down the law. Claris is destined for medical school and Mrs. Williams doesn't want her head being turned with any nonsense about being a writer, no point Swenson giving her any Toni Morrison bullshit, one black woman winning a prize doesn't mean the field is wide open.

What is Swenson supposed to say? She's got nothing to fear. Claris isn't a writer. She's a sharp and tactful critic, good at detecting what's wrong, excellent bedside manner, a first-rate diagnostician. But she doesn't have talent. Like Angela.

"Lord knows why Claris chose this place." Mrs. Williams sighs. "I warned her a million times. She got into Yale. Did you know that?"

"No, I didn't," says Swenson, chastened. "In any case, I promise you, I'll do everything in my power to discourage your daughter from wasting her life. Anyway, Claris is way too smart to want to be a writer."

"I hope so." Mrs. Williams raises one eyebrow. "Thank you," she says frostily, then picks herself up and leaves.

He looks at the clock. Eleven-thirty. Well, that's that. Nearly painless. Really, not bad at all. So why is he disappointed? Because he was looking forward to meeting Angela's family. He wants another parent conference? He *has* gone out of his mind.

Swenson hears a tapping on the frosted pane, the ping of metal on glass.

He knows they're Angela's parents before the woman says, "Are you Professor Swenson? Our Angela is in your class . . . ?" She's wearing almost as much metal as Angela, though in her case it's gold. Clunky bracelets, chains, earrings. She bears the weight as proudly and humbly as a Hindu bride, each carat a mark of distance traveled upward into the world. She's in her early forties, with wide dark eyes and a startled doll-like blink, dyed blond hair, black eyebrows. A royal blue dress and matching pumps, an outfit she'd wear to a wedding. Her slightly older, pudgy husband wears a shiny tan polo shirt, a checked jacket. He too has a gold ring.

"I'm sorry we're late," says Angela's mother. "We started out from Jersey at five-thirty this morning so we wouldn't have to pay for another night's motel."

Her husband says, "That's a little more information than the professor needs."

"Oh, is it?" she says. "I'm sorry."

"Oh, no," says Swenson. "You're right on time. They'll be serving that awful lunch for another hour and a half."

"Oh, is there lunch served?" the mother says. "Are you gonna want lunch?" she asks her husband.

"We can buy lunch," says her husband. "We're here to talk about Angela."

"I'm glad you came!" Swenson's practically shouting. "Please. Have a seat."

The mother sits, hooking her legs at the knees, shaking one shiny blue pump. Her husband crosses and uncrosses his legs, squirming with an angular clumsiness so reminiscent of Angela that Swenson has to remind himself that he isn't her biological father. The guy resembles Angela—something about the shape of his eyes, revealed when he takes off his glasses and rubs the bridge of his nose.

"Eight hours on the road," the man says. "How'd they find this place?"

He looks more like Angela than the mother does. Or maybe he resembles Angela's real father. The mother has a type. They're certainly not the parents in her novel, the distant imperious doctor and his moody wife. On the other hand, there's no guarantee that this isn't the guy in the poems, the child abuser and phone-sex addict. Swenson's prepared to hate him. But he has to keep an open mind. He's the one who warns against assuming that anything's autobiographical.

"Well," says the stepfather, rearranging his arms and legs until at last he gives up. "How's Angela doing? She told us to make sure and come here. She said you were the only teacher who would say anything nice. So, you know, I got to wonder why we ain't going to see the ones who *won't* have nice things to say. Not waste our time with the subjects where she's already doing okay. . . . Not that we're wasting our time here. Jesus. I didn't mean—"

"I understand," says Swenson.

"We meant to get here in time to see the other teachers," says Angela's mother. "But the drive took so long. At the end we got lost for an hour. . . ."

"*Who* got lost?" says her husband.

"*I* got us lost. We wound up right downstairs in front of this building." She holds up a creased campus map that appears to have absorbed all the sweat and stress of their recent trouble. "So we decided to come here first."

"I'm glad you did," Swenson says.

"So you said," says Angela's stepfather.

"She talks about your class all the time," says his wife. "Really! She just won't shut up about it."

"Good things, I hope," says Swenson.

"Absolutely," says Angela's mother. "You're . . . well, you're her hero! She thinks you're just the greatest writer who ever lived."

"Right," says her husband. "I'm sure the professor really cares what some little pipsqueak kid thinks about his work."

"Of course I do." Swenson can only pray that his pleasure and pride aren't visible on his face. "It's always flattering to have a fan. Especially such a talented one. I mean, I think Angela may be a real writer." Then he stops. It so rarely—never—happens that he gets to say this with any sincerity, he can't imagine how it sounds. Probably like he's lying.

"She's always been a writer," her stepfather says. "Back when she first learned, I got her a computer, and she started printing this little family newspaper. She'd put in stuff like how long she'd had to wait that morning for me to get out of the bathroom. I knew computers were going to be big. They've sure changed my business—I'm a pharmacist. I can't imagine how we lived without them."

Swenson can't manage to hate this guy. He's no more the father in the poems than he is the dad in the novel. But something's not computing. Didn't Angela say her father killed himself when she was a teen? Wasn't that why she liked *Phoenix Time*, why it saved her life? But this guy talks as if he's been around forever. Could Angela have lied about this? What point would there have been? Is there some way of asking the guy if he's her father or stepfather, if the real father committed suicide . . . without sounding . . . nosy? Surely, the truth—the explanation—will emerge on its own.

He says, "She's working on a novel. It's really very good."

"What's the story about?" asks her mother.

"A high school girl," he says at last.

"What about a high school girl?" Angela's mother says.

"Well . . ." How much does he want to risk? The closer to the edge he goes, the greater the chance that he'll look over it and see something he wants to know. "It's about a girl and a high school music teacher who is not exactly . . . er, always . . . professional in his conduct with his students. At least that's what I think it's going to be. I've only read a few chapters."

Angela's parents exchange glances.

"What is it?" Swenson fears he knows what's coming. The novel *is* autobiographical: the tragic drama of Angela and her teacher. He doesn't want it to be true, doesn't want to know he's dealing with a student who compulsively seduces teachers. "What is it?" Swenson repeats. "Something I should know?"

"Actually . . . ," says Mrs. Argo, "something like that—*sort of* like that—happened at Angela's school. There was this biology teacher . . . "

"Angela wasn't involved," her husband adds quickly. "But the guy was messing around with a whole bunch of girls. He had himself a regular harem. Friends of Angela's, too."

"Her best friend," says Angela's mother, "got . . . you know, involved with the teacher."

"But not Angela," says her husband. "Angela's too smart a kid."

"Also she's a big chicken," says her mother proudly. "Don't let all the body piercing fool you. Angela's a pussycat, really." A peculiar echo resonates from that last sentence—the faintest hint of meow or growl. I'm a pussycat, too. Or has Swenson imagined it? Is compulsive seductiveness a learned trait that Angela studied at her mother's knee? But what is Swenson thinking? Angela's the least seductive person he knows. In fact a big part of her appeal is the touching effort she puts into eliminating anything that might elicit desire.

"Actually," says her mother, "I've always thought that Angela was a little shy, a little . . . funny around boys."

"Funny how?" says Swenson.

"Well . . . she'd chase after some kid she liked . . . and the second he started to like *her*, she wouldn't answer the phone."

But what about her boyfriend? Is there some way to ask about that? Swenson's trying to formulate some sort of tactful, halfway-normal sounding question when Angela's father says, "Jesus Christ! This guy's her teacher, not her friggin' psychiatrist."

After a silence, Swenson says stuffily, "Well. Be that as it may, she's an excellent writer."

"Thank you so much," says her mother.

"Yeah, great, a writer," says her father.

"Thank you," says Angela's mother, standing. "We appreciate your time."

Her husband follows her cue, and stands. Swenson's up on his feet.

"Pleased to meet you, Mrs. Argo, Mr. Argo." If the guy isn't Mr. Argo, if neither of them are Argos now, maybe they'll tell him so. And he'll know that this guy is the stepfather—not Argo, the biological father. But what if he's adopted Angela and given her his name?

"Thank you," repeats her mother.

Her husband nods and, in his haste to escape, nearly plows into the door.

"Oops," he says. "I nearly ran into the door."

Angela's father, thinks Swenson.

The discussion of Makeesha's story goes reasonably well compared with the scene Swenson envisioned as he lay awake last night and imagined Makeesha denouncing the workshop's racist bias. In fact, the class has responded instinctively to the undefended sweetness of Makeesha's improbable transcription of a phone conversation between a black college student and her former high school boyfriend, the white guy who broke up with her the night before the prom, under pressure from his parents. From its first line, "I knew the dude's voice right away, even though we didn't be speaking for a year and a half," the story, like Makeesha, veers in and out of street talk, and is in every other way (its protagonist is a sophomore at an isolated New England college) so very much like its author that when Jonelle Brevard says, "I really believed these characters," there's a chorus of "I did, too," and everyone—including Makeesha—is relieved and happy.

Their positive comments go on for a while. Swenson's not going to chill these warm feelings by introducing the tricky question of how one transforms experience into art, or by pointing out the stiffness that results when narrative exposition masquerades as dialogue. (Early in the story, Makeesha's heroine says, "Dude, what you be calling for? We ain't talked since you broke up with me a year and a half ago on the night before senior prom.") Is Swenson's forbearance racist? Is he being unfair to Makeesha?

The only thing Angela says in class is, "I liked the moment when the girl and her boyfriend stop making small talk and fall silent, and out of nowhere the guy tells her he's been thinking about her non-stop for a year and a half."

After class, Makeesha hangs around for a final word with Swenson. Claris waits for her at the door. Angela remains at the seminar table.

"Good job, Makeesha," Swenson says. "It's obvious everyone thought so." He smiles at her but doesn't speak, though she's clearly expecting more. If Claris and Angela weren't watching, Swenson could be more falsely effusive. Their presence also makes this harder on Makeesha, makes her more eager to get out while she can, with her dignity still intact, before she's had a chance to beg for another compliment from Swenson.

"Well, thanks," she says, and hurries to join Claris. As they leave, they cast identically disdainful, competitive glances back at Angela. She watches them go, then turns to Swenson and says, "Jeez. Excuse me. What did I do?"

"It's what I didn't do." Apparently it's become quite normal for Swenson to engage Angela in these unprofessionally conspiratorial chats about the other students.

"I want to thank you," Angela says. "You did me a giant favor."

"What was that?" asks Swenson.

"Lying to my parents."

"Lying?"

"Telling them I could write."

"You can write. I was telling the truth."

"You don't have to say that," Angela says. "I spent the whole weekend crying because my novel's so bad."

"Every writer goes through that," Swenson says. Everybody, that is, but Swenson, who hasn't written a word in so long that at this point a crying jag would be a sign of progress. "Anyway, I enjoyed meeting them . . . your mother and . . . stepfather."

"Enjoyed? That's hard to imagine."

Swenson says, "That was your stepfather, right?"

"Right," says Angela. "Why?"

"Well, it was the strangest thing. He kept talking as if he knew you when you were a child, almost as if he were your real father. . . ."

"He *did* know me. He lived next door to us my whole life. He and his wife, that is. A year after my dad killed himself, the next-door neighbor—my stepdad—married my mom. Major neighborhood scandal. His wife and kids kept on living next door. Everything was the same, except they weren't speaking to us, and he was married to my mom. I know it's hard to imagine a hot romance, to look at the two of them now."

Swenson tries to summon their images so he can match them against this new information, but only unhelpful fragments appear—false eyelashes, jewelry, shoes—details that fail to cohere into a portrait of lovers who braved all New Jersey just to be together. Also, he's still not entirely convinced that Angela's telling the truth.

"I lied about something," Angela says.

"Oh?" says Swenson. "What's that?"

"My real father wasn't crazy. He was sick. With emphysema. I remember once he took me grocery shopping for my mom, and he got so winded helping me bag the groceries that he had to sit down. He was wheezing. He couldn't catch his breath, and for a while it looked like they'd have to call an ambulance. And I was like at the mercy of these checkout guys, my dad's *life* depended on them. . . . I saw one of those assholes roll his eyes at the chick who was bagging. Until then I'd been thinking that particular guy was cute. The worst part was: I was so embarrassed. I mean, about my dad. After he killed himself I couldn't stop thinking about that day, and I felt totally guilty." Tears well up in Angela's eyes. She scrubs them away with the back of her hand. "Why was I mad at him?"

She can't be lying. Or can she? That Swenson can't tell makes him painfully conscious of the distance between them.

"You weren't mad at your dad." He should be patting her shoulder, but a seminar table divides them. "You were angry at the situation. Life can be cruel and unfair."

Angela shuts her eyes, squeezing back tears, her fingers hooked onto the edge of the table. "Anyway, I can't believe how I'm repaying the favor. You were so nice, saying all that stuff to get my parents off my case. And now I've brought you another chapter. You don't have to read it. I can wait."

"Hand it over," says Swenson.

Alone in his office, after class, Swenson finds himself pretending—as if someone were watching—that he has many more pressing things to do before he can get to Angela's chapter. He has to open his desk drawer and then immediately close it. He has to wheel his chair back and forward. He has to pick up the phone and put it down. He has to think about checking his E-mail and then decide not to. Only after considering and putting off these many important tasks does he take Angela's manuscript out of its orange envelope and begin the first page.

> After school every afternoon I rushed out to the shed to see if the eggs were hatching. I searched the shells for fissures, the needle holes chicks poke with their beaks. But the shells were unbroken as I spun them in my palm. I knew they were dead and cold, that their warmth was from the incubator, not from life inside them.
>
> Incubation took twenty-one days. Three weeks passed. A fourth. I knew from Mrs. Davis, and from the pamphlets, how much could have gone wrong. Problems with the parent stock, old roosters, malnourished hens. Incubator malfunction. A few degrees here or there. And yet I couldn't make myself admit they were dead. What was I supposed to do with five dozen rotten eggs? Was my mother supposed to cook the little things I'd imagined as tiny pulsating blood-red creatures growing daily in secret, sixty fragile ovals from which I'd thought I heard sixty heartbeats?
>
> One night I asked my father to come out to the shed. I remember how pleased my mother looked that at last I was including him. I hated that it made her happy.
>
> So I said, "I think they're dead."
>
> My father said, "What do you mean, dead?"
>
> I said, "They were supposed to hatch ten days ago."

"Ten days ago?" my father said. "Christ. Where have I been?"

He pushed his chair away from the table, left his steak and potatoes. I had to run to keep up with him as he ran out to the shed. Emergency! He flung open the door as if something were hiding inside it. But of course there was only the red light, the silent eggs, the humming.

My dad said, "Have you been keeping charts?"

I said, "Look, Dad. Look how neat."

"None of them hatched?" he said. "Not one?"

I waved my hand around the shed.

"These things happen," my father said. "The point is to find out why, and redesign the experiment." He didn't want me to be discouraged. He wanted me to like my science project.

"First of all," he said, "let's verify our results." He grabbed an egg from the incubator and hit it against the rack.

The smell took a second before it hit.

"I'm throwing up," I said.

What to do with the broken egg? My dad transferred it, oozing gunk, to his other hand, and picked up an egg from another incubator. It broke. It smelled bad, too. He ordered me to get a trash bag from the house, and I held the bag for him while he dropped in the eggs. At first he was just efficient. But the smell got really bad. He began to slam them in hard. He said, "It's all about trial and error, goddamn it. Finding out what went wrong." He asked if I was sure the temperatures were correct. If I'd turned the eggs every day. I told him I'd done all that.

I knew what I had done wrong. But I couldn't tell him.

I was supposed to have candled the eggs. When they were a week old you held them up to a bright light and and looked for a veiny red spot that proved they were fertile. If they weren't, you threw them out. The blanks could spoil the others.

I couldn't do it. I didn't want to see what was inside the eggs. I didn't want to be the one to throw the dead ones away. Besides, Mr. Reynaud had said something about helping me with that part.

Instead of candling the eggs, I'd gone out to the shed and imagined a knock, imagined I opened the door—and there was Mr.

Reynaud. I pictured the look on his face: confident, as if he had every right to be there, and at the same time worried I might not let him in. I imagined he took off his jacket, replaced one of the red lights with a bright light bulb, and gently, one by one, held the eggs to the light. I imagined him saying, Come here. And I did. I stood behind him, so close I felt his rough jacket against my skin, and I leaned forward, against his back, looking over his shoulder until I could see what he saw: the egg as red as the blood in your hand when you hold it up to a flashlight, and the yellow yolk deep inside, and the tiny red clot.

By now I had to lean in so close that my breasts pushed against his back. I felt it, and he felt it, neither of us spoke. He replaced the egg in the rack and started to reach for another, but then he turned slowly. I was so close he could have thrown me off balance. He put his hand on my upper arm and steadied me as we turned against each other and meshed, his mouth locked into mine. We kissed. His hands ran over my back. Then his hands slipped under the waist of my jeans, and I made a sound so low in my throat that even the unborn chicks must have heard me. What did they think that noise was as they swam around in their shells?

Angela's thinking about him. He knows this with telepathic certainty. She's back in her room at the dorm waiting for him to call. He should call her. Tell her the chapter's fine, it's great, just keep on doing what she's doing. He picks up the phone. He puts it down. Good. He'll wait for a while.

Home early, Sherrie's cooking thin chicken cutlets, breaded, fried in butter and olive oil, arranged with slices of lemon, scalloped potatoes with prosciutto, a salad with walnuts and Gorgonzola. Are they celebrating again? Swenson certainly is— a miracle cure, the unbidden grace of coming to his senses, his recovery from a fleeting, inappropriate interest in one of his students. The evidence that he's cured is that he has a reason to call Angela. But he doesn't want to. Nothing could interest him less.

He sits in the kitchen, admiring the easy competence with which Sherrie flips the cutlets, checks the potato casserole bubbling in the oven. The sight of her tossing the salad by hand, lightly stroking oil onto each lettuce leaf, fills him with such longing that it's all he can do not to put his arms around her and lead her off to bed. He watches her wipe her hands on her jeans, imagines covering her hands with his, feeling her fingers underneath his, and beneath that, her thighs. He remains quiet, so as not to distract her and because he feels that their silence, together with the heat from the stove, creates a humid greenhouse in which his desire can thrive.

Sherrie lights the votive candles, then hands him a bottle of cold white wine, a corkscrew, and two glasses. He pours half a glass and tastes it, drinks what's left in the glass. A flush of intense well-being makes him think that all history and civilization has been preparation for this blessed moment of sitting across from his wife, inhaling the perfumes of wine, chicken, lemon, and melted cheese, while a gentle steam rises from his plate.

They bring their food to the table. Leaning forward to eat, Sherrie rakes her hair back from her forehead. The skin between her brows forms a vertical crease dug by years of focused attention, hours listening to students describe pain more intense than anything they put in the stories they write for Swenson. How moved he is by her frown lines, by the loveliness of his wife, the beauty that's grown stronger and stormier with the passage of time.

He takes a bite of chicken, potatoes, smiles inanely while detaching the strings of cheese that connect his mouth to the fork. "So? How was your day?"

"Kind of great," Sherrie says. "Nothing too awful went wrong. Arlene brought me a fabulous sandwich with cream cheese and some kind of spread she made from stewing red peppers practically down to nothing. She got the idea from a magazine. The sandwich was so delicious I didn't even mind her spending twenty minutes explaining the recipe and the changes she made in the recipe or thought of making in the recipe and how she never used olive oil before and how the smell took getting used to, and how long it took to reduce the peppers to this gummy paste, and how she knew I would like it because I like exotic foods. . . . How was *your* day?"

"Not bad," says Swenson. "We did Makeesha's story. It could have been a bloodbath, but somehow we all dodged a bullet."

Sherrie says, "Again. Well, that's a relief."

"Is this how low we've sunk?" says Swenson. "No disasters in class and a sandwich from Arlene is enough to make a day 'kind of great'?"

Sherrie laughs. "Well, also . . . Chris Dolan's echocardiogram report came in. The heart thing turns out to be nothing."

"Heart thing? Chris Dolan?" Swenson knows he's supposed to know.

"Don't you listen to anything? He's that adorable freshman. His family doctor heard some abnormal sounds during his last physical and told him to deal with it when he got here. Dumped the thing in our laps. And the kid's really lovely, really sweet. We were all terribly worried. I know I told you about him—"

Wouldn't he remember if she'd told him about some *adorable* kid, some *really lovely, really sweet* kid? His ears would have perked right up. Does Sherrie have a crush on this guy? Swenson will *give* him a heart thing. But who's he to cast the first stone? A guy who spent last month with the hots for some punk girl writer. But all that's over now. Finished. So what does Sherrie think *she's* doing?

Sherrie says, "He told me about a pizza place where he worked last summer for this crazy Syrian boss who thinks that America's just waiting for him to invent a more American pizza, a hot dog and mustard pizza, a peanut butter and jelly pizza, and how the guy made his employees recycle the leftover cheese from the half-eaten slices—"

Swenson waits till Sherrie stops laughing. "I guess you had to have been there."

"Oh, come on, Ted," says Sherrie. "Don't be like that. He's a kid. He could have been in real trouble. He's not. How could I not be relieved?"

Swenson takes another mouthful. The chicken's salty coating rips, spurting oil onto his palate, releasing its layer of breading under the garlicky crispness. He feels expansive, large enough to see that his crush (or whatever) on Angela is not so different from Sherrie's fondness for this kid. It's all so understandable, touching, and tender, really, the two of them sinking into middle age, their own child not only grown and gone but hardly speaking to them, wrenching herself away from their grasp, beyond the reach of their love.

No wonder he and Sherrie might find themselves drawn to students. It's not as if they're perverts out of *Dangerous Liaisons*, two old vampires conspiring to suck the youth from the young. Their hearts are heat-seeking missiles drawn to whatever's still burning. They're like those old men in the Kawabata novel frequenting the brothel where they pay to curl up and sleep beside the warm bodies of young beautiful women. Christ! It's all so depressing Swenson thinks he might weep. Age and death—the unfairness of it, the daily humiliation of watching your power vanish just when you figure out how to use it.

"Is something wrong?" asks Sherrie.

"Nothing," he answers glumly. Of course he can't tell the truth for fear of insulting Sherrie by including her among the aging and decrepit when, for all he knows, she may not be feeling that way at the moment. In theory, he and Sherrie are close. But now he sees that's a lie. Somehow it seems more honest to be around someone with whom there's no pretence of the intimacy that a shared history is supposed to confer. Sooner or later—sooner—he has to call Angela and tell her he's read her chapter. He can put it off as long as he wants, but it's his professional duty.

He smiles at Sherrie. "If I were forced to choose one meal to eat every night for the rest of my life, it would be chicken with lemon, and scalloped potatoes with prosciutto."

"Why would you have to make a choice like that?" Sherrie asks.

"Why would I?" Swenson says.

In the middle of the night Swenson feels Sherrie rubbing against him. Lightly, experimentally, he kisses the back of her neck. They make love urgently, silently, hardly moving, the way they used to when Ruby slept in the next room.

Afterward, Swenson sleeps soundly and in the morning wakes up in such a rare good mood that, fortified with coffee, he decides to go to his study and take a peek at his novel.

The opening chapter isn't half bad. He hasn't touched the manuscript in so long that it seems like someone else's work, someone's ironic, ersatz-nineteenth-century description of the downtown neighborhood—Soho—where Julius Sorley arrives with dreams of fortune and reputation. But as soon as Julius starts reflecting on his past and present situation, everything pales, falters, stumbles, drops dead on the page. It's worse than Courtney Alcott's "First Kiss—Inner City Blues." Swenson wills himself to stay calm. He'll get more coffee, shower. Then he'll decide if he can read the rest, assess the damage and the likelihood that he can fix it.

Showered and shaved, neatly dressed, he feels more in control. He returns to his desk, picks up his manuscript, puts it down, ransacks the house for his briefcase, finds it under his coat, gets Angela's manuscript, and goes back to his study. He needs to call her, she's waiting. It's cruel not to call.

A man—a young man—answers. "Hello?" Why does the groggy voice sound familiar?

Swenson hangs up. He takes some deep breaths. Inhale. Exhale. He counts to five.

The phone rings.

"I'm sorry for calling you at home," Angela says.

Does Angela have caller ID? Can you get that in a college dorm? It horrifies Swenson to think of Angela and her boyfriend waching his number come up on a screen.

"I know I'm wrecking your morning," she says. "But I couldn't stand it another minute. I know you read the chapter and hated it, that's why you didn't call—"

"Relax. I liked it fine. I've been busy, is all."

"Can we talk about this?" Angela says. "I need to talk. I think I'm going insane."

"Don't go insane," says Swenson. "Meet me in my office in twenty minutes."

Swenson's just wrestled off his scarf and coat when Angela falls through his office door. She's wearing her usual uniform: black leather jacket, pouchy black sweater, black boots. But today she's added a pair of striped men's boxer shorts rolled on top of her jeans and angled around her hips, like a bandolier. She drops into the chair and slumps forward, her elbows on her spread knees, her chin cupped in her hands.

"I was sure you hated the new chapter," she said. "I was sure you read it and hated it, and that's why you didn't call."

"I didn't hate it at all," Swenson says. "I . . . admired it very much."

"Know what?" she says. "You're a guy, after all. Not calling's a guy thing to do."

Wait a minute! A guy *after all*? When *wasn't* he a guy? And isn't his guy-ness beside the point? He's a teacher. She's a student.

"Angela, I know you kids all secretly think your professors leave the classroom and go to their coffins like Dracula and don't wake up until it's time to teach the next class. I hate to tell you, we have lives. I read your manuscript, and, as I said, I admired it. But I had a few things to take care of before I could get to the phone. I was going to call you. . . ."

"I'm sorry. What did you think of the chapter? Did you believe that part about her trying to hatch the eggs and all the eggs dying and—"

"I believed it. I was totally convinced."

"Then what? What about the other part?"

Swenson leafs through the pages. "Let's face it. It's very . . . um . . . erotic. If that's what you intended." What an idiotic comment! What else could she have meant? Angela's not a child. She worked at a tele-phone-sex line.

Angela writhes briefly in her chair. Finally she says, "All right, I'll tell you this one thing. Then we can act like I never said it. And you have to promise not to hate me, no matter what."

"I promise," Swenson says.

"For the past two days," says Angela, "all I've thought about every second of every minute of every hour was you having those new pages, wondering if you were . . . I mean, I've been thinking about you going through your normal day, eating breakfast, driving to work, and I keep wondering if you're reading—" She stops and stares at him, wide-eyed with horror at what she's just said.

Swenson says, "I hardly ever eat breakfast."

"Excuse me?" Angela says.

"You said you'd been thinking about me eating breakfast. And I said, 'I don't eat breakfast.'"

Is there some way to take that back? Swenson doesn't think so. Angela stares at him, then jumps up and leaves, slamming the door behind her. Swenson shakes his head as if to keep the memory from implanting itself in his brain. All he knows is that he's ruined every-thing by being so tight-assed and nasty. Ruined what? What else should he have said? Hey, here's a bizarre coincidence. I've been thinking about you, too.

A moment later, the door swings open. Angela pops back in, smiling.

She says, "I forgot to give you this."

She slides a thin orange envelope onto his desk, then takes off again.

Swenson counts: a page and a half. What did she mean when she told him she'd been thinking about him all week? He wishes she would come back. This time he'd have the nerve to ask, instead of making some dopey remark about breakfast. Well, at least he's got more pages to read, pages that may tell him more than their garbled exchanges.

It wasn't long after the eggs died that I got my new clarinet. We'd already started practicing for the Christmas concert. Handel's greatest hits scored for a wimpy high school band. It was my job to lead the woodwinds into the Hallelujah chorus. One afternoon I picked up my clarinet and counted the measures and blew, and the hideous fartlike squawk stopped the entire rehearsal. The other kids started giggling. They thought I'd made a mistake. They resented my being first clarinet—the music teacher's favorite.

Mr. Reynaud knew, right away. The kids stopped giggling as he looked at me just the way I'd imagined him looking at me in the toolshed. I ran my hand down the clarinet. The bell came off in my hand.

He told me to stay after class. He said, "The clarinet could be fixed. But you're far too good to be playing this cheap piece of shit. I'll put in the order today. I'll borrow something from the grade school you can work on until then."

That was Thursday. On Monday he told me to stay after class again, and handed me a long narrow box.

"Unwrap it," he said. He took out his pocketknife and cut the box open. "Go ahead."

The gleaming gold and ebony pipe of the clarinet lay like Baby Jesus in His creche, snuggled in a soft nest of curly wood shavings.

"It's beautiful," I said. "I know it's the school's clarinet, but thank you for—"

"Try it out," he said.

I put the clarinet to my lips. I looked over it, at Mr. Reynaud. He handed me a reed, and watched me put it in my mouth to wet it. I sucked in my cheeks, took it out of my mouth. My mouth was totally dry.

Wood shavings had clung to the clarinet and gotten into my hair. He reached out and brushed them off. He said, "Why so sad?"

I told him I'd ruined my science project. None of the eggs had hatched. For a moment he seemed puzzled. Then he said, "Why don't I come over and take a look at the incubation system? Figure out what's wrong. I grew up on a farm. I know about these things."

I said, "Oh, please don't. You don't have to." But that was

And that's where the manuscript ends. Swenson flips the page over to see if anything's on the other side. He feels—suddenly, unaccountably—like gnashing his teeth and weeping. Well, better not gnash his teeth, at least. Probing his ragged, fragile molar is a distraction and a pleasure. There's no need to blow this situation entirely out of proportion. It's simple enough to call her and find out what's up.

But she won't be home yet. Well, good, he can go home, too.

He drives home. He goes to his study. The machine is blinking. He knew it would be. Angela's called. Swenson hits the play button.

"Dad? Are you there? It's Ruby. Call me at school. Everything's okay. I just need to ask you something."

This is what Swenson's prayed for. Now this, *this* is important, *this* is his real life. And this is what a monster he is: He's disappointed that it's not Angela. There is no angry God, it seems, waiting to hurl Swenson into the circle of hell reserved for fathers who care about crazy students more than their own daughters. He can't pretend that he's not the scum of the earth, the lowest excuse for a human being.

All this goes through his mind in the few seconds it takes the machine to beep and to speak again, this time in the unmistakable voice of Angela Argo.

"This is Angela? There's, like, a problem with my manuscript? You've probably figured that out. Um. I wanted to tell you. So call me. See you. Bye."

Horrified by how pleased he is, he replays her imploring, slightly whiny message. He thinks he'll keep the tape for a while before he erases it. He likes the fact that he can hear her voice anytime he wants. It's as if he's trapped something wild and brought it indoors, a firefly in a bottle. And this is how depraved he is: With Ruby's message still on the machine—with, for all he knows, his daughter awaiting his call, primed for reconciliation, needing his advice and help, or just wanting to hear the sound of his voice—he dials Angela's number.

"Oh, hi," she says. "I hoped it was you. Probably you haven't had a chance to look at what I gave you, but I wanted to warn you. I've got the chapter finished. But my computer ate the last couple pages, and my hard drive crashed."

"Jesus," says Swenson. "How much did you lose?"

"At first I almost threw up," she says. "Then I realized I'd backed it up," she says. "Then I realized I'd backed it up. I back up my files every day. I have it on a floppy disk. I just can't print it, is all."

"That's amazing. No one backs their files up every day. I mean, we all know we're supposed to, but—"

"I do. Anyway, I wanted you to know I didn't just, like, space out. And I couldn't wait for you to read the new pages I had. But then I got home and started thinking how strange it was that I wrote about her clarinet breaking—and my computer broke."

"Stuff like that happens," he says. "You write it, and then you live it. Or you make up something that turns out to be someone *else's* real life."

"Right," says Angela, blankly.

The silence lasts so long he thinks the line's gone dead. "Angela?" She says, "Meanwhile I can't write."

"Can they fix the computer?"

"In this dump? I don't think so. Anyhow they never fix them. They're like doctors, right? They just charge you a fortune and tell you nothing can be done."

"You need a new computer," says Swenson.

"Tell me about it," she says. Another lengthy pause. "Listen. I need to ask you a favor, and the thing is, you can absolutely say no. I *expect* you to say no. It's absolutely fine. I need a ride to Burlington so I can get a new computer. I got my stepdad to say I could put it on his credit card. And thanks, that's sort of your doing, too. Whatever lies you told them worked. I can pay for the computer, but I need to pick one out. Try out the keyboard and stuff. Really. You can say no. I just thought I'd ask. . . ."

Swenson says, "Well, it's not impossible. But I'm trying to write, and I'm a little overwhelmed by how much I've got to do."

"I'm sure. That's why I knew you'd say no."

"I'm not saying no," says Swenson. "But . . . don't you have friends who could drive you?"

"Nobody has a car. Some of them *used* to have cars, but they've been, like, grounded by their parents. I seem to know a lot of people who've been grounded by their parents."

Swenson rubs the webbing between his forefinger and thumb—an acupressure point Sherrie told him about, but he can't remember if the effect was supposed to be energizing or calming. "What about your boyfriend? Doesn't he have a car?"

"He's one of the ones who got grounded."

Swenson resists the urge to ask why. "It'd be a real shame to quit now when your writing's going so well. Okay. All right. I'll take you. When do you want to go?"

"Tomorrow," Angela says.

"Morning?" says Swenson. "How about ten?"

"That would be great. Oh, thank you thank you thank you. I live in Newfane. Third floor. Should I meet you outside my dorm?"

"See you then," Swenson says.

He sets down the phone for a moment, then dials Ruby's number. After two rings, an answering machine picks up. He doesn't even want to consider the possibility that he might have reached Ruby if he'd called her before Angela. A few oily bars of Kenny G. ooze out of the receiver, followed by a female voice, not Ruby's, saying, "You have reached the humble abode of Alison and Ruby." How unhappy he and Sherrie were to learn that after a year at school Ruby hadn't found anyone she wanted to room with and so had to pick her sophomore roommate through the housing lottery. Obviously, some loser Kenny G. fan.

Swenson says, "Ruby, it's Dad. Your father. Returning your call. Call me when you get in." He puts down the phone and waits meekly to be overcome with frustration and grief. But in fact he's quite cheerful. Everything will work out. Ruby's called. She's talking to them. She'll grow out of this phase. It's just a matter of patience, of time. Time will take care of them all.

S wenson hardly sleeps all night. Shouldn't he wake Sherrie and discuss his plans for the day? Couldn't he have brought it up earlier, at any point during the evening? Why didn't he feel like mentioning it? What does that imply? Is it wrong to drive a student to Computer City without telling your spouse? Or to spend all night twisting in your bed because you're getting to spend a morning with some sophomore in Beginning Fiction? Swenson moans with shame. What if he wakes Sherrie and has to explain that moan? He'll say he just remembered some department business. He never lies to Sherrie. Here's where the betrayal begins.

But there's no reason for Sherrie to know. Not that she's normally jealous. But Swenson hasn't forgotten the effect that Angela's name had on Magda. Even if Sherrie understands that he's simply doing a favor for a talented student, it's still ammunition to stockpile for future use. What does he *mean*, he doesn't have the time to pay the bills or empty the dishwasher? He's got the time to drive some kid sixty miles to Burlington. But it's not just any kid. Try telling Sherrie *that*. Isn't he allowed to drive to town without having to clear it with her? What does Sherrie think he does all day? And what does Sherrie do? Flirt with cute students who turn out not to have heart conditions?

Although he hasn't slept, he pretends to be slumbering soundly when Sherrie wakes and gets out of bed. He ignores the seductions of coffee and burrows into the covers until he hears her car pull out of the driveway. Then he wants to jump up and run out and confess what he's doing today, because if he *doesn't* tell Sherrie, the trip to Burlington will appear to *mean* something, especially if someone sees him with Angela and tells Sherrie, or if he and Angela die in a car wreck on the road and his death becomes some Jackson Pollock horror legacy for Sherrie to live with forever. He longs to chase after Sherrie and shout what he always says when she leaves: Drive slowly! Be careful! Ruby used to say that what he really meant was: Please don't die. But doesn't it seem . . . counterintuitive to run into the driveway half-naked and tell your wife that you love her and, by the way, you somehow forgot to mention that you're spending the day in Burlington with a female student? Why say that the student is a female? Because by that point Sherrie will ask.

With rare, adult self-control, Swenson resists the impulse. After a while he gets up and showers and lets the hot water needle him into steamy bliss. So he's unprepared for the shock of wiping the steam from the mirror and confronting the smeary face of an ugly old man: graying, blotchy, with thinning pasted-down hair, wattles under his chin, thick whiskers sprouting from black craterlike pores. He angles back the tip of his tongue. That filling is really loose. Oh, dear God. He used to be reasonably good-looking. He picks up a jar of Sherrie's face cream, studies the label, and shudders. He finds a pair of clean blue jeans, sucks in his belly, zips his fly, puts on a black T-shirt, his brown tweed jacket. That's it. He's not going to change clothes again. Not one more peek in the mirror.

It's only nine forty-five. He's early. He drives slowly. He's still early. Who are all these voyeurs, detectives, and spies cleverly disguised as teachers and students, all displaying an unnatural interest in Swenson, peering into his car, stopping conversations to watch him cruise by? He feels like a pederast trolling the schoolyard. What if someone sees him? Does he stop and wave? Hey, it's not a crime to give a student a ride.

At precisely five after ten, he swings past Angela's dorm, convinced she won't be there. She'll have overslept or forgotten. They'll have gotten their signals crossed. He'll call her or she'll call him. They'll straighten the whole thing out. After that he'll be off the hook. They won't have to reschedule.

His breath catches when he sees her sitting on the hood of a parked car. She's wearing her black leather jacket and a short black skirt. An expanse of shockingly white leg reaches down to the tops of her black engineer boots. Something's different. She's dyed her hair an unflattering hornet-colored blue-black. Swenson's touched to think she might have done it for the occasion. Kicking the side of the car with her heel, she's smoking and glowering at the street. She tenses when she sees his car and peers warily inside. When she sees that it's Swenson she grins instinctively, like a kid, a lapse for which she compensates by flicking her cigarette butt over the roof of his car.

"Good morning," Swenson says evenly. Get in the car, little girl.

Angela slides off the hood, causing her black pleated schoolgirl skirt to ruck up almost to her waist, revealing the same striped boxer shorts she wore last week on top of her jeans. The shorts slide a few inches down her bare hips. Swenson looks away.

Angela throws herself into the front seat, winging her head on the door frame.

"Jesus Christ." She rubs her head.

"Are you all right?" he says.

"I'm fine," she says. "I'm great. Actually. I didn't think you were coming."

"It's only five after ten."

"I didn't know what time it was. I just didn't think you'd come."

"Why would you think that?"

"You're a guy," Angela reminds him.

"Well, here I am. Guy or whatever. Where to? Computer City?"

"Go for it," says Angela. "Thank you. Really. I mean it."

Swenson guides the car gingerly along the college road rippled with speed bumps. He doesn't have to wait long for his bad luck to show up, driving a black sedan. From the opposite direction. Bump bump. With any luck, they'll pass each other in the middle of a speed bump, slowly enough for the other driver to get a good look at him transporting a minor off campus.

It's more than bad luck. Look who's been selected from the entire Euston community to be driving that black sedan. If it's not going to be Sherrie, then how about Lauren Healy? He can't ask Angela to scrunch down in the front seat. He gives Lauren a hearty wave. Hi there, they haven't seen each other since Swenson disgraced himself at the Benthams' dinner party. Lauren scrutinizes Angela as if to make sure that she's not a kidnap victim signaling for rescue, then peers curiously at Swenson and makes a small, stiff gesture halfway between a wave and salute. Swenson waves and drives on.

"Whew," says Angela. "That was close."

"Fasten your seatbelts," Swenson says. "We're in for a bumpy ride."

Angela doesn't get his Bette Davis imitation. Sherrie would. But so what? There are more important things than having seen the same movies. Angela fastens her seatbelt.

"Thank you," Swenson says.

Even with the heat on, it's chilly in the car. Still, Angela struggles out of her leather jacket. Swenson reaches over to help her, and the backs of his knuckles graze her neck. She twists out of the coat, sending his hand down the length of her arm, bare beneath the short sleeve of her black T-shirt. She flinches as if he's struck her.

"Ow." She turns to show him a bandage on her upper arm. "I got a tattoo. I'd let you see, but it's still sort of swollen and gross."

Poor kid, she'll be stuck with it now. He hopes someone used sterile needles. Where did she get it, anyhow? Certainly not on campus. She found a ride to get tattooed but not to buy a computer.

"A tattoo of what?" he asks.

"I wanted to surprise you. Actually, it's your name."

Swenson says, "You're joking, right?" Is she out of her mind? She could be mad and he wouldn't know. He doesn't know one thing about her. Happily, the road's empty enough so he can have his moment of panic without plowing into an oncoming car. Angela laughs. He notices she's not wearing any facial jewelry except for one ruby dot in the white plush of her earlobe.

"Joke," she says. "Only kidding. The truth is: It's an egg. A cracked egg with a little chicken peeping out. I made a vow to God that I'd put the image on my body if He helps me finish my novel."

Does Angela really believe in a God who so wants her to get tattooed that He'll ghostwrite her book? "I guess it's a good thing we're getting you a new computer. Otherwise you could wind up tattooed head to toe." This makes no sense, but Angela giggles obligingly. They ride past the weatherbeaten barns, the herds of shivering cows picking over the bare meadows, the isolated trailers coughing tarry smoke.

The silence seems unbreakable. Swenson's heart skips warningly. Has he drunk too much coffee? He hasn't had any coffee. *That* must be the problem. Maybe they'll stop at a diner. He likes the idea of ordering eggs and home fries while Angela flips through the tableside jukebox and the farmers at the counter watch the free entertainment.

Finally, he asks, "So how's your semester going?" How could they have regressed to this point since Angela's confession that she thinks about him all the time?

"Mostly terrible. Except for your class, obviously. But you already know that. The real hell is studio art. Last week we had this assignment to do clay sculptures of American icons? All the other kids did these total clichés—torches, eagles, flags—"

Angela's nervous delivery—a breathy, rattling staccato—makes Swenson oddly happy. Why should he be the only one who's anxious?

"I did a McDonald's Super Value Meal Number 7. It was cool, I got the Coke and the straw and the french fries and burger perfect. And that asshole, excuse me, Professor Linder got totally pissed. He said I was being irreverent and trying to annoy him."

What kind of art teacher is that? How superior Swenson feels. He *orders* his students to break the rules. He isn't threatened by their talent. He should call that moron Linder and ask him what he's doing, though really he should be thanking him for making Swenson look good. So Angela's taking creative writing and studio art? What are her parents buying with the long hours her stepfather—or father—spends counting pills and typing labels?

"Do you know what you're going to major in?" he asks. Another loser question. The line that failed to pick up girls at mixers when *he* was in college.

"I have till the end of this year to declare. I don't know. What do you think about me majoring in creative writing?"

"The obvious choice. Except for one little problem. There *is* no creative writing major." The subject's been debated for years at department meetings. The rest of the faculty—especially Bernie—has fought against it, partly as a way of letting him know what they really think of his so-called field of expertise. Swenson and Magda don't argue too hard. Why would they want the extra work of reading student-thesis novels?

"Oh," she says. "I thought there was. I thought they said that when I applied. Well, then, it doesn't matter. I'll pick the easiest subject so I have time to write. That's all I care about. I get up in the morning and if I can write that day, I'm in a good mood. I'm happy!"

Swenson remembers how that used to feel: the pleasure, the excitement of starting a day's work, the almost physical sensation of slipping into another world, into madness, really, imagining voices, one of those psychoses that deludes its victims into thinking the world makes sense.

Already they're passing the burned-out shell of the Wendover Country Inn and Tavern. In its former life, as a roadhouse, always more tavern than inn, it marked the halfway point between Euston and Burlington. As a child, Ruby knew to look for it on their drives into town. Now, still boarded up, years after a suspected arson, the rambling, roofless structure fills Swenson with dread. Is it the thought of Ruby or the fact that the trip is half over?

Angela crosses and uncrosses her legs. She says, "Writing is better than anything. I mean, even better than sex."

Swenson shoots her a quick look.

"Well, maybe not that," she says. Once again they fall silent.

"Do you know what kind of computer you want?"

"I don't care about speakers and graphics. Fancy video games. All I want is a big screen and lots of memory so I don't have to keep deleting stuff to put more of the novel on it. That's what happened with the last one."

Swenson says, "You used up all the memory?"

"I write a lot," Angela says.

Why isn't Swenson jealous? She's writing, and he isn't. Why? Because he's grateful to her for reminding him what this little field trip is about. Student writer and dedicated teacher working overtime.

They ride in companionable silence the rest of the way to Burlington until Swenson pulls into the wasteland of Computer City's huge lot.

"Are they open today?" asks Swenson.

"Why wouldn't they be?" she says.

The cavernous hangar of a store is nearly deserted except for a cluster of salespeople in Computer City kelly green, clustered near the service desk, a manager yelling at a guy wheeling a hand truck loaded with boxes, a few customers taking early lunch breaks to shop for home computers, two high school techies cutting class to check out the new equipment.

Swenson scurries after Angela, who's striding fiercely across the vast store. The salesmen stop what they're doing to take in the flash of white thigh, the keys on a heavy cord bouncing against one hip, the black socks sticking over the tops of the boots. And who do they think Swenson is? Some old lecher purchasing electronics for his young punk girlfriend? What fool would try to buy the affections of a girl who, you can tell from aisles away, is pure attitude and trouble? They probably think he's her father. Well, go ahead, let them. Swenson *could* be her father. He might as well allow himself the pleasure Ruby cheated him of when she took her high school computer to college rather than speak to him for as long as it would take to ask him to buy her a new one.

A salesman approaches Angela. By the time Swenson catches up, Angela and a young man whose name tag says *Govind* are deep in conversation. The Indian kid's acne-scarred, friendly face is rigid with embarrassment as he tries to shrink his tall, skinny frame down to Angela's size. He wants to be helpful, to do his job and not have to deal with the shortness of the customer's skirt, the white legs, the boots.

Aside from that, Angela's the ideal customer. She knows exactly what she wants. The whole transaction takes minutes. Govind figures out what she needs and only then looks at Swenson—Dad— for agreement and approval. Swenson nods. Of course. By all means. My daughter's got this together.

When Angela takes out her credit card, Swenson discreetly drops back and lets her collect herself as the salesman dashes off to get printer cables. Smart girl, she politely refuses the in-store service plan.

Govind smiles. "I have tried," he says.

"I'll swear to it," Angela says.

He passes her the credit slip. "Enjoy," he says.

He gives them directions to the drive-in pickup window, presses the receipts into Swenson's hand, and wishes Angela good luck.

"You're a prince," Angela tells him.

"It is only my job," he says, glowing with bashful pride.

Angela and Swenson leave the store far less quickly than they walked in, an almost postcoital languor dragging at their steps.

"That was easy," Angela says. "Everything should be so easy."

Swenson drives around to the side of the building. Like circus clowns, they both jump out at once. Angela grabs one of the smaller boxes, shoves it into the trunk. All these cartons can't possibly fit, but it's Swenson's job to try. He wills himself into a state of physical competence in which he can muster up the testosterone-linked ability to judge spatial relations. He hasn't forgotten that story about her damaged, wheezing dad. At last he's able to close the trunk. See! She needed him here. She may know her way around the brave new world of megaherz and RAM, but he's had to walk her through the simple old-fashioned geometry of squeezing bulky objects into a small cramped space.

"Well!" he says. "All rightee now! Should we get some lunch?"

"I don't think so," Angela says. "I'd be nervous to leave this stuff out in the car."

"This isn't exactly the South Bronx. It's Vermont, remember? You could leave it in the backseat with the door unlocked, and it would still be there when you came out."

"That would be asking for trouble," she says.

"Okay," says Swenson. "How about we drive partway back to Euston and stop at some country diner where we can watch the car from the window—"

"I'd rather not. I'd be too worried to eat. Maybe if you're hungry we could find a McDonald's or something with a drive-through window."

"I'm not that hungry." Swenson can't believe he's begging this skanky kid to have lunch with him after he's driven her sixty miles and wasted his whole day. Still . . . he's disappointed. He'd so clearly imagined the shocking warmth of the restaurant after the cold outside, the smell of coffee, the soothing aromas of meatloaf and mashed potatoes, the jukebox. He feels like a kid whose date has announced she wants to go home early.

"The sooner I get back the better," she says.

"I understand that." He can't help sounding annoyed, or tromping on the gas as he pulls out of the lot. Angela has to brace herself to keep from falling against him.

Swenson turns onto the cloverleaf that leads out of the business strip. The highway narrows into the potholed two-lane county route.

"Anyway," says Angela. "Listen. You could say no. But I was hoping you could help me carry this stuff into my dorm room. And help me set it up. I'll understand if you say no. I don't want to take up your day."

Swenson waits a beat. "I don't think I'd be any help setting up a computer. My wife had to put mine together. I was totally useless."

Idiot! Why mention Sherrie? What's he trying to communicate? Any normal male would take on the task of computer setup, whether he knew how or not.

"That's all right," says Angela. "I could probably set it up. You could just give me moral support."

"*That* I can do," says Swenson.

"I know that. That's what's so great about you. No one's ever taken the time to encourage me or help me."

Swenson says, "It is only my job." Was the Indian accent a mistake? Will Angela think his Govind imitation is racist? Or is it a sign of a shared history that's accruing minute by minute, uniting them, a common past that's already a source of private jokes?

But Angela seems to be thinking of something else entirely. "You know . . . if I get the computer working, I could print out those missing pages and give them to you before you leave."

And that's the last thing either of them says until they're almost back at Euston. As they drive through the college gate, Swenson feels depleted. He wishes he could drive back into the country and pull over to the side of the road and take a nap with his head in Angela's lap.

Angela's exaggerated sigh is so much the sound *he* wants to make that for one alarming moment he thinks he might have made it. She says, "I feel like I've been out on parole and now you're returning me to prison."

"It's not so bad," lies Swenson. But that's exactly how he feels.

"That's easy for you to say," she replies. "You've got a car. You can leave."

"Look . . . if you really need to get away, if there's anyplace you need to go, please, feel free to call me. . . . We could take a ride." He can no longer pretend that this is part of his job.

"Thanks. That's so unbelievably nice. You might want to watch those speed bumps, what with all that stuff in the trunk."

Swenson slows down, comforted by the thought of the computer—exonerating evidence. They had an errand to do, and they did it. He no longer cares if someone sees him driving back with Angela. He's innocent. They've completed their mission, and nothing improper happened.

"Remind me. Which dorm is yours? They all look the same. My wife and I were dorm parents in Dover. Prehistory. Obviously."

There he goes, invoking Sherrie again. She gets the point. He's married. Angela, he notices, doesn't mention *her* boyfriend. Why isn't *he* waiting to help her bring her computer upstairs, some big strong kid with wide-open, pumping coronary arteries.

"Newfane. One dump named after another." Euston students think their dorms are named after Vermont towns. No one tells them that the towns were named after Elijah Euston's friends. In its effort to seem like an inclusive, democratic institution, the college has been underplaying the fact that its founder and his pals once owned most of the state. "Turn right. That one over there."

But of course, he knew that. He picked her up there this morning. He parks in front of her dorm. "Are gentleman callers permitted at this hour?"

"Are you kidding? It's a coed dorm. It's been, like, a trillion years since they had rules about visiting hours. Guys can come in anytime. Anyhow, you're a professor. You can do anything you want."

"Given the current climate," Swenson says, "that makes me all the more suspect."

"What do you mean?" says Angela.

"Forget it," Swenson says.

Angela gets out of the car. "Hey, maybe you should stay with the car. You could sit here and make sure nothing gets taken. I can carry the boxes up."

"I'd feel weird just sitting here with you busy working." He'd feel weirder if someone came by and saw him sitting in a parked car outside a student dorm. "No one's going to break into a locked trunk on campus."

"I guess you're right," concedes Angela. "But let's be careful, okay?"

Swenson goes around and unlocks the trunk. They each take one carton. Angela heads for the front door, and he hurries after, hugging the monitor box.

It's been ages since he's been inside a dorm. Ruby's dorm is more like a dilapidated housing project. The only time he saw it was when they moved her a year ago August, at the start of the semester, when every dorm has a ghostly, theoretical quality.

Now, as he enters the foyer—a soda machine, a bulletin board, bare but for a list of fire regulations—he's assaulted by the smell of sneakers, sweat, sports equipment. How can these kids stand being greeted, every time they come home, by this oppressive fruity rottenness, this edge of saline decay? Which only shows how far he is from their age. To them, this is the smell of life itself. The aromas he prefers—garlic, roasting chicken, wine, apple pie, flowers from Sherrie's garden—reek to them of parents and airless stifling boredom. Evenings trapped at home, away from their friends. The stench of living death.

They climb a flight of stairs, up past a deserted TV lounge furnished with a Ping-Pong table and a few grimy armchairs apparently chosen for the undiluted purity of their institutional ugliness. There's not one touch of hominess, not one poster on the wall, no sign that humans spend time here.

Swenson's still sprinting after Angela as they take off down the hall, rushing past doorways into which he can't help peeking. What if he meets one of his students, Makeesha or Jonelle or Claris?

At last Angela reaches her door and fishes for the keys on the leather cord hanging from her waist. On the door is a poster: a black-and-white photo of a Hell's Angel with long hair, a Nazi helmet, a beard, his thatched chest crisscrossed by menacing chains.

"Friend of yours?" says Swenson.

"Avedon," says Angela. "Isn't it terrific? It's like having a Beware of the Dog sign. Only not nearly so corny."

Swenson follows Angela into her room and stops, frozen by the hundreds of faces staring back at him. Every inch of wall—except for a few mirrors glittering among the photos—is covered with postcards of actors, writers, saints, musicians, artists. At first the order seems random, but after a moment he notices the patterns, grouped by theme (Janis, Jimi, Jim, Kurt Cobain) or by era (Buster Keaton next to Charlie Chaplin and Lilian Gish). The elderly Picasso facing the equally rakish, equally bald Jean Genet. Chekhov and Tolstoy, Colette, Virginia Woolf, and . . . is that Katherine Mansfield?

Across the room is a single bed, narrow as a monk's, covered with a monastic brown cloth. Running the length of one wall is a white formica desk, on which Angela sets down her box and motions for Swenson to do likewise.

"This isn't a room," says Swenson. "It's an . . . installation."

"Like it?" says Angela proudly. "Everyone else thinks it's a mess. Another reason so many chicks on the hall think I'm totally insane. They've all got, like, the one perfect poster of Brad Pitt over the bed. And you should see Makeesha's room. It's all done up with Black Panther shit, posters and rasta flags, and this huge blow-up poster of Snoop Doggy Dog. The thing is, everybody knows Makeesha's dad teaches at Dartmouth. They're way richer than my parents."

"Now now."

Swenson might *look* like a drooling lecher skulking around some nymphet's room, but in fact he's a consummate professional who never forgets his position, or the inappropriateness of joking with one student about another, even about another's interior decor.

"Where's your old computer?" he says.

"This is sort of retarded," Angela admits. "I got so mad when it ate my work I threw it out the window. That's how I knew it couldn't be fixed. The creepy part was that right after I did it I remembered seeing some terrible movie where Jane Fonda played a writer who throws her typewriter out the window. I couldn't believe I'd done it."

"Oh, I saw that movie. What was it? I can't remember."

"I don't know," says Angela. "Let's go get the rest of the stuff."

So they've got another gauntlet to run, or rather, the same one again. Swenson's luck can't possibly hold. This time he'll meet *all* his students, gathered to watch their professor race after Angela Argo.

They hurry back outside. Angela's still worried that her equipment might get filched from the locked trunk of Swenson's car. He's touched by how deeply, how passionately she wants that machine. No wonder her parents were willing to fork over the money. If Ruby wanted *anything* that badly.... He takes the box that contains the minitower. She grabs the bag of cables. Okay, this is the final trip. After this, they're done.

Angela opens doors for him and walks slightly ahead. In the room, she clears space for him to set the box on the desk.

"Let me help you unpack it," he says. "Got a knife? Sharp scissors?"

"Try this." Angela produces a bush knife from her purse. "Don't look so alarmed. I hitchhike. A girl can't be too careful."

"You shouldn't be hitching," Swenson says. "You could wind up like those girls that hunters find a couple of seasons after the serial killer picked them up."

He can't conceal his horror at the thought of something happening to her. Meanwhile he's aware of the irony of having these tender protective feelings while watching her slash heavy cardboard with a hunting knife. And really, for such a frail creature, she's got remarkable upper body strength, holding the boxes while Swenson wrestles the monitor and console loose from their Styrofoam liners.

"Okay," he says. "Okay. Okay. Is there a manual or something...?"

"Look," says Angela. "Do me a favor. Sit down on that bed over there and, like I said, just be there if I need moral support, if I start freaking out...."

Swenson laughs. "How can you tell I have no idea what I'm doing?"

"By how many times you just said *okay*."

Swenson does as he's told. He perches on the edge of the bed, then scoots his back against the wall with his feet sticking out before him. Angela's too busy to notice. She's hooking up power cords, finding parallel ports, shaking the toner cartridge, attaching the mouse, and massaging it around its brand-new pad.

The computer's behaving obediently. At each juncture Angela waits, tense. When the proper light blinks on or something begins to whir, she puts up her thumbs and says, "Yessss."

How fond Swenson is of this gifted, awkward girl! It's not just that he covets her youth, her talent, her good teeth, whatever she has that he's lost. It's genuine affection. At the same time he's acutely aware that he's sitting on her bed. Once more a drowsiness overcomes him, as it did in the car outside. He looks longingly at Angela's pillow. Perhaps he could just nod off.

Angela says, "I can't believe how well this is going. Setting up my old computer was total hell. It's like you're . . . lucky for me."

"I hope so," Swenson says.

"Yessss!" hisses Angela. "Yes yes yes. I think we've got it up and running. Let me try printing that last chapter."

Angela pops a disk into the floppy drive, skates the mouse, and clicks. The first five pages the printer spits out are bare but for a diagonal black stripe. Then the machines stops printing, and an error light flashes.

"Sonofabitch!" She flips the switch on and off. For a moment there's a hopeful whir, and then a daunting crunch sounds from deep inside the machine. The paper jam light blinks.

"I think the paper's stuck," says Swenson.

"Duh," says Angela, wheeling on him.

Wait a minute! Swenson's not her *friend,* not her father or stepfather or boyfriend, some random useless male she can talk to like that. He happens to be her teacher, her creative writing professor. He's doing her a favor way beyond his job description.

"I'm sorry," she says. "Please don't be mad. This shit drives me so crazy. I so wanted to get you those pages so you could take them with you. It meant so much to me, and now. . . ."

"That's okay. Try it one more time."

Angela shrugs and clicks on PRINT. The printer starts. The paper jams. She bursts into tears. Swenson gets up and crosses the room and puts his hand on her shoulder. Angela reaches back and covers his hand with hers. Swenson has an out-of-body moment, watching their fingers intertwine, as if his hand were an arachnid or sea creature with a life of its own.

It's not as if he doesn't know that one thing will lead to another, that his leaving his hand on her shoulder will lead to his sliding it up her neck to the base of her hair, to his running his hand through the soft down on the back of her neck. It's not as if he doesn't know that he is reaching down her T-shirt, down the smooth expanse of her back, and that, still sitting at her desk chair, she is arching her back against him. It's not as if he doesn't know that if he stays there and doesn't move away, Angela will stand and turn around and they'll be in each other's arms. He knows it, and he doesn't know it, just as he has and hasn't known all along that every word they spoke, every gesture they made was leading to this. Still, he manages to be surprised, and he watches, as if from a distance, as he kisses Angela Argo.

After a while, Angela pulls back. She says, "Are you sure you want to do this?"

He *is* sure, but only so long as he doesn't have to say so, which would mean it was really happening—with his full knowledge and participation. He could be one of those unfortunate girls who manage to get pregnant while convincing themselves they're not really having sex. Isn't *he* supposed to be the one asking Angela's permission? Swenson can't let himself think about that, he's got too much on his mind: for example, the challenge of moving, while still kissing Angela, across the room to her bed, navigating the obstacle course of discarded computer boxes.

Luckily, Angela's walking smoothly backward, guided by some sort of sonar. All he has to do is follow. How can this be the same person who's always tripping and flopping about, trying to get comfortable? She's in her element, Swenson thinks, a fish returned to water. She pulls him across the room, steers him round, pushes him down on the bed. There's no resisting, no evading her gaze. It's like being charmed by a snake, not a king cobra, obviously, but a tough little adder, weaving slightly, holding him in her unblinking stare. Isn't it the snake who gets charmed? Why can't Swenson think straight? Why? Because Angela seems to be taking off her clothes, crossing her arms before her and pulling her black T-shirt over her head. How budlike and perfect her breasts are. The nipples stand up from the chill.

She peels her miniskirt down over her boots and steps out of it, leaving it on the floor. She's wearing a lacy black thong. Is this what young women routinely wear to go shopping for a computer? Could Angela have planned this? She'd left off the lip rings and any of the facial jewelry that might have made kissing a problem. Well, it's not as if *he* didn't dress with special care this morning.

She's naked except for the leather boots. It's unbelievably sexy. And yet . . . how thin she is. Her body's so different from Sherrie's, about whom he should not be thinking as he sits here with an erection so big that Angela can see it through his jeans.

"Cool," she says admiringly, and comes over and straddles his thighs, facing him. For an instant Swenson catches what looks like fear in her eyes. Then she refocuses on his belt buckle, by which she's stumped for a moment until she figures it out and unbuckles it with a dreamy, sly abstraction. Abruptly, she slides off him, then sits down next to him and, leaning forward, yanks off her boots. Swenson slides one hand along the delicate bumps of her spine while, with the other, he struggles with his jeans and shorts.

When Angela has her boots off, he reaches for her again, but she motions for him to lie back on the bed and fumbles in the nightstand, from which she produces a little foil packet. It's been so long since he's used one—Sherrie's had a diaphragm for years since she went off the pill—that for one confused instant he thinks it's a tea bag. Well, it's a condom, all right. That's sex in the nineties, and a good thing for them both that Angela's careful. Not that she has much to worry about from Swenson. But who knows what *she's* been up to? Who was that boy who answered the phone? Swenson's the one at risk. It's a sobering thought, but not grim enough to make him lose his hard-on, which seems to be responding positively to the intimidating fact of how nearby Angela keeps her condoms. Isn't this how girls used to feel when Swenson was in high school, and, in the midst of the spontaneous passionate necking, their boyfriend turned out to have brought along a coolly premeditated rubber?

Angela gives him the packet, which he unwraps, mildly worried lest condoms have changed. What if he no longer knows how to use one? His high school years come back to him. It's like riding a bicycle. He slips it on, leaving room, and rolls back the rest.

Once more he feels the way the woman's supposed to as Angela lowers herself onto him and he thinks, What about foreplay? But it's only for a split second, until the pleasure takes over, the warmth pulsing up from his groin. For once he isn't thinking as he turns her over, and her legs fall open. He braces himself on his arms, then lets his chest sink against hers, feeling his chest against her breasts, her thighs pushing to get closer. And now his face is against her face, his chin against her cheek. . . .

There's an explosion inside his head. A crack, a crunch, and then a grinding, like stone turning to powder. It takes him a while to realize what's happened.

"What was *that*?" asks Angela. "I heard it through my skull."

"Nothing," says Swenson. "I broke a tooth."

That molar that's been going for months has chosen this moment to self-destruct. He hadn't realized he was gritting his teeth. This is dreadful! Unfair! At the moment he's been longing for and denying he wanted, when at last he gets what he hasn't dared to dream, he cracks a tooth. How middle-aged, how pathetic to be unmasked as a geriatric case with emergency dental problems! Still connected to Angela, Swenson moves his tongue to the back of his mouth and probes the jagged ruin.

"I lost a filling," he says.

"That's not all you lost," says Angela.

His hard-on's gone. Gone for good. He rolls onto his side. He looks down at Angela as desire drains from her face, ironing flat her expression. She blinks, then smiles uncertainly.

"Bummer," she says. "Does it hurt?"

"Only my vanity," he says. "My vanity's mortally wounded." It's important not to let her know how wretched he feels. And the fact that he can't tell her fills him with a loneliness so excruciating that tears pool in his eyes. He knows it's partly hormonal, the chemistry of frustration. Still, he's cogent enough to wonder what he's doing here naked with this child, this stranger. He should be with Sherrie, whom he knows like his own skin. What will he tell Sherrie about how he broke his tooth? Sherrie's sympathy will make his torment more exquisite—and more deserved. He wants to howl at his own stupidity, at this toxic cocktail of lust and self-deception that he's been consuming in sips so tiny that he could convince himself he wasn't drinking.

Meanwhile all he really wants is to stay pressed against Angela Argo. But now she's sitting cross-legged on the bed, against the wall. Swenson pulls his legs over to make room. In their neutral asexual ease, they could be two dorm pals gathered to do their nails and gossip. The fact that they're both naked makes surprisingly little difference. He looks disconsolately across the room, and his gaze is drawn to the mournful: Bert Lahr, Harold Lloyd, Buster Keaton. What's Chaplin got to look gloomy about? He slept with harems of women!

"I'm sorry about your tooth," Angela says. "But you know it's no big deal about the sex. I mean lots of weird stuff goes on. You know what happened to me once? I had an epileptic fit right in the middle of sex. A lucky thing it's *petit mal*. The guy really would have been grossed out if I'd started twitching and foaming. But I just spaced out and, like, disappeared."

How sweet of Angela to offer this confession of a sexual gaffe even worse than cracking a filling. On the other hand . . . what if Angela had had a fit while she was with *him*? Whom would he have notified? How would he have explained it?

"I didn't know you were epileptic," he says.

"I'm on medication," she says. "I'm fine."

"Like Dostoyevsky. Except that he wasn't fine. . . ." Swenson hears noises outside the door. He's naked in a girl's dorm room. He doesn't even know her. She could be a lunatic who's lured him here just to blow the whistle on him and make him lose his job.

"Does that door lock?" he asks.

"Yeah," says Angela. "I locked it. When we first walked in."

So she engineered this. But what is Swenson turning into? Another Adam blaming Eve for making him eat the apple? He knew better. It was his idea, too. He's the adult, the teacher. It was his doing as much as hers. A fine time to develop a consciousness, or, for that matter, a conscience. After he's already tried—and failed—to sleep with his most vulnerable student. Or was it his doing, really? Swenson has to wonder. What does it mean that she's writing a book about a teacher-student affair? Is this research for the next scene?

She scrambles toward him, monkeylike, and tenderly—or is it pityingly?—ruffles his hair. Her nipples brush against his face. He takes one in his mouth, from which she gently extricates it with a gesture so instinctive, so sure, that Swenson thinks—God help him—of how Sherrie used to reclaim her breast after Ruby fell asleep nursing.

As he dresses, Angela, still naked, goes back to the computer. She says, "Let's try it again." It takes him a moment to realize she means the printer, not sex. "Maybe we worked magic," she says, and now she *does* mean sex.

He watches her lithe, agile body. Her unselfconscious beauty. She double-clicks the mouse. The printer purrs. One by one, three pages drift onto her desk.

"Bingo," she says. "We shook it loose. We did do some kind of voodoo." She waits until he's fully dressed, then hands the pages to him.

"End of chapter," she says.

"Excellent," Swenson says, uncertainly. "I'll read it as soon as I can." The promise feels extracted—the price he's paid for sex. But wait! He *likes* Angela's novel. He wasn't faking enthusiasm just to trick Angela into bed. In fact it's quite the reverse. He began to like Angela *because* he liked her novel. And he should have kept it that way and not let himself blur the distinction between literary enthusiasm and sexual attraction. But it's not a catastrophe, only a misunderstanding. . . . He pauses, then can't keep from saying, "You know we can't tell anyone. It would be a giant scandal." Well, it's certainly going to be a challenge to keep on conducting the workshop as if none of this had happened.

"Right," says Angela. "Sure. I'm *really* going to tell everyone. I *really* want us both to get kicked out of Euston. Besides, I don't want my boyfriend to know."

Right. The boyfriend. Chances are *his* teeth don't crack in the middle of sex.

"It never happened," Angela says. "Later, you know . . . we could . . ."

"I'd like that," says Swenson, though he's not quite sure what she means. This is no time to figure it out. It's time get out of her dorm before he ruins his life completely.

"I'll call you when I read these." It's what he's always said. So maybe Angela's right, after all. They can go on the same as before.

"I'll be waiting," Angela says. But it's not the same. For starters, she's never before come over to him stark naked and, rolling her eyes—all irony—shook his hand.

"Bye," she says, and, without bothering to dress, returns to her computer.

Swenson stumbles into the hall without checking to see if it's empty. Luck, it seems, is still on his side, the fate that looks out for lovers, if that's what he and Angela are. Well, they're no longer just teacher and student. Something irrevocable's happened. His life will be changed after this—to say nothing of writing class. He turns into the stairwell and nearly runs into Claris.

"Hi, Claris," says Swenson.

"Hi, Professor Swenson," Claris says.

He can't even attempt the breezy explanation of how he came to help Angela with her computer. He can't bring himself to say Angela's name, partly because he's sure that Claris is already thinking Angela's name, that somehow she knows what just happened. She can read it on his face.

"Well," says Swenson. "See you in class."

"See you," Claris says, watching him lope unsteadily downstairs.

Swenson checks the mailbox. Nothing. Well, not *nothing*, exactly. A brown envelope of coupons that will languish on the kitchen counter where he and Sherrie will eye it, guilty for being too lazy to practice these small domestic economies, until one of them gets sick of looking at it and tosses it in the trash. He thinks of Len Currie, facing his stack of unanswered invitations to glamorous parties, to literary conferences in Tuscan villas and Sonoma vineyards.

The contrast between Len's undeserved popularity and his own undeserved exile generates a vapor of discontent and irritation that, for want of another solid object, collects around Sherrie, who's done nothing to deserve it short of having the bad luck to be sitting in the kitchen, leafing through a cookbook, no doubt seeking something soothing to prepare at the end of a long day he's spent cheating on her—or trying to—with a student.

Sherrie must have had a tough day, too. It's *The Cooking of Sicily*, roots she tends to return to when things are a trifle rocky. The cuisine of a culture in which a wronged wife's male relations are the vigilante marriage counselors practicing kidnap-murder therapy.

"What do we want?" asks Sherrie, without looking up from the book.

"A million bucks. A new life. Roll back the clock twenty years—"

"For dinner?" says Sherrie, impatiently.

"Oatmeal," Swenson says.

"Excuse me?" says Sherrie.

"I broke a tooth today." Swenson probes the jagged edge with his tongue. He's got to go to the dentist. What if he needs a root canal? What if he's exposed a nerve? Wouldn't he know that already?

Sherrie winces. "Oooh. How did you do that?"

"On an olive pit," says Swenson.

"Where did you get an olive?" says Sherrie. "An olive's way exotic for the Euston Commons."

Is that all the sympathy Swenson's going to get? The wince, the little moan. And now we're onto the olive. The worst student malingerers must get a few more seconds than that.

Anyway . . . Swenson hadn't given much thought to the nonexistent olive. He waits a beat, then watches the liar inside him get busy. "Well, it was the strangest thing. I got this craving . . . for olives. I went to the MinuteMart and bought a jar of olives and ate the whole jar, and you know how you save the pits in the corner of your mouth? And then forget they're there? Crunch."

It's pure adrenaline talking, but fine, whatever works. Often the most effective lies are the most unlikely.

"Are you pregnant?" Sherrie asks.

"What?" says Swenson. "What?"

"Weird food cravings. Ted? For a second it looked like you were scared you might be pregnant."

"It's not a joke, Sherrie. Breaking a tooth. When you're twenty-two, you think everything can be replaced. At forty-seven, you know better."

"I'm sorry," says Sherrie. "You should have come to the clinic. We could have fixed you up." Sherrie's flirting with him in that reflexive, unserious, conjugal way.

"I guess it didn't occur to me." Swenson seems to have lost the reflex.

"Does it hurt?"

"Only psychically. But let's not do the big juicy steak dinner tonight?"

"When's the last time we ate steak? Listen, I've got an idea. Chicken soup with pastina and egg and spinach and cheese.

Soothing and warm. No chewing. Baby food. I think I've got some chicken broth put away in the freezer."

Chicken soup! The adulterer's wife cooks him chicken soup. You couldn't get away with writing a scene so obvious and corny, a scene in which the cheating hero simultaneously wallows in guilt and luxuriates in uxorious admiration. How confidently Sherrie raps the eggs on the side of the bowl and pries apart the shells, letting the contents slide out with a satisfying plop. Obviously, he can't help thinking of Angela's novel.

He has done a dreadful thing that he can never undo. Not just morally wrong, but stupid. How could he have betrayed this graceful woman, who makes chicken soup with spinach and egg and cheese for her wounded husband? And it's not just a matter of culinary skills, but of beauty and soul. He's married to Florence Nightingale and Anna Magnani rolled into one.

What was it that distracted him? A self-involved, wounded baby bird who knows her way around a computer, a neurotic child writing an overwrought, precious little romance about a teenage girl and her sleazeball teacher? For that he's wrecked a tooth, and he'll be very fortunate if he hasn't totaled his marriage.

Now is when he figures out how easily—how inevitably—all this could blow up in his face. Angela could tell someone. It would be odd if she didn't. Sherrie will find out, the college will know, and that's the end of life as he knows it. *Now* is when he thinks about that, in the kitchen with his wife. Certainly not this afternoon, when he wasn't thinking.

He sits at the kitchen table and opens the two-day-old *New York Times*, which has come in today's mail. The front-page photo shows an Afghani with a rifle shooting a teenage boy at close range. Swenson skims the article, about the revival of Islamic justice and the cultural emphasis on revenge. The Sicilian uncles again. Swenson doesn't need this. He's got his own molar to dole out primitive justice. The newspaper shots of his father's death pop into his head. Flames, a cone of incense, tendrils of black smoke. . . .

All at once, he feels what he felt then, that intensity of longing to travel back in time and reconfigure the future. He couldn't have saved his father. But he could have stopped himself from trying to sleep with Angela Argo. Glancing around the kitchen, he can hardly bear to see Sherrie's Fiestaware pitchers, the cat clock with the moving eyes, the folk art whirligig of the mother feeding her babies. He feels as if his house has burned down, been swept away by floods. He thinks of Emily in *Our Town*, Bill in *Carousel*, the Jimmy Stewart character in *It's a Wonderful Life*. He's died, and an angel is showing him how smoothly life goes on without him.

He's lost it all, lost everything, and Sherrie, blissfully unaware—for now—grates Parmesan cheese and chops spinach. How much he has sacrificed for a kid with a scabby tattoo oozing under a Band-Aid. But why can't he lighten up? Guys used to do this on a daily basis and never think twice about it.

Swenson says, "When's dinner?"

"Anytime," Sherrie says. "Ten minutes. Whenever."

"I need to jot down some notes. Something I thought of today."

"For the novel?" Sherrie says hopefully.

"Yeah, right," he says. "The novel."

"Gee. Sorry I mentioned it. Let me know when you want to eat."

"Fifteen minutes." Swenson nearly runs from the kitchen because he can no longer sit there and talk about olive pits and when he wants his soup.

He needs to call Angela. He wants to know what she's thinking. He owes her a phone call—some gesture of care and concern. Isn't that what women want? He remembers a passage in an Isak Dinesen story, about how, in sex, the woman plays the part of the host and the man plays the part of the guest. The man wants what a guest wants: to make a good impression, to enjoy himself, to be amused. And what does the hostess want? The hostess wants to be thanked. Fine, but what precisely does he have to thank Angela for? Thanks for the chance to destroy my marriage and my career?

Anyway, he can't call. How would that little chat go? Oh, hi, Angela. I was just wondering . . . how's the new computer working? He used to be able to phone her, but now everything's been deformed, twisted into coils of discomfort and innuendo. Simple communication is no longer an option. Maybe it never was. Maybe he and Angela have never had a straightforward conversation. He might as well admit that now. Some element of flirtation or attraction was present from the start. Meanwhile, it seems, he's the kind of guy who can have no idea what's going on until after it's happened.

The only excuse to call her is that he's read her new pages. That's what their relationship's really about. Sex was just a distraction. That's why she'll make it easy for him, why she'll set the tone of their conversation so they won't have to deal with what happened this afternoon. Perhaps they'll never mention it. It will never happen again.

As always, he's eager to read Angela's work. Though now, for the first time, doubt creeps in. Is he merely looking for a reason to call her? No! He admires her writing and genuinely wants to know whether the heroine will sleep with her music teacher.

Swenson puts his head in his hands. I'm losing it, he thinks.

He rips apart his study looking for Angela's envelope. He must have left it in the car. Understandably, he was a mite confused—a first-time semiadulterer in the midst of a dental crisis.

It's perfectly normal for someone to go outside and get something from his car. Even so, he's glad he can use the side door without having to go through the kitchen. Outside, the icy mist carries a sharp edge of leaf rot. He turns to look back at the house. Lit up. Welcoming. Bright.

The pages are on the car seat, exactly where he left them.

Sneaking back inside, he goes to his study and begins from the top of the page, rereading the part he read before and this time reading straight through.

> Wood shavings had clung to the clarinet and gotten into my hair. He reached out and brushed them off. He said, "Why so sad?"
>
> I told him I'd ruined my science project. None of the eggs had hatched. For a moment he seemed puzzled.
>
> Then he said, "Why don't I come over and take a look at the incubation system? Figure out what's wrong. I grew up on a farm. I know about these things."

*I said, "Oh, please don't. You don't have to." But that was what I
wanted. It was the only reason I'd tried to hatch the eggs.*

Did I give him directions to my house? I must have. I can't remember.
*All that day and the next, I thought about him all the time, eating
breakfast, driving to work.*
*That night, someone knocked on the door. It was Mr. Reynaud.
Standing there, smiling but serious. Just as I'd imagined. Somehow
that made me less nervous, as if it had happened before. Still my
heart was beating so hard I thought I would literally die.*

Swenson finds his blue pencil and circles *literally die* and writes
"cut 'literally'" in the margin. What in God's name is he doing?

*Mr. Reynaud's face looked confident, pleased, but also apologetic. As
if I might be angry. I wasn't angry. I couldn't speak. I stepped aside. The
incubators hummed. The shed was warm and dark except for the blood-
red light. I helped him take off his jacket. He picked up one of the eggs.*
*"Come here," he said. I went and stood behind him and leaned my
stomach against his back, and he slowly turned toward me, still
holding the egg. He took my hand with his free hand and closed my
fingers around his hand, the one that held the egg. He pressed until
the egg cracked. The slimy sticky yolk and white slipped over our
intertwined fingers, and, as he rubbed his hand against mine, the egg
stuck us together. My fingers slid against his fingers until our hands
were joined and I no longer knew which fingers were whose.*
*I'd imagined him looking at me in the pulsing red light, but not
that he would go on staring, keeping my eyes locked on his as he
released my hand and reached down and opened his pants. Then he
took my hand again, still slippery from the egg, and wrapped it
around his penis. I assumed it was his penis. I'd never felt one before.
His was smooth and already hard, and he rubbed my hand along it,
closing my fingers around it, just as he'd closed them over the egg.
Actually, it felt sort of nice, velvety and warm. And also, sort of disgusting—rubbing egg on some guy's penis!*

He pushed me back against the wall and began to kiss me. His tongue squirmed in my mouth. His spit tasted like an old person's food. Liver and onions, fried fish. I choked down his bubbly saliva. I thought, This guy is my father's age. His stomach pillowed into me. His whiskers scratched my face. He was a whole other species than the smooth boys I'd kissed in school. Maybe he knew I was thinking that, because he got rougher, angrier, and he picked my skirt up and pushed down my tights, and pushed himself hard inside me, and now it didn't feel smooth at all, but sandpapery and rough. I began to cry because it hurt, and it was so unromantic to think that there was raw egg on his penis inside me.

At the same time I felt happy because he wanted me, wanted this so much he had risked everything to get it. My parents were across the yard. Our school loomed somewhere in the dark. And I was bigger than any of it. I alone had the power to make a grown man risk everything to do what we were doing in the warm light of the shed, with the trays of eggs humming around us.

Swenson puts down the manuscript, determined to have—for one second of grace—a purely literary response. Well, sex scenes aren't easy, and this one's pretty good . . . the detail of the cracked egg, for example. What were the lines he liked? *I assumed it was his penis. I'd never felt one before.* Swenson writes "good" in the margin.

Suddenly, he's gasping for air. What is this about? Where's his sense of humor? His distance? His perspective? Well, at least the poor music teacher didn't crack a tooth. The poor teacher? The guy's a pervert. But at least a successful one.

Swenson takes a deep breath, counts backward from ten. Angela doesn't mean him. She likes him. Loves him, maybe. She knows he's nothing—nothing—like that disgusting creep in her novel. She wrote it before they had sex, or whatever it was they had. It was on the computer when she got up from bed. All she did was print out what was already there.

So what? Who cares if life copies art, or if life imitates art?

Swenson does. He cares a lot. He'd rather that teacher not be him.

No one said it would be easy, teaching a class five days after you've slept with one of your students. It's a good thing Swenson's made such a production of his miniblackouts. Because now that he's sustained real harm, the class is cutting him some slack, a moment in which to collect himself and attempt to stop ping-ponging back and forth between the image of *that* Angela, naked except for her boots, and *this* Angela, across the seminar table, fully armored—rings, bracelets, spiked collar, the works. She seems to have reverted to an earlier, more ferretlike incarnation. Twitching, sighing, she alerts the class to her presence without anyone having to look at her, which is fine. Swenson can't look at her, nor can he look at Claris, which considerably narrows his visual range.

Meanwhile he's facing a session that under normal circumstances would test his pedagogical, diplomatic, and psychiatric skills. Today's ordeal is a discussion of Meg Ferguson's story about a man whose girlfriend leaves him after he (Meg's word) *batters* her, and the man takes revenge by kidnapping the woman's beloved cat, Mittens, taking Mittens to Manhattan, and dropping her out a thirtieth-story window. Everything in the story is maddening and false: The thin, implausible characters, the idiot-simple morality, the dishonest, judgmental cant masquerading as narration. It's what Swenson hates most about certain student work. This ideological junk is what some of his colleagues would write if they could. The ferocity of his distaste scares him into silence.

At least the chicken in Danny's piece was already dead. At least that was about love of a sort, not male brutality, vengeance, and murder, though maybe it was male brutality. The kid wasn't making love to the chicken, he was raping it, just as the music teacher rapes the girl in Angela's novel, just as the father rapes the daughter in her phone-sex poems. That's all sex is to these kids. Rape and abuse and incest. Magda told him, and Magda was right. Why didn't Swenson listen?

Luckily, the others are so busy mulling over Meg's story that they hardly notice Swenson drowning. Even Jonelle and Makeesha, who share Meg's disapproval of human nature in general and male sexuality in particular, must have been awed by the moment when the villain wishes that his girlfriend would come along and find Mittens splattered on the sidewalk. Danny and Carlos look at Swenson, as if they're hoping he'll tell them what to do if they don't want to wind up like Mittens.

Swenson's own anxiety is so multilayered, so sticky, he barely hears Makeesha saying she knows where the story's coming from, she knows there are dudes who would do that. She just wasn't convinced that *this* dude would do that. Carlos says it's total bullshit, he knows lots of funky bad dudes, but nobody does shit like that. This abstract philosophical conversation about whether or not a dude would do that goes on for a long time. Spared from literary scrutiny, Meg nods smugly, enragingly. She knows dudes would do that.

Swenson's left his body. He's floating above the table at which Claris is saying that it doesn't matter whether or not *someone* would do something like that, what matters is whether Meg has made them believe that the guy in her story did it. Even Claris is frightened of Meg. She's not saying whether *she* believes it or not. Though otherwise Claris seems normal—that is, not as if she's brooding about the fact that she's seen her professor in a classmate's dorm.

Suddenly they're startled by a sound so loud that Swenson thinks it's the bells, then realizes it's the hollow boom of Angela hitting her spiked wristband against the seminar table.

"Meg," says Angela, "let me ask you something. That guy in your story—what does he do for a living?"

"I don't know," says Meg, warily. "I mean. Wait. He's a contractor. That's right."

"Is that in the story?" Angela asks.

"No," admits Meg. "Not yet. I mean, maybe it was, and then I took it out.

The whole class is transfixed by the spectacle of Angela going after Meg. Who would have predicted that the feisty, righteously aggrieved Meg would be so easily routed?

"It's not in the story. Because the *guy's* not in the story, *nothing's* in the story except your stupid ideas about how men are disgusting pigs. We don't believe this guy for a second, not one thing he says or does, certainly not his taking the cat to the top of the building. Have you ever traveled with a cat?"

This is precisely the sort of thing Swenson's promised not to allow—this prosecutorial lunge for the throat, this reckless bloodletting. He should be wading into the fray, yanking back on Angela's leash, rescuing poor Meg, but he can only watch, mesmerized, as Angela says exactly what needs to be said. How relieved he is—for obvious personal reasons—to hear her say that men are not disgusting pigs. Meg answers each of her questions with a slight, almost involuntary nod of appeasement and supplication.

"Did you bother working that out, Meg? Or were you too busy thinking up some vicious thing for this asshole to do? A guy like that might kill a cat, but he'd stay in the neighborhood. Most likely he'd be nicer to the cat than he was to the woman."

The room's dead silent. No one blinks. Why can't the bells ring at the right moment, for once, and save them from this silence?

Finally Swenson says, "Well, I guess Angela didn't much like Meg's story."

Heh heh. After a beat, the others laugh.

Another silence. Then Claris says, "I agree with a lot of what Angela . . . but . . . I've got something to say. I'm sorry, Professor Swenson, but I think it's unfair that Angela gets to shoot her mouth off about everybody else's stuff, but we never talk about *her* work, so it's really safe for her, she doesn't have to play by the same rules we do."

Swenson must have been insane to think he'd get away with their encounter in the hall of Angela's dorm.

Carlos says, "That's right, man." The others nod. Why are they so eager to jump all over Angela instead of thanking her for freeing them from a gruelingly tactful discussion of Meg's story? Could Claris have told the others about seeing Swenson in the dorm? Swenson tries out a placating smile. "I made it clear at the beginning that no one would be forced to bring work into class. . . ."

This is not going over. No one's being persuaded.

"Fine," Angela says. "Whatever. If that's a problem for you guys, then fine, I'd be glad to bring my stuff into class. It's not that I was scared. I just didn't see the point. But if it makes you guys happy, we can do it next week."

"Thank you, Angela," Swenson says. "For volunteering. And extricating us from this little snafu."

"Snafu," says Carlos. "Beautiful."

"All right," says Swenson. "Meg? Anything else about your story?"

"No," says Meg, quickly. "I think I'll survive. Thanks."

"Good," says Swenson. "See you all next week. Angela, hang on and we'll figure out what you should hand in."

Slightly stunned, they file out. Footsteps gallop down the stairs. Swenson hardly hears them. He's searching Angela's face for some sign of what she feels, and whether that . . . mishap in her room was an end or a beginning.

He'd planned to pretend that nothing happened, but he's just so glad to be with her. He's missed her. He can't stop staring. Whatever happened, or didn't, between them, at least it's given him the right to look her in the eye. It seems to him that her face is flushed with feverish affection. Now they'll have to be careful lest her feelings for him—their feelings for each other—get them in serious trouble.

Meanwhile he's trying to reconcile the young woman across the table with the naked girl crawling up his body, the one whose nipple he took in his mouth. It just doesn't seem possible. Maybe he dreamed the whole thing. He probes his broken tooth with his tongue. It happened. It was no dream.

"Man," she says. "I am *so* sorry for going off like that in class. I don't know what got into me. One minute I was sitting there minding my own business and the next minute I was ripping Meg's heart out."

"Well, you were right," says Swenson.

"But way too heavy. Now look what I've got myself into. I just didn't want to put up my work for, you know, target practice—"

"You can still back out. We don't have to workshop your novel. It's not a requirement." Frankly, he wishes she would refuse. He'd rather not moderate a discussion of a novel about a student-teacher affair by a student for whom (as the least perceptive student can tell) he has some special feeling.

"I might as well bite the bullet. Let them tear it apart. Revenge for my trashing Meg. You want to know the truth? It wasn't Meg's story. It was *me*—the mood I was in. I was pissed before I walked in here."

"And . . . why was that?" Swenson couldn't be more eager, or more reluctant, to know.

"Because you didn't call all week."

Christ, thinks Swenson, bracing himself. Here it comes.

"To tell me what you thought of those pages," she says. "I mean, that scene was sort of . . . extreme. I needed to know what you thought. So, like, I'm sitting here in class defending males against Meg's bullshit while this week you demonstrated the worst shit about guy behavior. To tell you the truth, I'd rather see some guy throw my cat out the window than give you this really tough, hard-to-write scene and you don't even call."

Swenson can't keep from laughing. What a strange little creature she is. She's not even going to mention . . . whatever happened between them. It's all about the work for her. It was always about her work. But doesn't the rest mean anything?

"I promise I won't throw your cat out the window—"

"Fuck that," says Angela, shocking them both. "Did you *notice* that you didn't call?" Her voice is edging up toward the pitch at which she'd berated Meg. Slow down. This is going too fast. How did they get to the breakup stage and skip the middle steps? What makes her think she can talk to a teacher that way? He has only himself to blame.

He's sorry. He was wrong not to call. He's supposed to be the adult. It couldn't have been simple for her—what happened in her room. Actually, it's made everything hopelessly complex. He didn't call because he couldn't imagine saying, Hey, I really liked that scene of revolting sex with an older man.

"*Did* you even think about it?" she says.

"All the time." Was that a declaration of love? Swenson feels suddenly brave.

Angela doesn't return his smile. "Well, that's a start," she says.

"The fact is, I wanted to call so much that I couldn't call."

All right, then. He's said it. Let it all come down.

Angela seems unimpressed by what's just occurred, by the giant leap he's taken over the widening fault between himself and his life.

"That makes no sense, no sense at all. You couldn't call because you *wanted* to call? If you want to call someone, you call. Anything else is just guy bullshit."

Who *is* this girl, and what does she think is going on between them? What happened to the worshipful student who hung on his every word, the young woman whose favorite author, whose hero he was, whose life he saved and transformed? Something's ringing the faintest of bells, he hears Angela's mother's voice, *The second he started to like her, she wouldn't answer the phone.* . . . Now that she's let Swenson sleep with her she doesn't respect him anymore. That's the trouble with loving. It makes you act like a girl. Meg is right, Makeesha's right, Angela's right to hate men, to fear their power. He could flunk this little twit. Fail her for the semester.

"What *did* you think of the pages?" she says.

"Fine," Swenson says, idiotically. "At least the guy didn't break a tooth."

Angela claps her hand over her mouth, truly concerned and con-
trite. "Oh, gee, how's your tooth?"

"Fixable. I guess."

"Cool. So what about the pages?"

"I . . . liked them. They're risky. Very brave. The scene makes
your flesh creep. I guess you meant to do that."

"I meant to do that," she says.

"You did it," says Swenson.

Angela sprawls forward and leans her elbow on the table in a
parody of rapt attention. Her eyes are liquid and sincere, but her
voice is clipped and ironic.

"You know what?" she says. "None of this means anything.
Nothing that happens in this crappy little college amounts to jack
shit. The class could build a bonfire and burn my novel or get on
their knees and worship it, and it still wouldn't mean anything. I
care what *you* think. A lot. You know that. Obviously. But I need to
get my stuff beyond this . . . college, out into the world, and find
out if someone who doesn't know me thinks I should even go on
writing or tear it up in tiny pieces and throw it in the garbage."

"You can't ask anyone that," Swenson says. "Especially not at
your stage."

"What's *my stage*?" she says. "Listen . . . tell me if this is impossible. I mean, you don't have to do this, but maybe the next time you
talk to your editor in New York, you could sort of mention my
novel and ask him read it, just look at it, thirty pages, whatever,
enough so he could tell you something and you could tell me."

He should have seen this coming, taken his warning from her
being the only student in Euston history who claimed to love *The
Red and the Black*. What did he think *that* was about? Naturally
Angela loves Stendhal. And now she's Julien-Soreled him. But it
wasn't—it isn't—so simple. There's something deeper between
them than mere opportunism and ambition.

Len Currie might like Angela's book—it's young, sexy, transgres-
sive, there's no telling what the folks in New York are going for
these days. If that happened, it *would* be great—for her, for

Swenson, for Euston. A marvelous boost for everyone except the other students.

"Let me think about it," he says.

"Think about it," Angela says.

"What about the novel?" he says. "Do you have more pages for me?"

"I do," she says. "But it's weird. I forgot to bring them."

"That *is* weird," says Swenson.

"Who knows? Maybe my forgetting was Freudian or something. Maybe it's because I was so fried over your not calling me. I thought maybe you didn't read the pages I gave you."

"I read them."

"I got that. Well, I can hardly bring *those* pages into class next week."

She's right. She'd have to be mad to bring a sex scene into that bloody arena of gender combat. Not to mention the challenge of submitting a chapter about teacher-student sex when the student writer is having sex with the teacher. Is having? Has had. Will have? Swenson has never felt so alone. If he can't discuss this with Angela—whom can he ask? Let it go. He is not going to quiz Angela about their . . . relationship. The word gives him the creeps.

Angela says, "I guess the smartest plan would be to do that first chapter. It's fairly neutral compared to the rest of the book. Things haven't really started hopping."

Swenson chuckles. "Would that be useful? That first chapter's pretty polished."

"None of it's useful. It's just some initiation thing. I get to be part of the gang. The Latina Diablas."

"Wear earplugs to class," he says. "Ignore anything they say."

"I already do. Anyhow, I promise to bring you some new pages next time. I don't know how I forgot. It's been a strange week, I guess."

"That it has," says Swenson.

"Look, I'm really sorry I asked you about your editor. Why don't we just forget it?"

"No," says Swenson. "It's fine. I promise I'll think about it."

"Okay. See you next week," she says. And she's gone.

Swenson gazes after her. His grief is visceral—shocking. Well, he can't sit here forever, alone in an empty classroom, mooning over an undergrad with lip rings and a tattoo. He practically runs down the stairs, across the quad, and into Magda.

"Ted! How was your class?"

"Crazy," Swenson says.

"Normally crazy or especially crazy?"

"Normally," lies Swenson. "I guess."

If only he could tell her! How sweet it would be to grab Magda's wrist and hustle her off to his car and drive around long enough to tell her the story of the conferences, the classes, Angela's novel, sex, the broken tooth, and now her asking him to show her novel to Len.

He would end with the questions forming in his mind: Does Angela—did she ever—have a crush on him, or is she just using him for his professional connections? Is Angela blackmailing him, or simply asking a favor? What does a favor mean when you have the power to wreck someone's life? How devastated Magda would be to learn that he'd slept with a student. This is how criminals get caught. Sooner or later they talk. It's not the cops who bring them down, but their own urge to confess or boast.

"So when do we have lunch?" The jolliness of Magda's invitation fails to mask the intensity of her desire to see him.

"Maybe not for a while. Time's been sort of tight. I don't want to jinx things but . . . I'm working on my novel."

What demon made him say that? Now he will never write again.

"Oh, that's wonderful!" Magda says.

"I guess." Swenson's almost convinced himself. "In fact I may soon have a section to show Len Currie." And now he knows why he's lied. For practice, in case he recycles the lie when he calls Len and pretends to have work to give him—when the truth will be that he's calling about Angela's novel. And why not call Len, pitch Angela's book, find out if it's something he might want to look at?

It's fine to phone your editor and recommend a promising student. It's generous, noble. Passing on the torch to the next generation. And it's hardly a privilege Swenson has abused. He's never suggested anything to Len before, and Angela's novel is good enough so that his recommendation could hardly be seen as a consequence of his . . . involvement with its author.

Magda says, "Listen, Ted, I mean . . . you can say no. But the next time you talk to Len, do you think you could just maybe . . . ask him about my new book of poems? I know they publish poetry."

This is really too much. Two women in twenty minutes cozying up to Swenson as a way of getting next to his editor.

"I'd be happy to," Swenson says. In fact, it's unlikely that Len would do Magda's second book, but there's always a chance of catching him on a day when he's feeling guilty about how little real literature he's publishing. Still, Swenson can't muddy the waters by asking him to look at two books. "But . . . I'm pretty sure I heard that Len isn't taking on any new poets. I guess I could ask him, but it's a long shot."

The wintry afternoon light has bleached the color from Magda's face. She thinks Swenson hates her book. Why couldn't he have lied? Weeks from now he could have reported that he'd broached the subject with Len, who'd said his poetry list was full—

"If it were up to me I'd publish it," Swenson says. "I love your work. You know that. But Len's a businessman. He's got other concerns besides literary merit. . . ." None of this has anything to do with Magda's book. But if he told Magda the truth, would she feel better, or worse?

"I'll call you. I've got to go," he says, and hurries across the quad.

He feels as if he's being chased all the way to his office. He locks the door behind him and picks up the phone. Before he knows what he's doing, he's dialed Ruby's number. He's been trying to reach her for days, since she called and left a message and he missed her—he's still convinced—because he called Angela first.

The phone rings. Ruby answers.

"Ruby," says Swenson, "it's Dad." He wants to weep with joy at the sound of her voice, and with the corny pleasure of being able to use the word *Dad*.

"Hey, Dad," she says. "How are you?" As if they were normal people. Maybe they are—at last. Maybe Ruby's recovered from whatever has kept her so at odds with them for this long, terrible year.

"How's school?" he asks.

"Fine. Excellent. Really good." Ruby's voice rings out as if she always talks in sprays of cheerful adjectives instead of curt monosyllables. "I've sort of decided that I might declare as a psychology major. I'm taking this course I really like on the abnormal personality."

Has someone put his daughter on Prozac? Wouldn't they need his permission? Probably not. Ruby's over eighteen. And anyway, it's okay with him if some savvy college shrink has found a way to turn his child back into the bright spirit she once was.

"Hey," says Swenson, "having a dad like me must have given you plenty of experience with the abnormal personality."

There's a silence. Then Ruby says, "Well, I've kind of been thinking about that. You know I haven't been in the greatest shape. . . ."

Something in her tone of voice—a programmed, robotic echo—makes Swenson's heart start to pound. Is she gearing up to report a recovered memory of his having molested her in early childhood? Nothing could be further from the truth. In fact, it's occurred to Swenson that Ruby's growing up—overnight, it seemed—mystified and hurt and embarrassed him. He'd felt himself holding back from her, stepping aside so they wouldn't pass too near one another in the narrow hallway. Almost overnight, their easy kisses and hugs became perfunctory and self-conscious. How can he explain to her—or to himself—what happened? No wonder she's furious at him for abandoning her when she needed him most.

"I've been reading about all this research into hereditary patterns of illness—and you know that Grandpa was not exactly a healthy guy."

Swenson exhales sharply. But . . . whom is she calling Grandpa? *Grandpa*? She knows how his father died. When she was ten or eleven, she pressed for the information. Trying to be reassuring and calm, Swenson and Sherrie told her. More or less.

Does Ruby think she inherited anything from Swenson's crazy old man? Swenson's never seen the vaguest family resemblance. But now he finds himself deeply touched by Ruby's calling his father Grandpa. It's time to really talk to her about her grandfather—with more compassion and at greater depth even than in his novel. It would matter to Ruby more than it matters to anyone else.

"We can talk about that," he says. "When are you coming home?"

"Thanksgiving," says Ruby. How obvious.

"Do we have to wait till Thanksgiving? You're only forty miles away. I could drive over. We could have lunch."

"Thanksgiving's only two weeks away," Ruby says. Okay. He can accept that. She needs to feel like a successful, independent college student who has gone away to school and can only come home on vacations. He hopes he hasn't pushed too far—scared her off with his enthusiasm. That would make it three times in one day he's struck out talking to women.

He says, "I can hardly wait." There's another silence. Ruby's message said she needed to ask him something. "What's up?"

"Promise you won't get mad?"

"Promise."

"I got a call from Matt McIlwaine? You remember him, don't you?"

"Of course I remember him. What does he want?" Swenson's voice is steely with irony. He's got to stop this. Now. How many times has he regretted the arrogance with which he broke up Ruby's romance? How often has he said that letting her date Jack the Ripper would be better than turning her against them?

"I don't know," says Ruby. "He left a message on my machine and told me to call him back. But his old number's changed, and student information said his new number was unlisted."

Can students have unlisted numbers? Probably, if they're being tracked by disgruntled drug connections and the fathers of virgins they've impregnated. Enough! This is the chance Swenson's been praying for, the chance to do things over and finally get some of it right.

"I see him on campus," Swenson says. "Not often. Once in a while."

"Alone?" asks Ruby.

"Desperately alone," Swenson lies. "I'll get his number for you. I'll ask him to call you back."

"That would be great. Thanks. Love to Mom. Talk to you soon. See you at Thanksgiving."

"Love you!" Swenson says with such intensity he's afraid she'll change her mind.

"All right, see you then."

"See you then," Swenson says.

When Swenson hangs up, he feels like a fairy-tale hero who's just gotten through the enchanted forest by heeding a complex series of magic warnings and taboos. Everything seems conditional, as if he's on trial, as if the promise of Ruby's visit might be revoked in a heartbeat.

And so, when he looks out the window and sees Matt McIlwaine walking across campus, his first thought is that he's summoned him with some supernatural power. The sight of the movie-star handsome Matt—sickeningly entitled—jolts Swenson with enough adrenaline to send him racing downstairs. He's convinced that if he doesn't go after him, Ruby will somehow know and decide not to come home for Thanksgiving. If he's lucky he'll get downstairs just as Matt's passing by.

But Matt's already gone. Swenson takes off after him toward the edge of campus. His daughter's happiness depends on his keeping the kid in sight. From across the street he sees Matt go into the MinuteMart and emerge with a pack of cigarettes. Pausing near—too near—the gas pumps, he lights up, then walks on. By now, Matt's opposite Swenson on the far side of North Street. Swenson ducks into the drugstore and watches from inside the door.

Matt gets as far as the ragged lawn officially known as North Street Common, reclaimed a few years ago from a bottle-strewn lot in a failed attempt at village gentrification. In the park are two benches and a sculpture, donated by Euston College as a gesture toward amicable town-gown relations, a two-ton steel tarantula made by Ari Linder, the very same Ari Linder who gave Angela a hard time for doing the Super Value Meal as her American icon. Well, it serves the humorless shit right if his work has found its true purpose as the newly traditional target for townie kids to egg on Halloween night.

From the Rite-Aid doorway Swenson spies on Matt. Is he expecting someone? Why would you meet anyone here, when there are all those benches on campus, each with its own flower bed and plaque naming the alumnus who funded this or that irresistible place to park your butt? No reason—unless you were meeting someone you didn't want to be seen with. Your drug connection. Your jail-bait sweetheart.

Swenson pulls his collar up and strolls with phony nonchalance straight in Matt's direction. When Matt sees him, he looks so alarmed that Swenson thinks: He did come here to buy drugs or pick up an underage girl. But of course he's apprehensive. You don't forget a conversation in which your girlfriend's father threatened to get you kicked out of school if you didn't stop seeing his daughter. Swenson can still see Matt's smile dripping off his face as he slowly—it took him forever—understood what was being said.

Swenson has a lot of acting to do, pretending to just now see Matt, miming surprise, confusion, and then the resolve to be friendly and forgiving.

"Matt!" he says. "How have you been?"

"Fine, thanks, sir," says Matt. That *sir* enrages Swenson, as does Matt's smile: part goofiness, part calculated charm, part menace, and part ice.

"How's school?"

"Fine, sir. Very well, thank you. And how have you been?"

"Excellent," Swenson says.

Just then, Matt's attention is caught by something over Swenson's shoulder. Swenson turns in time to see Angela walking toward them.

"Hey, Angela, how's it going?" says Matt. "How's your semester been?"

"Sucky," Angela says. "My semester bites. Except for this guy's class."

"Oh, that's right," says Matt. "I remember. You're a writer."

Swenson can't stop himself from saying, "Angela's my prize student."

"Yeah, well," says Angela. "I'm going to get my ass kicked this week."

"Uh oh," says Matt. "Good luck."

"Oh, it won't be so bad," Swenson says. "I'll bet it goes just fine."

"Right," Angela says. "Well, I guess I'd better go. I'm on my way to the drugstore. To buy earplugs to wear to class."

Matt glances at Swenson, uneasily. "I told her to," Swenson says.

"Only kidding," Angela says. "I'm going to buy Tampax. Plus I've got to return this."

She holds up a videotape case, which Swenson takes from her. *The Blue Angel.* His hands shake as he returns it. He and Angela exchange a searching glance, which must be even more puzzling to Matt than it is to them.

"Good choice," Swenson says.

"It's a cool movie," Angela says. "But a little boring."

"I'm surprised the video store had it," Swenson says.

"Are you kidding?" says Angela. "That store's the best thing about this crappy town. So . . . okay. Gotta run. See you guys later."

Together, they watch her go. Swenson turns to Matt. "Can I ask you something?"

Matt tenses visibly. "Sure," he says. "No problem."

"Why would you want to sit here?" Swenson says. "It's the ugliest spot in the world."

Matt grins with a relief so genuine and boyish that Swenson catches a flash of the person Ruby must have liked.

"I can think here," Matt says. "Don't ask me why."

"Well," says Swenson, "thinking's always a good idea."

"And I run into the nicest people. Like you and Angela." Swenson wishes Matt hadn't said that.

"Well, I'd better be going," Swenson says, taking off down North Street. Only now does it cross his mind that he forgot to mention Ruby.

Swenson drives around aimlessly to work off the adrenaline rush for which he can thank his meeting with Matt and Angela. Finally, he's calm enough to go home, where he finds Sherrie napping by the wood stove. There's an open book in her lap, her head's tipped back. He longs to kiss the smooth white arc of her neck. Standing in the doorway, he can almost convince himself that he's the person he wishes he were, the one whose life is still in order, the one who hasn't yet pulled the pin on the grenade that's going to blow his happy home sky-high.

He doesn't move or make a sound, but Sherrie senses his presence and opens her eyes. She's happy to see him and at the same time, he's pained to note, annoyed at having had her nap disrupted. "Guess who I talked to today?" Swenson says brightly.

"I give up," murmurs Sherrie.

"Guess."

"The Nobel Prize Committee. Hey, congratulations."

Swenson winces. "Ouch." His marriage is in worse shape than he imagined.

"Sorry," says Sherrie. "You know I get crabby when someone wakes me up."

"Actually, it was better than the Nobel Prize Committee." Swenson waits a beat. "Ruby." Now let Sherrie be sorry that she made that nasty crack. "She's coming home for Thanksgiving."

Sherrie says, "You're kidding."

"I wouldn't. You know that. Not about this. Anyway, that's the good news. The bad news is she asked for Matt McIlwaine's phone number."

"Fine," says Sherrie. "Give it to her. It's got to be a good sign."

"I guess," says Swenson. "Unless she's coming home to tell us that she's just recovered a memory of our having abused her in some satanic ritual."

Sherrie says, "That's not funny."

Swenson knows that. He's only trying to dispel the heavy weather of grief and guilt that settles in whenever Ruby's name is mentioned.

"She was bound to come around," Sherrie says. "She couldn't stay mad forever."

Swenson sits and watches the fire. Sherrie glances down at her lap.

"Page one hundred and sixty." She shuts her book. "Remind me where I was."

"What are you reading?"

"*Jane Eyre.*"

"Why that?" Swenson manages to say.

"Arlene was reading it. Arlene who never reads anything but supermarket romance. I guess there's some new movie or miniseries or whatever. . . . I found your old copy in the den. And you know, it's amazing. What you remember is her marrying Mr. Rochester, you forget the stuff about her being so plain and poor and furious. . . ."

"I should reread it," Swenson murmurs, then pauses, staving off paranoia. He was never one of those men who believed in a conspiracy of females. But now suspicion nags at him: Arlene and Angela somehow in league, and they've enlisted Sherrie. A coven of vengeful harpies, their anger and resentment fueled by periodic readings of *Jane Eyre.*

As soon as Swenson walks into the classroom he senses something in the air. Something vile is about to occur. What maniac invented this torture, this punishment for young writers? Imagine a group of established authors subjecting themselves to this! It's not an academic discipline, it's fraternity hazing. And the most appalling part is that it's supposed be helpful. The bound and gagged sacrificial lamb is supposed be grateful.

But why is Swenson experiencing this acutely heightened compassion? Because his feelings for this particular lamb are unusually strong and complex. Meanwhile he can't help thinking that what's in the air isn't merely the normal, garden-variety, classroom blood lust and angst. This is something special. Just as Angela predicted, she's going to get her ass kicked.

"Whose head is on the chopping block today?" Swenson asks, rhetorically.

Angela grins at Swenson and shrugs. The others melt from the edge of his peripheral vision. Can he risk saying her name out loud? Better not even attempt it.

"Well then," he says, "would you like to read us a paragraph?"

Angela's manuscript rattles in her hands. A spasm flutters one eyelid. The others are never this scared. Swenson longs to reach over and take her hand. She doesn't have to put her heart and soul on the line to satisfy a spoiled college kid's whiny demand for fairness. And it's all his fault. His feelings for her have warped the entire class.

Angela begins to read: "Every . . . after . . . I . . . out . . . sat with the eggs."

It's a good thing they've read it before and that they're reading along as Angela mumbles, swallowing every other word. She swigs from her water bottle.

"Jesus, Angela," Carlos says. "Pull it together, okay?"

Scowling, Angela says, "Okay. I'm starting again."

"'Every night, after dinner, I went out and sat with the eggs. This was after my mother and I washed the dishes and loaded the washer, after my father dozed off over his medical journals, it was then that I slipped out the kitchen door and crossed the chilly backyard, dank and loamy with the yeasty smell of leaves just beginning to change, noisy with the rustle of them turning colors in the dark.'"

The long sentence has done Angela good. It's taken her briefly out of herself and made her forget the class. Still, she's not a great reader. She goes too fast, in a nasal monotone and a faint Jersey accent. Even so, Swenson's enchanted by the language and by the image of the girl dreaming of her music teacher among the incubators and eggs.

For one terrifying moment he thinks: Oh dear god, I've fallen in love. There is no remedy, nothing to do but try everything, risk anything to be with her. What a time to realize this—in the middle of class! Meanwhile his students are squirming. Angela's still reading.

"Thanks," he says. "That was great." Angela turns on Swenson with the grumpy face of a kid waking from a nap.

"What's the matter?" she says.

"Nothing. That was terrific." He never says anything like that. "Who wants to start?"

"I will," says Meg. "Well, first of all, I just didn't believe it."

Fine. They can write that off. Everyone recalls how Angela tore into Meg last week. It's payback time. That's how the system works, except in the rare cases of unusually generous, honest, or masochistic students who can get their hearts ripped out and the next week praise their attacker. But no one's that selfless in this class. No wonder they're all writing about having sex with lower life forms. It spares them the complications of love for their fellow humans. Well, some classes are just that way. It's chance, the luck of the draw, group dynamics. All of which means that Angela could be in for a very rough time.

"What didn't you believe, Meg?" Swenson labors to purge his voice of contempt.

"The whole thing," says Meg. "Every word. Even the *a*'s and the *the*'s were a lie. Like Mary McCarthy said about Lillian Hellman."

Comparing Lillian Hellman and Angela Argo strikes Swenson as so hilarious that he's afraid he'll dissolve in hysterics that may lead to wrenching sobs. "Yes, well, I suppose that before we get into Hellman and McCarthy . . . someone should say what's good about the piece."

"I thought some of the egg stuff was . . . okay," Carlos offers.

"Oh, come on, Carlos," says Claris. "It was all so heavy. So obvious and symbolic. And fake."

"You go, Claris!" says Makeesha. "Don't be giving us that egg shit, Angela."

Claris looks Swenson full in the face, and everything becomes clear. Cool appraisal flickers in her yellow-green eyes. He glances through Angela's manuscript. How well he knows those first pages. He can hardly remember how his own novel begins.

"I didn't believe the voice," Meg says. "A teenage girl wouldn't think like that."

"She doesn't use any teenage expressions," says Nancy. "It was, like, totally unrealistic."

"I have to say I felt the same way," Danny says. "I kept wanting this girl to say something that made me believe in her as a character, instead of which we get this weird . . . *old person* going on with this disgusting stuff about hatching eggs." Awfully high-toned sentiments from a guy whose hero has unnatural relations with the family dinner.

Jonelle says, "We don't hear anything about the narrator. I kept waiting to learn something about her . . . as a character."

"Well, it's only the first part of the first chapter of a novel," says Swenson.

"Still," says Meg. "All the more."

"Yeah," says Carlos. "I mean, a novel's got to have something to keep you reading, and I wasn't sure I was going to stay with this story about some chick, ha ha, some chick hatching eggs and having fantasies about her teacher."

Swenson's paging through the manuscript, this time with the vague intention of asking them to point out the parts they don't believe. But before he can speak, Courtney Alcott announces, "I totally agree with everything everyone's said. This is, like, the worst thing we've read in class all year."

Tears are shining in Angela's eyes. Red patches bloom on her cheeks. She's on the edge of breaking apart, and Swenson's let it happen. She can't just shrug the whole thing off, as the others have learned to do. This is Angela's heart's blood, and Courtney's drained the last drop.

Swenson feels the thrum that precedes the bells. As they toll, he closes his eyes, and the room disappears. The sound fills his mind, working its way into the folds of his brain. There's no space left for distraction, for trivial, useless thoughts. He enters a deeply meditative state. He could be a Tibetan monk blowing one of those six-foot trumpets, in search of instant enlightenment through oxygen deprivation.

When the bells stop and he opens his eyes, the world appears washed clean. Now, in his exaltation, he feels less like a monk than like a prophet or a madman or the . . . oracle at Delphi. All he has to do is open his mouth for pure truth to come burbling out. He's never felt so guided, so certain of his mission.

"Sometimes . . ." Swenson pauses to listen to the silence so deep it's roaring, or maybe it's the lingering echo of the bells. "Sometimes it happens that something new comes along, something fresh and original, unlike what's been written before. Once in a lifetime or once in a generation, there's a Proust or a Joyce or a Virginia Woolf. Almost always, hardly anyone understands what the writer's doing, most people think it's trash, so the writer's life is a hell."

How banal his little oration is! Every moron knows this. And what is he doing, mentioning Joyce and Woolf? Suggesting that Angela's novel is *Remembrance of Things Past*?

"As good as Angela's chapter is—and it's very good—you realize I'm not saying that Angela's writing *Ulysses*." A few students giggle. Do they know what *Ulysses* is? "But her writing's original, the rest of you need to see that, because if there's anything I want you to take away from this class, it's the ability—the generosity—to recognize the real thing."

Two hot dark coals of resentment glow in each student's face. Let them find out for themselves that life is unfair. Talent isn't doled out equally to everyone at birth. Plus, Angela, gifted as she is, works ten times harder than anyone else. How dare these little thugs presume to tell her how to write? He knows his anger isn't pure, or purely on Angela's behalf. He has his own reasons for being enraged: the hours he's spent in this hellhole, the pages of grisly prose that have furnished the text for hours of classroom discussion. The years he's sacrificed! How little time is left, and how much of it he'll have to waste in rooms like this one—in *this* one—pandering to these children's silly ideas about something that means so much, something he might be doing right now if he weren't watching time trickle away in the company of his adolescent jailers.

"What should be obvious to you all is that Angela's manuscript is a thousand—a million—times better than anything we've seen in this class this semester."

"That's bullshit, too," says Carlos.

The others are temporarily incapable of commenting on whether it's bullshit or not. Swenson stands and gathers his papers and—without a thought for how long the class is supposed to last—leaves the room before anyone can ask him whose story they're doing next week.

Hurrying across the quad, Swenson feels confident, energetic—capable, for the first time in weeks, of telephoning Len Currie. He

Francine Prose

won't be calling about himself, his book or lack of book, won't be asking for a favor or for personal attention, for patience or impatience with him for not having written his novel. He needn't wheedle or apologize, manipulate or boast, resort to the various strategies writers adopt with their editors. No, sir. He's doing something generous and large, something in keeping with his standing in the literary world and his vocation as a teacher.

Clearly, his classroom aria on the subject of Angela's work was a dress rehearsal for his conversation with Len. Every adjective he used was a dry run for what he'll say when he calls down to Manhattan. He unlocks his office door, throws down his coat, picks up the phone, and dials.

Some higher power must know that Swenson's on a crusade. Len's assistant asks Swenson's name and immediately puts him through. Len not only picks up, but sounds happy to hear from Swenson.

"Hey, man," he says. "How are you? It's been a million years. When are you coming down to New York? It would be great to see you."

Isn't that what you always hear: call your editor after lunch. After the two martinis, they're in more receptive moods. At least that's what you used to hear. No one drinks at lunch anymore. It's all Perrier and decaf. Even Swenson knows that. Or does he? What does *he* know? He's been away twenty years. For all he knows they're drinking again. Because the fact is that Len sounds . . . drunk. Or in some other sort of artificially assisted good mood. Maybe he's been carrying on a noontime romance with some assistant publicist. Which means that he and Swenson have a little something in common. . . . In any case, Swenson understands that this moment is unusual, and fleeting. If he wants to see Len, he should take him up on it now.

"Well, actually, that's why I'm calling. I'm going to be in town . . . the week after next."

"Let me check my calendar," Len says. "The week of the twenty-third? That's Thanksgiving week. Really?"

That's not what Swenson meant at all. Ruby's coming home for the holiday. It's the one time in the entire year Swenson can't come down. He could postpone classes, faculty meetings, student conferences. But blow off Ruby's visit? He just said the week after next without knowing what week it was.

Len says, "Actually, you know what, that Friday is perfect. It's the only lunch slot I've got free on my schedule for the next year. Only kidding. But it's almost that bad. That Friday would be fabulous. I'm not going into the office. By lunchtime I'll be climbing the walls to get away from the wife and kids." He pauses. "Don't tell anyone I said that."

Maybe, just maybe, it's possible. Swenson could fly into town Friday morning. Ruby would understand. She probably has plans of her own, plans involving Matt. Ruby and Sherrie could have some time together, and they'd all be heartened by this evidence that the man of the house has a life, a professional life beyond Euston.

Of course, it's just as likely that Ruby will hate him for skipping out on her first weekend home in a year, and Sherrie will never forgive him. Well, so be it. He'll have to live with that. He welcomes it, in a way. If he's going to do something wrong—cheat on his wife, skip out on his daughter—he might as well do everything wrong. Let's show the world how bad he really is: bad husband, monstrous father. What is this sick Dostoyevskian craving for punishment and expiation? Possibly something he inherited from his dad, like some late-onset degenerative disease, latent until middle age.

"Ted," says Len. "Are you still there?"

"Sorry," says Swenson. "I spaced out for a second."

"Jesus," says Len. "You writers. All right, then. See you Friday, at one. You know the Norma? On East Twenty-second? Twenty-second and Park Avenue South."

"I'll find it," Swenson says.

The protocol for Ruby's visit has been as elaborately orchestrated as the plans for the arrival of some volatile, powerful head of state. Sherrie's told him not to question Ruby's decision to arrive on Thanksgiving morning—after all, she's staying till Sunday. Sherrie doesn't have to point out that Swenson has lost the right to comment on anyone else's comings and goings, since he himself is ducking out in the middle of the holiday weekend, apparently the only day all year when he can have a business lunch with Len. Sherrie and Ruby each said something like that once, and then acceded to Swenson's plan with a speed and ease that he found demoralizing and ever so slightly insulting.

It's been decided that Sherrie will pick Ruby up at the bus station—Swenson's a little vexed that Sherrie so obviously doesn't trust him to handle this delicate overture—and bring her home, where Swenson waits, pretending to read, pretending to watch TV.

At last he hears Sherrie's car pull in. Should he stay in his chair, with his newspaper, and rise to kiss her, the classic, dignified dad? Or should he run outside and throw his arms around her in an effusive papa-bear hug? Why can't he remember what he used to do? He opts for a compromise position—outside, but on the doorstep, smiling, giving Ruby a choice.

Ruby's gained weight. Her face is a pale white moon, and there's a certain blurriness, a thickness around her chin. In her baggy jeans and sweatshirt, she looks like a student at State, some local kid—which is what she is. When Ruby sees him, a look comes into her eyes that he chooses to read as affection, though the alternate reading is distant pity. Has he shrunk, or aged drastically? The debilitated daddy, hovering on the doorstep? She hugs him dutifully—she can't get past him without submitting—and then pats him roughly on the head.

She stands in the living room, looking around. Who can tell what she's seeing as she sniffs the air, incuriously. "Hm, turkey," she says. "Cool. I'll go put my stuff away."

When they hear her door shut, Sherrie says, "This feels familiar."

"Back to square one," says Swenson.

"Maybe not," says Sherrie. "Maybe she's just putting her stuff away. Anyhow, it's her *room*."

Sherrie always takes Ruby's side. But what side is *that*, exactly?

After Ruby's been in her room for almost two hours, Swenson knocks on her door. "Can I come in?"

Ruby says what sounds like, "Sure."

Ruby's kneeling on her desk, which seems dangerously fragile. Swenson imagines the scenario in which she falls over backward, just as when she was small he used to visualize, obsessively, terrifying cinematic images: Ruby tumbling down the stairs, Ruby's school bus crashing. "Redecorating?" he asks.

"This stuff's kind of babyish." Ruby's prying out thumbtacks, letting her pictures of film and rock stars drift to the desk. Swenson can't help thinking of Angela's room, with its varied, stylish, attractive faces—Chekhov, Akhmatova, Virginia Woolf, all with their excellent bone structure. Ruby and Angela are the same age. There's no point dwelling on that. It crosses his mind that in the past, Ruby's changing her room decor meant she was entering some new phase that she wanted, or needed, to broadcast all over the walls. But now there's nothing going up, only coming down. He thinks: She's not redecorating. Ruby's moving out.

"So . . . how's school?" he asks.

"Good," says Ruby. Down comes Suzanne Vega, down comes Magic Johnson.

"What's happening with Magic Johnson's health? He seems to be doing fine."

"Yeah," says Ruby. "Sure, Dad. I guess." Down comes some empty-eyed kid with long stringy hair. "Who's that?" he asks.

"Beck," says Ruby.

"Right. I forgot." Why go on? Swenson's just about to leave when Ruby says, "How's your novel coming, Dad?"

He must have heard her wrong. But what else could she have said? "Great," he replies. "It's going great!" And for a moment, he thinks it is. All he needs to do is write it! "In fact, I was just going to go take a look at it. Call me when dinner's ready."

Jimi Hendrix slips to the desk as Ruby turns to face Swenson. "Doesn't Mom need help?"

"She probably does. I'll go and see."

"*I* will," says Ruby, combatively.

"Mom would love that," Swenson says.

"Whatever," Ruby answers.

Swenson slinks off to his study. *My Dog Tulip* is still in the living room, and he's hesitant to go get it. He picks up a chunk of his novel, stares at the first page, but is afraid to read it. So much for the resolution he felt when Ruby asked how it was going. He looks for Angela's manuscript. Where the hell did he put it? Here. It's in his briefcase, in preparation for its trip to see Len. He takes it out of the envelope and reads a few pages, reassured to discover it *is* as good as he thought. He holds the pages up to his face, as if they're an article of clothing on which he can pick up Angela's scent. He can't believe he's doing this. His beloved daughter is finally—at long last—back in their home, and he's off alone in his room, pining for a student his daughter's age.

He wanders into his bedroom and briefly falls asleep, dreams of bottles of olive oil with stained, greasy labels that, for some reason, he knows he's supposed to read. Then someone is reading them to him, a woman's voice, a genie that appears in a cloud of delicious smells. . . . It's Sherrie, calling him for Thanksgiving dinner. Calling him to carve the turkey that they will eat together as they always did, their little family on Thanksgiving Day, ever since they moved out of the Euston dorm, where they suffered through those grim cafeteria dinners with the students stranded at school.

Compared with that, this isn't bad. In fact it's pretty good. A warm house, his wife and child. They love each other. They're together.

Ruby heaps her plate as if she hasn't eaten since she left home. Hasn't she heard of seconds? Well, Swenson should be grateful, he has a dozen colleagues with anorexic kids. Ruby's manners have gotten worse. Perhaps it goes with the extra weight. A slippery wedge of meat disappears between her glistening lips.

"When did your classes end?" asks Sherrie and then looks in panic at Swenson. Please don't let Ruby take this as a criticism of when she came home.

"Actually we didn't have classes this week."

"Why not?" Sherrie asks.

"They had a teach-in," Ruby says.

"A teach-in," says Swenson. Perhaps that explains why Ruby was asking about his father. Maybe the teach-in was about Vietnam. Maybe someone mentioned the Buddhist monks and the guys, like Swenson's dad, who immolated themselves. "What kind of teach-in?"

"About the Mikulsky case."

"Oh, Jesus, no," says Swenson.

"Ted," says Sherrie. "Let Ruby talk. Okay?"

"I can't believe they cancel classes so they can spend two days debating whether that poor schmuck did or didn't smack his lips over a Greek sculpture."

"Ted," says Sherrie. "You've got to shut up now. I mean it."

"It's more than that," says Ruby. "He'd been saying stuff before that, and these girls went to his office and asked him to stop, to be careful what he said, and he just went on and on—"

"That's not what I heard," Swenson says. "I heard it was just that one word. If *yum* is a word. Or a syllable. I don't know—"

"You should have gone to the teach-in," Ruby says.

"You went to this? You went—"

"It's an assignment," says Ruby. "I'm taking this class, it's called Batterers and Battered, and the teacher said we should all go to find out about the abusive personality—"

Swenson can't believe she's his kid. *Batterer* is Meg Ferguson's word. He makes *fun* of kids like that. What if Angela heard her?

He's shocked to be thinking of Angela, or, actually, shocked that he's forgotten her for a good ten minutes. But really, it's not so surprising. Family takes you out of yourself, transports you above your workaday cares. For a few minutes, Swenson's been so mired in a political discussion with his daughter that he's forgotten about his unpleasant, risky, ongoing . . . situation. Here is his own flesh and blood saying that this poor schmo should get the death penalty for one syllable, and Swenson, her beloved dad, has had sex with a very unstable student whose book he is about to bring to his editor in New York. How awful, how unaccountable that his guilt and dread could be dispelled in an instant by the thought that tomorrow he'll be in the city with Len. A whole new chapter will begin. Let's see where we go from here.

S wenson finds the restaurant, a full half-hour early, driven there by a damp wind, through streets so eerily empty that the wind can push him wherever it wants, an icy wind so rough and cruel, yet so playful with the garbage, tossing stray sheets of newpaper like lettuce in a salad.

Half an hour is *early*. Probably he should walk around for, let's say, fifteen minutes, browse in a bookstore, then make his way back to the restaurant with a more reasonable amount of time to kill. But why should Swenson kill one minute? Why should he wander the cold bleak streets like the Little Match Girl when the restaurant is full of men in suits, young men, all younger than Swenson? The middle-aged and elderly have been erased from the planet. It's pure science fiction. Swenson's the survivor, the lucky guy who was out of town when the space aliens picked off every male over thirty-five so they could take over their gyms, health clubs, and restaurants. Swenson's the last relic of his generation. But so what? He's still here.

As soon as he walks in the door, his eyes lock into the tepidly welcoming gaze of a young woman in a pigeon-colored suit. With her book and lighted lectern, it's all vaguely religious, as if at any moment she might begin to preach. And in fact the woman's a saint. She searches her glowing bible and not only finds Len's name but says, "You're the first one here. Would you like to go to your table?" without the slightest suggestion that Swenson is a loser for being so early.

Well, it's not too early for the other customers to have ordered
giant slabs of charred meat, slopping over their plates, staining the
virgin white tablecloths with their gory juices. Swenson feels as if
he's traveled back in time to the 1950s when people still believed
that consuming huge hunks of animal flesh assured a long, vigor-
ous life. At the far end of the restaurant is a sort of greenhouse, its
windows fogged with the cigar smoke produced by the happy
crowd inside, each patron a polluter, a factory unto himself, while
the nonsmokers outside can watch the brave cigar puffers slowly—
proudly—snuffing themselves, their gradual public suicides like
some gladiatorial entertainment.

Have the space aliens abducted the women, too? There are
almost none around. It could be a Moroccan souk. Is this some kind
of gay bar? Len would never do that. Besides, too many heads are
swiveling to follow the round, gray-suited rear end of the woman
leading Swenson to his table.

A waiter appears and asks Swenson if he wants a drink. Why,
yes, thank you. He does very much. A glass of merlot would be
dandy. The wine arrives within seconds. Swenson sits back and
takes a sip, enjoying the warmth that spreads through him and the
mysterious optimism that shoots from his throat to his heart.

Who would have thought that happiness was so freely available,
obtainable for the price of a ticket from Burlington to New York?
The moment his plane was airborne, Swenson felt all his problems
falling back to the earth. Imaginary troubles! Phantoms, as it turned
out. Now, as the wine kicks in, blurring and blending the restaurant
noise into a soothing murmur, Swenson's little difficulties seem so
easily solved. If Len asks how Ruby is, or about his Thanksgiving,
he can say that Ruby came home—no need to mention how long it
had been since her last visit—and of course he'll say how glad they
were, how overjoyed to see her.

The mental picture that this will create (father, mother, daughter, relatives, and friends gathered around the turkey, the yams, the
brussels sprouts and chestnuts) won't be a *precise* representation of
reality: their rather more gloomy threesome, the bewildered par-

ents and the daughter who reminded Swenson—as he whispered to Sherrie in the middle of the night—of a brainwashed cult member. Sherrie said they shouldn't complain. Ruby was getting her life together. That was how Ruby had put it at dinner: she was getting her life together. Perhaps she'd become a social worker and work with battered women and children.

"It's a growth industry," Swenson had said. Neither Sherrie nor Ruby laughed. But Len will chuckle, if Swenson remembers to repeat it. One last brush stroke to complete the picture of the happy home: the indulgent, tolerant mom and daughter, the gently teasing, irascible dad.

How glad—how relieved—his womenfolk seemed to watch him pull out of the driveway this morning, to send the hunter-gatherer father off to bag the saber-toothed tiger. In his rearview mirror, he'd caught the two women leaning together with a conspiratorial grace that made him suddenly fear that they'd been talking about him, worrying about him, and had decided that a trip to see his editor in New York might be good for his mental health.

It bothered him that Angela's novel was in his briefcase beside him on the front seat. Suppose he died in a car wreck on the way to the airport and among the mementos in the plastic bag delivered to his family by the specially trained policeman was the blood-soaked manuscript of Angela's novel? But there wouldn't be blood on it. It was in his briefcase, so unless the car was incinerated, Sherrie or Ruby could open anywhere and read about a girl's affair with her teacher. A novel that Swenson just happened to have with him when he was supposedly going to talk about his own novel, which—if Sherrie or Ruby cares to look—is still on his desk.

He should have brought *his* novel. Suppose Sherrie goes up to his room and pokes through his desk and finds it. She'll think he took a copy. No one in his right mind would go off with the only copy of his novel. Anyway, she never goes through his desk. She's not that kind of person. But now . . . what if some disgruntled former dishwasher with an AK–47 comes blasting through the door of this steakhouse, and the bloodied pages of Angela's book are discovered among the carnage? That's not going to happen. The scene around him is the opposite of violence and disorder. Everyone's name is on the list, and there is always a table. The gray-suited young woman conducts one young man after another through the clusters of other young men.

It all goes so smoothly, so magically—sure enough, there's Len Currie, walking through the door. How bizarre that you could call someone long distance, write something on a calendar, time passes, and everyone appears precisely when and where they agreed. Len scans the room for Swenson. It could hardly be more amazing if pure coincidence had brought them to the same restaurant at the same time.

The way Len bounces on the soles of his feet makes him seem shorter and plumper, more boyish than he is. In fact, his hair has grayed and slipped back off his forehead, as if someone has been yanking lightly but steadily on his signature pigtail. How long has it been since he's seen Len? Swenson can't remember. He rises to greet him, unsteadily. Christ, that merlot was strong. He'll have to remind himself to stop at one glass. All right, maybe two.

"Man!" says Len. "You look great!" The most striking thing about him is the brightness of his eyes, glittering maniacally behind his round steel-rimmed glasses. He shakes Swenson's hand and then, as if the handshake is too formal, delivers an ironic cuff to Swenson's upper arm, a punch he follows instantly with a manly biceps squeeze. The whole complex gesture seems faintly ritualized, some arty, self-mocking soul-brother thing. "Country life agrees with you!"

Fuck you, Swenson thinks. Fuck you with your big steaks and cigars and beautiful women in pale gray suits, while I'm stuck up there with the moose, the spinster assistant professors, and pimply undergraduates. But what is Swenson's problem? Len's telling him he looks well.

"You look the same, man," lies Swenson. In fact Len looks drastically changed. Not sick or ailing or damaged, but dramatically aged. A dusting of fine ash seems to have settled on his skin.

"Sure." Len smiles stiffly. "We're all getting older."

On that jovial note, they take their seats. Len folds his arms on the table and leans forward, beaming his brights on Swenson.

"Another?" he asks Swenson's wineglass.

"Definitely," says Swenson.

Len points two fingers at Swenson's glass.

He says, "Could we have that right away? I mean *now*?"

The hostess says, "I promise."

"Don't you love this place?" Len says, when she leaves. "Time travel back to the days when babes were babes and men were men who died at fifty on the golf course. It might not be such a bad way to go. But enough of that morbid shit. . . ."

The wine comes, moments later.

"To literature and commerce," Len says.

Swenson raises his glass. To Angela's book, he thinks. It calms him to imagine Angela, just as it comforted him to remember her during that dinner at Dean Bentham's. Angela's like an amulet he brings along for stressful occasions like this one.

Swenson takes a sip of wine.

"What do they say in France?" says Len. "*Chin*? Or are they back to *Salud* again?"

"*À votre santé*," Swenson says.

"That was decades ago," Len says.

Did Len always make this much eye contact? Or does it come with the mature middle-aged married-guy-with-kids sincerity that he's laboring to project, together with the druggy puckishness so integral to his image: the wood sprite and former cocaine abuser who has gotten away with it, thanks to his killer literary and commercial instincts.

"How's the family?" Len asks, just as he always used to in his bachelor days, when he was rumored to be sleeping with a new publishing groupie every night. Back then, he'd said it with condescension and pity, but now Swenson detects camaraderie. Len has two small kids and a marriage, to a former agent, that no one dreamed would last.

"Quiet Thanksgiving," Swenson says.

Len says, "Congratulations."

"And yours?"

"*This* is quiet. Comparatively." Len means the noisy restaurant. He looks around, taking it in. Something or someone (a woman?) behind Swenson appears to have snagged Len's attention, and a long interval passes before he turns back again.

"Sorry," says Len. "I spaced out. LSD flashback. I *wish*. This place is a tomb compared to home with my kids. And that's when they're sleeping."

"Little kids," Swenson commiserates. "You gotta be young—" He stops. Will Len be offended?

Len leans forward again. "It's not just kids. Denny—you know, our eight-year-old—has been having some problems."

Problems has an ominous sound. "I'm sorry," Swenson says.

At that moment, the waitress appears. "Have you decided?"

"That's what I love about this place," says Len. "No waiters named Keith reciting long lists of specials. There's the twenty-ounce sirloin, the twelve-ounce sirloin, the nine-ounce, the rack of lamb. I'll have the twelve-ounce. Still mooing."

"Make that two." Swenson hates rare meat.

"Good man," says Len. "Eat, drink, and be merry. While we still have our teeth."

"What's the problem with Denny?" asks Swenson.

"ADD," says Len. "Attention deficit disorder."

"I know what it stands for," Swenson says. "Even out in the boonies we get all the new diseases."

"Easy, big fella," Len says. "Look . . . this is not a joke. . . ."

"Sorry," Swenson says.

"Where the fuck is that waitress?" Len says. "Wasn't she just the fuck here? It's been hell with the kid. Ellen and baby Andrea have pretty much taken to their beds. The living room's a battle zone. . . ."

"What does he do?" asks Swenson.

"The usual," Len says. "Totally distractable. Zero patience, zero impulse control. Can't concentrate for one second. Rips the joint apart. The kid's attention's all over the place. And he's got to have what he wants, the instant he wants it."

Does Len not know that he's described his own behavior, symptoms he's exhibited within the last five minutes? Swenson's not about to point that out, nor to suggest that Len sample his kid's medication. Maybe Swenson should try some, too.

"The diagnosis took forever. We dragged the poor kid to every goddamn specialist, psychologist, pediatric psychoneurologist. The poor little fucker spent weeks hooked up to electrodes. At least three-quarters of the doctors were certifiably insane, while we struggled, year after year, with his so-called teachers, bitches who shouldn't be allowed to be in the same room with children."

"That's terrible." Swenson's close to panic. What if Len—in his new incarnation as family man dealing maturely with the problems of raising a privileged Manhattan child—spends the entire lunch on his kids and they never get around to the shallow, careerist, unreconstructed male topic of the business they've come here to transact?

"It took us another two years of dicking around with the kid's dosage. Meanwhile he was bouncing off the walls. Smashing every dish in the house. We must have a zillion years of bad luck on our tab with all the mirrors he broke. He'd take his sister's Barbie and slam it into the mirror till the doll's head exploded. You'd be amazed what damage Barbie can do. Lucky no one got killed. So now the Ritalin seems to be working pretty well, though I think the new doctor's got the kid on enough drugs to tranq a baby rhino—"

"Jesus, Len," says Swenson. "That's child abuse."

It takes Len a second to take this in. Then a sort of milky film hoods his glittery eyes. By now, even Swenson realizes what he's said. He looks down at his glass and feels like one of the Three Bears. Who's been drinking my wine? Could he have drained another glass, and even so, how could it have happened that a few glasses of merlot could turn a hundred-and-eighty-pound man into a raving nasty drunk? Or a ranting truth-teller, depending on how you see it.

"Excuse me?" Len says coldly. Swenson always knew that Len could turn on him in a second for any number of reasons less serious than his accusing him of child abuse. "I'm sure if you'd had to live with the child and seen the way he suffers—"

"I was kidding," Swenson says. How lame can anyone be? "Isn't it scary how everything's child abuse these days? The entire population's remembering it happened to them. These days you feel like you're getting along with your kids if they're not accusing you of using them in ritual blood sacrifice—"

Now what glitters in Len's eyes is crystalline fascination, as if he's watching Swenson commit exquisitely slow public hara-kiri.

No wonder Len likes this restaurant. The waitress has somehow intuited that Swenson requires her intervention, needs her to slap two huge slabs of meat in front of him and Len.

"Wait!" Len says. "Should we do a half-bottle of something really good?"

"Whatever you think," says Swenson. On the one hand he should quit drinking. He's done quite enough damage. On the other hand . . . what has he got to lose? Anyway, his alienating Len—if that's what he's done—would be more of a problem if Swenson had come here to talk about his own book. The fact that he's here on Angela's behalf seems to diminish the importance, the relevance of whether Len likes him or not.

"What a great place," Len says. "Good food and speedy service. Move 'em in, move 'em out. One big revolving door."

Swenson looks around at the lunchtime crowd. None of *them* seem to think they're dining in a revolving door. In fact they appear to be taking their time, enjoying their steaks and all the muscular chewing that red meat demands. Only Len wishes the door were revolving. What does it say about Len's attitude toward Swenson that he's invited him to a place where you can inhale a steak and be out in under forty-five minutes? Swenson flew down from Vermont for this, left his daughter, gave up his day, and Len's trying to get it over with, fast but not so fast that some busboy's Heimlich-maneuver training will be put to the ultimate test.

They chew in silence for a while.

"So how's the novel going?" Len asks.

Swenson wants to think that the food has brightened Len's mood. Or is it yet another of Len's cultivated tics: the learned miming of the implication that the food has brightened his mood and given him the energy to broach the real business at hand?

"Microscopically," Swenson says. "Actually . . . the truth is . . . to tell you the truth . . . I didn't really come here to talk about my novel."

"Then let's not!" says Len. "No problem. Let's just chat. Have lunch."

"No!" Swenson says, too loudly, startling Len. "I actually *do* have a purpose. I've got this novel I think you should look at. Written by one of my students."

"Student writing," Len says. "God help us."

"It's not student writing," Swenson says. "It's very very good."

"I'm sure it is," says Len. He takes another bite of steak, which he swallows when the wine waiter appears with the requested half-bottle. Len sips it, swishes it in his mouth, and gazes, mock moonily, at the waiter. Swenson shields his glass with his hand.

"Better not," he says.

"It's too good not to try," Len says.

"Just one glass," concedes Swenson.

Len savors his wine contemplatively. "I'm glad we did this," he says. "I would have gone nuts if I'd spent the whole day at home, and work is the only excuse, the only way I can get away. God forbid I want to go for a walk, or worse yet, take in a movie. . . ."

If Swenson lets the subject of Angela's book drop now, he'll never get back to it again. "The novel this student's writing . . . it's hard to describe how good it is. To say that it's about a high school girl who has an affair with her teacher is hardly—"

"Well!" says Len. "No wonder you've got child abuse on the brain."

"No," Swenson says, "Trust me. It's not like that at all. The girl wants it to happen. She seduces him. You rarely see that written about, it's always the guy who's some kind of pervert, but in this case the girl. . . . It's like *Lolita* rewritten from Lolita's point of view."

"That's quite a claim," says Len.

"Well, maybe I'm overstating it. But listen—"

"What's she like?" interrupts Len.

"The character?" says Swenson.

"Please," says Len. "The writer."

"Spacey. Punky. Facial piercing. You know."

"Watch out for the spacey ones," Len says. "With women writers,
I mean. They're the killers. Without half trying, we could come up
with the names of a half-dozen women, household names, you'd
swear they had molasses for brains till they sit down at the computer,
and then it's watch out world. Better hang onto your balls. Did I say
computer? I meant typewriter. Half these women would have you
believing the electric typewriter's still way beyond their technological
skills, so they must be dipping their quill pens in little wells of poison."

It's not as if Swenson wouldn't like to share this moment of male
bonding at the expense of these famous women writers, whoever
they are. But Angela's book is the reason he's here, ditching his
daughter for the sake of a kid who will do fine without him.

"It's not just that she's spacey," he says. "It's weirder than that.
She may be a pathological liar. About the strangest things. Why
would someone tell you that her father is her stepfather and that
she has epilepsy when she hasn't? I don't know if she has or hasn't.
Why would a kid lie about that?"

"Is she from California?" Len asks.

"No, why? New Jersey," says Swenson.

"Your wife's from New Jersey, no?"

"Brooklyn," Swenson says.

"Are you fucking her?"

"My wife?" says Swenson, cagily.

"Ha ha, very funny," Len says. "I mean the girl. The student.
The writer."

"Certainly not!"

"Sorry to hear that," says Len, who in fact doesn't want to hear
that Swenson is toeing the politically correct line on sexual harassment. He would have respected Swenson more if he were screwing
the entire female student population.

"But you want to," Len says.

Swenson drains the final drop of his wine.

"Len," he says wearily. "It's not about sex. The girl's got talent. Believe me."

"Oh, I *do*," says Len. "And I'm sure she's very good. The thing is, to be perfectly honest with you, I simply don't have time to look at some chick novel about a girl with the hots for her high school teacher."

"Please," Swenson says. "Just read the first few pages. . . ."

He's begging. So it's decided. What he wants will never happen. Swenson picks up the orange envelope from the chair beside him and holds it out to Len, who pushes it lightly away, as if it were a credit card with which Swenson was offering to pay for lunch. Swenson puts the envelope down.

"Ted," says Len. "Do yourself a favor. Take the manuscript back. Tell the kid you'll show it to me if she lets you fuck her. After that . . . well, you can tell her I told you I wasn't looking at first novels. More wine?"

"Sure," says Swenson.

Len pours two glasses. Swenson drains his in three swallows.

"What about *your* book?" Len says. "Let's get serious here. Because if there's really a problem with the novel . . . You know, I've been thinking about your work. In fact, I've been giving it a lot of thought."

"You have?" says Swenson. "Really?"

"Have you considered a memoir?" says Len. "You don't need me to tell you that what's selling these days has to have the juicy gleam, the bloody smell of the truth. And half the people writing them, well, nothing ever happened to them. Maybe Mom got drunk once or twice, smacked them around a little. But you, my friend, you watched your father incinerate himself on national TV. Writers with childhoods not half so dysfunctional as yours are turning them into gold mines."

"I already wrote the novel." Not just any novel, Swenson thinks. Angela's favorite novel. What would he tell Angela? What would

Angela think if he betrayed everything they believe in to crank out some cheesy memoir? And what about all those other Angelas, his ideal readers, stranded, as she once was, imagining that no one else had ever had troubles like theirs? "You published it, remember?"

"Why should that stop you? It's not the same. Face it, Ted. Novels just don't give the reader the same kind of hard-on. You know how many people read a novel? Ten thousand's good for a novel. Eight, nine thousand in the stores, we're breaking out the champagne. And of the ten thousand—well, let's say the five thousand—people who read your novel, two thousand of them are probably dead and the other three have forgottten. You could start fresh, you're lucky. It's better to start over. Better a hot new memoirist than a middle-aged midlist novelist."

Swenson pushes his knife and fork to the side of his plate. Chewing's out of the question. As it is, he can hardly swallow. A hunk of steak would be suicide.

Len stares liquidly into Swenson's eyes. "I'm not doing this for the sake of the publishing house. I'm doing it as your friend."

"I appreciate that," Swenson says.

"Don't answer now," says Len. "Think about it. Look. I don't know you that well. We've been out of touch. But the best thing— the really good thing—would be if there were something that had been going on since your father's death, some ongoing problem, an update, dues you've paid later on. . . ."

"What *kind* of something?" Swenson says.

"Bad behavior. Drinking, drugs, gambling, spousal abuse. Sex addiction. Compulsively fucking students. That would be great. Maybe you could make it up. Just because it's a so-called memoir doesn't mean. . . . Anyway, something directly traceable to your dysfunctional childhood. And something, of course, you've recovered from."

What would Hemingway have done? Thrown his drink in Len's face. Swenson's glass is empty. Anyway, a gesture like that is way beyond his range.

He lets the silence linger. Then he leans back and says, "So, Len, are the medications still working? Is Denny doing better?"

Sitting in the LaGuardia departure area, Swenson opens his briefcase to take out his copy of *My Dog Tulip* and knows at once: something's missing. His heart starts to pound as he scrabbles frantically through his papers. He pauses briefly to glare at the elderly couple choosing the entertainment he's providing over their boring magazines, then resumes his futile search. He's lost Angela's manuscript. It isn't anywhere. He must have left it on the seat beside him in the restaurant.

He's got twenty minutes before the flight—enough time to find a phone, call information, get the restaurant's number, ask them to send it to him. Then he'll have to watch the mail so Sherrie won't casually open a package from New York.

As the phone rings and rings, Swenson pictures the empty restaurant bathed in golden late-afternoon light. At last a male voice says, "Hello," and Swenson breathlessly explains his problem into the silence before a tape recording tells him, in its unhurried bass, the restaurant's address, hours, its policy on smoking. Swenson knows all that and no thank you, he doesn't want to press *one* to be connected to the reservationist. He'll stay on the line all day until he reaches someone who can help.

A young woman answers. Finally. A sympathetic voice. She asks what's in the envelope. What business is it of hers? He supposes she has to look inside to find out which one of the dozen tangerine-colored envelopes left there that day is his. He should say it's a contract, something important, official. But suppose she *does* look inside. . . .

"It's my novel," he says.

"Oh, dear. Your novel! Let me see." He hears high heels clicking, then silence. She's taking forever! He'll miss his plane and get stuck here overnight while she flirts with the bartender. But now, at last, she's back, to say, Sorry, nothing like that's turned up. Would he care to leave his phone number? No, he wouldn't care to, he wouldn't care to stave off a panic attack every time Sherrie answers the phone.

He hangs up and grimly boards the plane, having the usual fantasy about his imminent death, his loved ones' grief. Today it expands to include the scene of Len appearing at the graveside to tell Sherrie how noble and unselfish her late husband was. Why the very last time they talked, he was trying to sell him some girl's novel. Len would never say that. And what if he did? It won't be Swenson's problem. He'll be in hell, a blessing compared to this.

Halfway to Burlington, the light drops out of the sky. Swenson's alarmed, then remembers. Winter. Sunset. Time passes quickly when you're wrecking your life. He's scared to go home, afraid he'll find that Ruby's decided it wasn't okay for him to go to New York. He wills himself into a sort of trance, in which he manages to get off the plane, find his car, and drive.

The house is dark. Where are they? Has some tragedy occurred? Wait. There's a light in Ruby's room. What could be nicer? Swenson imagines the women talking, sitting on Ruby's bed, the murmuring altos of their voices rising in splashes of laughter.

How thankful he is for his family, for his solid, inviting house, for not being Mr. Lonely Guy pacing the bleak chapped solitude of those wintry Manhattan streets. He grateful he is, and how well he knows that he doesn't deserve what he has. At least he's mature enough to have stayed in control and not totally alienated Len—that is, if you don't count that unfortunate exchange about the overmedicated kid. So why does he think something awful did happen? Because something awful did.

He left Angela's manuscript in a restaurant. Talk about acting out! Why not leave your adulterous love letters on the kitchen table? But now, with safety—refuge—in sight, it occurs to Swenson that he needn't be so upset. Finding someone's lost manuscript is not exactly the same as surprising that person in bed with its author.

Groping through the living room, Swenson feels as if he's burglarizing his own home. He flips on the light—and jumps when he sees Sherrie in her chair.

"What are you doing?" he says.

"I don't know," she says. "Sitting here, thinking."

"Is everything all right? With Ruby?" How ironic, how perfect if some disaster had happened while he was off trying to peddle his undergraduate paramour's novel.

"It's fine," says Sherrie. "Everything's fine. I thought you'd call from the airport."

"I just got there in time for my plane," Swenson lies, and now it seems like a miracle that some catastrophe didn't occur to punish him for all the small, incremental lies like this one. Swenson probes his tooth with his tongue. He's got to see a dentist.

"Is Ruby really okay?" Swenson says. "Was it all right with her that I went?"

"She's fine," says Sherrie. "I told you. Everyone would like to see you get this book done, Ted. Believe me. Oh . . . Ruby needs you to do her a favor? She needs a new computer. We can spring for it, right? She wants you to drive her to Burlington and help her pick one out."

There's a lag before Swenson understands what's being asked. He says, "Sure. That'd be great. I can use a drink about now." He means he can use the activity, the corkscrew, bottle, glasses, breathing space, a reason to leave the room.

"Me, too," Sherrie says.

He pries a bottle loose from the rack in the pantry, then opens the kitchen drawer and roots around for the corkscrew, all the while pretending to be a normal husband pouring wine instead of a madman slipping irretrievably into insanity. Shouldn't he be happy that his prodigal daughter wants his company, his advice, his two thousand dollars, that she's offering him the chance to win her love, to buy it back for the modest price of some home electronics?

So what if he has to take the same trip he took with Angela? Is he afraid he'll get caught? For what? No one's going to report you to the authorities for buying computers for two young women. Besides which, he didn't *buy* Angela's. He just went along for the ride. It's good that he went with Angela. Practice, in a way. Ironing out the bugs before he makes the trip—the real one—with his daughter.

He fills two glasses, gulps from his. Not a moment too soon. His hands stop shaking just as Sherrie appears in the kitchen doorway. "What about the computer she already has?"

"Christ, Ted. She's been using her desktop from high school. She told me it takes fifteen minutes to save a file."

It pleases Swenson to think of Sherrie and Ruby talking about something so normal as saving a file. "Fine. I'd love to. They're open tomorrow? Right?"

"They're open Saturday," Sherrie says, with the exasperation that must creep into her voice when a student makes her repeat medication directions. "By the way, one of your students called."

"Oh? Want some wine?" Swenson passes her a glass without turning around, so he won't have to meet her eyes, an avoidance he justifies by pretending that the cork is in urgent need of unskewering from the corkscrew. No reason to assume that "one of your students" means Angela.

"She sounded upset," Sherrie says. That narrows the list of suspects. But it could be . . . Jonelle Brevard, who hasn't handed in the story they were supposed to do after vacation; Claris had to volunteer to bring in something instead. He wishes it were Jonelle. The range of what Jonelle could want is so much narrower than the possibilities of Angela's phone conversation with his wife.

"Did she leave her name?" asks Swenson.

"No," says Sherrie. "She didn't. She just said she was one of your students, and that she needed to talk to you about her novel."

"Great," says Swenson, dully. "Her novel." A sudden updraft of happiness threatens to float him away. He didn't really wish the caller was Jonelle. Then he thinks, I lost Angela's novel.

"She left a number," Sherrie says. "Her home number. In New

Jersey. She said to call her. Anytime tonight. Is she the one who's so talented?"

Swenson says. "Students! They suck you dry, call any hour, day or night, Friday, Thanksgiving weekend, you're constantly on duty, at their beck and call. . . ."

It would look extremely strange if he rushed off to his study to return a student's call. Besides, he doesn't want to talk to Angela. He's just pleased that she called. If he reaches her, he'll have to say that Len doesn't want to see her book, and oh, by the way, he lost it somewhere in Manhattan.

"She can wait till Monday," Swenson says.

"So can you take Ruby tomorrow?" she says.

"Where?" Swenson knows that he knows. He just can't recall.

Sherrie frowns. "Computer City."

"Absolutely," says Swenson.

In Swenson's dream, he's standing before a table in the middle of nowhere, a void with a certain resemblance to a De Chirico painting. On the table are two goblets, a comb, a feather, a book, and an egg. He knows he's supposed to choose, and he picks up the egg, and the egg explodes in a hail of fire and pain that rockets him out of his nightmare and back into his bed, from which he looks up to see Sherrie standing over him, saying, "She's out there, waiting."

"Who is?" asks Swenson groggily.

"Jesus, Ted. Ruby's in the car. It's after nine. You slept late."

Swenson looks out his bedroom window and down into the driveway. "It's Saturday morning. Are we on some kind of tight schedule?"

"We're on Ruby's," says Sherrie. "Please."

There she is in the passenger seat, staring out the windshield. No point asking her to come inside, have a cup of coffee while he takes a shower. Naturally, Ruby will agree, but with a certain disappointment, an accusatory resignation. Swenson will fail all over again at the job of being her father.

But why should he feel guilty? He's giving up his Saturday and blowing a small fortune. And to compound his sacrifice, he's foregoing a shower, a shave. It's a miracle he doesn't throw out his back as he hops into the same pants he wore down to the city, then squirms into a black sweater he finds over a chair.

Last night, gazing into the fridge, he noticed that Sherrie had bought bagels and smoked salmon, which he's been savoring in his mind, a reward in advance for having to drive to Burlington. Well, there's no time for breakfast now. Anyway, he doesn't deserve it. He didn't need breakfast to console himself when he went with Angela Argo.

He throws on his jacket and rushes outside, jumps into the driver's seat. Ruby turns to look at him. She's gathered her hair in rubber bands, a little spray over each ear. Pigtails—an unfortunate choice for her full pink face. Swenson sees too much of his own face in hers, and not enough of Sherrie's, as well as that rabbity underbite that's always reminded him of his mother. Still, Ruby could be pretty if she'd just stop telegraphing her wish to disappear. She's dressed in blue jeans several sizes too large, and a baggy sweatshirt.

Ruby says, "You didn't have to rush."

"I didn't," Swenson lies.

"Thanks for doing this, Dad," Ruby says.

"My pleasure," Swenson tells her. Then, partly to cover the hollow echo of his words, he leans over and kisses her cheek. It tastes perfumey, of makeup. Ruby stiffens and flinches.

All right. Let's do it Ruby's way. He's giving her his day. The idea floods Swenson with the peace he imagines people feel when they decide to turn their problems over to Jesus.

"Chilly." Swenson shudders.

"Yup," says Ruby. "Nasty."

They turn onto Route 2A, which takes them into the woods. The black branches stream past above them, oozing droplets of ice.

"How's school?" It's not as if Swenson hasn't asked forty times this weekend. But that's one privilege of family life—the right to ignore good manners and the fear of boring others, to repeat things and get the same answers. "Aside from everyone getting sued?"

"Pretty good."

"It gets easier," Swenson says. "Are you having fun?"

"Fun?"

"You know. Friends. Hanging out."

Ruby says, "I work at a rape crisis center, Dad. I wouldn't call that fun, exactly."

"I wouldn't either," Swenson says.

Ten, twelve miles of silence go by, simultaneously tense and boring. As opposed to his drive with Angela—also tense, but fascinating. Swenson inhales audibly.

"Is something wrong, Dad?" Ruby asks.

"Toothache," Swenson says.

"Do you want to go back home?"

"No, I'm fine." After another pause, he says, "Is there that much rape on campus to keep a whole center going?"

"Not really. We also do battered women outreach into the community. We just try to give them a place where they can feel safe, and share."

Feel safe? Share? Who *is* this person? She sounds like Lauren Healy.

"But there was one incident. . . . It's pretty gross. Sure you want to hear this?"

Well, now that she asks, he isn't sure. "Of course I am."

"There was this fraternity party? The whole lacrosse team was there? It was Keg Day, which is this really stupid tradition at my school, like, you're supposed to start chugging beer the minute you get up in the morning and keep drinking till you fall asleep or pass out or whatever. Anyhow, one of the guys had this date. Supposedly his high school girlfriend. She'd come for the weekend, but really she'd come to tell him that she wanted to break up. So . . . this guy gets all his fraternity buddies together, and they drug this girl's drink, and they stretch her out in the frat house living room, and they all take turns pissing on her."

"Christ," says Swenson. "That poor girl."

"I mean *really*." Ruby warms to the heat of her father's outrage. "And the really disgusting part is, she wasn't going to report it—

women always blame themselves and don't come forward in these situations—but two friends of hers witnessed the crime and convinced her that her healing process would go faster if she nailed the guys."

"I'm sure they're right," mumbles Swenson, knowing perfectly well that he should be feeling sorry for the victim instead of for himself and Ruby. He can't believe that his only daughter, the light of his life, goes to a school in which there are students who could piss all over a woman. This kind of thing doesn't happen at Vassar or Harvard. Or Euston, for that matter. How can his daughter be caged in that zoo while, just a few miles away, kids no better than Ruby, girls like Angela Argo, are enjoying the freedom to cultivate their tender feelings? Carlos and Makeesha are in college to have their rough edges sanded off, to prepare for easy lives, good jobs, cocktail parties, while his daughter is being schooled in downward mobility, taught to keep her elbows tucked in and her eyes lowered as she slithers down the chute that leads to subsistence-level employment.

Where did he and Sherrie fail her? *She* didn't want to go to Euston. That would have been a disaster of another sort. It was Ruby's decision to go to State. They couldn't have changed her mind. He tells himself that the future masters of the universe are, in fact, more likely to have been fraternity animals from State than creative writing students from Euston. But why is he even thinking about this? The story Ruby's just told him is far more serious and troubling than the question of where his kid goes to college.

A gray blur streaks across the road. Swenson twists the wheel. The swerve sends Ruby flying into the passenger door. She runs her hands down her upper arms—checking for damage, thinks Swenson. He recalls a grade school drama in which Ruby played a male character. King Midas? The giant in "Jack and the Beanstalk"? Who knows. What he does remember is that something about her performance seemed puzzlingly familiar, and later Sherrie pointed out that Ruby had copied all of Swenson's gestures.

"Dad? Are you sure you're all right? Would you like me to drive or something?"

"I'm fine," he says. "Fine and dandy. Okay?" By now they've

reached the Wendover Inn, and he's mortified by the contrast between the relief he feels—the trip is half over—and how disappointed he was, for the same reason, when he came this way with Angela. He deserves to be in this car hurtling sixty miles an hour down a glorified cow path, on a suicidal journey with this sullen, unhappy young woman pretending to be an older version of the happy little girl who used to bounce up and down, singing her unintelligible songs, beside him in her car seat. It's all his fault. He knows how evil—how unforgivable—it is to be spending the day with his daughter for the first time in more than a year and secretly wishing he were with his little slut of a student girlfriend. Let whatever happens, happen. Let it all come down.

"The school didn't want to press charges," says Ruby. "The Women's Studies Department had to threaten a class-action lawsuit before they'd even investigate."

Another symbol of the vast divide between his daughter and his students: at State, a girl gets pissed on and the school does nothing. At Euston, they have meetings to warn the faculty about saying an unkind or ambiguous word.

Swenson says, "It's only right. Someone has to take responsibility."

"It's not about responsibility," Ruby says. "It's about not having secrets. Everyone knows that secrets can kill—"

You can say that again! The secret that Swenson's keeping is a real killer, as it happens. What if he told Ruby, floated it by her, just to relieve the pressure? Hey, you know, the last time I was here, I was driving around with this student, and we got her a computer and then went back to her room and had sex. *Tried* to have sex. . . .

"Dad," says Ruby, tremulously. "Don't you think you should open your eyes?"

Swenson needn't have worried so about his return trip to Computer City. The place is unrecognizable. It takes him five minutes to find a parking spot. The fluorescent wasteland has turned into a hive of buzzing shoppers, wheeling carts and baby carriages, arguing, discussing, comforting screaming babies. Swenson spies a

toddler whacking at a neatly stacked pyramid of boxed diskettes.
The kid sees Swenson watching, pauses, then slams it again.

The difference has nothing to do with Angela and Ruby. He
came here with Angela on a weekday morning, and now it's the
Saturday of Thanksgiving weekend, the busiest shopping day of the
year. Furled patriotic bunting announces holiday specials.

Ruby pauses near the entrance, disconsolately studying the
crowd. As Swenson heads for the computer department, she lags a
few steps behind him. She takes it for granted that he, the grown-
up, knows where to go, which, as it happens, he *does*, if not for the
reasons she thinks. She gazes at the rows of keyboards and screens,
but can't quite focus or commit herself to trying them out. She
looks autistic, thinks Swenson.

Several grueling minutes pass. All the salesmen are busy or pur-
posely refusing to make eye contact. At last a nervous boy approaches.
His terror of Ruby seems sexual, and clearly the feeling's mutual. She
has no idea what she wants, or needs, or what the confusing specifica-
tions mean. Swenson thinks of Angela reeling off gigabytes, RAM.
Why doesn't Ruby know that?

Ruby looks at the kid, than at Swenson. She's on the brink of
tears. Even the unconfident salesman is moved to awkward gal-
lantry. With a sweet, fraternal reassurance that Swenson feels certain has nothing to do with inflating his commission and everything
to do with keeping Ruby from flying apart in front of their eyes, he
shows her a computer that he says may suit her needs—as if she
knew what her needs were and had managed to make them clear.
It's the third cheapest computer. Swenson wants to hug the kid,
which, he knows, would only increase their collective discomfort.

Somehow they get through the transaction with minimum
embarrassment and join the long queue shuffling toward the cash
register, shoppers trudging forward in silence, like deportees.
When he'd come with Angela there hadn't been a line. The salesman had borrowed her credit card and flown across the store while
Angela browsed the computers and Swenson watched her brows-
ing. The card flew back, and Angela signed.

Nothing's that simple this time. The machine rejects Swenson's card while he watches in growing panic, certain that his life has crashed and burned without his suspecting, some fresh disaster related to Angela or to his trip to Manhattan.

The teenage girl at the cash register says, "I never had this happen before."

Swenson says, "Try it again."

The second time it doesn't work, Swenson says, "What *is* this?"

The third time, he says, "What the *fuck is* this?" The register girl won't look at him but stares fixedly at the LCD screen. At last she grins. The card goes through. Swenson signs the slip, and he and Ruby leave.

As they wait in the long line of cars inching past the pickup window, he scans the radio stations. Ruby says, "Dad, could you turn that down?" Annoyed, he turns it off.

"Sorry," Ruby says.

"Don't be sorry," Swenson says.

The guys at the pickup window can't find Ruby's order. Five, ten minutes go by. Swenson attempts to stay calm despite the pressure building behind his eyes. He taps his palm on the steering wheel. Some small, childish part of him wants Ruby to understand what a giant inconvenience this is. Let her feel guilty for once.

Ruby stares straight ahead, while Swenson twists around, shooting furious glares into the warehouse window. He wants to take her in his arms and swear that everything will be fine, that he and Sherrie love her, they will always love her. At last someone produces their boxes and goes to the apologetic extreme of sending a young bodybuilder out to load them in the trunk.

It's not till they're back on the road, moving at a decent speed, that Swenson feels able to attempt conversation. "I think you made a good choice," he said. "I think it will be useful, make it easier to write your papers—"

"Case histories," Ruby corrects him.

He thinks, I have to call Angela.

"Case histories," Swenson repeats.

Three sharp taps rattle the glass on his office door. He'd know Angela's knock anywhere.

On the afternoon he got back from Computer City with Ruby, he'd called Angela's dorm room and left a message on her machine telling her to meet him in his office Monday morning. If he'd reached her at home, he'd have had to explain over the phone what happened with Len. Better to do it in person. At the time, it had seemed a smart solution. But now he wants to bolt and run, hop the first flight to Tahiti. Or anywhere. Downtown Seattle! He pictures himself in a seedy hotel over an XXX video store, registered under a false name, sitting—happy, compared with this—on the edge of a lumpy bed.

Angela stumbles into the room. What has she done to herself? Devoted her Thanksgiving to advanced facial piercing, adding a tiny ball bearing to the center of her lower lip, another ring in one nostril, a triangular silver billy-goat beard bubbling from her chin. The holes must have been there before. She must have put in the extra jewelry as a holiday surprise for her parents. Her *Mad Max* look is emphasized by the vampire makeup: white geisha powder, black lipstick, sooty kohl smeared on her eyelids. Actually, the total effect is less *Mad Max* than *La Strada*. There's a glint of fear in her eyes, as if she's being chased. Did something traumatic happen at home? Did her parents deceive him with their goofy goodwill?

Angela flings herself into the chair. And then, in an unusually loud and strident voice, she says, "I hate it when you look at me like that."

Has she gone mad over Thanksgiving break? A weekend with her parents has driven her over the edge. The extra facial piercing is merely the external symptom. Swenson has read descriptions of how schizophrenia can strike suddenly, unpredictably, in early adulthood, often in association with a young person's first leaving home. Something horrible *must* have happened. Swenson longs to touch her shoulder, to comfort her in some way, but remembers how, the last time he did, one thing led to another. Their history has made it impossible to distinguish a simple gesture of concern from a sexual come-on.

"Look at you like what?" says Swenson.

"Like dinner," Angela says.

"I'm sorry," says Swenson. "Believe me. I didn't think I was looking at you like dinner."

Maybe she's just worked up about Len having seen her novel. Maybe she senses that if the news were good, Swenson would have called her at home. Her fate is at a crossroads, and it's his happy job to tell her it's taken a turn for the worse. Really, he should just lie to her. He's gotten so good at lying.

"I left your manuscript with Len Currie. He said he's terribly busy, but he'll try to take a look at it. Of course he may be *too* busy, and he'll pretend he's read it and just send it back." It's not a total lie. He did leave her manuscript with Len. Or somewhere.

"When can I call him?" Angela says.

"How was your Thanksgiving?"

"Grisly. So how soon can I call your editor? And, like, ask if he's read it?"

"That just isn't done!" says Swenson. "I don't think he'd like that. I'm afraid that might make him decide not to read it at all."

As Angela tilts her head back quizzically, Swenson thinks he sees something metallic wink high up in one nostril. The energy rushes out of him so fast he feels as if he's deflating. He should have told the truth in the first place. It just seems more peculiar now.

"Look, I lied. I didn't leave it with Len. Len's not reading first novels. So it isn't personal. It's not like he read it and didn't like it—"

"I knew that," Angela says. "I knew if it was good news you would have called me. I knew something terrible happened."

"Nothing terrible happened. Come on. You're young, the book isn't even finished. Besides which, you and I know that this isn't what matters. Publication, reputation, fame, none of it matters as much as the work—"

"Fuck you," Angela says.

"Wait," Swenson says. How dare she? He left his family and flew to New York—at considerable personal expense—to try and do her a favor, and this bitch is saying *fuck him*? "Fuck *you* is more like it. I went out of my fucking way for you, I went all the way into Manhattan to have lunch with my editor so he could treat me like shit, so he could tell me to write a memoir about my early life, all the stuff I already covered in *Phoenix Time* but this time telling the so-called truth—"

"What did you tell him?" Angela asks.

"Of course I won't write it," says Swenson. "I'm a novelist. An actual *writer*. I've still got some . . . standards." Oh, listen to the fatuous, grating drone of his voice!

"*I* would have written the memoir if someone said they'd publish it," Angela says. "If someone said they'd pay me for it. It's easy for you to have standards, you and your nice fat teaching job, your tenure forever and ever. You never have to write another word, you'd still have time to write, whereas if I wind up working in a drugstore—and with my parents' connections, that's the best-case scenario—I will not have time to write, while you sit here making your little moral distinctions about not selling out your fabulous talent."

Angela approaches the desk, leaning so close to Swenson that he sees red patches marbling her face under the rice-powder white.

"I can't believe you let this happen," she says. "I can't believe you didn't fight harder for me. The only reason I let you fuck me was so you would help me get this novel to someone who could do something—"

Swenson feels his spirit separating from his body. Now he knows what he was dreading, but this is worse than whatever he'd feared. He feels as he does when he hurts himself, cuts his finger or stubs his toe, and in that first moment understands that the real pain is still to come, taking its own sweet time, waiting until the adrenaline goes and leaves him unprotected.

"I didn't know it was about that," he says. "I didn't think it was about you *letting* me fuck you. I thought it was what we both wanted, and we both knew that all along."

"Well, let me know if you figure it out," Angela says, and rushes out of his office. Swenson listens to her boots pounding down the stairs. A short time later the noise stops. Has she paused halfway down? Is she considering running back up, telling him she's sorry? The footsteps continue, growing fainter, until he can no longer hear them.

On Tuesday, Angela isn't in class. Swenson half expected her to be absent. But when he walks in and sees that she's not there, he's shocked by the intensity of his disappointment.

"Who's missing?" he says, unsteadily.

"Angela," says Makeesha. They know he knows that, they can read it on his face. No one's forgotten the session before Thanksgiving break—Swenson's impassioned oration on the subject of Angela's talent. And now they seem to be taking a sour triumph in her absence. She's gotten the praise she wanted, heard what she wanted to hear. Why should she waste any more precious time slumming among her inferiors?

Swenson takes a deep breath. "Anybody know where she is?"

"I saw her in the dining hall at lunch," says Carlos. "She didn't say anything about blowing off class."

Claris says, "I saw her leaving the dorm this morning." Is her steely, meaningful look a reference to the time she saw *Swenson* leaving the dorm?

"Well, that's too bad," says Swenson brightly. "It would have been nice to hear what Angela thought of Claris's wonderful story."

He's not supposed to say *wonderful*, to register his approval before they've all delivered their unbiased critical opinions. But why not let them know that Claris has written something good—that is, good for Claris? Angela isn't the only one whose work Swenson likes.

Claris's story is about a boarding school freshman, a rich white girl from Bloomfield Hills, assigned to room with a black student—a plastic surgeon's daughter from Brentwood. They get along perfectly well. But when the white girl goes home for vacation, her parents grill her about her roommate, a pseudoliberal, pseudoconcerned expression of interest in their daughter's life that is actually an attempt to make sure they're not paying twenty-eight grand a year so their darling can room with a gangbanger from Watts. Exasperated, the girl gives them what she thinks they want, a story about her roommate being a former gang member who quit when the gang did something awful. Of course, the story's invented, but after she tells it, the girl realizes that now she won't ever be able to bring her roommate home for school vacation. Her parents will never believe that she lied, that the gang story isn't the true one.

"Read us a paragraph, Claris." Swenson's beginning to think he can do this. Before he knows it, an hour will have passed, and he will be free to leave this room where Angela used to be, this room without Angela in it.

Claris pages through the manuscript to find the story within the story—the lie that the girl tells her parents.

> "So I told them that my roomate burst into tears one night and told me about this guy she liked, the first boy she ever kissed, and how he was a gang member, and they wanted her to join, and she was all ready to go through these dangerous, disgusting initiation rites until one night she found out they'd done something so bad she wouldn't even tell me.
>
> "'Are you sure she wouldn't?' said my mom. 'Or is it that you won't tell us?'"
>
> 'I told her I didn't know. I could have made it up, just like the rest. But I didn't want to give them that."

Claris says, "I guess I'll stop reading here."

After the obligatory silence, Makeesha says, "Well, I'll jump in. I think it was really cool, man. Really *real*. You know what I'm saying? White folks wanting to hear that shit about a sister." Makeesha means it as praise. Too bad she's zeroed in on the worst thing about Claris's story: Its obvious political point.

"What about the rest of you?" Swenson says.

"It was kind of bitchy," Carlos says. "I liked that."

"I liked it a lot near the end," Danny says. "When she had to go back and deal with her roommate after she tells those lies to her parents."

"I liked that, too," says Nancy, who likes anything Danny likes.

Courtney raises her hand and wiggles her fingers. Her nails are painted a frosted purple, like grapes afflicted with some sort of silvery blight.

"Courtney," says Swenson, "chime right in. You don't have to raise your hand."

"I have one teensy criticism," Courtney says. "That story about the gang. Maybe it could have more detail so it could be like one *particular* gang and not *any* gang."

Does Courtney not know that she's repeating word for word what the class said to her about *her* story? It's not uncommon for students to parrot advice they've received—the mark of the successfully brainwashed prison-camp survivor. What makes it all the more piquant is that Courtney doesn't seem to realize that the lie the rich girl tells her parents, the bullshit white-folks dinner-table version of black experience, is a summary—a conscious parody—of Courtney's story. And what's stranger still is that Swenson hadn't noticed until this minute. He's horrified, and at the same time it seems kind of funny. The other students sneak worried looks at Swenson and Courtney. Let them worry. Let them look. Who cares where the class goes from here. Why not end this charade right now? What's the point of pretending that Claris's decent but mediocre effort—written for all the wrong reasons—can be greatly improved? He picks up Claris's manuscript, then puts it down.

"Well, I guess that's it," Swenson says. "Anyone else?" It's neither a question nor an invitation. The discussion is over. "See you next week." He doesn't ask whose story they'll be discussing. The students are upset, and they're right to be, especially Claris, who has worked hard at something and done well, and for whom he has not come through.

"You mean that's *it*?" says Carlos. "Coach, we've been here, like, twenty minutes."

"That's it," Swenson repeats. "Beat it. What's wrong with you? If some teacher told *me* I was getting out of school early, I wouldn't be sitting staring at him with my mouth hanging open."

Slowly, hesitantly, one by one, they zip their backpacks, stand, put on their coats.

Carlos says, "Get some sleep, Coach."

Claris's "Thank you" is icy.

"Bye-bye now," Courtney says.

Dazed, they slouch out of the room. Swenson thinks of a story he heard when he first came to Euston, a cautionary tale about a teaching fellow who started coming into class drunk, scheduling her student conferences for midnight at a Mexican restaurant in Winooskie. Her students were so frustrated that at last, when she passed out in class, they put a paper bag over her head on their way out of the room. This story used to comfort him. He'd think, As long as I got through class without a bag over my head, things are under control. But now, as his students file past him, he knows that if they had a large enough bag, they wouldn't hesitate to use it.

Back in his office, Swenson finds the light on his telephone blinking. Obviously, Angela's calling to explain her absence. He pushes the button and for a moment can't understand why Angela's speaking in a male voice with a British accent.

It's Francis Bentham saying he needs to see him, asking him to call his secretary. ASAP. Why does the dean want to talk to him? He hasn't done anything wrong. Maybe he's been chosen Teacher of the Year. The dean can't wait to tell him. Or he's been put on some committee that's supposedly a huge honor, and he'll have to find a way to say thanks but he doesn't feel worthy. Still, he doesn't like the sound of *need*. I need to see you. No one *needs* to see you to say you've been chosen Teacher of the Year. He doesn't like that ASAP, nor, for that matter, does he like the fact of Francis Bentham calling him in his office. Could Claris have told the dean she saw him in Angela's dorm?

Swenson dials. The way Bentham's secretary says, *"Oh,"* when he gives his name increases his unease. She says, "Tomorrow morning at nine? Can you come in then?"

Swenson doesn't like that, either.

"Would nine-thirty be better?" the secretary says.

"Nine would be perfect," says Swenson.

The dean's office always makes Swenson think of some exclusive London brothel where members of Parliament can request the fantasy rooms. The scenario to be enacted here is "the headmaster's private office," and whatever's going to transpire between the naughty schoolboy and the punishing principal or, alternately, the punishing schoolgirl and the groveling headmaster, will do so amid props designed to heighten the pleasurable illusion: the leather chairs, the spooky lighting, the bookshelves, the enormous mahogany desk so perfect for bending over, all guarded by the faithful spaniel staring out from the painting burnished during its previous life in some gentlemen's club. Doesn't it bother anyone that the dean of a liberal arts college has no art on his walls except for a portrait of someone else's dog?

Rising to shake Swenson's hand, Bentham shuts the door and tells his secretary to hold all his incoming calls. "Ted. Please. Sit down." He goes back behind his desk. "I appreciate your coming in on such short notice."

Swenson says, "No problem. I don't have much on the calendar for this hour of the morning."

"Yes, well. Good. Well, then . . . maybe we should dispense with the small talk and get to the point. Let me show you what we've got here, and we can proceed from there." Bentham opens his top drawer and takes out a tape recorder, sets it on the desk, exactly halfway between them. For a moment Swenson thinks he means to record their conversation. Then Bentham pushes a button and slides it closer to Swenson. Static, a faint hum of voices. Eventually, a female voice emerges from the white noise:

"I hate when you look at me like that."

"Look at you like what?" says a man's voice.

"Like dinner."

"I'm sorry," the man says. "Believe me. I didn't think I was looking at you like dinner."

In the blare of static, Bentham stares at Swenson. His usual air of ironic bemusement has solidified into contempt. All right, if Swenson has to, he'll admit it. That's his voice. And Angela Argo's. How did they get on tape? He listens with voyeuristic fascination, as if he has no idea what's coming.

"I left your manuscript with Len Currie," says Swenson's voice. "He said he's terribly busy, but he'll try to take a look at it. Of course he may be *too* busy, and he'll pretend he's read it and just send it back."

"When can I call him?" Angela says.

A subdued roar of static. Something's been edited out. Probably the crucial words that will make it instantly clear that these exchanges aren't at all what they sound like.

"Fuck you," says Angela.

"Wait," Swenson says. "Fuck *you* is more like it. I went out of my fucking way for you, I went all the way into Manhattan to have lunch with my editor so he could treat me like shit, so he could tell me to write a memoir about my early life, all the stuff I already covered in *Phoenix Time*."

Another gap. Then Angela says, "I can't believe you let this happen. I can't believe you didn't fight harder for me. The only reason I let you fuck me was so you would help me get this novel to someone who could do something—"

"I didn't know it was about that," says Swenson. "I didn't think it was about you *letting* me fuck you."

On the tape, more static, the crash of a slamming door. Then footsteps running downstairs. How strange that a tape would be sensitive enough to pick up footsteps in the hall. And only now does it dawn on Swenson that the recorder was attached to Angela.

The footsteps stop. Swenson remembers thinking she'd hesitated on the stairs to consider turning around and coming back. In fact she'd only paused to switch off the machine.

Bentham turns off the recorder.

"Holy Christ," says Swenson. "That little bitch came to that conference wired."

None of this makes sense. Why was Angela out to get him? How could she have been taking revenge for what hadn't happened yet? Before their conference, she didn't know he'd failed with Len, so her making the damaging tape was a little . . . premature. But now he remembers her saying that she *did* know, that his not having called her was a sign. Still, no one would be cold-blooded enough to have it all figured out—to calculate that she'd have this useful evidence, in case she needed it later. Useful for what? Evidence of what? What was Angela doing? Arranging a little blackmail to make Swenson hang in there and not give up—and try again with his editor? But then why didn't she blackmail *him*? Why did she give it to Bentham?

"That little bitch," repeats Swenson—the only words he seems to know. Bentham flinches, delicately. Rolling his eyes upward, he tells the ceiling, "Ted, maybe it's premature to warn you that everything you say can be used against you. But . . . "

"I see," says Swenson. "So am I under arrest? Are you reading me my Mirandas?"

"Miranda?" Does Bentham think it's a woman's name? Another student Swenson's dating?

"My legal rights. It's that little problem we Americans have about our constitutional protections."

"Ha ha," says Bentham. "Of course. Ted. Well, the evidence . . . "—he points at the recorder, his face at once regretful and accusing—"looks pretty damning."

"Meaning what?"

"Well, that depends on you." Bentham taps his fingertips together. "We have several options. Look, this is unpleasant, so let me come right out and say it. The student is charging you with sexual harassment. She's threatening to sue the school. And given what she's presented us with, I really think you might consider—for everyone's sake—resigning. I wouldn't ask you to do it just for the college, old chap. I'd say go ahead and fight if you want. But you have a family to consider, and a professional reputation."

Old chap! Swenson never realized just how much he hates the academic British, with their phony Marmite-smeared *politesse*. What does Bentham expect him to say? Yes, sir, I'll be right on my way, just give me a second to clean out my office. What about justice? Swenson's innocent. It was Angela who dragged *him* to Computer City, Angela who lured *him* into her room, Angela who rolled up her skirt. Though of course he could have declined. Just say no. He knows about the power differential between teacher and student. But this wasn't about power. This was about desire. Mutual seduction, let's say that at least. He's too embarrassed to let himself think, This was about love. And he's not going to think that, not with Bentham watching!

"And my so-called options?" He folds his hands in unconscious mimicry of Bentham.

"Well," Bentham says, "I suppose we'd have to form a committee to look into this. Gather testimony. Interview students. Faculty. Put together a report. Make recommendations. Then, if necessary, hold a hearing. I assume it will be necessary." Another nod at the tape. "And so forth." Bentham shudders.

"And if this committee decides I'm guilty. What then?"

"We'd have to let you go, Ted. It's grounds for dismissal."

"What about due process? Should I be calling my lawyer?" What lawyer? He doesn't have a lawyer.

"This isn't a court of law," says Bentham, wearily. "It's strictly intramural. It's spelled out in the faculty handbook under sexual harassment."

"Wait one motherfucking minute!" Swenson says. "This is *not* sexual harassment. I didn't make this girl sleep with me in exchange for pimping her novel."

"Actually, it sounds like the textbook *case* of sexual harassment." Bentham nods familiarly at the tape recorder. "And by the way . . .

Miss Argo has asked me to ask you not to contact her until this matter is settled."

Miss Argo? And that's the moment when Swenson decides to take the college down with him. He's not going to go meekly. He'll make sure the damage spreads until no one can contain it. Let's see what this does to Euston's endowment! He'll be damned if he rolls over. Meanwhile, the implications are sinking in. His life is ruined, his marriage is finished. Sherrie will leave him, he'll be all alone, jobless, out on the street. Sell the house, hire lawyers.

"What do you say, Ted?" asks Bentham.

"Let's do it. Let's have the hearing. How long will the goddamn thing take?"

The dean looks at his calendar, but only for punctuation. He knows what the date is. "Well . . . Christmas vacation's coming, then reading period. I think we ought to move fast and not let this drag on. Maybe by the second week of the new semester."

"Excellent," Swenson says.

Bentham says, "You know, this sort of thing can function like a . . . malignancy in the community, spreading all sort of rot. Early detection, early cure. In the meantime, your paycheck will keep coming, of course. But it might be better for everyone if you take a break from teaching. I'll ask Magda Moynahan if she'd mind taking over your class. I believe there are only three classes left until the semester ends. Think of it as a minisabbatical. Get some writing done."

On this note of jolly faux levity, Bentham rises and puts out his hand. Swenson refuses to shake it. He stands there, glaring at Bentham. One corner of Bentham's thin mouth is twitching, because *this* really appalls him, this breach of good manners, of gentlemanly conduct. Screwing a student is nothing compared to refusing a colleague's handshake.

Swenson knows it's infantile, declining Bentham's handshake. But it's not nearly so regressive as the fact that, despite the trouble he's in, he's thrilled to have been excused from teaching three whole weeks of classes. School's over for the semester! Or . . . possibly forever. Swenson's childish elation gives way to foreboding and adult regret.

"We'll talk soon, Ted," says Bentham.

"I'm afraid so," Swenson says.

Swenson gets as far as the top step of the administration building, where disorientation and paralysis bring him to a full stop. It's the strangest sensation, really. He doesn't know where he should *be*. He won't be teaching for a while. So what is he doing on campus? He can't go to his office, where the telephone will only remind him that there is no one he can call to talk about what's just happened.

He could leave town. They'd like him to leave town. But this may be the first time since he got here that he *hasn't* wanted to leave. All he wants is to go home, but he can't go home, where every room, every object will confront him with the evidence of how recklessly, how pointlessly he's destroyed everything, with the fact that he has to tell Sherrie—and how is he supposed to do that?

As it turns out, he's able to get in the car and drive. He circles the campus several times. This must be what people mean when they talk about a fugue state. This is how you wake up and find yourself in Caracas. He goes home and gets into bed, fully clothed. He gets up twice to piss, takes his shoes off, falls asleep, wakes at noon, sleeps again, wakes at three, showers, and drives to the clinic.

Arlene Shurley's at the reception desk.

"Oh, hi there, Ted," she says. The sea of tears in her voice has risen to a new level, and just for a moment Swenson thinks she knows about his problem. That's pure paranoia. Arlene's not exactly the college's most plugged-in person. And yet she's barely able to speak as she waves him back to the treatment room, where Sherrie's filing charts. When he sees her, he wants to throw himself at her feet and tell her the truth right here and now, to swear his undying eternal love and beg her forgiveness.

He says, "Want to go out to dinner?"

A flicker of wariness glints in her eyes. So this is what it's come to. He can't even ask his wife out to dinner without her suspecting him of having some secret agenda.

"Are we celebrating something?" Sherrie asks.

"A day without disaster."

"That's worth celebrating."

"Maybelline's?" says Swenson.

"Yikes," says Sherrie. "Burlington? We might want to save that for a *month* without disaster."

"There won't be any months like that," Swenson says. "We might as well go tonight. Want to go now?"

"Ted, it's four in the afternoon."

"Oops," says Swenson. "Alzheimer's. Sorry."

Sherrie's almost finished her shift. Arlene can take over. It's arranged they'll meet at the house so Sherrie can shower and change. Swenson rushes home, determined to get there first, as if there's some evidence of wrongdoing there that he needs to clean up fast. He feels like a kid who's had a party with his parents gone, except that he's a middle-aged man who's spent the day in bed. Alone. Sherrie doesn't need to know that yet. Who can tell where *that* revelation might lead?

He makes and unmakes and remakes the bed, but still it doesn't seem convincing. He feels like the victim of an obsessive-compulsive disorder. He gets back into bed, still clothed, though this time he takes off his shoes. He can admit to *this* nap, but not to the last one, though this nap is the phony one—clenched eyes, watchful awareness, listening for Sherrie's car, a state in which he finds himself frozen even as he hears Sherrie call his name. She tracks him to the bedroom. He keeps his eyes closed tight.

Sherrie goes into the bathroom. He hears the shower running. He waits a few minutes, then follows her. He knocks, makes a point of his presence. Sherrie hates being surprised.

Through the veil of the shower curtain and the cloud of steam, Sherrie's body works on him: that old Pavlovian magic. They regard each other through the haze. Sherrie steps out of the tub. In the moments before he stops having second thoughts, or any thoughts at all, Swenson thinks how this might look to someone watching from outside: a man who can sleep with his wife on the evening he's going to tell her that he'll probably lose his job for sleeping with a student. But what would be harder for those stranger's eyes to see are the depths of desperate love that Swenson feels for Sherrie.

At seven on a weekday night, Maybelline's is almost empty. But as luck would have it, Swenson and Sherrie are seated next to a young couple so madly in love that they've left their food untouched and can hardly speak, or move, but stare at each other tremulously over the tops of the wineglasses from which they are too preoccupied to drink.

Would they notice if Swenson grabbed the wine from their table and drained the bottle before the waitress has time to bring him his own? He needs it more than they do. Ordinarily, Maybelline's sound system plays its signature mix of Chuck Berry and Vivaldi, another symptom of the bipolar disorder that has inspired the fairly new, successful restaurant to serve its expensive chef-driven takes on Vermont farm food. But tonight the CD player is silent, out of order perhaps, ripping away the cover of background noise under which Swenson had imagined confessing to Sherrie.

In his dread and confusion, Swenson has reverted to the conventional wisdom that if you're going to deliver shattering information to a loved one, it's best to do it in a public place that will preempt or at least forestall tears, recriminations, hysterical scenes, murder attempts, and so forth. Instantly, he sees the numerous pitfalls in the plan. But it's too late. He's made up his mind. He's going to see it through. If he doesn't do it now, he will have to eventually, and the longer this goes on. . . . He should have come clean months ago.

How much luck can one guy have? The waitress could be Angela's slightly older sister. As she extends one skinny hand to pass out their menus, Swenson glimpses a flower tattooed between her thumb and forefinger.

Swenson studies the menu. Everything costs a fortune. If Sherrie ever stops hating him for what he's about to tell her, she can hate him all over again for spending so much to do it. In spring and summer Maybelline's specializes in hard-to-find items—morels, fiddlehead ferns—gathered by local hippies hired to comb the woods, but now, in the dead of winter, the "seasonal" dishes are mostly game birds and forest creatures glazed with maple syrup.

"Are there any specials?" Sherrie asks.

"No." The waitress shrugs. "I don't think so."

"Think so or *know* so?" asks Swenson.

"No," says the girl. "There aren't any."

"Fine," says Swenson, "We'll take a bottle of the Chardonnay. Now."

"Organic?" says the waitress.

"Toxic," Swenson says. "Please."

The waitress smiles unhappily. The sympathetic look with which Sherrie watches her slink away hardens as she turns back to Swenson. "Christ, Ted, you promised."

"Promised what?"

"To take it easy on people. That kid could be one of your students."

Swenson looks at her, terrified. But this is not about Angela. Sherrie's just stating the obvious.

"Maybe that's the problem." Anyway, he doesn't remember promising any such thing.

"You knew she meant there weren't any specials. She just didn't want to disappoint us."

"She doesn't *think* there are any specials. Is everyone's brain turning to jelly? You don't *think* some kid has strep throat? Try getting away with that. Someone has to set them straight. Just once."

"My God," says Sherrie. "You sound like you're about eighty."

"This is great," says Swenson. "We're spending a hundred bucks to talk about whether the waitress did or didn't *think* there were specials."

On cue, the waitress brings their wine and pours it, sloshing a little ice water out of the bucket into which she plunks the bottle. "Are you ready to order?"

"I'll have the venison," says Sherrie.

Please, prays Swenson, let the deer be tough and claim so much of Sherrie's attention that she's not even looking at him when he says what he has to say. Swenson orders the salmon, realizing, the minute he does, how far it would have had to swim to Vermont. He doesn't have the energy to change his mind, or his order.

Sherrie raises her glass. "To nothing getting too much worse."

"That's probably impossible," Swenson says. "Let's drink to . . . let's drink to patience."

"Absolutely." Sherrie clinks glasses. "To patience."

They drink rapidly and without speaking, then smile gratefully at each other. The mood is almost mellow as Swenson pours out two more glasses and says, "Listen, today I read this weird story in the science section of the *Times* about a new disease, some brain function thing." Despite all his intentions and resolutions, he seems to be lying again. He read it in *yesterday's* paper. He didn't read the paper today, he was too busy finding out that his life is over. He fully expects Sherrie to say that the science section was yesterday, but mercifully, she lets it go, and he proceeds with his story, though without the slightest memory of why he's telling it. "Anyhow, some part of the brain gets damaged or something, and the result is that the patient is constantly smelling fish."

"Fish?" asks Sherry.

"Fish."

"I don't believe it," says Sherrie.

"You don't believe it? It was in the *Times*. Why don't you believe it?"

"Because fish is so obvious. Why couldn't it be like . . . diesel fuel? Coffee? Nail-polish remover? Lilies?"

If Sherrie thinks *that's* obvious, what will she think of the fact that he's taking her out to dinner to confess having had an affair with a student? Well, not exactly an affair, a distinction she might miss, especially when she finds out that a complaint has been filed with the school.

Sherrie says, "I thought Thanksgiving went pretty well. With Ruby, I mean. What do you think about Christmas?"

"I can hardly remember Thanksgiving," Swenson mutters darkly. "I hardly remember anything." Swenson hates knowing something Sherrie doesn't, something that will change everything. It's as if he's watching her, a character in a movie, about to turn the corner behind which the killer waits; he feels a childish desire to cry out and warn her, even though *he* is the murderer lurking around the bend.

"This is not about the past," Sherrie says. "This is about the future. Look into your crystal ball. Do you think she'll come home for Christmas?"

"I hope so," is all that Swenson can say.

After a moment, Sherrie says, "I'm so glad we're in this together."

Swenson has to tell her now. But he makes himself wait until their dinner arrives. He hopes that the food will increase Sherrie's sense of well-being and somehow cushion the shock. He's glad to see their plates come, not because he's hungry, but because it seems to insure a long stretch of time before the waitress will bother them again. He's repulsed by the oily ease with which the layers of salmon divide. He spears a tiny piece on his fork and can barely choke it down.

"Your tooth still hurt?" says Sherrie.

"Sometimes."

"You've got to get it fixed. I can't even offer you any of this venison chop. And it's really delicious."

"I promise," Swenson says. "I'll call the dentist tomorrow. Speaking of promises . . ." He takes a deep breath. "I've got to tell you something. Do you promise not to hate me no matter what?"

Sherrie says, "I can recognize a lose-lose deal when I hear one."

"I mean it." Swenson's tone causes Sherrie to put down the rib bone she's been sucking.

Her gaze is cool and level. "Have you been sleeping with a student?"

Well, that certainly solves the problem of how Swenson's going to put it. And somehow the fact that Sherrie has said it herself makes it sound less serious. She knows about it already.

"I didn't exactly sleep with her," he says, and sees, too late, that she *didn't* know.

"And why didn't you . . . *exactly*?"

"My tooth broke." It's the worst thing he could have said, attaching his sin to a specific time, a memory, to a specific lie, to something that Sherrie does know about, and about which she's so far been sympathetic.

"Let me get this straight," Sherrie says. "You were *going* to sleep with her except your tooth broke."

"Something like that," says Swenson.

"So what did she do? Punch you in the mouth?"

"No," says Swenson. "She should have." Maybe then she wouldn't have needed Dean Bentham to do the punching for her. Only now does he understand that he's made a huge mistake, telling Sherrie in public, as if she were some new girlfriend whose stability was so dubious that he dare not risk doing it in private—where Sherrie might at least have retained some shred of dignity and grace. The drastic speed with which all traces of pleasure and relaxation drain from her face is as obvious, as hard to ignore as a scream, so that even the transfixed lovers beside them turn to watch the train wreck in progress at the next table.

"How did you know?" asks Swenson.

"You think I'm stupid," Sherrie says. "You've always thought I was stupid."

"Never," says Swenson. "That's not true. You're the most intuitive person I know."

"Go fuck yourself!" says Sherrie, and now the happy young couple is staring nakedly at this painful soap opera of true love gone bad.

"Look at me, goddamn it!" Sherrie says. "Why are you looking at them?" The couple scans the room for the waitress. "Tell me something. One thing. Was she the one who called that day you were supposedly in New York?"

"I think so," Swenson says. "I *was* in New York."

"And do you *think* that's who you went to see that day when you told me and Ruby you were going to New York?"

"I was in New York. Having lunch with Len." How glad he is for each occasion to tell the truth. "I'd never lie about something like that. I'm way too superstitious. Suppose my plane had gone down—"

"Too bad it didn't." Sherrie is way beyond being amused by a personality quirk that once—ten minutes ago—might have extracted a smile. "Is she pretty?"

"Not at all."

"Then what is it? Youth? Great body? What?"

"Nothing like that. She . . . can write."

"*She can write*? This is about *writing*? And it never once crossed your mind that your wanting to sleep with this kid might have clouded your . . . literary judgment?"

"It wasn't like that," Swenson says. "I don't think I would have thought twice about her if not for the book she was writing." He shouldn't have said *thought twice*. *Once* would have more than Sherrie could bear, more than he could ask her to bear.

"Oh, I get it," she says. "You didn't fuck a student. You fucked a book. You're like some groupie, like one of those chicks who used to come up to you after readings and be all over you because they *thought* you were some famous writer." Now it's Sherrie who shouldn't have said *thought*. "You're worse than a groupie. You're like some kind of vampire, sucking this kid's blood. A guy whose own daughter won't talk to him because he forgot she existed, he was so self-involved, so in love with his own problems, so interested in his own little ideas about this or that meaningless bullshit, so the only way she can get his attention is to start going out with a guy whose reputation is so bad even her father will have heard about it, even with his head so far up his ass."

This would not be Swenson's version of Ruby's adolescence. But when Sherrie says it, it sounds obvious. Simple common sense.

"You don't have to be Sigmund Freud to see that this has something to do with Ruby." Sherrie has put down her fork and is gripping her steak knife. "So you got a replacement daughter. Which is why it's happening now. And I thought it *wouldn't* happen because of all the times it almost happened and didn't, all those pathetic little crushes you used to get on students, and you'd start simpering about how Little Miss Such-and-Such is really very talented, and you'd start asking me if anyone would still think you were attractive, as if you hadn't asked this each time some little girl, some child flattered you for half a second. . . . And each time we dodged a bullet. You talked yourself out of it, took cold showers, I don't know how you did it. But I knew what was going on. And I thought because it hadn't happened that it wouldn't happen this time, either. But I should have known better. Because every time you hear about some banal guy shit, don't fool yourself into thinking that your guy won't do it. The reason it's such a cliché is because all you guys do it sooner or later. Guys turn out to be guys."

"I guess you could see it that way. . . ." If you wanted to be cruel and reductive. Because it wasn't that way at all. It wasn't about Ruby, or daughters, or youth, or even about sex. It was, he thinks, about love. Which of course is the one thing he can never tell Sherrie. No desire to confess and redeem himself could tempt him to do that to her. And in return for being that large, he wants something larger, too. Forgiveness, some godlike, all-encompassing knowledge. That moment in a Chekhov story when a character sees that God and time are eternal, greater and more enduring than any human problems.

"What's her name?"

"Angela," Swenson says, carefully. "Angela Argo?"

"You're kidding," Sherrie says. "You've got to be joking."

"You know her?" Swenson asks, with such curiosity and enthusiasm that his feelings for Angela are suddenly, nakedly clear.

"Of course I know her," Sherrie says. "She spends half her life at the clinic."

"You do? She does?" Swenson's having trouble breathing. "Is there some problem?"

"She's suicidal," Sherrie says. "Oh, Ted. Jesus. How could you pick on the weakest, most vulnerable, most unstable girl on campus? How could I live with someone for so long and not know him, not know him at all—"

Swenson says, "That poor helpless little girl is suing me for harassment."

"Good," says Sherrie. "I hope they crucify you. I hope they make you pay."

They finish their dinner in silence. Finally, Swenson says, "So what's going to happen now? Do we get to go on being married?"

"Let's see what happens." Sherrie's answer fills him with panic and the almost unstoppable impulse to cry out, like a child, What do you mean we'll see? I want to know *now!*" Repeating it until the grown-up gives in. . . . For some reason, Swenson finds himself thinking of his father and how, near the end, even language fractured for him, words turned into pure sounds whose meanings he could ignore, enabling him to hear a parallel nonsense-conversation of puns and double entendres. At least Swenson was old enough not to bother trying to make sense out of what his father said.

The couple sitting beside them seems to have gotten up and left. At some point when he and Sherrie were at once so engrossed and distracted, the lovers must have retreated into their cocoon of protection and light and grace, of chosenness, of being singled out and granted the singular blessing of being allowed to live in a world in which what's happening to Sherrie and Swenson will never happen to them.

S herrie stays for two weeks, fourteen days that seem longer than their whole life together so far because time stretches out in a sequence of discreet, dreadful moments, no major blowouts, surprisingly, but a steady killing politeness. Every over-careful exchange is a boulder in their path, which they must either squeeze around or gracelessly stumble over. Every conversation dead-ends, every effort they make—Sherrie telling a story about the clinic, Swenson summarizing something he's read—requires a heroic, futile effort to appear natural and normal. When Swenson reaches for Sherrie's hand, he stops himself and draws back; every instinctive, affectionate gesture has come to seem like a calculated ploy, or worse, a heartless insult.

Laughter is impossible. Every motion's a strain: waking, cooking, opening the mail are like acting-class exercises. Their sense of being on stage persists even when they're alone. Sherrie—the confrontational one—is obviously trying to get through this without open antagonism, which means not bringing up his affair with Angela or the upcoming hearing. But there is no other subject, everything is about that.

This is why God made alcohol. Though plenty of people, the guests at Bentham's, maybe Len—and Sherrie, for all he knows—probably think Swenson has had a drinking problem for quite some time, Swenson disagrees. But now is when a drinking problem would solve a lot of more serious problems. This is the moment for which God *created* drinking problems. Swenson watches the cases of wine empty, wrapping the world around him in Styrofoam, cushioning voices and objects as if for the shock of a move, a spongy buffer zone between Swenson and his life. Alcohol keeps him numb and paradoxically energized with an oddly pleasurable anger: white noise that drowns out the dangerous whispers of pain and fear and sorrow.

So he's not paying quite the attention he might when Sherrie comes home and tells him that she'd gone to the library, and there'd been a rally on the steps, the Faculty-Student Women's Alliance with their placards demanding that Euston be made a safe place for women. In preparation for that happy day, they've started redecorating. Banners drape the women's dorms. STOP SEXUAL HARASSMENT NOW. NO WHITEWASH FOR SEXUAL HARASSERS. It's given the bleak, wintry quad a splash of Mardi Gras color.

Poor Sherrie had to walk right by the demonstration. She stood and watched the speakers ranting in that shrill, strained warble that she says could make you understand why guys hate women. Swenson wonders, Was Angela there? When Sherrie passed the demonstrators—they were blocking the steps—Lauren Healy invited her to come up and speak, and the other women cheered.

Sherrie says, "I couldn't get up there and argue with them as if I was on your side. But I've been on your side for so long, I've had so much *practice* being on your side, I couldn't figure out which side I was on, or how to be on anyone else's."

Wine or no wine, Swenson hears Sherrie say *that*. He's still reeling, he hasn't quite caught his breath, when Sherrie tells him she's had it, she's leaving, she's going to stay in the large farmhouse that Arlene Shurley has lived in alone ever since her husband quit knocking her around long enough to miss a curve in the road and plow into a cinderblock shed.

Sherrie's right. You can live with someone forever and not know them at all. Personally, he's astonished to discover that the woman with whom he's spent his life prefers Arlene to him. If, as Sherrie said, guys always turn out to be guys, maybe women turn out to be women, with their *Jane Eyre* and their covens.

On the night after Sherrie moves out, Swenson's a little looped when Ruby calls. But he distinctly hears her say, "I think it sucks, what you did to Mom."

Then she tells him she didn't call to talk about that. She called to say she won't be coming home for Christmas. She's decided to spend the holidays with Sherrie at Arlene Shurley's. Fine. They can have their own private battered women's shelter. Ruby can do an internship with her mom and her mom's weepy friend. Besides, he knows that Ruby is the last person on earth whose mind he would attempt to change with logic or persuasion.

For a few nights, Swenson tries cooking something Sherrie would have made, a simple omelet, or spaghetti carbonara. But the sauce refuses to coat the pasta and sticks in the pan, grainy lumps of butter and cheese, a thick coating of bacon grease. Each culinary attempt involves at least one moment of panic—he can't find the pasta server, the butter's smoking under the omelet—and eventually he gives up. Why not live like the rest of the world? Frozen microwave dinners. Actually, they're not so bad. He and Sherrie should have done this before, instead of making such a *production* of their middle-class gourmet life. But the exotic charm of the freezer section wears off, and after a while he stops eating, though from time to time he heats up a can of baked beans or creamed corn, healthy vegetarian stuff.

Most afternoons, he doesn't drink till five, though sometimes it's closer to four. During the day he reads. Engrossed in his book, he forgets to listen for Sherrie's car, for the noises that will announce she's had second thoughts and come back. He stops waiting for Magda to call and assure him she's still his friend even though it was stupid to get involved with a kid. He stops dreading that Magda will hear about the tape—or worse, that she'll find out he tried to give Angela's manuscript to Len Currie.

Swept along by some plot turn or revelation of character, he can forget his grief over Sherrie and what he'd foolishly thought was his life, and almost convince himself that this apparent curse is really a blessing. He can read as much as he wants, he doesn't have to teach, he is filling up the cup that will spill all over his writing! Meanwhile, he can't help noticing that he's reading the great classics of adultery, or, depending on one's personal interpretation, the great classics of inappropriate, tragic, ennobling, life-changing love. He dips into *Anna Karenina*, rereading his favorite scenes, looks at *Madame Bovary*, tries *The Scarlet Letter*—which he can't get through at all. Passion and its punishments: poison, prison, a train. Not much slack for the sinners. Tolstoy would say that Swenson should find the nearest train to jump under. Which may not be a bad idea. But Swenson won't let himself go there—where his father went.

No one forgives the liars, the cheaters. Except for Chekhov, of course. That's what Swenson wants: the end of "The Lady with the Pet Dog," Gurov and Anna deceiving their mates, neither of them perfect despite their great transformation by love, the love that has lifted them out of the shallow pond in which they'd dog-paddled all their lives. Gurov is still a delusional poseur, Anna still passive and whiny, but they're not just small and ridiculous in their low-rent lusts, but humans, acting out of their mortal desires and dreams and fears, and therefore lovable and forgivable. The hardest part is still before them. Swenson has no trouble believing the hardest part's in front of *him*.

Maybe Tolstoy and Flaubert are right, he should be diving under the train or drinking some poison that will make him swell up and turn blue. But when he lets himself imagine that all of this is being observed and forgiven because he's only human, with all his flaws and imperfections, well, then he can actually get himself up off the couch and make some token attempt to wrest control of his day from the suicidal kamikaze who most times seems to be driving.

During one such attempt to act like an adult whose future is at risk, Swenson returns Angela's book of poems to the library. He doesn't know or care, really, if this will help or hurt his case. His instinct is purely expulsive. He wants it out of the house. He goes at eight, when the library opens, an hour when no self-respecting Euston student would be studying, when even the members of the Women's Alliance are still snuggled in their beds, dreaming of

Amazon utopia. Not even Betty Hester has come to work, but is home trying to dislodge those half-dozen children from their nest under her skirts.

Amazingly, no one's at the desk. The sanctuary is unguarded. Anyone could steal anything from the magazine rack. Swenson rushes out of the library, so energized by the ease with which he's aced this dangerous mission that he feels emboldened to attempt a trip down Main Street. Since Sherrie left, he's avoided town, not for fear of meeting someone he knows, but rather from an irrational terror of Christmas decorations. If he stays home, avoids the radio and TV, and confines himself to books whose authors are dead, he can generally manage not to notice what season it is. Not that he's ever had a particular attachment to the holidays—quite the opposite, in fact—but he's sure that his already low spirits will dip further if he remembers that his wife and daughter have left him just in time for Christmas.

Once again, Euston comes through. His dear little country town! What was he imagining—the gaudy splendor of Fifth Avenue department store displays? A string of lights flickers weakly around the edge of the awning at the convenience store. On the napkin of frozen grass in front of the Congregational Church, the Adoration of the Magi is being enacted by a group of store-window mannequins in golden crowns and purple terrycloth bathrobes. It's hardly a scene to bring tears to one's eyes, and Swenson passes by unscathed, so heartened by this that he decides to stop at Video Village. Miraculously—this *is* his lucky day—the store is open early, possibly for stay-at-home moms who have dropped off the kids at day care and are facing the gloomy hours ahead.

Swenson evades the glittery enticements of the new arrivals, sails past the siren song of the depressing romantic comedies, and heads for the classics section. *Brief Encounter, Rules of the Game*—his principles of selection seem to be roughly similar to those that currently govern his choice of reading material. He takes *The Blue Angel* off the shelf and considers renting it, then puts it back with a sort of shudder, not of distaste but attraction. He tells himself he'll save that for when he really needs it, for when he needs to see another pitiful self-abasing slob transformed by the magic of art into a tragic hero.

And yet for all the care that Swenson takes to cushion his fragile psyche from the shock of holiday cheer and the grim reality of family celebration, he knows, he would know in outer space, when it's Christmas Eve. He buys a gallon of good rum and several cartons of supermarket eggnog, which he mixes together in a crystal punch bowl—if he's going to do this, he might as well do it right—but then, unable to find the ladle, dips his coffee mug into the eggy mess. After several cups, he finds himself thinking with amusement of all the terrible Christmases, strung out like some freakish popcorn-and-cranberry chain, reaching back to his boyhood. The Christmas when his father gave him, as his only gift, an impressive selection of nasty old bottles containing specimens of algae from the coastal waters; the Christmas that Ruby's brand-new doll came broken from the store and refused to talk or wet itself or perform in any way, and Ruby spent the day wailing that she wanted a new one *right now*.

How much better this is! Privacy, peace and quiet, enough eggnog to make himself puke, a library of comforting, suitable books. It's been years since he's looked at *A Christmas Carol*. So why is he sitting so near the telephone, in case Sherrie or Ruby decides to call to wish him a happy holiday and better luck for the coming year? He lets himself imagine that Angela will phone to tell him she's thinking about him. What else has she got to think about, stuck home with her parents in New Jersey? Of course she's thinking about him—about testifying against him. Even the eggnog reminds him of Angela's book.

The time begins to drag again. Swenson feels like some lovelorn high school girl waiting to hear from a boy. He *has* turned into the heroine of Angela Argo's novel. Before the eggnog's worked its magic—he's on the cusp of still being able to drive—Swenson heads out on the icy, deserted road between his house and the video store.

The rum has mercifully blurred the edges of his peripheral vision, allowing him not to register the Christmas Eve lonely guys edging their way to the curtained-off "adult" area. Though he himself could be looking for child porn, that's how guilty he feels as he slinks down the aisles of the classics section. *The Blue Angel* isn't in, isn't anywhere. He frantically searches the shelves. Who could have taken the goddamn film? No one's borrowed it for years—except for Angela Argo. Maybe she's brought it home for vacation and is watching it over and over, thinking of him, of . . . Oh, what has he done to deserve this? He helped her with her work.

He rushes to the cash register, behind which a pretty girl with long blond hair and blue eyes, a Botticelli cherub, is secretively nibbling potato chips from a bag hidden beneath the counter. If he had to get involved with a student, why not some sweetie like this instead of a shark with facial piercing and an eye on mainstream publication?

Swenson says, "Is *The Blue Angel* in?"

"Gee, I don't know," says the cherub. "*The Blue Angel* . . . Hey, what about *It's a Wonderful Life*? Have you seen that? It's the best angel movie there is. We've got ten copies just for Christmas Eve. And they all went out. But someone brought one back already. I guess they couldn't wait."

And now Swenson remembers: why Angela and not this girl. He says, "It's German. From the thirties." It is very important to think of himself as someone who wants to see *The Blue Angel* and who would never ever watch *It's a Wonderful Life*. But what difference does that make? Who cares what movies he likes? He's ruined everything, over nothing, because of some embarrassing, pointless obsession with a difficult, dull girl, an amoral, ambitious child, literally scrambling over his body—

The girl says, "I read in the papers where ninety percent of Americans believe in their personal guardian angels."

"That seems awfully high," Swenson says. "I mean, a high percentage."

"I know *I* do," says the girl. "Years ago I had this boyfriend who got mean when he was drunk? And one night he was coming for me with this two-by-four? And I saw this angel with a long white robe fly into the trailer and squeeze his hand till he dropped it."

"That's amazing," says Swenson. Where was the angel with the flaming sword barring the door to Angela Argo's dorm room? "So . . . is the tape in?"

"It should be there," says the cherub. "I looked it up on the computer."

Swenson nearly runs back to the classics shelves, and this time finds the tape at once, hiding from him, in its unglamorous black-and-white melamine case, too venerable and distinguished to stoop to selling itself with a sexy photo of Marlene Dietrich.

"Enjoy!" says Miss Botticelli. Neither she nor Swenson can hide their relief and pleasure in this transaction, which so easily could have gone the other way, the angel having to disappoint a stranger on Christmas Eve, perhaps with dire consequences.

"Merry Christmas," says the girl.

"You, too," Swenson mumbles.

But first, a good deal more eggnog. A toast to Sherrie, Ruby, Angela, Magda, and while he's being Christlike, to Dean Bentham and Lauren Healy and all his students. It's proof of God's existence that not only isn't he kneeling on the bathroom floor with his head over the toilet, but he's even capable of working the VCR. And now come the trembly, hand-lettered credits that last forever. He could fast-forward through them, but he needs to prepare for that first scene: the geese and ducks squawking in their cages. Then comes the cut to the classroom, the riotous students snapping to attention when Herr Professor Rath walks in (Swenson wishes *he* got that response), then the confiscated dirty postcards of Lola Lola with her feathered skirt, that downy slip of erotic couture that inspires the professor to seek out its wearer at that petri dish of vice, that snakepit, the Blue Angel Club.

Swenson settles into his chair, dips another mugful of eggnog in preparation for that backstage meeting between Rath, who introduces himself, "I am a professor at the gymnasium," and Marlene

Dietrich, aka Lola Lola, who appraises him coolly—so what if he's in a topcoat and she's in frilly bloomers?—and says, "In that case you should know enough to remove your hat." And that's it for Herr Professor. That tiny power reversal, that tiny tweak of S&M, and he's a goner before she says, "Behave . . . and you can stay," all of which is being observed (Swenson can hardly bear this part) by the professor's students, hiding in Lola Lola's room.

Nor does he find it much easier to witness Lola's refusal to sell her favors to a customer for money. "I'm an artist!" she says. And he watches through spread fingers as she sings her famous song, in English "Falling in Love Again," a song of helpless passion from a woman obviously in control, but still it makes the whole audience fall for her—the professor and Swenson, too. What a sucker Swenson is for these women and their . . . art. And now it seems—has he missed something?—Rath and Lola Lola have spent the night together, and even the preposterous, blustery, unsexy professor appears to have made it through a night of love without totaling a molar. So Swenson should quit feeling so knowing, so superior.

When Lola Lola tells Rath, "You're really sweet," Swenson grabs for the remote and replays the scene, searching for some clue. To what? Does Lola love the professor? Is her tenderness real? It's as if the vulgar, graceless, boyish, sexy Lola were the boyish, graceless, sexy Angela, and the film—that is, Swenson's ability to replay it—can somehow solve the mystery of his so-called real life, which passed too fast, and only once, and now he will never know.

The twisted path down which he chased Angela seems to have veered away from the route that Professor Rath and Lola Lola—who have gotten married—are taking together. Soon enough the professor is selling those spicy postcards of the singer. Is that so different from trying to get Len Currie to look at Angela's novel? Yes, it's completely different! What is Swenson thinking? He was never down on his knees, putting on Lola's stockings, in that gesture of self-abasement, intimacy, and surrender, never crowing like a rooster, never playing the clown, letting the magician crack eggs on his head.

He thinks, with grief, of the broken eggs in Angela's novel. Oh, wasn't he, wasn't he playing the clown, and isn't he, isn't he still? That's why he's going through with this hearing instead of gracefully resigning. He knows there's no chance of winning, of proving his innocence. He wants that public humiliation, that one-man orgy of shame and repentance. He needs his fifteen minutes of playing Hester Prynne or Professor Immanuel Rath, the tragic figure of grotesque, masochistic self-debasement. And this is what the movie has done, this is the power of art, to make him recognize himself, understand and forgive. He never knew he was a masochist, but apparently he is one. He never really thought much about the way that Angela dressed, but maybe some secret part of him was attracted to all that hardware. He never saw himself as a clown. The world is full of surprises.

The film keeps running. Professor Rath, in his clown suit, has returned to play his hometown. There, he's beaten by an outraged mob for assaulting Lola Lola after he catches her in the embrace of that oily, faux-continental slime, Mazeppa the Strong Man. Bruised and humiliated, Rath staggers off to his former place of work and past glory, sneaks into his classroom in the middle of the night, and slumps over, dead at his desk. Swenson certainly hopes that's not going to happen to him.

His life is not Professor Rath's life. The story of a teacher who throws everything away for some heartless low-life slut is not his story. Rath's death will not be his death. We already know how Rath's story ends. The jury's still out on Swenson's. At least he'll see Angela, once more, at the hearing. . . .

With those final words, The End, still lingering on screen, the blanket of the film is rudely pulled from Swenson, and the chill of his situation rushes in and makes him decide to watch it all over again, this time keeping in mind that Angela watched it, not so long ago. He met her bringing back the tape, in that lost, sweet, other lifetime.

On the night before the hearing, Sherrie calls and says, "This is not a real conversation. This is to wish you good luck." This is to prove that Sherrie is, after all, a good person, a generous, large-souled woman who phones her husband on the eve of his public mortification. It only makes him feel worse to know that he has done something so awful that someone with such an excellent character is still so angry at him. Lots of guys have done worse, they've been doing it for years. Swenson didn't start early enough. Maybe that was his big mistake.

He goes to bed hoping that sleep will replace these cynical grumblings with pure bright thoughts of misguided but genuine love, with the hope of being forgiven for what was just a misunderstanding. If it *was* a misunderstanding, which is not his real opinion. He believes that it all meant something, that Lola Lola loved her professor, that Angela loved him. Once. Even if Angela, unlike Lola, came wired to see her beloved.

It's too big a task for sleep to take on, and sleep eludes him, hour after hour, while he lies in the dark orating to the committee, composing and revising speeches about what he thought he was doing, about his respect for Angela's novel, about the erotics of teaching, and the dangers of starting to see one's student as a real person. *Seeing her as a real person*—surely that will win the hearts of the women on the committee, and might even make Angela think twice about what she had and lost. But after he falls asleep around five and wakes at seven, exhausted, he can't remember a word.

He puts on his dark suit. Defendant clothes. Get real. This is a trial, not Joe College Professor chilling with his academic homies. Not some panel, some interdisciplinary brunch dreamed up by an ambitious chair. This is his future. Why not preempt the inevitable, dress early for the grave? The closet has left a chalky stripe on both shoulders. Swenson rubs at them. The stripe widens. Tough. Who will see the tops of his shoulders—unless he gets down on his knees?

Swenson pulls out of the driveway without looking back, Lot's wife, forbidden the briefest glance in the rearview mirror. He knows it's pointless to see himself as a biblical figure when in fact he's just an English teacher about to be tried and found guilty by a jury of his peers. He'd much rather feel like a tragic martyr, shedding the chrysalis of his old life as he prepares to stand trial, emerging so pure, so righteous—he could be Joan of Arc.

In the car, halfway to the college, he realizes that he forgot to shave. Why not give them the grizzled old pedophile, the child-rapist they're expecting? If Sherrie were here, she would tell him: Breathe deeply. One step after another. As if his private tragedy were some yuppie Lamaze class. Terror and panic, at least, seem like honest instincts.

But what does instinct have to do with what's about to happen to him in Cabot Hall, which has been, from its inception, a monument to anti-instinct, a grim multipurpose Puritan hell, sometime chapel, lecture forum, torture chamber, and now in its latest guise, courtroom? There will be more and more of this. Better get used to it now. Though maybe Cabot's already hosted a witch-burning event, the incineration of a Puritan teaching assistant caught reading Shakespeare on Sunday.

He can't believe they're holding the hearing in Cabot. It's so theatrical, so excessive. Why do they need a small amphitheater better suited for corpse dissection than for a civilized inquiry into Swenson's professional conduct? Not for Swenson the clubby warmth of Bentham's office, with its collegial promise that matters can be peaceably settled in the judge's chambers. They've gone for the chilly public space, the full-scale Kafka blowout. How many people are coming to this? For all he knows, the entire school. Why not hold it in the gym?

Such is the power and the mercy of denial that it's not until Swenson gets out of the car in the parking lot near Cabot that it finally occurs to him how little he *does* know. How many people *will* there be? Who is on the committee? How long will this last? *Could* he have brought a lawyer? Anyone would have asked that, but not Swenson, apparently, whose bid for taking control of his life went as far as returning Angela's dirty poems and watching some pompous old geezer's romantic problems turned into a German film classic. He could have asked the dean's secretary for more information when she called, but he didn't want to, he couldn't, and she was glad. All he asked was when and where the hearing would be held. He should have done his homework, researched in detail the biography and personal quirks of each committee member as he calculated his chances, readied his defense. And what defense would he have made? The tape was edited. Slightly.

Swenson arrives exactly as the college bells ring ten and carefully picks his way over the path booby-trapped with patches of ice that could send this sinner straight to hell. He imagines falling, hitting his head, lying dead on the walkway while the committee waits inside, assuming he is late. Then they'd hear the tragic news. How could they live with themselves, knowing they had convened to ruin a dead man's life?

He's got to try and think of this as a long dentist appointment. It can't last forever. At some point it has to end. Which naturally reminds him: He should have gone to the dentist and gotten his tooth fixed while he still had dental insurance. Is he holding onto his broken tooth as a sentimental souvenir, as proof that something happened between him and Angela Argo? That is what *he* wants to prove and yet another reason, he suspects, for why he's going through this—this inquiry into the mystery of what did happen, and why. If he just resigns and leaves town, as any adult would, his infantile need to know what Angela felt will never be satisfied.

Obviously, his agenda could hardly be more different from the committee's. . . .

He reaches the tastefully faded brick building, half expecting a mob. But no one's around as he goes inside, pausing to admire the spare austerity that makes the hall seem almost intimate despite its cavernous dimensions and the long flight of stairs leading down to a small proscenium, like some sort of Puritan bullring. The steam that rises off the snow behind the wavy old glass fills the lecture hall with powdery white light.

At a long wooden table at the bottom of the amphitheater, the committee—six of them—fills every seat but one. A few spectators, witnesses maybe, occupy the first row.

Swenson makes his way down the stairs, then stops, three rows from the bottom. The ever-gracious Bentham rises from the table and bounds up to shake Swenson's hand, then—always the good host—motions for him to be seated, right there, three rows up, on the aisle.

Don't the others want to shake his hand? Who are they, by the way? Three women and three men. Francis Bentham. And isn't that . . . Lauren Healy? One-third of the committee despises him already. Isn't it jury-rigging, a major conflict of interest to include among its members the first person to have heard the incriminating tape as well as faculty chairperson of the Faculty-Student Women's Alliance?

He supposes it could be claimed that Bentham's especially well informed. And it makes sense that Lauren's here. It's her gang of thugs that must be appeased. The hearing might not count without Lauren present to witness that justice has been done. Still, doesn't it matter that one of the judges saw him in a car with Angela on the fateful day that marked the beginning and the end of their affair? The innocent trip to Burlington, just before it all fell apart. He could have been Adam, absentmindedly turning the apple in his hand.

And could that other woman at the committee table really be Magda Moynahan? Is Magda here to represent his side? To balance out Francis and Lauren? So what if she doesn't have tenure? So what if he lied to her, his so-called best friend on campus—and hand-carried Angela's book to the editor to whom he refused to show Magda's poems?

And there's Amelia Rodriguez, the tight-lipped, beautiful head of the Hispanic Studies Department. Maybe that's a good sign. At least she's Puerto Rican and might have, he hopes, a laissez-faire Latin anti-Puritan attitude toward relations between the sexes. Swenson remembers wishing she'd been invited to that dinner at Bentham's, speaking of which: one half of the committee was present at a social occasion on which the accused disgraced himself and ruined the entire evening. Too bad you couldn't make it that evening, Amelia, glad you can be with us now, in your austere black suit, your black hair slicked back so tight your eyes looked yanked, your neat hands patiently folded, stern, graceful, inquisitorial, like some judge from the court of Philip II in sleek Armani drag, the evil spinster sister in a García Lorca tragedy. What's Amelia doing in this New England interior designed by and for dead white males, John Winthrop and Cotton Mather?

So who are Bentham's male buddies? How typical that Swenson should know all of the women and hardly recognize the two men besides Bentham. That's been Swenson's whole problem here—not enough male bonding. Okay, that's . . . Bill, Bill Grissom, from the anthro department, a pleasant, wonky guy still capitalizing on the few years he spent in the early seventies on a Navajo reservation. Level-headed, just goofy enough not to be cowed or swayed by the current mood on campus. And the other is—this takes another minute—Carl Fenley, from chemistry. Both are reasonable, rational men, a little on the nerdy side. Fair-minded, rule-abiding. Swenson might be better off with the football coach up there.

The six of them have his fate in their hands, so why can't Swenson focus, or pretend that he has any real interest in them—or in anyone here, except Angela Argo?

She's sitting in the front row. That is, he assumes it's her. It's Angela. But different. She's dyed her hair, replaced the squid-ink black with a shiny, authentic-looking auburn. How vulnerable her head looks, egglike and terribly fragile. And how bizarrely she's dressed—bizarre, that is, for Angela. Neat khakis, a red velour sweater, ordinary college-girl "good" clothes. For all he knows, the piercing and the black leather were always the costume, and this is the real Angela, restored to her true self. For all he knows. He doesn't know. All right. He gets that now.

Even her body is different. She's sitting up straight in her chair, a well-behaved girl turned expectantly toward the kindly parental committee. Her mother and father surround her. The balding head, the platinum head lean tenderly toward Angela's, two pale bulbs hovering over her, wary and protective. They've learned how to do this, how this should look, on the news, on Court TV.

Swenson wishes they'd turn and look at him. Their faces would have to betray some sign that they remember the conference in which they told him that Angela talked about him all the time, that she adored him, that she thought he was the greatest writer who ever lived. But what if they've successfully erased it from their minds, and Swenson, alone in all the world, knows what really happened? He can't take the risk of meeting their eyes. Swenson's heart is thrumming. Chest pains. Shortness of breath. The embarrassment, the chaos, the rush to the college infirmary, and that's how Sherrie, who's working today, will see him for the last time. . . .

Francis Bentham smiles and says, "Hi. Ted. Thanks for coming in."

"Hi, Ted," chorus the others. Hi, Ted. Hi, Ted. Hi, Ted. Thanks. What's Swenson supposed to say? Don't mention it? I'm delighted? As if he were gracing their party with his optional presence. There's nothing he can say. He nods but doesn't speak. Will that be interpreted as a hostile act?

Francis Bentham glances at Lauren, the same look Swenson's seen him shoot at Marjorie. Let the hostess do the honors, try and remember the names.

Lauren says, "Thanks for coming in. You know Magda, Amelia, Francis and myself, Bill, and Carl. Thank you all for coming. And thank you, Angela. And Mr. and Mrs. Argo. Well, I guess everyone knows the drill. The committee will call the slate of agreed-upon witnesses." *Who* agreed? Swenson would like to know. Who is lining up to take turns slandering him? "Cross-examination is not allowed. This is not, after all, a trial." So they don't have to worry about bothersome sticking points like due process.

Angela nods vigorously. Overacting, thinks Swenson, who looks over just in time to see Angela's father put his hand over hers and to feel jealous of this guy who can touch her whenever he wants. If he *is* her father. How could Swenson have been *inside* a woman he knew—and trusted—so little? And does her "father" know he's the subject of a poem cycle about a daughter he molested and hurt so badly she wound up pursuing a promising career as a phone-sex worker?

Swenson nods weakly, playing his role: the sullen guilty lecher. Let's get this over with. He can't wait to see who has volunteered to come forward and get him fired.

When Bentham's secretary telephoned, she'd asked if he had a list of witnesses he would like to appear in support of his case. What case? Whom could he enlist to convince a faculty committee that tape or no tape, he was such a great teacher that they should overlook the misleading evidence suggesting that he'd pressured a student into trading sexual favors in return for his pimping her novel? Maybe he should have subpoenaed Govind, the salesman from Computer City, to ask *him* if Angela seemed like Swenson's cowering sex slave. The fact is: Swenson prefers the committee's version—its image of him as the predatory harasser—to the truer story of obsession and degradation, the humiliating real-life update of *The Blue Angel*.

"All right, then," says Lauren. "Probably we should begin. Ted, we need to find out what exactly has gone on here. And we're sure you want that, too."

Already it feels less like a trial than like the boilerplate adolescent primal scene: Mom and Dad confronting you with the drugs or bad report card. Swenson never experienced that. His father was way too crazy, more likely to be ranting than reading his school reports.

It's taken this long for Swenson to turn into the misbehaving teen, facing Bentham and Lauren, the steely punitive parents.

"Fine, then," says Bentham. "Let's begin. We all know why we're here, to investigate the charges of . . . er . . . sexual harassment"—he speaks rapidly, somehow communicating both his Old World sophistication and his willingness to take this seriously enough to throw Swenson out of Euston—"brought by Miss Angela Argo against Professor Theodore Swenson."

So now it's Theodore. After all these years of Ted.

"The committee has already taken a number of depositions under advisement." What number? And where has Swenson been while all this was going on? Oh, right, watching German videos, returning Angela's poems, drinking eggnog, and somehow forgetting to find one single person willing to vouch for his character.

"Do you have any questions, Ted?"

"No," says Swenson. In fact, he has plenty of questions, none of which, he's quite certain, the committee plans to ask.

"And you, Miss Argo?"

Angela turns to scan the room. The pivoting beacon of her pale scrubbed face sweeps right over Swenson. "I'm fine with it," she says.

"Well, good," says Lauren. "Is Dave ready?"

"I believe so," Bentham says.

Bentham gives a tiny nod, and everyone looks up as the door opens and Dave Sterret walks purposefully downstairs. In his neat chinos and sneakers, his slightly too small navy blazer, Dave's the very model of a certain kind of gay man, circa 1960: a guy you could imagine as a friend of Frank O'Hara's. What is Dave here to say about him? And who is Dave to say it? Dave, who used to have affairs with every handsome kid in the Gay Students Alliance, has come to testify against Swenson for making a pass at Angela Argo. But Dave did all that before it was wrong, before anyone thought twice about it. Bentham shakes Dave Sterret's hand and ushers him to the empty seat at the end of the committee table.

Lauren says, "Thanks for coming in, Dave. We appreciate your time."

"That's okay," says Dave. "Though I can't say I'm glad to be here."

Lauren bites her lip and nods. Amelia and the two men grimace mournfully. Magda leafs through her papers. Why won't *she* look at Swenson? Where's the wave, the wink?

"Dave," says Lauren, "why don't you tell us in your own words what happened at Dean Bentham's house on the evening of October eighteenth?"

"Well, it was a perfectly normal evening," says Dave. "A perfectly pleasant dinner. Most of the evening was flawless. There'd been a little accident with the dean's new stove—"

"Oh, my good man," says Bentham flirtatiously. "Don't tell them *that*, please—"

Dave smiles. "And Marjorie performed the most marvelous rescue, some kind of shepherd's pie with mashed potatoes, pure British-nanny comfort food, if one *had* a British nanny . . . and then this extravagant dessert, positively Dickensian, flat-out British sugar with all the bells and whistles." Dave forgot to mention the Marmite!

"Professor Swenson was there?" asks Carl Fenley. Lauren and Magda and the dean—half the panel—know that.

"Ted was there. With Sherrie."

Silence. No one wants to touch this.

"And how did Professor Swenson behave?" says Bill.

"Fine," says Dave. "Really. For most of the evening . . . impeccably."

"For the whole evening?" prompts Lauren, who knows very well what happened. But this is not for Lauren. It's for the record, the committee.

"For almost the whole evening. It was late, we were tired, we'd all been teaching hard. A good deal of wine was consumed." Dave smiles again. "Any one of us could have acted badly. It just happened to be Ted."

What a stand-up guy Dave Sterret is! Dave doesn't want to do this. He's working hard to let Swenson off easy. It was late. The wine was flowing. But what Dave wants doesn't matter. Who knows what dirt Bentham has on Dave? Years of dalliance, for starters.

"We all understand how these things happen." Lauren understands nothing of the sort. She doesn't believe that any substance could trounce *her* superego.

"And what did Professor Swenson do that you think the committee should know about?" asks Amelia. Swenson searches his conscience. What did he do to her? Those few failed conversations at faculty gatherings couldn't have ignited the flicker of rage glinting in her anthracite eyes. Amelia's only doing her job, playing by the rules of this cult to which she's surrendered her life.

"Well, the odd thing," says Dave, "given what's happened since, the truly ironic thing is that the trouble occurred during a conversation about sexual harassment. I remember because later . . . I recall telling Jamie that Ted's behavior was so extreme it made me wonder if Ted might not have some sexual harassment issues."

A volcanic rage boils in Swenson, fueled by the idea of Jamie and Dave gassily discussing his *issues*. Anyway, he would like to object to this whole line of inquiry. A dinner party is private time. Let's stick to the classroom, the hostile workplace environment.

Dave says, "We were sharing experiences we'd had in class around gender issues. Tensions. Rough moments. We all know how things are lately." The committee nods. It knows. "And suddenly, Ted began to use the most disturbing language. . . ."

"What language?" asks Lauren gently. "Can you remember?"

"I would prefer not to," says Dave. Lauren, Magda, and Francis smile at Dave's "Bartleby the Scrivener" reference. The chemistry and the anthro guys merely look perplexed.

"We understand," says Magda. Magda's first contribution to all this could hardly be more benevolent, assisting Dave off the hot seat, ending this part of the hearing. Still, Swenson's disturbed to hear her use the plural.

"Thank you, Dave," Lauren says. The committee concurs. Yes, thank you thank you thank you. Bentham shakes Dave's hand once more, and as Dave walks past Swenson, he winks and says, "Good luck, man."

Everyone watches Dave ascend the stairs. Oh, how they wish *they* were free to leave! The door at the top of the steps slams shut. Are lectures here interrupted every time someone exits? Bentham should be nagging Buildings and Grounds instead of persecuting Swenson.

"Who's next?" Bentham asks Lauren. Lauren checks her notes.

"Betty Hester," says Lauren.

As Betty makes her way downstairs, her full skirt parachutes out. How tiny Betty's feet are! How could Swenson never have noticed? All at once he sees in Betty the chunky girl heading bravely off to the torment of ballet lessons. Every cell in Betty's body wishes it were back behind the library desk and not here, exposed to the committee watching her navigate this challenging descent, mined with potential stumbles. Betty stops and shakes Swenson's hand. Her soft face swims before him. Enragingly, the tears in her eyes almost bring tears to Swenson's.

"Ted," she says. "How are you?"

He wants to fling himself on her pillowy breast. He wants to kill her for asking.

"I'm fine," he says. Jim Dandy, Betty. Frankly, I've never been better.

Betty pauses, then impulsively leans down and whispers, "I wish this weren't happening!"

"Me, too," says Swenson. "Believe me."

Betty smiles and sighs, then goes over and shakes Bentham's hand, carefully maintaining that fragile smile as she sinks down into the hot seat. Come on. This isn't Betty's fault. She's got a job. Kids to support.

"Thank you for coming in, Betty," says Lauren.

Betty sighs dramatically. "I think it's a shame," she says.

Shame! What does she think the shame *is*? Swenson having sex with an—allegedly—innocent student? Or Swenson's life being ruined by the not-so-innocent student? The panel members study their folders again.

"All right, then, Betty," says Lauren. "What you agreed to tell the panel concerns the book that Professor Swenson checked out of the Euston library on the afternoon of November first."

"That's right," Betty says.

Lauren settles back into herself, signaling her fellow panelists that someone else has got to take over. After a stall, Amelia says, "And what book did Professor Swenson borrow?"

Magda can't hold out any more and looks searchingly at Swenson, her taut pretty face drawn several notches tighter than normal. Strung-out attractive Magda now just looks a mess. Magda loves him, sort of. And they alone in this room know how this book borrowing came about, the intense lunch *à deux* at which Magda told him that Angela's book was shelved in the poetry section. Shouldn't Magda confess that she told Swenson about it? Why did Magda mention the book? Just to have something to say, to make herself more *interesting*? Swenson knows that's cruel. They were talking about a student. He detaches his gaze from Magda's. If he looks at her too long the committee might think he's sleeping with her, too.

"Can you describe the book?" Lauren prompts Betty.

"Well . . . ," says Betty. "It's a book of poems. A pamphlet, really. Self-published."

"What kind of poems?" Lauren asks.

"Well . . . ," says Betty. "I'd say they have a fairly strong . . . sexual content."

"Excuse me!" Bill Grissom clears his throat. "Maybe I'm just a simple literal-minded Joe from the social sciences, but I don't get exactly what this book of student poems is doing on the shelves of the Euston College Library."

Bill, that's a very good question! Why doesn't Magda tell them? She explained the whole thing so well to Swenson. The last thing Magda wanted was trouble—trouble exactly like this—about work that Angela did for her class.

"It was a gift to the library," says Betty. "She wanted us to have it so badly. Out of politeness, I couldn't refuse. And it's certainly not the only racy book we have. . . ."

Politeness. Swenson knows all about that. Politeness has got him sitting here and not punching out Francis Bentham. And as always, the impolite are winning. Angela's strong-arming poor Betty

Hester into putting her dirty poems in the library should tell them something about Angela, a pornographer and careerist terrorist, an ambitious maniac blackmailing her way into those hallowed stacks. Naturally, a snake like that would wriggle her way into Swenson's heart and convince him to peddle her novel. And is that what Angela did? Swenson wishes he knew.

"I have the book here with me." Betty produces the bound manuscript from her voluminous eggplant-colored tote. Holding it at arm's length, she gives it to Lauren, who, sniffing with distaste, passes it down the line. Swenson shouldn't have returned it. But wouldn't it be worse if the book were still charged out to him and they subpoenaed it for the hearing? He waits for Lauren to ask some brave committee member to read Angela's verse into the minutes. But she won't do that to her colleagues.

"For the record," says Lauren, "Ms. Argo's manuscript has been introduced as evidence."

Evidence? Against *Swenson*? Naturally. Who else? By definition, a nineteen-year-old student sex poet is innocent compared with a forty-seven-year-old professor using her poems to get off. But why is Swenson complaining? He should be thanking his lucky stars that no one's reading Angela's poems aloud, or sending them down the table for the group's appalled inspection. Actually, if he could distance himself, that could be entertaining, watching each committee member gingerly leaf through the book, deciding how much smut to peruse before passing it on. Magda wouldn't have to look. She knows what's inside. Lauren slips the book into a folder as if it were a used condom. And the book disappears. How conveniently all this has worked out for everyone concerned. It's the ideal solution to Betty's pesky little problem of how to spirit Angela's book off the Euston library shelf. Why couldn't she have let Swenson steal it when he tried?

Then Lauren says, "Betty, can you tell the committee . . . for the record . . . in a bit more detail . . . what these poems were like?"

What is Lauren thinking? Doesn't she know how this looks? This heartless interrogation that keeps bringing fresh tears to Betty's eyes? Is Lauren suggesting that Betty Hester rattle off the hottest moments of Angela's raunchy sex poems?

Desperation saves Betty. She says, "Well, really, I just got a chance to skim through them. I believe that Professor Moynahan was working with the student and probably would know. . . ." Betty falters, and her silence bullies Lauren into looking at Magda.

"Magda?" Lauren says.

Sure. Magda's the perfect choice. Dear Magda can just barrel through this with no agony and no bullshit, just say what the goddamn poems are about, and let this circus resume.

Magda says, "They're a related series of poems about a young woman who works in the phone-sex industry, with subthemes of child abuse, incest. . . ."

Child abuse. Incest. Swenson sees a fine glaze come over the male committee members' faces. Strangely, he wants to defend the poems, and he's annoyed at Magda for leaving out the fact that the poems have a certain . . . intensity. Intensity. God help him.

Meanwhile, Lauren's not about to let the committee imagine that Angela's poems are just ordinary expressions of romantic undergraduate angst.

"Professor Moynahan, would you describe these poems as graphic?"

"Graphic?" Magda smiles. No one smiles back. "I'd say they were fairly out there."

Fairly out there is apparently a signal for them all to stare at Swenson. Why aren't they watching Angela and her parents to see how they're absorbing the information that she's written a collection of lurid verse about incest and child abuse? How could the esteemed committee manage to look Angela's way when it's practically inspecting Swenson for a bulge in his pants? Well, sorry. It's not there. Not today.

Lauren says, "Thank you, Magda. And thank you, Betty. Is there anything else you would like to tell the committee?"

"Well . . ." Swenson's disturbed by what he hears in Betty's voice: the tone of someone with a morsel of gossip so juicy it can't be suppressed.

"Yes, Betty?" coaxes Francis Bentham.

"Well, when Professor Swenson borrowed the book, I couldn't help but notice that he was acting rather strangely."

"Strangely how?" Bentham says.

"You know, I had the funniest feeling that he was trying to, well, not *steal* it, exactly. Just not . . . properly check it out."

"Did anything Professor Swenson do give you this feeling?" asks Amelia.

"No," says Betty. "It was just a feeling. Anyway, maybe he changed his mind, or maybe I was wrong. He gave it to me, and I checked it out for him."

What did he do to Betty? A moment later, he knows.

"The other thing is that . . . Professor Swenson didn't return the book until a week or so ago." Well, there it is. Case closed. He's guilty of the ultimate library sin, keeping a book out past its due date. Betty isn't the kindly, generous, Mother-Hubbard librarian, after all, but the retentive bad-witch librarian, longing to send you to the electric chair for that overdue fine. But wait a minute. Senior faculty can keep books forever. Stacks of overdue books and unread papers are part of every professor's office decor. So the sin must be that he'd taken it out at all. Not just any book. The priceless first edition of Angela's dirty poems.

"Thank you, Betty," Lauren says. Betty stands and leaves, this time without the tremulous pause for a heart-to-heart with Swenson. He will never forgive her, never go into the library and pretend this hasn't happened. Not that Betty will notice, since this is most likely the end of his library-going life at Euston.

Bentham waits a few beats, then says, wearily, "And speaking of phone sex . . . let it be entered into the record that Professor Swenson made a call to a . . . 900 line, a . . . phone-sex line. From his office telephone."

Swenson hovers briefly on the edge of hysteria. What about his privacy? His First Amendment rights? Since when does this committee have a mandate to examine his phone bill? Well, *their* phone bill, actually.

"Next witness," murmurs Bentham.

Carlos Ostapcek bounds down the stairs—Rocky Balboa in reverse. Jogging past, he punches Swenson's arm, a declaration of brotherly solidarity. Carlos is no Betty Hester, wimping out under pressure. Carlos is here on Swenson's side, on behalf of his coach. Touchingly, Carlos has put on a suit. He's more dressed up than Swenson, who half expects Carlos to pump his hands in the air when he finally reaches bottom. But he simply takes his seat and plunks his elbows on the table.

"Welcome, Mr. Ostapcek," Lauren says, and the committee members mumble greetings, a process that by now they've got down to a mild mass exhalation.

"Can't say I'm happy to be here," says Carlos, with a pointed look in Francis Bentham's direction.

"None of us are," says Bentham. "Believe me, Carlos." It's not lost on Carlos that the dean is calling him by his first name.

Son of a bitch, thinks Swenson. Not even he suspected just how slimy Bentham is. How else does someone get to be dean of a pretend college? This hearing's an education on the subject of his colleagues' true natures.

"Carlos," says Lauren, "I know this is tough for you. But in the interests of the college and your fellow students, there are certain questions we need to ask. And a number of your classmates have chosen you as their spokesperson."

This news encourages Swenson. The students—many of whom, he fears, have resented him all semester—have picked, as their representative, the one most likely to defend him. Swenson thinks of them, every one, with tenderness and regret. They're his class. They're sticking together. Swenson's been too hard on them—and himself. Clearly, he's taught them something. They've all learned together.

"I don't know about spokesperson," says Carlos. "I just know what I know."

"And that's all we're asking from you," Amelia says. The aristocratic señorita patronizing the dumb little campesino.

"All right, then," says Lauren. "Has Professor Swenson done anything in class that seemed peculiar to you or that has made you feel uncomfortable in any way?"

"No, ma'am," says Carlos. The *ma'am* is priceless, really. All those years in reform school and the military have given Carlos the strength to hang in there and not crack under torture administered by the likes of Lauren Healy.

"Nothing at all?" prods Bentham.

"Nothing, nope," says Carlos.

Is Swenson's teaching on trial? He's still under the misguided impression that they have convened to discuss the matter of his sexual relations with Angela Argo. The sex did not take place in the classroom, though now it occurs to Swenson that what passed between him and Angela in class was considerably more satisfying than what they finally did in her bed.

He shuts his eyes for a moment and through the darkness hears someone ask, "Did you ever notice anything unusual or surprising, anything unprofessional in Professor Swenson's behavior toward Miss Argo?" It takes him another moment to realize that the voice is Magda's. Magda doesn't sound like herself. Why does Magda want to know? Did she notice something on that very first day when she ran into Swenson and Angela walking across the quad? If so, would she please tell *him*. *He'd* like to know what she saw. Because despite everything Angela's done, Swenson longs to hear Magda say that when she saw him and Angela together, she sensed some current of . . . mutual attraction between them.

"Nope, can't say as I did," says Carlos.

"And what was his attitude about her work?" Good old Magda, trying to get this back on track. Teaching. Learning. Work.

"He liked it," Carlos says. "And I could see why. It was pretty good. Okay. She had a kind of tough workshop. But I think everyone secretly liked her stuff."

"What *was* Miss Argo's work?" Bill says.

"A chapter from a novel," Carlos says. "At least that's what we were told."

"And what was the novel about?" Surely Lauren knows: the oppression of the female sex by the phallocentric male hegemony.

Francine Prose

"Well," says Carlos, "it was about this girl. This high school girl. And she's hatching these eggs for her science project." Carl and Bill perk up slightly at the mention of something so tangibly, reassuringly concrete as a science project.

"And what else?" says Lauren. "Can you remember anything else?" Lauren knows what she's looking for. She's heard about the book. Who told her? Magda? Angela? Has Lauren read it? Swenson hopes she has. He hopes they all have. It will, as they themselves would say, alter the terms of the discourse.

Carlos says, "There was this part about the girl having a crush on her teacher."

"And did any of you find it strange?" says Bentham. "Did it make any of you uneasy that Angela was writing about a student with a crush on her teacher?"

"No," says Carlos. "Not at all. Professor Swenson taught us, like, practically the first class, that we should never assume that anything's, you know, autobiographical."

What a good boy Carlos is! In this crowd he seems like a pillar of moral rectitude, setting everyone straight, little Jesus lecturing the elders in the temple.

"I see," says Bentham, chastened. "Yes, I suppose that's a wise idea."

"And besides," adds Carlos, "half the stuff that college chicks write is about having a crush on their teacher. They've never been anywhere, done anything. What else can they write about?"

All right, Carlos. That's enough. Meg Ferguson, wherever she is, will revoke your authority to speak for her and the others.

"And Carlos . . . ," says Lauren, "did you and the others have any reason to suspect that Professor Swenson was involved with Miss Argo?"

"No," says Carlos. "But we do now. And you know what? I can't see what the big deal is. Shit happens. People get attracted to other people. It's not that big a deal."

Carlos's moral authority is slipping here. The committee's not about to be convinced that their ethical standards—the principles they're putting in all this time and energy to uphold—can be challenged by Carlos's goony common sense.

"And I assume that the class also knows by now," presses Bentham, "that Professor Swenson may have talked Miss Argo into having sex in exchange for certain favors."

"What favors?" asks Carlos.

"He promised to show her novel to his editor in New York. To get her novel published."

No, sir. The class did not know this. No way. Carlos doesn't need to answer. The truth is all over his face.

This is Swenson's payback for having enforced a sadistic system in which students are required to keep silent while their hearts and souls are ritually dismembered. The committee should have offered Swenson the option, the kindness, of a gag, to prevent him from shouting out: Carlos, don't listen to them! That's not what happened. And what should he say? What *did* happen? I showed her work to my editor because it's so much better than yours, Carlos. In any case, it's no longer clear that he *has* an editor in New York, besides which he would never have suggested trading a professional introduction for sex. Not only because of his own moral scruples, values, vanity, and pride, but also because, as it turned out, he couldn't be sure that he could collect on the sexual part of the bargain.

"No," says Carlos. "We didn't know. Gee. Let me get this straight. Sorry. I didn't mean to . . ." Everyone watches Carlos's perception of unfairness—Angela's gotten a special break denied the rest of the class—warring against his belief in loyalty and in not betraying his captain. Swenson wants to tell him that the real unfairness involves the distribution of talent and has nothing to do with whatever happened between him and Angela Argo. But that would hardly endear him to the committee, or to Carlos.

"That's all right, Carlos," says Bentham. "Take a minute. Tell us, are you a writer too?"

"I hope so," says Carlos.

"Well, it's been my impression," says Bentham, "that writers generally have excellent memories. It's one of the tools of their trade."

"I guess so," Carlos says.

"Then search your memory," says Bentham, "and tell us if anything happened in class this semester that seemed even slightly . . . odd or . . . out of the ordinary."

Every ounce of Carlos's training and life experience is pressuring him to stand tall and not disclose anything except his name, rank, and serial number. But nothing has prepared him to resist the seduction of having the dean of his college calling him a writer and a half-dozen faculty members hanging on his every word. How can he disappoint them? How can he not offer up any scrap of information he can recall?

"There was a joke going around the class. I mean, we were getting a lot of stories about people . . ." Carlos shakes his head. He can't believe this. Not even in the navy did he encounter anything this wiggy. "Um, there were a lot of stories about people having sex with, you know, um, animals."

Yes, and Carlos started it with his piece about the young voyeur, his tattletale neighbor, and the German shepherd. Let's enter that into the record.

"With *animals*?" repeats Bentham, in honeyed tones of ironic Brit disbelief.

At this, Bill the anthropologist comes—just perceptibly—to life. What interspecies intercourse is part of the secret rituals of this creative writing tribe?

"What animals?" Bill says.

Carlos shakes his head again. "Actually, sir, a chicken."

Bentham is having fun with this. "Are you telling me, Carlos, that a student in Professor Swenson's class submitted a story in which a character—a human—had sex with a chicken?"

"A dead chicken." Carlos can't help himself. Everyone chuckles, appalled. Bentham looks at Swenson, who shakes his head. Damned if he gets it, either. First phone sex, now animal sex. Obviously, he's been having an interesting semester.

"I see," says Lauren. "A theme seems to be emerging."

"What's that?" says Carlos cagily.

"Didn't you say Miss Argo's novel was about eggs?" Lauren's been trained by years of graduate school to look for patterns of metaphor. "And now chickens . . . ?"

"No one was having sex with the eggs in Angela's novel," says Carlos.

Not in the part you read, Swenson thinks. Another sign of how lost he is that he's proud to have read more of Angela's book than anyone else in the class or on the panel.

"You said *animals* . . . plural," says Bill, the statistically conscious, quantifying voice of the social sciences. "So there were . . . *other* animals."

"A cow," Carlos says. "And a dog."

"In the same story or in separate stories?" says Amelia.

"Separate stories," says Carlos.

"From different students?" Carl asks.

"Yep," Carlos concurs. "The dog was in my story, actually." Finally, the truth.

"All this in one semester?" says Bentham.

"This semester. Yeah."

"And you're telling the committee that, in one semester, students in Professor Swenson's class wrote fiction in which humans have sexual relations with cows and chickens and dogs."

"*A* cow," says Carlos. "*A* chicken. *A* dog."

"That's remarkable," Bentham says.

"I guess so," says Carlos. "We used to say we'd finally figured out what got Professor Swenson's attention."

That's what they thought got his attention? There's been a gigantic misunderstanding about those swamps of boredom Swenson slogged through reading their wretched stories, spiced by the dread of having to figure out how to teach them without getting charged with sexual harassment, which he *is* getting charged with, so he was right to worry. What got his attention was Angela Argo's novel.

No one can speak for several minutes as they consider Carlos's latest disclosure. Lauren makes relentless eye contact with her colleagues until she's sure they have no more questions.

"Thank you, Carlos," Lauren says. "We appreciate your coming here today and being so straightforward and honest."

"Look," says Carlos, "Let's get something straight. I personally don't think there's anything wrong with writing stories about having sex with animals. I think students should be allowed to write any stories they want!"

But it's a little late for Carlos's impassioned First Amendment defense.

"We agree," says Bentham. "Of course. Thank you for your help."

How many more of Swenson's loyal student defenders are going to be paraded before the committee? All of them, perhaps. The hearing isn't over. Carlos jogs back up the aisle, avoiding Swenson's gaze.

After a pause, the door flies open. Claris Williams glides down the stairs, transforming the chilly lecture hall into a fashion runway along which the gorgeous Claris skims, hardly touching the ground, turning her giraffe's neck toward, and away from, imaginary flashbulbs. Swenson thinks he can hear the committee catch its collective breath as they wonder why students like that don't sign up for *their* classes.

"Thank you for coming in, Miss Williams." Even Bentham is awed by Claris's beauty

"You're welcome." Claris gives away nothing. No regrets. No gloating.

"I know this may be difficult for you," says Lauren, "so we'll try to make it as quick and easy as we can. In your dealings, in class and out of class, with Professor Swenson, did his actions toward you ever seem . . . inappropriate?"

"No." Claris shakes her lovely head. She's sticking up for Swenson and at the same time discrediting her own testimony, because no one in the room can believe that a normal, healthy male would hit on Angela Argo when there was a woman like Claris around. Clearly, she is lying, or else Swenson is insane. Shouldn't an insanity defense be permitted in sexual harassment cases?

Swenson and Claris know it's true. Swenson thinks, How pathetic. What *is* wrong with him? He never even entertained a sexual thought about Claris and spent months mooning over Angela Argo? How abject, how ridiculous. He isn't a normal male.

Bentham closes in for the kill. "And did Professor Swenson ever do anything to cause you to suspect that he was behaving inappropriately with another student?"

"What do you mean?" asks Claris.

Bentham says, "Did you ever see Professor Swenson with Miss Argo in a . . . venue that surprised you?"

"Once," Claris whispers, and they all lean forward, except Swenson, who leans backward. "I ran into Professor Swenson leaving Angela's room in the dorm."

"Leaving Miss Argo's room?" repeats the incredulous dean.

Even now, Swenson expects the truthful Claris to amend her statement to say that she didn't actually see him leaving Angela's room. She only saw him on the stairs and assumed he'd been in Angela's room. Circumstantial evidence!

"Yes," says Claris. Hasn't Swenson taught Claris how crucially details matter?

"Do you remember when that was?"

"Actually, I do. It was just before Thanksgiving, because for a second I thought Professor Swenson was somebody's dad, helping load the car, bring stuff home for the holiday. So I was really shocked when I saw that it was Professor Swenson."

He *is*, by the way, someone's dad. Just not Angela Argo's.

"Did you and Professor Swenson exchange words," says Lauren.

"Just hello," says Claris.

"Did he see you?" Bill asks.

"Yes, he did," says Claris.

"And did you tell anyone about this?" says Lauren.

"No," says Claris. "Why would I?"

Why would she? Oh, why would she indeed? The question's a bit much, really. No one but a saint could keep that kind of gossip secret. So how did Bentham know enough to ask Claris? And then it occurs to Swenson that Claris must have told them, that she volunteered when she heard that the committee was soliciting information. Now he knows how bad it is, and that things will deteriorate from here, a rapid descent from Carlos's unwilling betrayal to the spectacle of students lining up to kick him when he's down.

"And how would you describe Professor Swenson on the occasion when you saw him leaving Miss Argo's residence hall?"

"I'd say . . . uncomfortable," replies Claris.

"Would you say . . . guilty?" presses Bentham.

"I'd say *uncomfortable*," repeats Claris.

"Thank you, Miss Williams," Bentham says frostily. He's not used to being corrected by the likes of Claris. "The committee appreciates your help."

And now the swell of tormentors and accusers can no longer be contained by the tidy protocol that has so far determined the order and the pace of their appearance. Claris is nearly knocked down the stairs by Courtney Alcott, barreling in. Like Angela and Carlos, Courtney's changed her look, lost the homegirl lipstick and earrings, the big pants and baggy sweater. She's wearing the sort of navy blue suit that her mother must put on when she consents to leave Beacon Hill for a ladies' lunch at the Ritz.

Courtney flings herself into a chair. She doesn't want to be thanked for coming, nor does she wait for a question. A spray of words explodes from her like champagne foam from a bottle.

"Nobody's going to say this," she begins. "I know nobody's going to come out and say this, so I just thought that somebody should. We all knew something was going on. Because we all got trashed in the class. Either Professor Swenson would trash our stuff or he would encourage the others to dump all over it. Especially Angela—he would get her to say all the mean stuff he really wanted to say himself. But when *her* story came up, her novel chapter or whatever, nobody was allowed to say anything bad, and when we tried to talk, he just told us how retarded we were and how Angela was a genius. So we all figured he had to be sleeping with her or something—"

"Excuse me," Swenson says. "Surely the committee realizes that there might be other reasons for admiring a student's work."

It's Courtney who's gotten through to him, the ultimate torture of being judged and accused by this dim, ungenerous girl. Surely the committee sees that listening to this silly young woman discuss his professional conduct has driven him over the edge. Yet Swenson's outburst so startles Bentham that for an instant he seems uncertain of who Swenson is.

"We understand that," he says. "But Ted ... if you could just hold your comments till we're through—"

"Sorry," says Swenson. "But this was just too much."

"It doesn't matter," says Courtney, forgivingly. "That's all I had to say. I just wanted to say that because I knew nobody else would have the nerve."

"We appreciate that," Lauren says. "Thank you, Courtney, for your courage."

Passing Swenson, Courtney gives him a dazzling smile of right-eousness and triumph. Why shouldn't she be happy? The truth has set her free. She can go on writing her sensitive meditations on ghetto life, and no one will tell her not to. Swenson's learned his lesson. He'll never criticize another student. Not that he'll get a chance.

Silence. Next witness. Could it be that Courtney's subnormal outburst will be the final voice they'll hear—the prosecution's sum-mation? The committee checks its folders, its lists. Angela, too, has lists. Everyone does, except Swenson. Bentham checks his Rolex. Swenson looks at his Casio. An hour has gone by. Lauren drums her fingers. Everyone mimes impatience. Swenson wishes some-thing would happen. Any lag in the drama creates a gap in which he can confront the disturbing question of what will become of him after this hearing is over. No wife, no job, no home. He cranes his neck and sees only the back of Angela's head.

Bentham says, "According to my list, the next person who wants to talk with us is a ... Matthew McIlwaine. Perhaps he's forgotten or changed his mind. ..."

Matt McIlwaine? What does Matt have to say? He ran into Swenson and Angela outside the video store. Swenson supposes the committee needs to hear from anyone who ever saw them in the same place at the same time. Matt could say he ran into them on North Street, where they passionately kissed hello and strolled off arm in arm. Matt has a million reasons for wanting to see Swenson get screwed.

"I'll go see if he's out there," Bill Grissom says in his ringing Boy Scout tenor. He stands before anyone else can offer and takes the stairs two at a time. Bill's gone for quite a long while. The lucky guy's taking a piss.

He comes back not with Matt, but with Arlene Shurley, whom he's holding by the arm, partly as if he's supporting her, partly like a cop making a collar. Suited up in her shiny uniform, Arlene's cringing and shivering. What's she doing here? This is getting too close to Sherrie.

Bill practically has to stuff Arlene into her seat. She's way beyond eye contact with anyone as Francis Bentham shakes her hand. The ritual thanks for coming in are lost on Arlene, who scowls guiltily at her knuckles.

Bentham knows not to go near this. This one belongs to Lauren.

"Arlene," says Lauren, "could you please tell us if Ms. Angela Argo ever visited the clinic?"

"Several times," says Arlene.

"On what complaint?"

"She . . . had medical problems."

"What sort of medical problems?" Lauren will take all day if she has to.

Only now does Arlene look questioningly at Francis Bentham, seeking out the alpha male to see if this is permitted. What about nurse-patient confidentiality?

"Betty . . . ," Bentham says gently.

"I'm Arlene," Arlene says.

"Betty was the librarian," says Lauren. She doesn't like Francis Bentham, either. But she likes Swenson less.

"Arlene, then," concedes Bentham "Our students' medical charts are a matter of college record. . . ."

Is that true? What would the lawyers say? Arlene's not going to ask, nor is she going to challenge the dean.

"Well, for one thing, she had epilepsy. Mild epilepsy, but still . . . It was controlled pretty well with medication. But one side effect was depression. This one time she came in, Sherrie Swenson and I were on duty—"

The mention of Sherrie's name stops Arlene dead in her tracks. In fact, it's a real showstopper. The committee knows who Sherrie is. The tension and the intensity in the room ratchet up several notches. Swenson suddenly notices that he's quit breathing for a few moments.

"And the patient said . . ."—Arlene's tremolo intensifies—"and she said she'd been having suicidal thoughts. It scared me, I'll tell you. I called Sherrie in. Sherrie got us all Coca-Colas. I remember Angela talking about how worried she was that she would never meet a man she could love, and she would never have kids, and that her being epileptic would make everything worse."

That doesn't sound like Angela. Swenson cannot imagine the tough, self-determined young woman he knew being—or pretending to be—so mired in adolescent girl bullshit. But the teenager in her novel was. Was Angela just doing research? Was Swenson research for the character of the music teacher? Hasn't he learned his own lesson about maintaining the distinction between fiction and autobiography?

"And what did you tell her?" Lauren says.

"It's a funny thing," says Arlene. "I actually remember Sherrie and me talking about how we met *our* husbands. Trying to comfort her. You know."

The committee members glance at Swenson, or more accurately, at his shell. He's vacated his body. His mind is taking a little break to absorb this information.

A mystery has been solved. So that's how the story of his meeting Sherrie worked its way into Angela's novel. He wasn't crazy or paranoid. Everything had an explanation. Well, not everything. Some things did. All of which strikes Swenson as interesting, and hardly painful at all compared, let's say, with the excruciating thought of sweet, generous Sherrie offering the romantic story of how she met her husband to a girl with whom her husband just happened to be romantically obsessed.

"And then?" says Lauren. Good question. *He* could tell them what happened then. Angela went home and wrote a scene based on how Sherrie and Swenson met in the St. Vincent's emergency room. But he's the only one who knows that, the only one who cares. None of them would have any idea about how this relates to the charges against him. She was sucking details from his life, using them in her work. Which was proof that she cared about him, that she was paying attention. Swenson himself feels slightly dizzied by the manic speed at which his passions are tracking back and forth between Angela and Sherrie.

"After that Angela seemed fine," Arlene says.

"Excuse me," interrupts Bentham. "Are you saying that when a Euston student comes to the clinic with suicidal impulses, you and your colleagues sit around drinking Cokes and discussing your romantic histories?"

"We're understaffed," says Arlene. "Gosh. We did refer Angela to the consulting psychologist in Burlington."

"In Burlington? You're telling us that we advise our suicidal kids to get themselves down to Burlington?" Bentham's tone is threatening. After they clean up this Swenson mess, they can look into the clinic. That's how they'll get rid of Sherrie next. Oh, what has Swenson done? Not only ruined his own life, but Sherrie's as well, Sherrie who has done nothing, nothing to deserve this!

"And did anyone ever check up to see if Miss Argo contacted this therapist?"

Why didn't Sherrie? wonders Swenson. Because all of them— except him—knew that Angela was lying. Sherrie, Magda, even Arlene. Women knew, apparently. Magda even warned him.

"You can't hold their hands every minute!" snaps Arlene. Does anyone but Swenson notice that class warfare has erupted? Arlene's working-class country passions have finally been stirred by these brats she's been coddling for years, and by these phony Brits who invaded her kingdom and think they can boss her around.

"Of course not," Lauren says.

"Is that all?" says Arlene, petulantly. Yes, it is, and it isn't. It's all Arlene will be asked to say, but it's not all she's done. Her testi-

mony has added to the weight of moral repulsion the committee
feels for Swenson, who has not just offered a student a chance to be
published in return for sex but has offered a *suicidal* student a
chance to be published in return for sex.

"Any more questions for Mrs. Shurley?" No, there aren't, no one
wants to touch this. Except Amelia, who seems to have missed that
sour note of class conflict that has made Arlene and Bentham's brief
exchange so jarring and discordant.

Amelia says, "Did Miss Argo ever mention her relationship with
Professor Swenson."

Arlene looks dumbfounded. "I don't think she would with
Sherrie . . . with Ted's *wife* there. Do *you*?"

Amelia shrugs. It's too much trouble to try to explain what Latin
women might say—or not say—to each other.

"Well, then!" says Lauren. "Arlene, is there anything else you'd
like us to know?"

"Maybe one thing?" says Arlene, whose voice has by this point
become a thin, sharp needle for delivering its precise dose of
venom. "I just think you people ought to know how hard this
has been on Sherrie." Arlene's looking directly at Swenson. He
buries his head in his hands, though what he really wants to do is
put his fingers in his ears and chant nonsense syllables to drown
out the sound of her voice saying, "Sherrie's strong. She's very
strong."

Swenson feels like the cuckolded one! Sherrie's left him for
Arlene. And now Arlene, not Swenson, has the right to talk about
Sherrie—what Sherrie's like—to this roomful of strangers. He
wants to go and grab Angela and make her look at what she's done!
But he knows that the point is: *he* did it. That's what this trial's
about. If he throws back his head and howls, can they all just quit
and go home?

"Thank you, Arlene," says Lauren.

"Don't mention it," Arlene says. She looks at Bill, as if she expects
him to help her out of the room the same way he helped her in. But
there's nothing wrong with Arlene—a sixtyish, healthy nurse who

has just shown great vigor in hammering yet another nail into Swenson's coffin. She can exit on her own steam, pick herself up and leave. As Arlene passes Angela and her parents, Swenson looks to see how the news of Angela's "suicidal" thoughts have affected her mom and dad. Not at all, apparently. They're too focused on their mission. They are here to support their daughter and to make sure that justice is done.

The committee looks at Angela—that is, at Angela and her parents. No one's surprised by any of this. It's all been arranged in advance.

Lauren says, "Angela, are you ready? Do you feel strong enough to address the committee?"

Angela, are you ready? The other witnesses weren't asked if they felt strong enough to speak. They were just trundled in and out at the committee's convenience. But it was Angela who started this, Angela who wants it. Angela's always been ready. She was present at the creation.

Angela gets up shakily and goes over to the table. As she moves, Swenson thinks he can still see sharp angles of sullen punkhood poking through the fuzzy eiderdown of that Jane College getup. He waits to see her trip or hit her hip on the edge of the table, but she glides into a chair like a debutante. Even with the makeover, wouldn't her gestures be the same, her body language speaking the unchanging language of self, like the kidnapped child's shoes in Arlene's ridiculous story? Wouldn't the body be slower to learn a whole new set of directions? Actors do it all the time. Angela's multitalented.

It's as if the whole committee takes a step backward, giving Angela over to Lauren, the only one qualified to take responsibility for handling this fragile creature and her sensitive testimony.

"Now, Angela," says Lauren, "perhaps we should start by saying that everybody in this room understands how difficult it must have been for you to come forward. How brave you are for helping make sure that this kind of thing is stopped. I also want to say, we've all heard that upsetting tape of your . . . conversation with

Professor Swenson. And we agreed, unanimously, that there is no compelling reason for us to sit here and listen to it together. Ms. Wolin"—she nods at Bentham's secretary—"has transcribed it for the record."

So they're not going to be forced to endure a public performance of the tape. Swenson's woozy with joy. He'll never have to hear the tape again, that crude low-tech forgery, that lie, that accident of timing that made it sound as if he'd persuaded her to trade sex for showing her book to Len. Angela's wringing her hands in her lap, reflexively searching for rings to twist. She should have anticipated this when she got dressed this morning. On her face is that combustive chemistry of wild irritation and boredom so familiar from those early classes, but now it's become a martyr's transfixed gaze of piety and damage, lit by the flames of the holy war she's waging against the evils of male oppression and sexual harassment.

"Well, Angela," says Lauren. "Suppose you begin by telling us how you became acquainted with Professor Swenson."

Angela curls her lip in disbelief. Are these people stupid? "I'm in his class. I mean, I *was*."

"How many students were in the class?" asks Carl. Just faculty checking up on who might have a lighter load.

"Eight," says Angela. "Nine, counting me."

Amelia and Bill shoot looks at Swenson. His teaching load *has* been light.

"And you and Professor Swenson developed a . . . relationship."

"Well, it was kind of weird," says Angela. "He kept wanting to meet me for these private conferences. Everybody thought it was strange, because he wasn't having them with anybody else. In fact it was pretty well known that he was, like, never in his office."

Lauren gives this damning information a moment to sink in. Swenson's not just a child molester—he's a lazy teacher.

"And what did you discuss in these 'conferences'?"

"My work, I guess. I mean, sort of. I mean, he never suggested any changes, exactly. He just said my stuff was so good I should just keep on doing whatever I was doing."

They might as well end the hearing right now. Every self-respecting academic knows a professor has never liked a student's work that much unless he was trying to arrange a little extracurricular activity.

"Now tell us, Angela, in your own words, how this relationship developed."

If Lauren says *relationship* one more time, Swenson will have to kill her. *Re-lay-shin-ship*. He hates how her tongue lingers on the second syllable.

And now the old Angela reappears inside the new Angela's clothes, and begins to writhe. But for all her squirming, Angela won't twist his way. He could jump up and down in front of her, and she wouldn't spare him a glance. He feels that if Angela looked at him once, something would have to change. She would call this whole thing off, she would drop the charges. He's thinking like a stalker. Is that what he's become? A stalker who's not even obsessional enough to stop being self-conscious, who's mortified to have this group know that he had a *relationship* with this bizarre wriggling girl.

"I began to get the feeling that he was, well, like . . . well, interested."

"Interested?" repeats Lauren. "Interested in having a relationship?"

Angela says, "Well, you know . . . I'd catch him looking at me in class."

Of course, he was looking at her, or at least in the direction of her aggressive silence, of the rings and chains and studs—where are they now?—that she'd tap on the table while her fellow students poured out their hearts and souls. Swenson hopes the committee is taking all this to heart. From now on, they'd better be careful before they even look at a student. Though how could anyone *not* have looked at Angela, whose whole performance was geared to *make* you look and at the same time make you feel that your looking was a violation of her right to slink, invisible, through the world?

Swenson needs to remember that. He needs to recall what happened so as to retain his grip on the truth—on his version of the story. A grip on recent history. On reality. The young woman he was "involved" with barely resembles the person before them. It's disorienting to keep translating from this Angela to that. Which one is the real Angela? Astonishing, what you don't know, not even when a person's writing allows you, apparently, intimate access to her soul. But as Swenson's always warning his class: don't assume that soul is the writer's.

Lauren says, "Did Professor Swenson say anything to you during this time?"

Angela says, "Sure, he talked to me. I brought him my stuff. My writing."

"And what did Professor Swenson say about your writing?"

"I already told you," says Angela. "He really liked it."

"I see," Lauren says. Then, after a moment, "How did you know he *really* liked it?"

"Well, he would leave messages on my answering machine saying how much he liked it."

"On your an-swer-ing ma-chine?" repeats Lauren.

"And he kept asking to see more of my writing."

Let the committee get this straight. A teacher asked to see *more* of a student's writing? Swenson only wishes they knew how good her book is. That's what he wants to say now, to set the record straight, establish that there was a reason he was asking to see more. But it will hardly help his case if he stands up and declares that. It will just make him look delusional. Which he was. But not about her novel.

"And what *kind* of writing did Professor Swenson ask to see?"

"My novel. Chapters from my novel."

There's just the faintest swell in her voice when she says that word: *novel*. Can't the committee pick up the signals that the blood-thirsty killer is transmitting from inside that deceptively guileless girl? Swenson's kidding himself. They hear nothing. None of them—except Magda, and she's not talking—can possibly imagine how this inarticulate, subliterate child could write a novel that a grown man would ask to see more of. Their moods sink just as his did when he first heard that word. *Novel.* Swenson watches Carl and Bill conclude: she's not the one *they'd* risk their jobs for.

"Perhaps you want to tell us a little about your novel."

"Like about what?"

"The plot?" Lauren prods gently, in the hope of forcing another inarticulate grunt to plop out of Angela's mouth.

Angela says, "It's about this girl who gets, like, involved with her teacher."

Yes, well, let's tell the committee about the scene in which the girl and her teacher fuck among the broken eggs. Let's point out that this demure, virginal young woman did an amazingly accurate rendering of all that groping and fumbling amid all those sticky fluids.

"And where did you get this story?" Lauren asks. "Where do you think it came from?"

Angela looks puzzled. Where does Lauren think stories come from? "I made it up."

"We understand that." Lauren smiles. "But do you think that reading your novel could have given Professor Swenson the idea that you were . . . willing to get involved with one of *your* teachers?"

"Sure," says Angela. "I guess."

Can six reasonable men and women believe that Swenson decided to have a "relationship" with Angela because he read it in her novel, as if he were some psycho teen who shoots up a schoolyard, and whose lawyers claim he got the idea from a video game?

Lauren says, "And was there anything else that made you think that Professor Swenson was interested in initiating a relationship with you?"

Angela has to consider this one. "Well, I did sort of find out that he'd checked my book of poems out of the library."

So Angela knew he was reading her poems. Swenson's still trying to grasp the implications of this—When did she find out? How long she did she know? Why didn't she ever tell him?—when Lauren says, "How did you discover that?"

"Every so often I kind of cruise that part of the shelves. To see if anyone's borrowed it. No one ever does. And then one day it was gone. So I asked this kid I know who works in the library to look it up on the computer. And it was Professor Swenson. I figured something was going on. You don't expect there'll be this teacher with nothing better to do than check out your really embarrassing poetry book."

No, you certainly don't expect *that*. But hold on. Back up. Has no one noticed that Angela's just admitted to persuading an accomplice to commit an act that may not be strictly illegal, but still just isn't *done*? Isn't your library checkout file privileged information? Not if your phone bills and medical records aren't. Nothing's sacred, nothing's private.

"And how did that make you feel?" Lauren says. "When you found out that Professor Swenson checked out your poems?"

"Creeped out," Angela says. "And also . . ."

"Also what?"

"Also, I remember thinking that if Professor Swenson had been, like, a guy, and I'd found out he'd borrowed my poems, I would have thought, it would have meant that he, you know, *liked* me."

If Professor Swenson had been a guy? And where did this little twit get the idea that borrowing a book from a library is a sign of sexual interest? Well, there is something sexy about reading someone's work: an intimate communication takes place. Still, you can read . . . Gertrude Stein, and it doesn't mean you find her attractive.

"And when was the first time you sensed that Professor Swenson wanted something beyond the nature of an ordinary student-teacher relationship."

From their first conversation, Your Honor, from the first time he looked at her in class, while the bells were ringing. Their eyes met across a crowded room. Not that he realized it was happening then. But that's what he thinks now. How did *he* become the romantic? Once more, the committee's version of him—the scheming dirty old man—seems less degrading than the truth. But if Angela knew what he wanted, why couldn't she have told him? Told him how he felt about her and how she felt about him, and spared him all the time and trouble of trying to figure it out? Saved him from the confusion, the pain of not knowing. Even now. But of course she couldn't have mentioned it. How could she have brought it up? Because he was the teacher, she was the student. That's what this trial's about.

"I guess it was when I told him that my computer crashed, and he offered to take me down to Burlington to the computer store. That seemed a little, you know, extra. But I kept telling myself he was just being nice."

"And was he?" asks Lauren.

Well, yes, absolutely. He was certainly being nice, taking a morning out of his life to drive this kid down to Burlington. All right. There is a God, and He's punishing Swenson for having wanted that drive to last forever, and for liking it so much better than the same trip he took with his daughter.

"And what happened that day?" asks Lauren.

"Nothing at first. Professor Swenson seemed nervous. Like he was scared that someone would see us. Like we were doing something wrong."

Is Lauren forgetting that she was the one who saw them, that she was driving straight toward them as they left the campus?

"Until . . . ," Lauren says.

"Until we were on the way home and he was saying something . . . I can't remember. Anyway, he started talking about his editor in New York. He asked me if I would like the guy to see my novel, and that's when he put his hand over mine . . . and then he moved it to my . . . leg."

Angela takes a moment to steady herself. The room is utterly quiet. Anyone would break in now, any normal person would say: she's lying! But if Swenson interrupts, he'll disrupt everything, he'll lose his only chance to hear what Angela says. To find out what she was thinking. Or anyway, what she claims she was thinking.

"And he asked me again if I wanted his editor to see my novel, and I knew what he was really asking, and . . ."—Angela's whispering now—"and I told him *yes*."

She looks down at the desk for a long time, no doubt gaining encouragement from the waves of understanding and forgiveness streaming at her from the committee, every one of whom—even Lauren, most likely—would have slept with anyone who promised them an introduction to a New York editor at a major house. And they're supposed to know better, have lives, they're older, Angela's just a kid. What could she—what would *they*—have done? *Yes*, they would have said, *yes*.

"And then what, Angela?" asks Lauren.

"And then we drove back to my dorm, and he offered to help me carry the computer up to my room."

Offered? Angela *asked*.

"And you told him yes?" says Lauren.

"Yeah," says Angela. "I didn't want to hurt his feelings. I wanted to be nice. I wound up feeling really, like, totally passive, like everything was out of my control."

Passive isn't Angela's word. She can hardly say it. She's trying out some jargon she learned in the last few weeks.

"So you would say that you didn't feel very much in control on that day when Professor Swenson suggested coming to your dorm room?"

"Not at all," Angela says.

No, sir. She just pushed him back on the bed.

"And did you and Professor Swenson wind up having . . . doing . . . whatever you assumed you had to do so he would help you with your book."

Angela can hardly speak. "I don't know if I can talk about this."

"Try," says Lauren. "Take a deep breath."

How pornographic and perverted this is, a grown woman—a professor—torturing a female student into describing a sexual experience to a faculty committee, not to mention her parents. Swenson could have slept with Angela on the Founders Chapel altar, and it would have seemed healthy and respectable compared to this orgy of filth. Meanwhile he has to keep it in mind that Angela started all this. Angela chose to be here.

"Well, we sort of had sex. I mean, we began to have sex. And then Professor Swenson had this . . . accident."

"Accident?" Has the committee not heard of this? There's some riffling of papers and notes.

"His tooth sort of cracked."

The whole committee pivots toward Swenson, who just at that instant happens to be probing his broken tooth with his tongue. They observe the telltale bulge in his cheek, the incriminatory pull of his mouth. Fascinated, they watch his own reflexes testifying against him.

"And?" says Lauren.

"That ended it," says Angela.

"And how did you feel?" asks Lauren.

"I was relieved," says Angela, as is everyone in the room. How do Angela's parents feel? What must they think of Swenson? "Anyhow, it wasn't my fault. I kept my part of the bargain."

"And did Professor Swenson keep his? Did he take your book to his editor?"

"Yes. I mean, I guess so."

"And how do you know he did?"

"He told me. But he lied."

"What did he lie about?" says Lauren.

"He said he gave it to his editor."

"And the truth is?"

Angela falls silent. Perhaps they'll sit here forever, watching her perform her party piece: psychic self-erasure. But now, as if to compensate for their daughter's withdrawal, her parents stir from their stupor of discomfort and politeness. A tremor—a sort of hiccuping— seizes her father's (step-father's?) body. His wife attempts to restrain him, to keep him from breaking some rule of decorum, but the man has something to say. His voice is rusty as he shouts, "Come on, honey, tell them. Tell the people your good news."

His daughter turns and glares at him—now *there's* the Angela Swenson knows! She closes her eyes and shakes her head. Why can't her father just vanish? When she opens her eyes, she seems annoyed that he's still in the room.

"Angela?" Lauren's improvising. "Good news?" Good news is not on the prearranged agenda of sin, abuse, and damage.

"The thing is, I believed Professor Swenson when he told me that he couldn't get his editor to look at my book, that the guy wasn't interested. I was kind of upset. Disappointed. After what we'd . . . you know . . . done. And then, like two weeks ago, I got this call from a guy named Len Currie, Professor Swenson's editor? He said he'd found my manuscript on a chair at the restaurant where they had lunch and he picked it up. He was going to send it back. But he started reading it in the cab going home. And now he wants to give me a contract and publish it when it's finished."

If this were a real courtroom—or better yet, a courtroom in a movie—a wave of shock and astonishment would ripple through it right now. But these academics are too refined, too repressed to whisper or gasp. Still, Swenson thinks he can hear the stifled buzz emanating directly from their brains. Doesn't anyone *get* it? The girl's a pathological liar. This wishful-thinking sick little joke about Len Currie and her novel. . . . The committee isn't laughing. Their faces are parched and drawn. They haven't had a chance to hide their separate pained responses to the jabs of envy and resentment. They'll need a moment to conceal their private jealousy and grief behind the mask of unselfish happiness for a Euston student's success.

Magda's mouth is open, but Magda doesn't know it. Swenson looks at her and looks away. That Magda asked him to bring Len her book and Swenson refused and brought him Angela's instead is more than their friendship can sustain. Magda will never get over this: so many different tiny rejections streaming into one. He's flattering himself. She'll recover. It's their friendship that won't make it. It's something else he's losing, yet another precious part of his life that he's never valued enough, just part of the water he didn't miss until his well ran dry. Only now does he realize how much he loved, he *loves* Magda. So why was it *Angela's* book that he tried to persuade Len Currie to publish?

Len Currie is publishing Angela's novel. So what is this hearing about? Angela should be kissing Swenson's feet instead of ruining his life. As she must have decided to do when she still believed that Swenson, her white knight, had failed to get her manuscript published. If that's when she decided. Who knows what she did, and why? Why did Lola Lola want a bumbling overweight professor selling dirty postcards—of her?

From now on it will be Len who gets to read Angela's book in installments, Len who talks to her about it, Len who will be the first to find out how the novel ends. But Len won't fall in love with her, he doesn't have to, he isn't that bored, that weird, that pathetic. Why would he sleep with Angela with a whole city of beautiful women to choose from? And Angela doesn't have to bother *making* him fall in love with her because she already has a contract.

Another thing Swenson wants to know is: Why didn't Len Currie call *him*? Why has he been cut out of the loop? What conspiracy is at work? He'd been mooning over *The Blue Angel*, how typically lame and romantic, when the film he should have been watching was *All About Eve*. Be careful. . . . That way madness lies. He'll never publish another book. Angela will take over the world. Well, let her. She can have it.

"That's . . . wonderful, Angela," says Lauren.

"Here, here," Bentham cheers. "Congratulations, Miss Argo! You'll be sure to let the alumni newsletter know, and of course freshman admissions."

How smoothly Angela's triumphed! Whom will the committee favor? The student with the success story to impress prospective students and alumni donors? Or the used-up, erotically restless, loser professor whose very existence must be hidden from the same applicants and donors?

"Congratulations," Magda says. The committee echoes: well done, congratulations. This is all working out wonderfully. They're extracting the thorn from their side—and getting good press for the college.

Quietly now, soothingly, as if to a baby, Lauren says, "Angela, how has this thing affected you? Have there been lingering effects?"

"What do you mean?" Angela says.

"You've mentioned sleep disturbances. . . ."

"Oh, that?" says Angela. "Well, yeah. I mean, I've been having these terrible nightmares. Practically every night I dream that I'm looking out my window and I see these white shapes floating across the quad, women in long white dresses with this long flowing hair. As they get close I somehow know they're Elijah Euston's dead daughters. And I have this feeling they've come for me, and I start to scream and wake up screaming—"

Welcome to *The Twilight Zone*. Really, it's appalling, Angela's hokey performance on the theme of Euston mythology, its spooky Puritan ghosts. But the committee goes for it. Angela *is* multitalented. She can act, as well as write. Swenson can't—he *won't*—believe that she was always acting with him. Not about what he meant to her. At least in terms of her work.

Magda puts on her sweater. Shivers all around. Lauren looks flushed, exalted. This is what she teaches her students, what she believes in her soul: the restless female spirits, floating up through the centuries, wailing.

"Am I done?" says Angela, the sulky teenager again, asking to be sprung from the hell of the family dinner table.

"Yes, of course, thank you," Bentham says.

Lauren's not about to let it go so quickly, so unceremoniously. "Angela, let me say again that we know how tough it was for you to come in and say what you did. But if women are ever going to receive an equal education, these problems have to be addressed and dealt with, so that we can protect and empower ourselves."

"Sure," Angela says. "You're welcome. Whatever."

"And congratulations about your book," says Bentham.

"Thanks, I guess." says Angela. "Now I have to finish it."

"I'm sure you will," says Magda, her tone so neutral that only Swenson can hear the icy sarcasm beneath it.

"Angela," says Lauren, "are you sure there's nothing you want to say? This may be your last chance."

"Just one other thing," says Angela. "It really hurt my feelings. I thought Professor Reynaud really liked my book. And then to find out it was because he just wanted to sleep with me—"

Reynaud. Did the committee hear *that*? That's the name of the character in her novel. Now Swenson's the one with the shivers. Angela called him Reynaud. Have them put *that* into the record!

The girl can't tell the difference between living breathing humans and the ones she's invented. It proves she's a raging psychotic.

Angela stands up shakily and practically limps to her seat. Her parents hug her and thump her back. After a suitable silence, Bentham turns to Swenson and says, "Ted, I imagine there are some things you might want to say."

It's *just* like the end of the writing class. The moment when students thank their tormentors and acknowledge their wrongdoing. Thank you for helping me figure out how to improve my story. Thank you for teaching me to sit still and shut up while what I care about most is defiled and mocked.

It takes Swenson a while to figure out that Bentham is not waiting for an explanation, or an expression of gratitude and self-abasement, but for an apology. This is Swenson's big chance to make his Dostoyevskian confession of sin, his impassioned, reckless plea for foregiveness and redemption. And in fact, Swenson *is* sorry. Sorrier than he can ever begin to say. He's very very sorry that he wrecked his marriage and his career, that he sacrificed his beautiful, beloved wife for some adolescent fantasy of romance. He's sorry he fell in love with someone he didn't know, who couldn't be trusted. He's sorry that he ignored Magda's warnings and his own suspicions and doubts. But, as it happens, he is not particularly sorry for having broken the rules of Euston College, which is what he is supposed to say. The committee couldn't care less about the rest. But he can't possibly tell them the painful details, nor would they want to hear them. Which brings up something else that he is sorry about. He is extremely sorry for having spent twenty years of his one and only life, twenty years he will never get back, among people he can't talk to, men and women to whom he can't even tell the simple truth.

That is, if he knew what the truth was, or why exactly he did what he did. It's become progressively more mysterious to him, increasingly harder to fathom, as each new version of Angela has obscured and erased the one he was drawn to in the first place. He can't imagine how he'd begin to explain. The will to argue leaves him. He doesn't bother to go the table. He can speak from where he is.

He says, "I admit my behavior toward Angela was unprofessional. But I don't agree with the way it's been presented here today. It was personal. And complicated. It was never a business transaction."

Transaction. What kind of word is that? And what does he mean by *complicated*? He supposes it's one way of describing how one thing led to another.

"I guess that's it" is Swenson's stirring summation of his rousing self-defense.

"Thank you, Ted," says Bentham. "We appreciate your honesty. Your forthrightness. We know this hasn't been easy for you. It hasn't been simple for any of us." The others mumble, in chorus, Thank you thank you thank you.

"Hey, any time," says Swenson. He gets up and, turning to leave, casts one last, long, burning, melodramatic look in Angela's direction. But she won't return his gaze, not with her parents there. Their eyes seek him and find him, bore into him, shielding their daughter with preemptive strikes: defensive earth-to-air missiles. He climbs a few steps, then ducks and sits, pushed into the nearest seat by the shock of seeing rangy Matt McIlwaine—charged up, pink-cheeked from the cold—bounding straight toward him. Matt's eyes are bloodshot, puffy. Obviously drugs. Or perhaps he's just woken up.

"Am I too late?" he says. "My car broke down." The lie is so reflexive that no one pays attention. It seems more like a tic than a conscious act. Why would he need his car to get across campus? Doesn't it bother the committee to depose a witness who's lying before he even takes the stand? Bentham looks at Lauren. Lauren looks at Magda. Swenson's the one they should check this with; he knows why Matt might take real pleasure in destroying him. They probably know that already. The committee's done its homework. They also know enough about Matt to suspect that he could make plenty of trouble if his testimony's not heard.

"Better late than never, I suppose," Francis Bentham says. In for a penny, in for a pound. What's it to him? It's nowhere near time for lunch.

Lauren takes one look at Matt and hands him over to Bentham.

"Matt," says Francis, "why don't you tell the committee what you told me in my office?" So they're in collusion. Whatever lies Matt's come here to spread are no surprise to the dean, who's permitted—advised—him to add his evidence to the rest. Swenson's trying to remember how the dean responded earlier, when it had seemed that Matt wouldn't show up for the hearing. Was he disappointed or relieved?

"I'm not actually a student of Professor Swenson's," says Matt. "That would be pretty stupid. Because I'm, like, a friend of his daughter's—"

"Ruby?" says Magda, proprietarily. Swenson can hardly stand to hear his daughter's name spoken aloud in this room, among these people who wish him and Sherrie ill, and who would wish Ruby harm, if they knew her.

"Ruby," says Matt. Swenson steels himself for whatever new torture awaits him.

"And I just thought the committee would want to know that Ruby used to talk about how her dad, like, messed around with her when she was a kid—"

"Messed around?" asks Bentham.

"You know," says Matt. "Sexually."

"I see," says Bentham.

But what does this have to do with this case—with Angela's complaint? This is a violation of Swenson's human rights. Besides which, the kid is lying. Anyone can see that! Swenson loves Ruby. He would never hurt her. And he never has.

But the committee doesn't understand. Swenson's all alone here. They all, very suddenly, have a lot of paperwork to do, notes to scribble, papers to check. So perhaps they do know it's a lie—or, in any case, irrelevant. Then why don't they say that? Because they have taken off their masks. Jonathan Edwards, Cotton Mather, Torquemado. Swenson's crime involves sex, so the death penalty can be invoked. No evidence is inadmissible. They're hauling out the entire arsenal for this mortal combat with the forces of evil and sin.

Swenson lets himself wonder: Did Ruby tell Matt that? He wants to believe she didn't. He can only pray that she didn't.

"That's it," said Matt. "That's all she wrote."

"Thank you," Bentham says. "And thank you all." Class dismissed. "Ted, the committee will be letting you know its decision in, shall we say, two weeks?"

The committee members nod. Two weeks would be grand. As long as it isn't tomorrow, they'll agree to anything.

"Thanks." Swenson's on autopilot. He stands and grabs his coat. Then he sees something that stops him. The committee members' preparation to leave is just background activity, the bustling of extras behind the important scene in which Matt goes over to Angela, who stands on tiptoe and kisses him on the cheek.

They turn to chat with her parents. Matt's arm is around her shoulders. Is Matt her boyfriend? Was it Matt who answered her phone? Did they cook all this up between them? Were they pretending to be near-strangers when Swenson met them outside the video store? Maybe they weren't faking it and hardly knew each other then, and Swenson introduced them, brought the happy couple together. He feels like Herr Professor Rath seeing Lola Lola entwined in the arms of Mazeppa the Strong Man. Angela's too smart for Matt. She'll chew him up and spit him out.

Angela's parents stand, and Matt places a steadying hand on Angela's father's shoulder. What hell they've been through together! Angela's mother gazes at him. How thrilled they are that young Sir Lancelot has rescued their fairy princess from the pervert professor King Arthur. Who wouldn't want Mazeppa as a family member? Matt would make the ideal son-in-law. He's rich. He's going to be richer. Why didn't Swenson see that? Sorry. His mistake. Perhaps all this was Matt's revenge. But that seems unlikely. Matt isn't nearly that competent, nowhere near that together. Angela is. But why would Angela want to destroy him? Her only agenda was to get published.

But that is just how it appears now. Not necessarily how it was. Angela's the only one who knows—who will ever know—the truth.

Swenson's not planning anything as he walks downstairs. If his mind weren't empty, he couldn't move at all. There's a flutter of uncertainty, he's heading in the wrong direction. Hey, that creep in the camouflage pants is unpacking his weapon! But he's a civilized professor, so they must assume he's coming up to shake his colleagues' hands.

Instead he goes over to Angela. He knows he's standing too close. Angela's father and Matt tense. Swenson can feel it without looking. He puts his face next to Angela's. Matt puts out his arm, protecting Angela, not quite touching Swenson. Her father does the same. Their reflex, their posture, the entire scene is patriarchal, biblical. They should be bare-chested, wearing turbans and beards in some Renaissance painting.

Then the men and Angela's mother float out of Swenson's peripheral field, and his gaze swims toward Angela, past her clothes, his clothes, her skin, his skin, her body, his body. His soul is swimming toward hers like some desperate little sardine looking for that ocean they navigated together, when she was bringing him chapters and wanted to know what he thought, and he put off telling her until he couldn't wait any longer.

Angela's eyes take in everything and give nothing back, certainly not the slightest sign that she's ever met Swenson before. All the air has been sucked from the room. Swenson feels like he's drowning.

He says, "Just tell me one thing, okay? What the fuck were you doing?"

"Huh?" says Angela. "What?"

"Ted!" says Lauren. "Control yourself. Please. Act like an adult." Her request—or is it a warning?—is taken up by the other committee members.

Maybe what they're objecting to is Swenson cutting so directly to the chase. Or maybe all they hear is Swenson saying *fuck* to a student.

Francis Bentham, their fearless leader, wades into the standoff. He gently grabs Swenson's elbow. Swenson shakes off his hand. He's breathing shallowly, something's blurring his vision, but unfortunately, consciousness hasn't deserted him. He understands that if he takes this further, makes a fuss, it will only get worse. Sadly, he's aware enough to know that he couldn't bear it, couldn't stand being hustled out of this joint by Matt and Angela's father. Oh, where was that sensible, self-protective voice when he went to Angela Argo's dorm room?

What a favor they're all doing him, showing him their true selves. What could he have been thinking to have wasted almost twenty years here? But he's still got time left. He should be thanking Angela! Had this not happened, he'd have stayed at Euston, secure, pre-embalmed—till he grew old and died and never noticed that he was in hell. He's not being fired, he's being promoted from the inferno to purgatory. Swenson knows he's not having an optimistic moment so much as an intimation of what an optimistic moment might feel like.

He won't allow Benthan to touch him, but he lets himself be walked upstairs. Professor Rath being driven from the Blue Angel by the angry mob.

"We'll be in touch," says Bentham, but Swenson doesn't answer. Hunched against the shocking cold, he walks onto the snowy quad.

The lawns and paths are empty. Soft curls of mist rise above the snow and give the edges of things an unfocused cottony blur. The college buildings have never looked so lovely, their austere white clapboard, colonial brick, and gothic stone beauty untainted by nostalgia or by personal sadness at his being about to leave them. Swenson feels like a tourist visiting some historic site. He feels chosen, privileged to be here!

Just at that moment, a deer—a doe—appears and gingerly minces along the path. She looks at Swenson, who looks back. The doe stares at him calmly, with something like—he could swear it—the affirmation or understanding he tried and failed to get from Angela. Which medieval saint saw the cross between the horns of the stag? Obviously, the deer is a sign of hope, of possibility and forgiveness. Perhaps a reincarnation of one of Elijah Euston's daughters. Suddenly, the doe lifts its head, and stands there. Attentive, listening. What does she hear that Swenson doesn't?

A moment later, he does hear. The bells tolling, joyously raucous. What victory are they celebrating? The beginning of Swenson's new life? Somehow that seems unlikely. How beautiful they sound! All his years here, he never listened, never responded except with impatience and annoyance. But who could blame him? He was up too close. The bells interrupted his classes, resonated in his skull. He remembers staring at Angela while the bells tolled the hour. He checks his watch. It's twenty-five past, so why are they ringing now?

Then gradually, it dawns on him. It's the Women's Alliance, announcing their triumph over another male oppressor, one small step along the path toward a glorious future. He's glad to be out of that future and headed into his own. Not that he's sure what his will bring. He'll just have to wait and see.

Why didn't the bells frighten off the deer? Even as their ghost echo fades, the doe calmly crosses the quad, delicate, flamingo-like, poking her nose in the snow. From farther away, she turns again, and looks through the mist at Swenson. What is she seeing? What does she expect? Swenson has no idea. But how strangely lighthearted he feels, what a relief it is to admit, even just for one moment, how much he will never know.